TREMBLING RIVER

Also by Andrée A. Michaud
(in translation)

The River of Dead Trees
Boundary (The Last Summer)
Back Roads
Mirror Lake

TREMBLING RIVER

ANDRÉE A. MICHAUD

TRANSLATED BY J. C. SUTCLIFFE

ARACHNIDE

First published as *Rivière Tremblante* in 2011 by Éditions Québec Amérique
First published in English in 2023 by House of Anansi Press Inc.
houseofanansi.com

House of Anansi Press is committed to protecting our natural environment. This book is
made of material from well-managed FSC®-certified forests, recycled materials,
and other controlled sources.

House of Anansi Press is a Global Certified Accessible™ (GCA by Benetech) publisher. The
ebook version of this book meets stringent accessibility standards and is available to readers
with print disabilities.

27 26 25 24 23   1 2 3 4 5

Library and Archives Canada Cataloguing in Publication
Title: Trembling River / Andrée A. Michaud ; translated by J. C. Sutcliffe.
Other titles: Rivière Tremblante. English
Names: Michaud, Andrée A., 1957- author. | Sutcliffe, J. C., translator.
Description: Translation of: Rivière Tremblante.
Identifiers: Canadiana (print) 20220409730 | Canadiana (ebook) 20220409757 |
ISBN 9781487005894 (softcover) | ISBN 9781487005900 (EPUB)
Classification: LCC PS8576.I217 R5813 2023 | DDC C843/.54—dc23

Cover image: EyeEm / Alamy Stock Photo
Text design: Alysia Shewchuk
Cover design and typesetting: Lucia Kim

*House of Anansi Press respectfully acknowledges that the land on which we operate is the
Traditional Territory of many Nations, including the Anishinabeg, the Wendat, and the
Haudenosaunee. It is also the Treaty Lands of the Mississaugas of the Credit.*

 Canada Council
for the Arts   Conseil des Arts
du Canada

With the participation of the Government of Canada
Avec la participation du gouvernement du Canada | Canadä

*We acknowledge the financial support of the Government of Canada through the National
Translation Program for Book Publishing, an initiative of the* Action Plan for Official
Languages — 2018–2023: Investing in Our Future, *for our translation activities.*

Printed and bound in Canada

MIX
Paper from
responsible sources
FSC   FSC® C103567
www.fsc.org

To all the children who didn't come home for dinner

PART ONE

Night was falling over Rivière-aux-Trembles. In the maple-lined cemetery, my father lay sleeping amid the mist created by the recent mild spell. Soon enough, February would once again blanket the ground in a layer of ice, encasing pebbles and bits of twigs severed by the frost. Behind the cemetery, a cloud had settled on Wolf Hill, so dense it seemed to be raining on the hillside, and only on the hillside, right above the black pines. The final birds of the dying day chirped a few solitary notes into the still air, while I stood motionless, wondering what to do with this sombre beauty caught between death and the looming darkness.

I'd spent all day walking along the little muddy lanes that led to the village — or led away from it, depending on whether you wanted to go home or escape the sadness of abandoned places. After hours of wearing myself out, my hands and feet were frozen solid, but I was still second-guessing myself, unable to decide which direction to head in. I'd only returned to Rivière-aux-Trembles to pay final homage to my father, resting in the chapel where he would be shut up until the spring, and to place a few of his favourite Mary-Jean roses on his coffin, where their speedy blanching would allow me to see death for what it really was: a new state of matter. Because that's all death is, a transformation of flesh and blood; this is what I kept repeating to myself to avoid thinking of the end of all things and all people. My father's body had been emptied of all thought and could now soar up to a new kind of communion with the world, a state where the perception of light, heat, and cold would not be hindered by pain or knowledge.

But what did I know of the pain of matter, or of the state of putrefaction's soul? I imagined potential resurrections and reincarnations that precluded suffering because I refused to believe that death was a definitive, immutable state. My father's passing had forced me to think about the fact that I would die too, and wonder what I was doing with myself, stalled in the middle of a life just like any other life at whose end there would be no possibility of appeal. I'd promised to leave Rivière-aux-Trembles the minute the funeral ceremony was over and never set foot there again, but the feeling of no longer having much time left myself overwhelmed all my plans. I was surprised at my inability to summon up the strength to tear myself away from this village where my childhood had ended so brutally.

As I crouched near the tombstone of a stranger who now faced the sunset for eternity, I asked my father to come to my rescue. I prayed to the mother I'd never known, who'd died too young, crushed in full sun; I implored the heavens to send me a sign, and at that very moment the shout rang out, a cry of fear that could just as well have come from the depths of the earth as from the recesses of my memory.

"Michael," I murmured, my voice husky from the rain and the cold, "is that you, Michael?"

But silence fell over the countryside once more, even denser than the stillness preceding the shout. So I ran, I took one of the four roads that cut through my village in the shape of a cross and vanished into the twilight. After a few minutes I stopped, out of breath, resting my hands on my knees. As I lifted my head, I noticed a deer grazing near a thin strip of forest marching over the fields, lost in the fog descending over Wolf Hill. It was like one of those life-saving visions that lead people away from the abyss they were just about to hurl themselves into.

I took a few steps forward into the field, deep in melting snow, and as the deer slipped into the forest, I let the tears I'd been holding back since the morning flow over the now-sealed abyss. It was finally time for me to go back home.

I.

THE STORIES

MARNIE

He was twelve and I was eleven, and just like knights in tales of chivalry, we had sworn never to leave each other, unaware that the forever of our promise might be brief. But while Michael Saint-Pierre had kept his promises — his memory had never left me — the forts we built deep in the forest and the intergalactic trips we used to plan now only exist in those increasingly rare dreams in which Michael, perched on the highest branch of an enormous tree, talks to me in childish words about the universe's endlessness.

Michael Superman Saint-Pierre, son of Jeanne Dubé and Victor Saint-Pierre, went missing in the Rivière-aux-Trembles woods on August 7th, 1979. I don't know what happened in the woods; nobody knows, except for Mike and his putative attacker, but sometimes I believe he's still alive, that some force whose power I can't even conceive of came to find him on his branch to take him to Krypton's twin planet or some distant star humans haven't yet discovered. At these times, I tell myself I'll receive a message from outer space one day, something shining out among the myriad stars I sometimes watch until I feel dizzy, a sign telling me that Michael Saint-Pierre is getting ready to come back to earth.

The truth is that Michael probably died deep in the woods, his disintegrating body swept along by the river into the mouths of coyotes and wolves, unless some predator with an all-too-human face threw himself on Michael for reasons that can only be explained by insanity. But in the absence of a body, I continue to hope that my friend Mike is still wandering around the mossy floor of some distant forest, trapped by thunder-induced amnesia. And if this is the case, perhaps his footsteps—propelled by some fuzzy childhood memory—will end up leading him here, to Rivière-aux-Trembles, this place I decided to move back to after twenty-nine years away from it, all because of a shout of unknown origin.

Michael and I had heard this same cry on two occasions that summer, the summer of 1979, the summer he disappeared. The first one happened a little before nightfall, when a lack of wind allows sound to travel through the humid air. We were messing around and throwing stones into Catfish Lake—whoever misses the rock on the point is a loser—when a scream ripped through the dawning darkness, making even the birchbark shiver. One last rock sank into the still water and Michael froze on the spot, his arm in the air, as I dropped the flat pebble I'd unearthed from under a pile of driftwood. Our eyes met, and without having to discuss it, we raced to the lake path and ran as fast as our legs could carry us towards the village.

Before we could reach Morin Sisters Road, where we'd hidden our chrome bicycles, blue with red handlebars for Michael—Superman's colours—and black for me, because it was the only one left in the store the day my father had bought it for me, I stumbled on a root lying across the path and wiped out in slow motion. My Pippi Longstocking braids, tied with lemon-yellow elastics, flew in front of my eyes, preceded by my Expos cap, while my hands scrabbled at the air, and then the section of sky where my cap was spinning disappeared. With my nose in muddy earth, rotting leaves, and pine needles, I'd felt sure a hand was gripping my left leg and pulling me backwards, towards the lake and its depths.

This was a first warning, I realized afterwards, the first sign of the fate that would come crashing down on Michael and me, putting an end to all our games. I was imagining the cracked black nails—like the talons of the witches in Phantom Swamp, a mythical place invented to keep children away from the peat bogs east of Wolf Hill—sinking into my ankle when Michael's hands grabbed me under my arms to help me stand up.

"Hurry up, Marnie, quick, it's going to catch us, it's coming, I can feel it."

But it had already arrived, it was already there, this thing that would make even the sun in Rivière-aux-Trembles go crazy.

The next day, we found out that Martin Bouchard, the oldest son of the mayor, Jos Bouchard, had drowned around eight the previous evening, as he was pulling out the fishing lines he'd cast at the mouth of Blueberry River, five kilometres by road from Catfish Lake, less than two kilometres as the crow flies, and within shouting distance when the air is humid.

"We heard the cry of death, Marn," Michael murmured, spitting his gum onto the sidewalk, and we stood frozen to the spot, staring at the forest where death had screamed.

The second time this shout rang out in the area would also be the last, at least that summer. It was August 7th, a torrid August 7th, and the sun occasionally flickered through the increasingly dense thunder clouds. We were sprawled on the porch, killing time and counting the flies stuck to the front of Michael's house. Michael was also supposed to be watching his little sister, Émilie, Emmy-Lou, Emmy-Lili, while his mother went over to Mrs. Tremblay's to teach her how to make a strawberry cobbler using a recipe in which the strawberries could be switched out for raspberries, blueberries, blackberries, plums, apples, or redcurrants, essentially for any small, medium, or large fruit that grew near us.

The afternoon stretched out endlessly in a humid heat that seemed to affect even Emmy-Lili's rag dolls, who were lolling with their legs akimbo on the porch floorboards. Our clothes stuck to our skin, Emmy's fine blond hair formed damp little commas on her forehead, and the mass of crickets gathered in the yellow hay had silenced all the birds. We resented Denise Tremblay, who'd got married in June in a wedding dress like something out of a magazine and didn't even know how to boil an egg, and we were annoyed with Michael's mother, who'd got it into her head to transform this newlywed into a cordon bleu chef. When we saw her old Datsun appear in the laneway, we ran to find our swimsuits. Michael called out that we were going swimming, without listening to her admonishments or even bothering to say hello.

Behind us, Emmy-Lili started crying. "I want to come with you, Mike. Take Mimi, take Lili..."

These were just the innocent cries of a child, but they would be forever engraved in the memory I would retain of that day. Years later, these same cries would yank me from sleep — little Emmy-Lou's sobs as she begged her brother not to abandon her, not to leave her alone during the storm, to take her with him into the woods some people never returned from. Perhaps she'd guessed from the greyness of the sky that she would never again see Michael, her brother, her god.

Michael patted her on the head and handed her a toffee lollipop that had been lurking at the bottom of one of his pockets. "Mike won't be long, Lili," he said, and we straddled our flying bicycles to head down the 4th Line, then along a path to where the river formed a little basin where we could dive without hurting ourselves, avoid the eyes of the forest monsters, and float on our backs as we gazed through the leaves at the changing shapes of the clouds. This was our secret place, our oasis, far from the dull, strict adult world. Michael had named it "the magic swimming hole" and claimed this was where a fortress would rise up out of the water—the fortress in which he would live in solitude once he turned eighteen.

While we were waiting for the glittering proof of Superman's distant origins to emerge from the river, we'd built ourselves a shelter out of branches under the pines, facing the swimming hole. That's where we were when the storm broke out, sorting the stones we'd fished up from the bottom of the water by size and colour. The first drops hit the shelter roof as Michael was arranging white pebbles beside the circle of black rocks whose powers would make us untouchable.

"It's going to thunder, Marn," he said, as he glanced through the opening that served as the shelter's doorway, and then he ran out to grab our swimsuits from where they were drying side by side on a flat rock.

He could only have been gone a few seconds, but when he didn't come back I went over to the doorway and looked out. Mike was standing near the rock, his back to the shelter, swinging from right to left as he lifted one leg and then the other, like the old rusty metal robot he finally got rid of at the beginning of the summer. Our bathing suits dangled from the ends of his outstretched arms and his head flopped down over his chest as if he no longer had the strength to hold it up straight. Looking as though his neck was broken, he seemed to be staring down at his left running shoe, whose lace had come untied.

At first, I thought it was a joke, that Michael was trying to wind me up, but something didn't sit quite right. He looked like one of the zombies in *Night of the Living Dead*, which we'd secretly watched a few weeks earlier. He looked like Emmy-Lou's dolls, with their slack limbs and drooping necks.

"What are you doing, Mike? This isn't funny!"

But he didn't react. He carried on swaying from left to right, and then started taking cautious steps backwards, his arms still raised, until a light flashed across the sky above the water. Then he leapt back, flapping his arms like the robot in *Lost in Space* that cries, "Danger! Danger!" Except Mike wasn't shouting, but, like the robot, he was afraid of a shadow I couldn't see heading towards him, hidden from me by the trees, his body, and the rain. I looked around for the shadow of this zombie that wanted to devour Michael, but I could only make out the movement of the branches in the wind, behind which multitudes of powerful, threatening arms might well be moving. Just as I thought I could make out the hairy arm, all scratched and slashed, about to rise out of the trees, I heard, over the grumbling of the thunder, the piercing cry of the drowned young man of Blueberry River, the scream that had announced Martin Bouchard's death. A second flash of lightning immediately ripped through the clouds and Michael froze on the spot, letting our bathing suits fall to his feet in such a slow gesture I thought the damp fabric was going to remain suspended from his open hands and never touch the ground.

My throat was as dry as if I'd raced non-stop from the village to the Mailloux pond. I repeated that I didn't find his playacting the slightest bit amusing: "Stop messing around, Mike, you're not funny at all."

When the wind started whirling around our swimming hole, I tried to tell him to come back to the shelter, wanting to say, quick, Mike, it's coming, it's here, there's werewolves and witches, but I had no voice, paralyzed by Mike's immobility, his petrified body standing in the rain.

"You're scaring me, Mike," I managed to murmur, or maybe sob; I don't even know anymore, but my fear wasn't strong enough to rattle his torpor.

After a few endless seconds, he finally turned to look at me, whiter than the freshly laundered sheets tousle-haired women hang out in the Rivière-aux-Trembles backyards on summer mornings. I thought he was going to faint, but he said a few words to me, or maybe to the invisible spectres standing in front of his vacant, staring eyes. In the howling of the wind that made the trees bend and bow, I didn't hear what he said, I only saw his mouth open mechanically, his lips purse around strange sounds, *Foggy day, ma'am, foggy day, how can you manage?* And then, as if he had suddenly come out of a trance, he flashed me a desolate smile, discreetly raised his hand in a gesture of goodbye, and ran off between the trees, pushed by the arms that were multiplying in the storm. I should have run to catch up with him, followed the dark corridor he was disappearing into, but my legs were as soft as cotton wool, while my feet felt as though I was wearing concrete shoes.

I came out of the shelter on all fours, thinking only of Mike's absurd words, *foggy day, ma'am, foggy day*, and then of his unlaced running shoe, all of it mixed up together, all chaotic, imagining how his beat-up shoe that was slapping against his bare heel would get stuck between two roots and make him stumble. When I succeeded in getting myself upright, my mind as confused as if I'd just woken from a nightmare, the red splash of Mike's T-shirt had already disappeared in the jumble of the forest. Another streak lit up the sky, which was darkening as the wind catapulted clouds across it, and I was still alone, futilely calling out for Michael Saint-Pierre.

I waited for him in the shelter until the storm was spent, walled in by the echo of the scream that had broken the sky with a mauve flash, then I pedalled my chrome bike home with trembling knees, struggling with each revolution of the pedals against the unknown force trying to drag me backwards.

One hour later, thirty-odd men, led by a child wracked by spasms, headed down the path to the magic swimming hole, where they branched out in different directions like the arms of a star, at the centre of which was the spot where Michael had dropped our wet bathing suits. Inside the shelter, the rock circles had been broken.

BILL

I washed up in Rivière-aux-Trembles like a stone tossed around by the current. I could have ended up in Chicago, Sept-Îles, Timbuktu, or Maniwaki, but this is where my fall from grace led me. It was exactly what I needed, some godforsaken hole where Lucy-Ann couldn't come and harass me with her accusations, a place where I could stew in my misery, bending Billie's ear with the stories this bitch of a life hadn't allowed me to finish.

During Billie's lifetime I'd told her so many stories I sometimes felt as though reality didn't exist anymore, that it was nothing more than a pale imitation of the movie spooling in the somewhat twisted minds of guys like me. We would be sitting nice and warm in the sunshine on the verandah, I would pick up a book at random, *Moby-Dick*, the *Odyssey*, *Cinderella*, or *Hop o' My Thumb*, and for my daughter I would reinvent Captain Ahab's journey, Cinderella's nocturnal jaunts, or Ulysses' adventures with the Cyclops. For her, I mingled together history and its thousands of stories, and was always messing around with

18

these classics by having Pinocchio stand at the prow of the *Pequod* or by marrying Hop o' My Thumb off to the princess who slept with the pea under her mattress, because, basically, Billie liked it, because it made her laugh and dream, and because the dreams of small girls are some of the most beautiful things in the world. Nobody can take that away from me.

Her favourite stories were, however, the same as mine, *Ronie the Flying Toad, The Noutes Dynasty, Alice and the Seven Cats*, those short stories that had made my fortune and carried me to places as far away as Iceland. *Ronie* had been translated into seventeen languages and adapted into a cartoon during the '90s; it had done so well that when I met L.A., Lucy-Ann, I was able to buy us a fancy house in a neighbourhood where proper, well-educated people lived, the kind of people who didn't spit on the sidewalk and who got drunk on expensive wine.

At the age of forty I could have lived off my royalties, but I applied myself to writing more stories about Noutes and polyglot toads, at the same time trying to inculcate in jaded students a few theories that they would try to apply to fiction before they realized that nobody was interested in it.

My life revolved around these three elements: my students, oblivious to everything that eluded them; my notebooks; and Billie-Billienoute, the only princess in my kingdom, who jumped onto my lap at every opportunity so I could invent some new tale of a toad, alligator, or snowy owl, right up until she discovered Harry Potter, the young

Indiana Jones, Pippi Longstocking, and a whole host of heroines and heroes, none of whom looked like a toad who'd just stepped out of an enchanted swamp. From that day onwards, my batrachians, Homer, and the Brothers Grimm faced some stiff competition.

I could have been jealous, or annoyed with Billie for preferring the adventures of an apprentice sorcerer, or a little girl who could pick up a horse while she sang in Swedish, over the fairy universe of my talking bestiary, but how could you be irritated with a princess who turns you into a Prince Charming every day? "Love you, Papanoute," she used to call out as she jumped onto my bed, and my nightmares and anxieties ebbed away under the covers.

Billie's sudden attraction for these stories in which childhood comes up against human stupidity showed me she was growing up. I preferred to ignore this fact, as long as she didn't start getting cigarette burns on her princess dresses, but she was also showing me it was time to reskill. But the idea of abandoning my toads for cowboys who get to meet Sigmund Freud and Gertrude Stein, or for futuristic metal creatures who communicate by tapping their heads together, inspired me about as much as the idea of becoming a gravedigger in Azerbaijan. My desire to elicit Billie's admiration being stronger than my literary inclinations, my plan for her next birthday was to concoct an adventure starring the young Indy and Billie Longstocking, because, I confess, I had a soft spot for Indy, as well as for Pippi, who'd travelled through the decades without getting too scratched and dented, kind of like a punk Joan of Arc. However, the birthday in question never arrived. I waited for her, God knows I waited for her, convinced that Billie would never willingly miss out on her cherry cake or her nine red candles, sure that it was simply impossible for her not to come racing down the stairs with her party hat yanked down over her tangled hair.

I waited in vain, and I never wrote my *Billie and the Lost Ark*, which was probably all for the best, since I would no doubt have failed in my attempt to measure up to George Lucas and Astrid Lindgren in one fell swoop. The last story she'd asked me to read to her was from the Harry Potter series. I remember it because I left the book lying around, and it fell off the side table at the exact moment Lucy-Ann burst into the house shouting that Billie had never arrived at her ballet class, that she'd left school at 3:30 as usual but had never shown up at the dance teacher's studio. She was screaming and gesticulating hysterically, and I had to grab her arms before she strangled herself with the scarf she was trying to rip off her neck.

Once I worked out what Lucy-Ann was trying to tell me, I raced to Billie's room just in case she was hiding out there to escape the chore of ballet lessons. After searching the whole second floor, I ran down the stairs four at a time and noticed Lucy-Ann's scarf, lying in melted snow on the floor, next to the much-trampled novel. I pushed the scarf aside and grabbed the book, frantically wiping the cover, where one of Lucy-Ann's heels had crushed Harry Potter's face and glasses. For a moment I had the impression that the young Harry, behind his broken spectacles, wanted to cast an evil spell on me, turning me into a *petrificus totalus* victim. And I wasn't completely wrong, because I stood there paralyzed while Lucy-Ann bawled behind me, telling me to get my ass in gear and find her daughter.

It was Lucy-Ann who'd insisted on signing Billie up for ballet lessons, despite Billie's protests. She ought to have known not to force a plumpish child to face a peloton of little matchstick girls ready to open fire on anyone who didn't fit the mould. That's how armies work, that's how we get the first victims of wars. But L.A. didn't want to hear about it. L.A. had always been slim, L.A. was as ignorant as all slim women are when it came to self-image and had no idea whatsoever of the burden of a round body. After two months of dance, Billie was basically existing on carrots and vegetable juice. So the day the little Dumas boy was run over by a car, I brought my fist down on the table and said, "That's enough, we're done, we're not going to force a child—who might get run over any moment by a ten-ton truck—to dress up in a ridiculous itchy tutu just so she might get cast as a loser mouse in some miserable little production of *The Nutcracker*!"

L.A. slammed the door in my face and Billie had carried on with her lessons and her diet until the day she cracked in front of a chocolate eclair, with me egging her on furiously by stuffing three of them down my own gullet. At a mere eight years old, Billie was too fragile, too sweet, too cheerful to be corseted by images out of the glossy magazines that had spent three or four decades perpetuating the vicious lie that the ideal woman looks like a barely pubescent girl in the last stages of anorexia.

The battle of the carrots versus the eclairs, which ended with chocolate's calorific power knocking out vitamin C's virtues, took place a few days before Billie disappeared. L.A. was having a few friends over for brunch, and Billie and I took advantage of the time to slink off for a stroll. We couldn't decide between the botanical gardens and the movies, but then Billie decreed it was too cold to go hunting for alien tracks in the botanical gardens' snowy paths as we had planned.

This alien-spotting business went way back with us. Billie, who must have been four, was perched on top of one of the kitchen bar stools, looking out the window, when she noticed the little marks on the white ground made by the snow that had fallen from the trees around the house. These prints, which she'd never noticed before, fascinated her, and I told her they were Martian tracks, which was the modern version of the goblin footprints of my own childhood.

Some parents try to explain everything very rationally to their children from the moment they cut their first tooth, teaching them the law of relativity at the age of four, banning the Cartoon Network. They even refuse to let them wander in magical dream worlds filled with ethereal creatures, monsters or fairies, ogres or sprites, where they might learn that reality is not always what it seems and that there are universes where the trees are red, and where flowers the size of sperm whales roam the oceans.

L.A., unfortunately, was among that faction of parents who only believe in educational toys, fluffy rabbits who count to one hundred, alarm clocks that wake you with opera music, or chunks of earwax that recite *Aesop's Fables*. Seeing that she was about to explain to Billie where the marks in the snow really came from, I shot her one of my most killer looks, preferring to wound L.A.'s pride rather than prevent Billie's imagination from flying free and creating a world that could belong to her and her alone, and which she would remember, years later, as one of the most beautiful parts of the earth.

Once tracking down aliens was off the table, Billie started hopping and prancing around me and asking if we could go back and see *Ice Age*, even though we'd just watched it a week earlier. I've never understood why children feel the need to be told the same stories over and over. When I interrogated Billie on the subject, she just gaped at me open-mouthed, and then gave me the most logical answer: "Well, because I like those stories, Papanoute." So then I would open the picture book or the novel she was showing me, and think to myself that it must make her feel safe to know in advance that the Big Bad Wolf was going to be neutralized, that Indy's genius would let him conquer the enemy, come what may, and that no real danger could be lurking under her bed as long as good triumphed over evil. I suppose this ritual of repetition gave the illusion of a kind of stability which she could already tell did not really exist.

The reason children beg for the story of the Three Little

Pigs four nights in a row is that they want to live for as long as possible in an illusion protecting them from the vastness of the world and the incoherence of time. At least, that's my guess. As you get older you forget so many of the basic things, you sometimes wonder what the point of being young was if you're too foolish to remember where happiness comes from, true happiness, the sort that overflows because of a three-scoop ice-cream cone with a cherry on top. With Billie, I solved the problem of repetition by combining stories with happy endings or by changing the endings of the ones that made no sense to a child who was dropping off to sleep while clutching a teddy bear to her chest. In this way, the stories I told her were always the same and never the same, which kept me from annoying the slightly dopey adult I'd become.

"But Papanoute, how come Snow White was sleeping in Goofy's house?" She used to fire questions at me, and I replied that Snow White had had enough of her damp castle, lost in the depths of the Forest of Nowhere, so she decided to get on a plane and go sunbathe on the Florida beaches with Goofy and his buddies. Billie then laughed her mischievous little laugh and slipped into a Technicolor dream that gave her access to Goofy's house and the long sandy stretches lining the Florida coast.

We did go back and see *Ice Age* that day. Billie laughed in all the same places she'd laughed the week before, as did I, although we weren't always laughing at the same moments. Whenever I guffawed at a joke that left her — and all the other children ensconced in the movie theatre's darkness—indifferent, she looked at me as if I was hopeless, which only made me laugh harder and simultaneously confirmed her fear that her father, just like most adults, sometimes behaved like an idiot. I laughed so much during the movie I almost choked, to Billie's great displeasure. She quickly pinched my thigh and glared at me like Mantan Moreland, an old American comic whose eyes were bigger than their sockets.

I don't know if Billie was ashamed of her cretinous father, but I didn't care, because Billie loved me, I knew she did, and because I was suddenly developing an enormous fondness for mammoths and sloths. If I'd watched *Ice Age* for a third time, my growing compassion for these endangered species would perhaps have inspired me to change a few of the stupid habits my peers and I obstinately insisted on keeping up while burying our heads in the sand. That was what was wrong with adults. They forgot the stories that had formed them instead of reciting them over and over again until the best parts became engraved on their brains.

By the end of the movie, I was hungry enough to eat a horse, so I took Billie off to a patisserie where they also served soup, salad, and sandwiches. I ordered the daily special, cream of asparagus soup accompanied by a kaiser bun stuffed with melted cheese, alfalfa sprouts, grated cucumber, and a creamy sauce specially designed to dribble down your chin and stain your Sunday jeans. I wanted Billie to have the same thing, but she ordered a sad little carrot salad, with that stubborn look on her face that meant she'd freak out if I interfered. So I shut my mouth and swallowed my kaiser down with difficulty, because I knew Billie was as starved as I was.

She gobbled up her bowl of salad with the greed of a prehistoric squirrel on the verge of starvation who's just discovered a stash of giant acorns underneath a glacier. When I asked her if she wanted anything else, she shook her head and pressed her lips together, quickly wiping away the two little tears that had managed to escape from her hazel eyes. When I saw those tiny, undernourished tears, I was the one who threw a fit, just quietly, a wimpy little tantrum, because an adult should know how to control himself in a public place.

"That's enough, Billie," I murmured, "I can't take this anymore, you have to eat," and I asked our waitress to bring us two chocolate eclairs, the two biggest ones she could find in the display case.

More tears flowed down Billie's cheeks, the kind of tears that break the hearts of fathers the world over, but she ate her eclair, and so did I. I even wolfed down two more with the eagerness of a father ready to make his stomach burst just to coax a smile out of his daughter. And then it happened. With a mouth full of chocolate, Billie smiled at me and I smiled back at her, we burst out laughing and hid our mouths behind our napkins, and I swore Billie would never eat carrots again, in any shape or form. My reaction was stupid, but I was happy.

It was this unrestrained laughter I was thinking about when I called the police to report Billie's disappearance, a crazy laugh so candid it convinced me that the temporary absence of this child could be nothing more than a monumental error, a farce with clowns throwing cream pies at each other's faces or stuffing chocolate eclairs down their throats.

After I hung up, I forced L.A. to sit down. I gave her a double Scotch and reeled off the platitudes people with normal constitutions trot out when a bomb lands on their house or an undertaker shows up right in the middle of dinner to announce that the world now has several billion people minus one. I squeezed her hand and swore to her in all the languages I knew that it was impossible. I told her the undertaker didn't exist, we could erase him with a wave of the hand and get rid of the ludicrous words twisting his damn pale face. The undertaker belonged to a nightmare, period, to a stupid, shitty nightmare, and the alarm clock would interrupt it as soon as the first rays of the sun appeared.

One hour later, two police officers disguised as apprentice undertakers knocked on the door, a bleached-blond woman whose ponytail twisted to the left, and a tall redheaded man who was missing one of his front teeth. They asked us a ton of questions about Billie, her routines, her friends, people she knew, and then they left with the most recent photo of our baby, a photo where she was wearing the pink coat with the hood that Lucy-Ann had bought her at the beginning of the winter, the one she'd put on that morning before she headed off to school. And she was smiling her puckish little-girl smile that rose higher on one side than on the other. Her little hazel eyes with the cute sprinkling of freckles underneath.

MARNIE

Less than twenty-four hours later, the dogs arrived—three German shepherds called Rex, Chet, and Lucy, trained to sniff out fear, death, blood, and to track scattered smells so barely there it was hard to believe they'd managed to linger amid the stench of the peat bogs. As soon as the animals were let out of the police van, the village was filled with a frenzied barking and howling that expressed better than any human cry the weight of the drama casting its shadows over the lightness of summer. Even when the dogs stopped howling, the echo of their multiple laments continued to ring out. Several days after they'd left, their barks still resonated on the trampled paths where no children were allowed to roam any longer. They were now confined to the narrow strip of light just outside the windows so that people could keep an eye on them, watching anxiously for the possible incursion of evil, and shooting without warning at point-blank range at anyone who came to disturb their safe home.

On the first day, the dogs were released near the magic

swimming hole from the centre of the star the men had traced when Michael's father had abruptly dragged them from the tranquility of their houses the day before. As for Jeanne Dubé, Mike's mother, she refused to leave the house just in case her son turned up, in case he was hungry; boys eat non-stop at that age. While the men were tramping through the damp forest, the Rivière-aux-Trembles women were keeping an eye out on their stretch of sidewalk, just in case, just in case... A few of them gathered at Jeanne's house, thinking they might be able to help, but she barely even registered their presence. Over and over, she made egg sandwiches, Mike's favourite, and baked cakes, constantly repeating that the boy would be starving when he got home. She muttered as she sieved the flour, wiped her hands on her apron, or adjusted the oven's temperature, convinced that any minute now she'd be hearing the squeak of Mike's bike tires in the yard.

"Everything needs to be ready," she would say to Emmy-Lou. "Go on, pumpkin, go and see if he's coming."

And Emmy-Lou would go out onto the porch with her favourite doll in her arms, a lollipop stuck deep in the pocket of her yellow dress.

The searches lasted until sunset, but as soon as the dogs were released in a new direction, they doubled back to follow a sinuous path towards the river, at which point they halted, trembling and sighing. It was always in the same place, two kilometres from the swimming hole. Not long after noon, a canoe was brought, and the dogs and their handler were taken across the river. Once on the other side, the dogs behaved the same way, staring at the river, accusing the river, barking that Michael was there, beneath the calm waters. A team was immediately ordered to drag the water, because the conclusion to be drawn from the dogs' innate knowledge was obvious: Michael Saint-Pierre's trail, with its childlike odours, vanished into this seemingly inoffensive water.

While everyone was out scouring the woods, two police officers, along with Michael's father, came and rang our doorbell. They had a hushed conversation with my father, who then asked me to come downstairs.

"These men want to ask you a few questions, Marnie," he declared, borrowing his line from a cheap crime novel or a television series from the fifties.

We all sat around the kitchen table, the tall moustached inspector on my left, the shorter one on my right, and my father in front of me. As for Michael's father, he remained standing in the doorframe, twisting his cap around in his hands, as if by crushing the sides and turning it around in all directions it might reveal the answer that would stop his heart from cracking under the pressure of his terror.

His presence was intimidating because I knew his pain—which he was trying to hide by lowering his head—held me responsible for his son's disappearance. Every time he raised his eyes to look at me, I had to look elsewhere, because this man, whose face was ravaged by fear, was right. If I hadn't been there, if Michael and I had not been inseparable, and if we hadn't gone together to the river, none of this would ever have happened. I was guilty of being too attached to

Michael, I was guilty of not having run after him, and above all I was guilty of not having disappeared along with him. If I had evaporated into thin air, leaving behind only the ribbon that tied back my hair, nobody would ever have entertained these half-spoken accusations about me leaving the forest without holding Michael Saint-Pierre's muddy hand in mine. I'd have been a victim too, just as he was, and my photo would have been pinned up next to his, in the hall at school, above a little description of my academic and sporting achievements. But I was denied victim status for the simple reason that I was alive, and the frightened child in me sided with those who essentially resented me—either out of pain or unspeakable stupidity—for having escaped the evil that had taken Michael away. I was the one who got away, the one who had no right to compassion or the warmth of outstretched arms. This is how a childhood ends, by learning about guilt from the shame of having survived.

I answered the police officers' questions mechanically because I'd already been asked the same questions at least three or four times already. I described the storm; I described the way Michael had swayed and then frozen, the rain soaking his red T-shirt, the slow fall of the swimsuits as they dropped to his feet; then, as I saw my bathing suit crumple on the ground yet again, I remembered Mike's left running shoe, which had come untied and was totally mud-soaked. I'd forgotten this detail, and it suddenly seemed to me to be of tremendous importance, because you can't run if your shoelace is untied. I tried to explain to the police officers how Michael had run anyway, how he sped off into the intertwined trees after murmuring a few words, but they were largely unconcerned about the loose shoelace; all they wanted to know was what Michael had said to me.

"What were his words, Marnie?" the tall police officer asked gently. "What did he say? Try to remember."

In the heat of the moment I couldn't remember anything further. The four pairs of eyes all turned desperately towards me were hoping for a miracle, some magic formula capable of bringing Mike back, and their staring scared me. I forced myself to read Mike's lips, but I could only make out an absurd stream of words being absorbed into the bated breath all around me.

Then Victor Saint-Pierre thumped his chest the way people do in church, *mea culpa*, and the words appeared, such unlikely words I was ashamed to repeat them.

"It didn't mean anything," I murmured, "it didn't mean anything, and I didn't really understand."

"We still need to know, Marnie, it's important," the tall police officer, who smelled of mint, said softly, his face so close to mine that I moved back in my chair as I said, "*Foggy day, ma'am, foggy day*, that's what Mike said, *foggy day, how can you manage?* I didn't really understand him."

Everyone remained silent. The tall policeman cleared his throat before asking me to concentrate very hard and listen again. I tried, but it was useless.

"I didn't hear anything," I admitted eventually. "I just saw the words, the ones I told you, *foggy day, ma'am*."

The tall policeman sighed while the shorter one took

notes and got back on track by asking if we'd built other forts, if we knew other hiding spots, and if we sometimes played in places that were forbidden. After a few moments of hesitation, I mentioned Catfish Lake. I shouldn't have said anything. I shouldn't have said anything because this story then became even more incomprehensible, more unreal than it already was, because that was the exact place, on the brush-covered shores of a lake that had long since been emptied of catfish, that Michael's left running shoe, the one with the untied shoelace, was discovered the very next day.

Lucy, the dog whose howls had ripped apart the Rivière-aux-Trembles night, found the running shoe after she was let loose on the path Mike and I used to take to the lake. She pulled up short by the little blue shoe, let out the long sigh of a dog that has suddenly been wounded by the silent weapons of humans, and then waited for her master to catch up. As he rewarded her and relieved her invisible wound by giving her bone-shaped biscuits and throwing a ball for her, the police officers put the shoe in a bag and took it to Michael's father to be identified. When he saw the shoe sealed in a bag just like the ones used for storing meat in a freezer, Victor Saint-Pierre recoiled as if the cops were holding a poisonous snake out to him. Then he grabbed the bag out of Officer Desmarais's hands and clutched it to his chest, then folded over double and collapsed at the foot of a tree, emitting shouts mingled with senseless words.

As I knelt on the back seat of the police car into which

my father and I had been ushered, I saw Victor Saint-Pierre's enormous body crumple and then start swaying at the foot of the tree, front to back, back to front, in the same mechanical way Mike had done at the river's edge. He looked like a horse kicking against his cart or against his stall, cornered by a raging fire trying to devour him. I pressed up against my father and noticed that Victor Saint-Pierre was holding in his powerful arms the Superman-blue running shoe Michael had lost as he ran. This was predictable because no child can run for long if their shoelace is untied. Thus, in my head, the words and the pictures began to sway backwards and forwards. The raging torrent of the Trembles River crashed out into the languor of Catfish Lake, the sun plunged north of the horizon, and I looked at my father so he could explain to me how Michael's running shoe had ended up there. Then everything went white, as white as snow in a blizzard, as pale as freshly washed sheets flapping in the wind.

I woke up under the high branches of a leaning tree, snuggled in my father's arms as he hummed *Lili Marnie, Lili Marleen* without even noticing what he was doing. This song he'd invented was as old as me, as old as my mother's voice as she leaned over my crib, singing "Lili Marnie sleepytime, Lili Marnie has gone to sleep, goodbye hello Lili Marnie." There were tears in his eyes; there were also tears in the even redder eyes of Victor Saint-Pierre, who was now holding his head in both hands, ready to explode, ready to let bloody chunks of his brain scatter among the grass at the side of the road, and I could have sworn there were tears too in the grey eyes of Officer Desmarais, the tall cop with the gentle voice.

I'd been unconscious for barely a minute, but during that minute the world had changed. In the before-world, Michael was wearing two shoes and running. In that world, west was over behind Wolf Hill and the sun hid behind it every evening, ready or not, here I come. In the new world, Michael had fallen into a hole and the sun had jumped right in after him, oblivious to geographical reality. A phenomenon far beyond human understanding had hijacked Michael's route during the night. There was no other possible explanation; God had colluded with the devil, otherwise Michael would have made it home, for the simple reason that it's not possible to get to the magic swimming hole at the edge of Catfish Lake without making a detour through the village, and then through the street where little Emmy-Lili was keeping her eyes peeled for Michael's return, Michael her brother, Michael her god.

The men gathered under the trees softened by the August humidity could not understand how Mike's trail could have petered out at the edge of the river and yet the child ended up here. Victor Saint-Pierre didn't understand it either, nor did the dog handler, nor the dogs that were sniffing at the sand where grasshoppers were jumping. But in my mind, it was all perfectly obvious. Someone had lied, someone was still lying, and it wasn't me. So it could only have been the river and the sun. It could only have been Mike's shoe, or even Michael himself.

BILL

Lucy-Ann spent the night making phone calls, waking up our friends, neighbours, close acquaintances, not-so-close acquaintances, screaming at the parents of Billie's few friends to go and drag their damn kids out of bed and shake them until they revealed where our daughter was, with no result other than creating chaos and fuelling the children's nightmares. As for me, in minus-twenty-degree weather I roamed the streets around our house, then the ones around Billie's school and the building where her dance studio was located, yelling her name loudly enough to bring a bunch of pale faces to peer out the windows, roused by the fury of the maniac disturbing their night's peace. I shouted out to Billie that I loved her, I loved her more than was even possible, as I climbed snowbanks, porches, fences, climbing everything that could be climbed, after which I showed her photograph to everyone walking past and all the convenience-store workers in the neighbourhood. With tears in my eyes, I even accosted a group of drunks staggering out of a bar until a flashing light forced me to protect my eyes from the red and blue glare spinning in the frozen air by placing my left hand, the one holding Billie's photo, in front of my distraught-father face.

It was then that I felt the warmth of tears on my face, the sweet relief this warmth brings to tensed muscles. Crying doesn't alleviate suffering at all, but it does allow you to let yourself go for a bit, to spread yourself out in salty little rivulets on your cold skin, while the metal band gripping your solar plexus loosens just a notch or two. The few tears that broke through the barrier of my anger gave ballast to my pain, and I sat down on the icy sidewalk in the flashing light. I showed Billie's photo to a police officer who was barely in his thirties and stood in front of me with one hand on his baton and the other stretched out towards the photo I was refusing to relinquish.

"We'll take you home, sir," he said as he gripped my shoulder. My tears dried up immediately. I leapt to my feet and shouted that it was out of the question, I couldn't possibly go home while my daughter, my little eight-year-old daughter, all pink with hazel eyes — "Here, look at her picture" — was lost somewhere in the dark.

"All right sir, let's go, I'm sure she's home by now," the cop said, signalling to the officer standing on the other side of the flashing police car to come over. But I knew Billie hadn't made it home. My fatherly intuition and my naked terror as a father who was trembling from head to toe told me the exact opposite. Before the cop pushed me into the car, I tried to punch him with my fatherly rage-filled fist, but he ducked. The other cop, a short, nervous guy, scooted over, his right hand moving towards his holster. I was afraid he'd get even more annoyed and maybe a little trigger-happy, so I gave up and lowered my arms because the last thing Billie needed was a father with a bullet through his heart.

Fifteen minutes later I was contemplating my Kodiak boots behind the bars of a temporary detention cell, in the company of two drunks and a guy dressed like an insurance salesman.

The cell across from mine, which was reserved for women, had a single occupant, a permed redhead who looked as though she'd been walking the streets for so long her high heels had sunk into the tarmac and fossilized there. Maybe some future archaeologist would one day pore over these artefacts to try to understand the strange customs of this period, in which women had to perch on top of instruments of torture. She wore nothing on her feet but a pair of socks full of holes that showed the scarlet polish on her toes, and she was also yelling, but for different reasons than I was. She was fulminating against the police, against men, against the injustice of the world that had created girls like her and couldn't even give them a fucking pair of shoes and treat them with a modicum of decency.

I don't like to diss women, and certainly not broken women, but my nerves were totally frayed and her nasal voice was interfering with Billie's voice, which I was listening for beyond the walls. Her rantings were boring into me like a gimlet with a concrete drill bit drives into a two-by-four, and in the end I yelled at her to shut her stupid trap. A dead silence fell over the two cells, the girl's mouth started to twitch at the corners, and she went off to cry in a corner. In other circumstances I would have tried to console her, because I felt like total crap, as overbearing as an angry pimp, but at that moment I didn't have the strength to reach through the bars to stroke the damp cheek of a girl who'd spent her whole fucking life hating the first man who ever touched her and every man since. I made do with stammering some feeble excuses and curled up on a metal bench while I waited for Lucy-Ann to show up and bust me out of there. I might have been tempted to cry too, but the sordid spectacle of drunkard number one drooling down himself, the insurance-sales guy buttoned up all wrong, and the girl with holes in her socks made me suppress my tears by calling on what pride I still had left. I improvised a balaclava with my sweater and dropped my head between my knees, where everything was dark.

We always think these kinds of horror stories only happen to other people. We feel compassion for the tearful parents whenever we see a photo of a child in the newspaper or plastered to a wall, but you never imagine it might be your own child one day. If the idea crosses our minds, we push it away immediately, saying it could never happen, convinced we'd be there to protect him or her; that nothing could happen while we were looking out for them. We feel sorry for those poor people who wander around with the photo of their little girl's first communion or her most recent birthday, showing a child puffing out her cheeks in front of a bunny-shaped birthday cake with seven or eight candles on it. We pity the women with rings around their eyes, zombified by sleeping pills or antidepressants or the big bottle of gin tucked at the back of the kitchen cupboard, within easy reach, for those moments when the awareness of time is too overwhelming, but we can't really understand their distress. This kind of terrible event only happens to people whom Destiny has singled out for misery, and we aren't that kind of people. Or so we think.

And then, one glacial January night, we wind up in the slammer in a fug of rancid sweat, wondering if we'll ever see our bundle of joy again, if she'll grow up, if she'll bring some pimply loser home the day she turns fourteen, if she'll end up treating us like dirt. And right then is the moment we wish most ardently that our daughter will one day have the chance to treat us like senile old cretins, that she'll bring sixty losers home if she feels like it, that she'll play bass in a punk band if she wants, convert to Islam, get twelve nose piercings, or sign up for the Foreign Legion. Whatever she wants to do with her life, we don't give a flying fuck. All we want is to be able to watch her breathing, growing older, crying at romantic movies from the fifties, with mascara down her cheeks and her hair all dishevelled. All we hope for is to be broken-hearted when she's sad, and to tear out our own guts to make her happy. Nothing else matters, too bad if she doesn't turn out to be the adult we imagined.

On the days when archaeology and witchcraft lost

their appeal, Billie would declare she wanted to become an astronaut. She dreamed of travelling into space and discovering in the weightlessness a drug that would cure trees and sick cats, mangy dogs and crocodiles. There was something of Mother Teresa in her, or Saint Francis of Assisi, she was so damn kindhearted. Maybe she'd have become a great protector of the weak, ugly, and socially outcast if this wretched life hadn't pulled the rug out from under her feet.

She'd adopted a cat the year before, a gutter tomcat in pretty rough shape. She'd given it the name of a mouse — Pixie, after the Hanna-Barbera cartoon *Pixie & Dixie & Mr. Jinks*, which I'd shown her not long before on the internet. Billie had immediately fallen in love with Pixie, the mouse who wore a blue bowtie, and she gave its name to her cat without a moment's hesitation. "That way he won't eat any mice, Papanoute," she said, because Billie loved mice, alligators, deer, rats, any four-legged creature, with a boundless love that made her forget that most quadrupeds only survived by gobbling up other quadrupeds or bipeds, and vice versa.

Pixie must have been lying on Billie's bed right then, anxiously awaiting her return, pricking up his worried ears every time Lucy-Ann opened the front door to yell out Billie's name into the darkness. I was just telling Pixie to hold on, don't get upset, Pixie, she'll be back, it's just a nightmare, when a cop took me out of the cell and led me to what he called the welcome desk. I don't know if he was trying to be ironic or wanted to inject a little humour into the situation, but I didn't have the heart to laugh, and neither did Lucy-Ann, who was waiting for me on a narrow fake-leather couch, gnawing at her nails.

I'd never seen her chew her nails. In our family Billie was the nail-biter, although Lucy-Ann had almost cured her of the habit by coating her fingertips in some product that smelled vile and tasted just as bad. I wasn't too keen on the idea of letting Billie suck on some poison whose side effects we didn't know, which might cause cancer or behavioural difficulties, who knows, but on this topic, L.A. invariably had the last word.

But since late afternoon, all rules had been in abeyance for Lucy-Ann. She was chewing the nail of her right index finger as if she wanted to rip it clean off and at the same time apologize to Billie for having hassled her about such nonsense and bits of dead skin. She was pitiful to watch, with her puffy eyes, her coat on askew, her messy hair, but I couldn't do anything to help her, or myself, or Billie. I'd been cornered into the kind of powerlessness that makes you utterly crazy, bringing out a violence you would never have believed could exist inside you. If I'd had some way of converting this violence into energy, I'd have invented a time machine and brought Billie back right away, I'd have intercepted her as she left school with all the other little Billies, Cédrikas, Victorias, and Ashleys, with all the young Davids whose smiles had been wiped away on the corner of a deserted street, but I wouldn't have done it for L.A. or for myself. I would have done it for Cédrika, Victoria, Ashley, and David, I would have done it for Billie, so she could grow up and travel in the purity of interplanetary space.

Lucy-Ann waited for me to gather my things, then she stood up. I followed her, and we didn't say a single word between the police station and the car. It was only when we left the parking lot that she exploded. She pulled a U-turn to avoid a one-way street and slammed on the brakes.

L.A. usually expressed herself very carefully, to set a good example for Billie, and rarely let herself stray far from proper language, but once the dam had been breached, all the sailors in the world would be unable to stop the flow. I knew her well enough to recognize when she was about to spark what I thought of as a kind of linguistic combustion. Even before she opened her mouth, I saw a gang of naked sailors swallow their gum, and then the dam exploded with cursing. To sum it up, I was a fucking fucking sicko irresponsible parent who managed to fucking fuck shit up every day including the day his daughter disappeared. I was an asshole, a bastard, a douchebag, an imbecile, and a fucking jerk who simply didn't deserve to have an amazing daughter like Billie. "If I was starting over," she spat in my face, "I'd find another fucking sperm donor, not you. You're a totally useless father, Bill Richard!"

In terms of low blows, it was hard to imagine a lower one, and it whipped my breath away as effectively as taking a boot in the balls. I wasn't a perfect father, but I defied any other sperm donor to prove he might have muddled through better than me in ensuring Billie's well-being. I bit the inside of my cheeks so I wouldn't jump out of the car and rip the door off. Then a moment later, a further storm of curses crashed around inside the overheated car, originating in my seat this time. I only stopped when I realized that Lucy-Ann was crying and that the windows were completely fogged up.

I wasn't the one who needed to apologize, but I did it anyway, for Billie, who needed a father and a mother ready to tear each other's eyes out about as much as she needed a father pierced by a 9 mm hole. Instead, she needed two adults standing shoulder to shoulder ready to turn the world upside down to find her. I reached my hand out to Lucy-Ann. She didn't flinch when I rested it on her shoulder to massage her neck, very gently, with all the remaining tenderness I could muster for this woman who didn't love me anymore. She let her head fall forward onto the steering wheel and I held out a pack of Kleenex to her. She shredded the first one before filling the other three and chucking them onto the back seat. After that, we drove back to the house at full speed, because it was the first place Billie would head if she managed to escape the night's density.

Pixie was there, keeping an eye out for Billie's return from one of the sunroom windows, lying on the back of a child's armchair in which Billie sometimes sat to watch the snow falling. Lucy-Ann started sobbing again when she saw the cat. She ran over and pulled him into her arms, sighing, "Poor Pixie, poor kitty, poor baby Pixie." She didn't associate her pain with mine, but with that of the mangy cat, who would slowly let himself die if Billie didn't come home to pet him and tell him how Puss in Boots and the Little Match Girl had met.

If Lucy-Ann hadn't beaten me to it, that's what I would have done too. I would have taken the old fleabag in my arms and rocked him like Billie does, giving him little nose kisses, "Way more fun than mouth kisses, Papanoute," as Billie would say as she rubbed her nose on Pixie's.

L.A. had never liked the cat, but that night he was the only living creature linking her to Billie. As for me, I didn't exist anymore. I was nothing but a man, just one among thousands of scumbags who approach young girls, offering them flowers or candy, just flowers or jewel-toned sweets, the kind kids like and men just happen to have hidden in their pockets. For a split second I hated Lucy-Ann for having made this animal — which she'd never petted even with her fingertips — an accomplice in her misery, but then I thought how happy Billie would be to see that her mother was finally taking an interest in Pixie.

Then I realized I was behaving as though Billie was never coming home. My fear of never holding this child in my arms again was such that I was anticipating the worst instead of doing something. Before I smashed the house to pieces, I put my hat back on and told Lucy-Ann I was going back out to look for Billie.

When I returned, Lucy-Ann was slumped on the kitchen table, asleep, my bottle of Jack Daniel's Gold Medal 1981 next to her. I pulled off my boots and went upstairs to sleep on Billie's bed, with her dolls, her stuffed animals, and Pixie, whose big green eyes already contained the knowledge that our house had come tumbling down.

MARNIE

I should never have mentioned Catfish Lake. If I'd kept our secret, maybe nobody would have found Mike's running shoe, and the compass points would have stayed in their proper places. In less time than it takes a raindrop to hit the ground, I'd become a schemer and a liar, and all the gentleness with which people had been handling me disappeared in a flash. Officer Desmarais's soft voice hardened, Michael's father's face became like Lex Luthor's when he realizes that Superman has yet again wrecked all his Machiavellian plans, and the whispering of the men who'd come to offer their assistance to the police morphed into a hostile buzz. "The little girl lied," the murmurs said. "The little girl made it all up, go figure why she did that, the little girl made a mistake and she wanted to cover it up."

In the opinion of all those men, the little girl who kept jumping out of her skin at the slightest sound like a nervous squirrel had entirely invented the bizarre tale of the magic swimming hole so she wouldn't have to reveal that she'd been near Catfish Lake with Victor's son, and because she refused to confess the bad thing that had happened to the boy. Only my father, who couldn't understand what had happened any more than I could, continued to believe me. "I'm sure there's a logical explanation, Victor. I know Marnie. She wouldn't have lied about Michael. Those two are joined at the hip, you know that as well as I do."

But Victor Saint-Pierre refused to listen to my father's arguments. To his mind, my father just wanted to protect his daughter and so couldn't be trusted. In just a few hours his mental state had changed radically, to the point where even his friends could no longer recognize him. This usually calm man, who could be heard humming Beatles tunes in his workshop on Saturday mornings, the man who came to ruffle our hair, calling Michael a little bugger, was now all hostility and anger.

After the cops took his son's shoe from him, I saw him push my father roughly away and stride towards me. I instinctively pressed up against the police car, whose metal, burning in the August sun, drew a cry from me, and I closed my eyes, convinced Victor Saint-Pierre was going to slap me. But someone stopped him before he reached me. "Don't lose it, Victor," is all I heard, and then the sound made by my father's big, calloused hands slamming down on the car roof. But my father didn't say anything. He simply stared right into Michael's father's eyes and took me by the hand to lead me down Morin Sisters Road. We hadn't taken ten steps when Desmarais showed up. He couldn't just let us go like that. They had questions they wanted to ask me, serious questions, million-dollar questions, even though the money in my pocket was only enough to buy Michael a Sprite when we got back from the magic swimming hole the day before.

That was our ritual that summer. Every other day before dinner we would head to Yvonne Leclerc's depanneur to buy a Sprite or an orangeade to drink on the porch. We used to sit on the old Pepsi Cola fridge purring away in a corner, pop the tops off our bottles, imitating the thirsty men at the Hotel Plaza opposite the post office, and glug back a few sparkling swallows that shot back up into our noses. Afterwards we chatted about our day, what we were going to do that evening, our projects for the next day—we were never short of ideas, dreams, or plans. Michael Saint-Pierre and I were two halves of the same person, joined at the hip, as my father had put it, like a bat and a ball, a bike and its wheels, and the police ought to have understood that you can't lie when you've just had a piece of your own head ripped off. But once adults grow up, they don't understand childhood relationships, those loves that are stronger than flesh and blood, grimy little paws reaching out to each other when the sun goes down.

While a dozen men were busy dredging the river to the northeast of the village, a team from the city was combing the banks of Catfish Lake under Officer Desmarais's supervision. He'd set up some kind of headquarters at the edge of the road with a picnic table and some folding chairs that one of Victor Saint-Pierre's friends carried around in the trunk of his car, and Desmarais and his partner, McCullough—I think, not a French name anyway—took me there to interrogate me. Since there were only two chairs, McCullough and my father remained standing in the sun and made me sit down next to Officer Desmarais.

It must have been nearly noon because the shadows were short, gathered around the feet of trees and men. To begin with I wasn't really listening to Desmarais. I was fascinated by McCullough's shrunken shadow. His head passed through his neck every time he took a few steps back to avoid the wasp buzzing around him, attracted by his aftershave lotion. I was also trying to find the wasp's shadow, which was getting lost among the bigger shadows. If it had been gathering pollen in the middle of a field, we'd have been able to see its minuscule silhouette on a meadow hawkweed or wild chicory flower, but out here the sun denied its existence. McCullough was waving his arms about so much that Desmarais finally asked him to go and look for something in his car, and then Desmarais took my hand in his big bear paw so that I had to look him in the eye.

He wiped away the sweat trickling down his forehead with a handkerchief embroidered with two letters the same colour as his eyes, a blue that had seemed inoffensive to me the day before, like the blue of a sky slowly clouding over, but which now had the glint of cold metal in his heat-reddened face. Actually, Desmarais had three pairs of eyes. He kept one pair for his wife and children, a pair that he pushed back into their sockets with a flick of his hand if he had to speak to victims or poor people, and then his cop's eyes, reserved for assassins, bandits, thieves, and liars. The cop's eyes, burned by sweat and lack of sleep, were waiting for me to tell them what had really happened after Michael and I had abandoned Émilie on the Saint-Pierres' porch.

What could I say that would convince him our only destination had been the magic swimming hole, that it was the storm — preceded by the cry of death — that had set everything in motion? I looked to my father for support, but he was staring at the truncated shadow at his feet, wondering how he'd ended up here, and if he would be able to extricate himself from this place where his body had been reduced to powerlessness, compressed by the sun just like his shadow.

I'd often seen my father in this state. Now and then he used to stop abruptly in the middle of the garden, looking around to see the voice that had called out to him, then lowering his head sadly and standing still until his shadow lengthened out again. Sometimes he would shuffle over to the Mary-Jean bush, drop his rake or his trowel, and kneel beside the bush. I think he was praying or crying, imploring the Mary-Jeans to answer him.

There were a lot of roses named Mary in our yard, Mary-Jean, Mary-Kay, Mary Mackillop, but the Mary-Jeans were my mother's flowers — she had preferred peach-coloured roses to the ones the colour of their name, finding the latter too obvious, too closely aligned with what was expected of them. She liked flowers to surprise her, the same way she liked it when a man's name didn't match his appearance. For example, she used to claim my father looked absolutely nothing like an Alex, and the fact that he and his name had nothing in common was the source of his charm. "I'd never have agreed to marry you if your parents had named you Paul or John," she used to say, before bursting into laughter and plunging the bucket into the rain barrel to draw water for the Mary-Jeans.

Most of what I knew about my mother, Marie Beaupré, were things my father had told me. The rest I'd either guessed or invented, or learned from the few letters she'd written to my father before she joined him at the altar in a cloud of peachy perfume. But death had carried her away so long ago that for me she barely had a real shape. She was nothing but a shadow in the garden over which my father would bend when a voice from the past called out to him, a voice from beyond. It was useless to try to reach him at these moments. He was travelling through the kingdom of the dead on Marie Beaupré's arm.

This is the way my father was standing under the midday sun, a prisoner of his own shadow and that of Marie Beaupré, while Officer Desmarais waited patiently for me to start confessing. Since I couldn't hope for any help from my father, and since I didn't actually have anything to confess, I fell back on what seemed the most logical explanation. "Maybe he flew away," I murmured, blushing despite myself. "Maybe he found a cape and swooped off to the lake like Superman."

As Officer Desmarais stared silently at me, I instinctively stiffened and tried to sink into my chair, aware that my childish logic had just hit a brick wall. Desmarais didn't like my hypothesis, and he was struggling to contain the anger welling up from his neck and spreading across his face like a red tidal wave pulsing with his heartbeat. He closed his eyes, lifted his cap to wipe his head, and in so doing accidentally knocked over the glass of lukewarm water he'd got for me a few minutes earlier. Hearing the sound of glass against metal, my father quickly came back to the world of the living; Officer McCullough chose this moment to come back from the car, cursing the wasp that had adopted him; and I burst into tears.

I'd sworn I wouldn't cry, because in the adventures of Superman Lois Lane never cries, and because if Superman had disappeared it must mean he was carrying out some mission, the importance of which neither Victor Saint-Pierre, nor Officer Desmarais, nor my father could under-stand. But he would return, of that I was certain, to tell them that they were all wrong, that Lois Lane didn't lie.

As I wiped my face with McCullough's handkerchief and tried to choke back my tears, my father informed Desmarais that the interrogation was over, that no other cop would be coming near me, then he took me by the hand and we started walking towards the village under the leaden sun.

Behind us, near Catfish Lake, the earlier buzz of rumours began swelling again. We heard it billowing up under the groundcover and then curling towards the trees before rising to their summits. After that, the wind carried it off towards Rivière-aux-Trembles, where it slipped in through the open windows and straight into the ears of the men and women who were clutching their children fiercely to them. By evening, the whole of Rivière-aux-Trembles had decreed that nasty little Marnie Duchamp was behind Michael Saint-Pierre's disappearance.

BILL

We searched for weeks, we harassed the police, we even hired a private detective, then fired him unceremoniously and hired a different one, but Billie's trail fizzled out right by the school, just as if she'd evaporated into the last rays of the January daylight, leaving nothing behind her, not even a grubby little mitten or one of the butterfly hairclips she was always losing.

Every time the phone rang or a child's cry was heard in the street, Lucy-Ann rushed to the phone or the door. I stayed in my corner, my heart beating wildly, hoping to see Lucy-Ann faint, her knees buckle, and her hands grab onto the kitchen counter or the door frame. I thought if L.A. swooned it would be a sure sign Billie had come back, or was racing towards the house with her arms stretched out, or sobbing on the other end of the line saying, "Maman, Maman, it's me, Billie." But Lucy-Ann never fainted. The light of hope that had flashed across her face just a few seconds earlier disappeared instantly, and her face took on its habitual death mask, ever harder and more impenetrable. Fear and pain had made her ugly, and I almost hated her for not making an effort to do her hair and for wearing the same dirty, wrinkled clothes day after day. I kept trying to tell her that letting herself waste away wouldn't help us find our darling girl, but she told me to fuck off as if I were worth no more than the discarded underwear lying on the floor next to the bed.

At the beginning, we'd had some friends helping out, we'd been surrounded by warmth, affection, smiles that said "I understand" without understanding, but at least they were there, fully present. Warm hands rested on our shoulders, held out glasses full to the brim with alcohol—*Here, drink this before you dry out*—cooked us meals that smelled of living houses, and then, little by little, the hands cooled down and the house emptied out. Those good souls had beaten a retreat and I couldn't even bring myself to resent them for trying to protect themselves from our unhappiness.

Only Lucy-Ann's mother, Régine, and her childhood best friend, Patricia, had remained despite L.A.'s hostile attitude. They showed up regularly, arms laden with food that would end up in the garbage, books and magazines that would never be opened, and they tried to inject a little order into the chaos building up around us. But every second visit, Lucy-Ann kicked them out, yelling that she didn't need a cleaner, and then collapsed as soon as the door closed behind them, and I was the one who had to pick up the pieces. I needed someone to pick up my own pieces, I needed Lucy-Ann to embrace me once in a while and whisper sweet words into my ear, "Don't cry, Bill, our little girl will come back, I know she will." But Lucy-Ann only had the strength to bear her own pain and never imagined I could be feeling so bad I wanted to rip out my own hair and my scalp along with it. I could have died and it would have made no difference to her, because she'd got it in her head that whatever had happened to Billie, it was my fault.

She claimed I should have been there when Billie came out of school to meet her and take her to her dance lesson, that I should have waited for her there because that's what normal fathers do, the ones who love their daughters and don't waste their days imagining how they might get a damn frog to fly. "Toad," I corrected her, ducking the pencil, cup, book, or porcelain elephant that came flying at me.

I protested just for the sake of it, so as not sink into the pond of stagnant water that was widening around me, and just so I wouldn't hate myself any more than I already did, but I was sadly lacking in assertiveness because I addressed the same reproaches to myself, and more vehemently than Lucy-Ann did — if that was possible. I *should* have been there, I knew it, good weather or bad, my feet sunk in slush or mud, my umbrella dripping down my neck or my T-shirt soaked with sweat, keeping watch for the appearance of the little corner-of-the-mouth smile that could send my father's heart spinning. But Lucy-Ann and I had discussed it for hours before deciding the opposite. Since the Studio Lenoir was right next door to the school, we fell in line with Billie's arguments. Every time we showed up to lead her by the hand from the school to the building next door, she balked. "I can walk by myself, you don't need to hold onto me." So we'd agreed that Billie could get herself there from then on. It was a way of showing her we didn't think she was still a baby and that we trusted her. We'd made the stupid decision together, but L.A. seemed to have forgotten this. She probably felt as guilty as I did, so she was twisting reality and erasing certain sections of it to protect herself, to suppress the voice that was crucifying her conscience.

So I became the guilty one, the one who should have been there holding Billie's hand. L.A. threw it right in my face when we got back from the police station that first night, and her accusations only got worse in the days that followed, after the cops had subjected both of us to fearsome interrogations. In the absence of any clear leads, the parents are always the prime suspects, and then the spotlight focuses on the father, the person most likely to rape or fatally injure someone. At the beginning I wanted to strangle all those guys who thought I could have attacked my own daughter. I came so close to leaping at their throats or kicking them up the ass, but then I calmed down. The men were just doing their jobs; their goal was the same as mine: to find Billie, even if it meant bulldozing the entire city to the ground.

The case had been entrusted to a team headed up by two investigators, Michel Dubois and Gilles Ménard, who'd worked on missing children's cases before. That much became obvious when they instructed me gently but firmly to just answer their damn questions. "Is that clear, Mr. Richard? We're the ones asking the questions." You could also see it in the way their big fingers gently touched the child's photos gathered on the metal table where the interrogation had taken place. These men had seen it all before and their only concern was what happened to the child. As for the parents' suffering, frankly, they couldn't give a shit.

The day after Billie disappeared, they bombarded me with questions for a good two hours, endlessly circling back over the same details and keeping a hawkish eye out for the moment when I might contradict myself, or the word that would betray me and allow them to knock me to the ground. Twenty times over, they asked me where I'd been when Billie finished school, and twenty times over I told them I'd been at Jack and Jack, a shabby café I'd been going to for years because I felt at home and I had my own table, in a corner behind a pillar, where I could think in peace without some cop double act attacking me instead of tracking down the bastard who'd snatched my child. They could check with the waitress; she'd confirm what I was saying. There were also two or three regulars who'd seen me at the café that day, all they had to do was track them down and ask.

"Take it easy, Mr. Richard, that's what we're planning to do," Ménard grunted, as he indicated that our interview was over.

Before I left the interrogation room, he jotted down on

a scrap of paper the three phone numbers where I could reach him and Dubois, just in case I remembered something later on.

The next day, though, Ménard showed up at my house, accompanied by the stoic and silent Dubois, to inform me he'd checked up on my alibi and nobody remembered having seen me at Jack and Jack on January 20th around three in the afternoon. As a result, he and his colleague wanted to ask me some more questions. Despite my protestations, they took me to the police station, interrogated me once again, and kept me hanging around for three hours in a grim room that smelled of disinfectant or Clorets gum.

At the end of the afternoon, they had another go at me, but I didn't crack for the simple reason that I had no reason to crack. I had been at Jack and Jack and if nobody remembered seeing me there it was because I'd been tucked away quietly in my corner, blending into the décor, or because someone was lying or had simply got the dates mixed up. We should just all go there together. Once she saw me in the flesh, the waitress would remember me. Ménard had a different idea. He'd summoned the girl while I was counting the holes in the ceiling tiles. She was in the next room, behind the two-way mirror, and she'd recognized my red scarf, just like the one her grandmother knitted her two years earlier. From the scarf, she moved up to my anonymous face and ended up stating that I had indeed been at Jack and Jack on January 20th, at a table at the back, table 12 or 17, she couldn't say which.

For Ménard and Dubois, however, this girl's testimony

wasn't worth much, because she'd recognized me on the basis of a scarf that didn't look anything like those big woolly scarves grannies knit. Dubois had been insistent on that point: grandmothers knit patterns, stitches on the right side, stitches on the wrong side, not the kind of scarves you can buy in a store. And luck wasn't on my side; as well as not knowing her table numbers, the girl didn't know any of the café's regulars. She was just filling in for the regular waitress that day, a friend who was studying for an exam, and she couldn't even remember the appearance of the guy who'd treated her like a dumbass because she gave him a mocha instead of a cappuccino.

This witness couldn't be trusted, so they suggested I take a polygraph, convinced they'd catch me out if they studied my cerebral activity. But they were shit out of luck. My brain waves agreed with me: I wasn't lying. This lie detector was my ticket out of there—without it, I'd still be in that room that reeked of disinfectant, trying to convince two men who'd seen other such cases that I was telling them nothing but the truth.

When I arrived home, L.A. was coming down the stairs to the ground floor, loosely holding a cup of coffee that was threatening to slop out onto the sixty-bucks-a-metre carpet. She stopped dead in the middle of the stairs and stared at me as if I was the worst monster the earth had ever produced.

"What did you do to Billie?" she whispered, clutching the banister. "What did you do to our daughter, you fucking sicko?"

Then her knees buckled under her, her head dropped, the cup of coffee bounced down the stairs, its noise muffled by the carpet as L.A. fainted, but no Billie appeared behind her in her bear-print pyjamas. Nobody at all appeared behind L.A., not even a small ghost blowing me a kiss to tell me not to worry anymore.

I picked L.A. up and carried her to the couch in the living room. I cleared up her mess, and then I wiped her café cognac–laced tears away as well as the acrimonious reproaches that burst out as soon as she opened her eyes. L.A. knew as well as I did that I hadn't laid a finger on Billie, but she needed to blame someone, needed to lash out at someone, so she'd let Inspector Ménard's insinuations creep in.

Frankly, this behaviour was grotesque. I couldn't believe that my own wife, the mother of my daughter, a woman who'd never seen me raise a hand against Billie — and who could tell if I was lying just from the timbre of my voice through the phone from three thousand kilometres away — could entertain such doubts about me when it came to the child for whom I'd have slashed my own throat or ripped off my own balls if need be.

"Jesus, L.A., wake up!" I yelled as she trotted out another one of her moronic arguments, and then a fog of anger descended, the kind of anger that blinds you and makes you see red as a headache seizes you. I even knocked over a chair and then hurled it across the room, which only served to prove my violence to L.A.

For days I pleaded my innocence in every way I could think of.

"Come on, L.A., Jesus, L.A., for fuck's sake, L.A., you can't seriously believe I harmed my baby girl?"

But it was a lost cause, my pleading wasn't worth shit. In Lucy-Ann Morency's mind as well as that of Inspector Gilles Ménard, Bill Richard would remain the sole and impossible suspect in the disappearance of his daughter, Billie Richard, aged eight years, nine months, until further notice.

During the following weeks, I called the numbers Ménard had scrawled down for me dozens of times, so often that Dubois's smooth voice on the other end of the line started cranking up a notch and he allowed himself a few demonstrations of impatience. But I didn't give a shit about his cop petulance, his stomach pain, his prostate issues, or anything else. All I wanted was for his team of assholes to work a miracle.

As for Ménard, he would turn up at the house unannounced at every opportunity, perhaps hoping he might surprise me as I was packing my daughter up into a suitcase or spiriting away some compromising evidence. He showed up looking like he thought he was Columbo, never bothering to take off his coat, and sitting down uninvited at the kitchen table. Then he would draw schemas, or build absurd groupings with the items that had accumulated on the table. He placed a knife on a plate, rested a fork perpendicularly on the knife, and set it swinging above dried-out pizza crusts. And then, apropos of nothing, he would clear his throat and ask if Billie liked pizza and burgers, and if we ever took her to McDonald's. His own daughter loved

McDonald's, he added, and he enjoyed taking her there, watching her order her cheeseburger all by herself like a grown-up, even though he hated the plastic décor and the overly harsh lighting that made it impossible to conceal from his daughter the fact that her father was old.

"Children's survival instincts are stronger than ours. Letting them eat what they want now and then won't do them any harm," he would murmur as he added a second fork to his impromptu see-saw, this time at a different angle, forming a star, and once again I saw Billie leaving for her ballet lesson with her shoulders hunched over, carrying her healthy snack in her lunchbox. I would have given anything in these moments to be able to wind back time and light an enormous bonfire into which Billie and I would throw her pink tights, her pink tutu, and her fucking ballet slippers while we toasted an entire bag of jumbo marshmallows.

If he noticed that L.A. and I couldn't take any more, Ménard wheeled out his arsenal of questions. "Where? When? How? Why? Louder, I can't hear you!" Then he left just as he'd arrived, without giving us the tiniest scrap of hope. Sometimes he would stop and stand in front of Billie's drawings on the fridge and ask if the green house in two of these pictures was the house of a relative or a friend, or if the giant bearded person in another drawing looked like anyone we knew, maybe someone Billie had mentioned to us.

I told him the green house was a picture of L.A.'s father's cottage in Mauricie, and that the giant was a hybrid character Billie had invented based on Oscar Wilde's *The Selfish Giant* and a giant from my own fairy tales, the blue giant, who lived partly in the ocean and partly on dry land. A gentle giant, half man, half fish. Ménard frowned, following the outline of the giant with an ink-stained index finger and murmuring that perhaps the giant was a man Billie was afraid of, a stranger she'd tried to tell us about. "Why don't you think back on that?"

After Ménard left, L.A. cried for a few minutes and then started yelling at me, asking where I'd dredged this fucking giant up from. Then she ran to shut herself in our bedroom, which had become her bedroom, a place I only entered to get clean clothes and pick up the discarded underwear she'd thrown into a corner. She never came into Billie's room — she couldn't — and now she was trying to avoid Pixie as much as possible, because he reminded her too much of our sweetheart. So Pixie had become my friend, my own confidant, the only living creature in front of whom I could cry my heart out in peace.

The final time Ménard came to the house, I was sitting with Pixie on the porch, telling him one of the stories that used to make Billie laugh. I was as pitiful as an old man talking to his wife's corpse. As usual, Ménard headed straight for the kitchen table and waited for me to join him there. He picked up a torn envelope and folded it in two, making a little tent, under which he slipped an orange crayon, one of Billie's, which neither L.A. nor I had had the strength to put back in its box. Then Ménard said he wouldn't be coming back again unless any new elements turned up in the inquiry. Billie had now been missing for three months and the investigation was going nowhere. He wasn't going to close the file but, given that there were no new leads to explore, he would have to give it some time and see if anything new came up. "I'm sorry," he mumbled, and then walked to the door.

I leapt up and shouted after him that he couldn't drop it now, he had no right to abandon Billie, it was his job to take care of her, that's what he was paid to do, and I would go straight to the top if the case was shelved. He gently raised his arm to stop me, and retorted in his twisted way, "All right then, Mr. Richard, how about you tell me where you really were on January 20th?"

MARNIE

There's a story I remember in which the main character, Lucas, I think his name is, tries desperately to get rid of a port wine stain that covers the left side of his face with a purplish cloud in the shape of a wolf's mouth opening around his right eye. "It's the mark of the devil," Lucas's mother had muttered over his crib, thus conferring satanic powers on her son, powers he would be unjustly accused of using until he threw himself into a well, dragging with him the beast that had been clinging to his face since he was born.

And that's what ended up happening to me too. Michael's disappearance imprinted the mark of the devil on my face, and from that time on I became a pariah, an untouchable, a child everyone had to stay away from. The conclusions of the inquiry led nowhere. There were too many hypotheses, and they were too unlikely. Mike's body hadn't been in the lake, the divers were clear on that point. And he wasn't in the river either. Given the weakness of the current, if he'd drowned, we'd have found him somewhere on a muddy shallow or near the swamps bordering the banks. If the dogs were right — and how could we doubt the dogs? — Mike had walked into the water, or someone had made him walk in, before taking him, who knows why, to Catfish Lake. It made no sense.

Most people opted for the theory that the dogs had simply followed an older trail of Mike's scent. The boy often played in that area, his scent was everywhere. He hadn't walked into the water. He'd covered the two kilometres the dogs had tracked on a different day, another time, and then he'd retraced his steps. I disagreed; there was no real path to get there, Mike never went that far. But people only half-listened to me, wondering why I refused to admit that the storm had taken place near Catfish Lake, where someone had abducted Mike, causing his scent to simply trail off into the middle of nowhere. People looked at the question from every angle, frowned, and then stared at me with a sigh: the little girl is lying, Marnie must be hiding something.

My father thought the rumour would die down over time, that people would come back to their senses and understand that I was simply the innocent victim of a mystery that time would reveal, but he was forgetting that the mark of the devil is indelible, and that a mystery, by definition, leaves its survivors in the dark.

We held out in Rivière-aux-Trembles for just under a year, Papa and I, attempting the impossible — ignoring the whispers that trailed off in long drooly streaks as we passed, the silent meaningful looks, the conversations that stopped abruptly when my father pushed open the door to the post office or Jos Bouchard's hardware store. Bouchard himself actually stole away to the back room as if he thought I was also responsible for the death of his son Martin, who had been carried off by the cries of Blueberry River. A constant stream of mean words trailed in my wake, spat out or barely audible, but the thing that scared me the most was the word "witch," a word only spoken by the children, who took it from those tales where princesses prick their fingers on the thorns of poisoned roses — Betsy Rose and Black Velvet — roses the exact same colour as the blood they cause to trickle.

"People burn witches in fires in the middle of the night," Germain Leblanc shouted after me as we came out of school one day. Ever since, I'd been waking up, sweating, in the middle of the night, convinced that men with soot-smudged faces were preparing a pyre for me outside. I could hear the crackle of the piled-up branches, I would imagine the aroma of my roasted flesh mixed with the scent of the wild rose under the dew. But I never mentioned these nightmares to my father. I waited for dawn to break, keeping watch from behind the curtains on the flickering lights into which they would throw me alive. Then, one night in late May, a storm broke out, lighting up my bedroom with the glow of burning logs, and transporting me back to the edge of the magic swimming hole, where the rumbling of the thunder mixed with Martin Bouchard's cries. In the background, very far behind the rain, Michael swayed mechanically, his pale face disappearing bit by bit, feature by feature, until it formed a smooth disc in the fog against which the thunder reverberated.

I must have cried out when I saw that white circle, because a few moments later my father came running into my room and took me in his arms. Through my tears and my trembling, I told him about the witches, about Lucas, about the devil and the rolling thunder, about the furious storms that had been rumbling ever since Michael disappeared because I escaped the plan fate had made for me.

"The lightning took Mike, Pop, it's my fault, the clouds are going to come for me." I had evaded the thunder, and if I escaped the pyre it simply meant I'd be snatched up later through a rip in the sky.

Three weeks after that, a truck with *Bob's Movers* in enormous black letters on its side pulled up in front of the house. If my father couldn't protect me from the storm, he could at least take me away from the whispering. The Mary-Jeans and the Sparkling Scarlets would just have to bloom without Alex Duchamp's care and attention for the next six years.

I didn't cry when the heavy truck door slammed shut definitively on the dozens of boxes piled up in front of our furniture, nor when my father locked up the fence around the garden, nor when our elderly Oldsmobile passed the sign saying "Welcome to Rivière-aux-Trembles," because for me the village no longer represented anything but the memory of a childhood that had ended at the edge of an evil swimming hole. The thousands of photos I kept from that time were nothing more than moments of life frozen on glossy paper, thousands of moments of happiness shut up in an album whose last page was dated August 7th, 1979. After that date, the paper cracked, the light deserted the pictures, and my memories were no longer anything but a series of black-and-white snapshots that resembled boring textbook illustrations. The light had left Rivière-aux-Trembles at the same time the sun fell in the north sky with Michael, and the place was emptied of everything that allows time to follow its course. The trees didn't grow anymore, children no longer ran in the paths lined with alders, ferns, and ragweed, or in the fields sown with rye and cow pats. Rivière-aux-Trembles was shut up in a past that had drawn its wealth from a land that was now sterile.

We drove for more than four hours, my father and I, barely saying a word, then we crossed an enormous bridge and entered the place of perpetual hum that would be our refuge from memories for a few years.

At the end of this period, when my father had become as grey as the concrete all around us, I rummaged in his drawers looking for the keys to our old house. I tossed them on the kitchen table and ordered him to go home before he became fossilized in the square of asphalt shadowed by our building. I was eighteen years old, and I too wanted to open the blinds, to get as far away as possible from this apartment where, despite our best efforts, we had not succeeded in forgetting Rivière-aux-Trembles.

As my father drove north to take care of his wilderness garden, I headed south, following the Canucks' route to the United States border. From there, I would wend my way down along the Appalachians, from Maine to Alabama, in the hope of finding some vast field of ripe wheat where I might want to put down roots. My journey lasted a year, a long year during which I tried to delude myself about the liberating virtues of poverty and disorientation, before I travelled back up to New York to find out if the Big Apple was as rotten as the Big Apricot of Jerry Siegel and Joe Shuster, Superman's fathers, and to see if maybe I could make out the fleeting silhouette of Michael Superman Saint-Pierre in the rectangular corridors created by the buildings.

I did happen to spot him once or twice, getting off a bus wearing his red T-shirt, or playing the harmonica on a street corner and counting the coins that landed in his dirty cap. I also saw him at the Metropolitan Opera, in Greenwich Village cafés, or in dusty cul-de-sacs, but every time I got closer, his eyes changed shape or colour and his face disappeared behind the hostile expression of a lanky teenager yelling "Fuck you, man!" in a Queens accent.

Over time, his T-shirt shrank and I stopped seeing him. But I ended up staying in New York for twenty-three years, sending gladioli, roses, and daisies to chic Tribeca clients until my father's death brought me back to Rivière-aux-Trembles, only for me to realize that running away had been an illusion, and that I wouldn't see Mike's corpse rise out of the water on the polluted banks of the Hudson River. It was here, at the very site of the drama, that the story of Marnie Duchamp and Michael Saint-Pierre would be resolved.

BILL

It hurts to think you're alone, when even the wife to whom you so often said "I love you" no longer thinks of you as anything other than a piece of shit. It's true that our relationship had been floundering for some time. Lucy-Ann and I weren't exactly poster children for the perfect relationship; we were no pair of turtle doves on permanent honeymoon. Candlelit dinners, hands slipping discreetly underneath sweaters, meaningful smiles across a room while half a dozen political geniuses reeled off nonsense with the seriousness of a pope—for us, all that stuff was way in the past. We did still fuck, because fucking was in our blood, because this kind of carnal confrontation allowed us to take possession of the other while also reproaching each other for simply existing, with just enough violence to make up for the lost tenderness. But I can't remember the last time Lucy-Ann said something nice to me, something genuinely nice, like "You look pretty good this morning, Bill," or "Your hair's all sticking up," with an amused smile and a finger gently brushing back the rebellious lock.

The reason we were still together was Billie, so that she didn't have to pack a Mickey Mouse suitcase or a Snoopy backpack every Friday night, wondering which teddy bear to take with her and which things to abandon to the sadness of her empty room until Monday. L.A. had experienced this double life, which forces children to rip themselves apart to satisfy what she referred to as parental egotism, and she didn't want that for Billie.

Neither did I, I didn't want that kind of parcelling out for my pumpkin. But I still thought that sometimes it was better for small children to trail their luggage around rather than have to watch out for knives flying across a room while being subjected to the sad and banal spectacle of conjugal hatred. But in every case, children end up footing some of the bill, which adds up and up the more the passion of the marriage unravels. When children arrive, the partying ends. Nights of love interspersed with night feedings invariably give way to night feedings only, which would have to be particularly amazing experiences to compete with the visits to bars, late-night movies, and weekends in New York or Los Angeles that the parents used to enjoy before the children were born. They have to balance the deficit and the end of their carefree lives with bursts of laughter, two-syllable words, and wonky little footsteps that elicit cries of enthusiasm and applause from the old folks whose under-eye suitcases practically reach their chins.

L.A. and I started growing apart not long after Billie was born, transferring the large part of our potential love onto that chubby-cheeked, peach-purée-spattered little face. As the months went by, we realized we might not love each other enough for the equation two plus one to augment the tenderness we felt for each other. The distance grew slowly, without any real ruptures, brawls, or blood on the white walls—so slowly, in fact, that we didn't always understand why the other person seemed so lacklustre, why their voice suddenly irritated us, why the bed had become too narrow.

It took months for the truth to leap out and stare us in the face: our honeymoon had taken place on a stage set, and the illusion had only been sustained because it was based on the image of an artificial happiness, a state to which anyone who doesn't want to be swept away by the current should aspire.

Although she'd outed the lie our union was based on, Billie had also plugged the breach, and it was because of this child that we hadn't yet started sending lawyers' letters or spiteful messages through mutual friends.

We'd established something of a status quo that suited us both; you mind your business, I'll mind mine, and everything will work out. In this way, we managed to tolerate each other, to look each other in the eye, even manage to laugh and have fun with our munchkin like a real family, and it would have taken next to nothing for us to start loving each other again, to put our arms around each other's waists, for us to become a team once more against the world's imbecility. It would have simply taken L.A. diluting her wine and me diluting my Scotch, my manly drink, but now that Billie was no longer there everything was in turmoil. Instead of reaching out to each other, we moved apart at supersonic speed. We snapped for the minutest of reasons, we popped old pus-filled zits, we let all the bad stuff out, but for all that, we felt no relief— quite the contrary. Each time I walked by a mirror after an argument and saw the poisonous spittle drying on the edge of my lips, I wanted to throw up, and I'm sure L.A. was equally disgusted.

Once it became clear in L.A.'s mind that I was the sole person responsible for Billie's disappearance, I had to take off before the treacherous doubts that occasionally attacked me could become a neurosis. I refused to become one of those innocent men who have been pushed to their limits, one of those fragile guys who end up with a noose around their neck just so people will leave them in peace and stop torturing them with questions they don't know the answers to. Because of course doubt sometimes slipped in the back door just when I was least expecting it, jumping on my back, grabbing my head in its two hands and shaking it until I started screaming that it couldn't have been me who made Billie disappear in the January mist.

Ever since Ménard had started bombarding me with questions so absurd that I could no longer remember my own mother's name, I spent entire nights worrying about my mental health and wondering if he was holding back some information that would have given me a heart attack if he revealed it. I was so afraid this cretin was right when he accused me in so many words of withholding information that would have helped the search for Billie that I became crazy. My memory was shrouded in a kind of loose veil, and I was getting things mixed up — the days and the years, Billie's pink jacket and her polka-dotted raincoat. Ménard's harassment methods were so effective they removed all certainty and at the same time twisted the purest truth. This cop was dangerous. One time I almost suggested he inject me with a dose of Pentothal so we could be done with it, but I came to my senses in time. Ménard was off the rails, and he was going to drag me with him if I didn't pull myself together. I hadn't touched a hair on Billie's head, and I wasn't insane.

The lie detector had confirmed what I said, the waitress had recognized my scarf — a red scarf, yes, that's right, blood red, Billie, the colour of the rose whose poisoned thorn pricked Sleeping Beauty. I loved my daughter, and I was correcting poorly written assignments at Jack and Jack sipping a cappuccino at the table in the back, with foam on my upper lip, when the monster who had kidnapped my daughter started his car and headed for the dark roads.

I had reluctantly come to the conclusion that Billie had been kidnapped, that she hadn't simply atomized or been taken on board a spaceship on a mission to seek out the best specimens of humanity. Abduction was still the most likely hypothesis, even if it was the one I most hated to believe. I turned the idea over and over in my head, and the first image to pop up was that of a man, a single faceless man who looked gigantic next to Billie, leaning over to enclose her in the shadow of his dark coat and muffle her cries. I imagined an overcoat, or an anorak, or a large raincoat that tumbled down to his knees, then a dark-coloured car driven away into the night by the man in the dark coat. An icy fog pressed up against the windshield, building up until it hid the horizon, and I breathed in the kidnapper's putrid scent as his big, coarse hands operated the windshield wipers. This was where Billie had been taken, inside this car in which the silence was shot through with hoarse breathing and the regular rhythm of the wipers.

As for me, I was in that miserable café, and if nobody remembered having seen me there it was because the place was only frequented by wrecks of men who started drowning their disappointment in cheap wine at ten in the morning. I'd forgotten nothing. I was of as sound a mind as a desperate man can be, and I left Lucy-Ann so I could remain that way. If I stayed just one month more in her zone of influence, I would end up agreeing with her accusations, and then confirming Ménard's theories—the man's doggedness teetered on the edge of obsession. This cop, who basically thought he was God, would grind me down and make me confess to a crime I hadn't committed, that I could never have committed, never in a month of Sundays.

I rented myself a small apartment not too far from our house, not too far from Billie's school, not too far from the places she might reappear, and I took Pixie with me. It's never a good idea to uproot a cat, but our house was in the process of leaving its foundations in any case, and the poor creature would have starved to death if I'd left it with L.A., who no longer seemed to comprehend that a living being needs feeding. If she hadn't transferred all the bitterness inside her onto me, I might have been able to help her, to put a little bit of flesh back under that previously firm skin, but that was far in excess of the authority she accorded me. I zipped up my suitcases, asked Régine and Patricia, the mother and the faithful friend, to take care of what was left of L.A., and I shut Pixie up in the travel carrier Billie had made for him from a crate of Campbell's tomato soup that evoked an Andy Warhol painting.

Once I was settled in my new apartment, I handed in my resignation at the university, where I'd only set foot a few times since Billie had disappeared. I also carried on harassing Ménard and Dubois, who had turned, respectively, into a voicemail and a wisp of air, and I continued my search, wandering around the city street by street, neighbourhood by neighbourhood, gazing at the lighted windows, doing a bar crawl to chat to guys I didn't know from Adam as I showed them photos of my little girl. In the evening, when I'd finished my Billie tour, I sat down in my makeshift living room with Pixie on my lap and told him a story while I listened to John Coltrane, Django Reinhardt, or Billie Holiday on my old CD player.

I kept this regime up for almost three years: street tour, bar crawl, Coltrane and Holiday, and by the end of it I knew the décor of almost all the apartments and houses in the city, and the few people I used to know — whom I saw less and less often — had decided I was crazy.

On January 20th, 2009, the third anniversary of Billie's disappearance, I phoned Lucy-Ann to tell her I was leaving town. She wished me good luck with a sniff, as if she'd stopped hoping and stopped hating me at the same time. L.A.'s abdication should have inspired compassion in me, but all the words to describe my desolation — I could have still loved you, L.A., I could have held your hand in mine for another stretch of the journey — had been carried off in the upheaval. Ever since the barbarity of the world had descended on our house with the fury of a hurricane measuring force 5 on the Saffir-Simpson scale, all possible words of encouragement had been crushed in the debris. In the silence following the storm, I searched in vain for a few words that might have survived the disaster, and then, idiotically, I told Lucy-Ann to take care of herself. No mention of Billie or any acknowledgement of the macabre anniversary we were celebrating that day. Neither L.A. nor I were capable of bringing up the anniversary, because January 20th would always remain in our minds a day of mourning, one day we just didn't need, a date that would have been better erased from the calendar, eradicated like some kind of infestation, one of those dark days when hell's entrails open up. Neither L.A. nor I had the strength to evoke the funereal music that would have suited the day.

After I hung up, I shaved and went to a real estate agency. The guy who dealt with me seemed surprised by my lack of enthusiasm and my unfussy requirements, but I was offering him an easy sale so he was hardly going to object. He showed me photos of four or five houses nobody wanted, and I opted for the fourth hovel, once he'd reassured me that the Rivière-aux-Trembles region was so deep in the sticks even the bears got lost. The house would be vacant in a week or two and I could move in whenever I wanted after that. I agreed without even discussing the price or asking to see it first. Then I shuffled off to a nearby bar where, surrounded by the aroma of chilled beer, I could ruminate on the disabused thoughts of a man who was leaving for nowhere.

On the television hanging over the bar, Barack Obama was a few seconds away from giving his investiture speech. Normally I was a big fan of American politics, but I'd barely followed the last presidential campaign. I knew the United States and the whole world were about to see the dawn of a new era, not only because Obama was Black but because the United States rarely put into power a man who could say the word "poor" without being amazed when half the country put its hand up.

"We, the People," Barack declaimed a little way into his speech, picking up on the first words of one of the world's oldest constitutions, and reminding the entire planet that Jefferson and Washington's America had based its laws on a democracy that, according to some people, still stood on two legs tattooed with dollar signs. The applause came thick and fast, everyone from Afghanistan to Zimbabwe via Australia who owned a television or radio was listening in, and for a brief moment I felt as though I belonged to these people, to this great North American family whose colours Obama was listing off from the top of his rostrum.

When I caught sight of the imbecilic smile lighting up my face in the bar mirror, I wanted to hurl my glass at it. The only family I had left until recently no longer existed, all my ideas about family had fucked off and died, and even if I could exist on junk food and potato derivatives while watching Hollywood series until the end of time, I would never again belong to what people call a family, North American or not. Family was busted, kaput, pulverized in a collision of atoms as unpredictable as the next explosion of Yellowstone's supervolcano.

I downed my drink and ordered another one for the road, to forget I was breathing the air of a planet that also allowed child murderers to inhale it. When my glass appeared in front of me, I raised it in Obama's direction as he smiled with all his white teeth, and I let out a moronic "Yes, you can!," which garnered me a look of disapproval from the young dude tending bar, along with a grunt that might have expressed either solidarity or disagreement from the only other customer in the joint, who was glancing distractedly at a crossword puzzle next to his Molson Dry, from which he was scraping the label shred by shred, his mind visibly miles away from 12 across, *Short letters in a big case?* I was tempted to ask him if he had also lost a child and could no longer concentrate on anything other than his memories, but his unapproachable expression dissuaded me. Let him get drunk by himself. I already had the immense sadness of Billie's loss to cry over, and I couldn't add to this another kid whose father had forgotten what a smile looked like.

Thirty seconds later, I realized I was crying into my fries and mayo. I wiped my eyes with the serviette and asked for another one, because the tears just wouldn't stop pouring out. The sluice gates had opened, and behind the barrage I'd erected between the world and me there was enough to flood half the city and drown the young barman, who was still a jerk who didn't know what to do with this big guy wailing at the end of his counter, another nutcase, another one who ought to be locked up. I stole a whole pack of clean napkins, and by way of an excuse I told him that my daughter, who had disappeared three years earlier, was officially dead as of today, January 20th, 2009, the day of the inauguration of the 44th president of the United States, to the accompaniment of the confident acclamations of the crowds that poured into Washington. To prove Billie had existed, I slid a photo of my little girl, wearing her most beautiful smile, across the counter towards the bartender and left it there, next to the crumpled napkins, until the douchebag could bring himself to dole out some kind of formulaic sympathy. A few days later, I left the city that had killed Billie.

II.

THE NAMES

WILLIAM, BILLIE, AND LUCY-ANN

I took possession of the shingled house from the realtor Max Lapointe on February 9th, just as two wildfires were devastating the heatwave-struck Australian southeast. Despite the cold that pummelled Quebec, I had no trouble imagining the fires because I myself was ravaged by a fever that tinted all the curves and steep slopes surrounding Rivière-aux-Trembles orange and red.

The flu had viciously attacked me on the Friday, making the mercury in my thermometer almost boil, while Australia hit a record-breaking 46.4 degrees. The mercury dropped a little on the Sunday, but that Monday morning, neither Australia nor I had yet come out of "hell in all its fury," as prime minister Kevin Rudd described the inferno that was razing parts of his country to the ground.

I was barely able to stand when I hit the road at the wheel of a moving truck, which a few idle Samaritans had helped me load up. Anyone with half a brain would have told me to get my mattress out of the truck and go back to bed, but staying just one minute longer in the empty apartment seemed to me as senseless as trying to breathe underneath a pile of flour. Ever since I'd admitted to myself that if Billie ever did show up again it wouldn't be in the schoolyard or in her bedroom, the city had become a hostile organism that was trying to expel me, a combustion engine jostling me towards its exhaust valve. If I tried to resist this repelling force, they'd probably have to fish me out of the sewers.

I ought to have seen this unexpected burst of fever in a man who'd never swallowed an Aspirin in his life as a sign: the city had changed its mind and now wanted to keep me somewhere in its intestines and its bilious liver instead of spitting me out. But I'd long ago passed the stage when hope made me prick up my ears at the tiniest snatch of birdsong that was just a little too piercing in case it was a message sent by Billie from the indistinct limbo where her body and her mind were floating. This was how I imagined the place where Billie was, some nebulous space situated in a dimension parallel to our own, where time no longer moved and where Billie had stopped too, waiting for someone to penetrate the mystery of the beyond and deliver her from the clutches of stagnating time. I refused to allow myself to be invaded by the image of a crying Billie, a screaming Billie, a wounded Billie, or one lying under the snow's whiteness, or by any of those gossip-rag images your memory of the horror bombards you with every time a child disappears in the darkness, because that is truly what happens when a child disappears, when her body is suddenly snatched far away from your field of vision. She's propelled out of time and space, towards an unknown whose clouds envelop her, minuscule in the immensity of the cold. I imagined Billie in a place like this, where evil could not mortally hurt her, and from where she could call me through the song of a chickadee or the tu-whit, tu-whooing of an owl that had brushed the coldness of the clouds.

For more than a year, half-lucid and half-blind, I believed she was sending me signals, until the day I knelt on a shit-encrusted sidewalk and realized that I'd become utterly insane, that irrationality had gained the upper hand, and that the camel's back was just one straw away from breaking.

It was a particularly mild day, the sun was shining, and spring was warming up the people who strolled by. I had gulped down my breakfast, which consisted of a dry croissant and two sugary coffees that would have killed a diabetic stone-dead, and then gone out to lose myself in the crowd of walkers. In the air was a scent you couldn't quite pin down, couldn't quite associate with a memory, but that nonetheless reminds you of a moment of extreme purity, back when life wasn't so complicated, when you could grab the morning light bodily and there was goddamn meaning in the word joy.

I was walking along a busy street when I noticed a dusty, half-ripped Billie Holiday CD case on the ground. I bent down to pick it up and saw a painted orange arrow under the case, the kind used to indicate a construction zone. I knew full well what those arrows were for, but it didn't prevent me from following this one to a pile of junk the wind had pushed into the recess of a sealed-off doorway. Crawling over the dirty ground on all fours, I rummaged in the heap of greasy papers, ripped newspaper pages, and cigarette butts with a desperate energy, looking for a trace, a clue, a sign, when three coins landed beside my left hand, the noise of their fall muffled by the trash.

This was the sign I'd been waiting for, the gong announcing the end of the match, telling me I'd lost my mind. I picked up the three quarters with the idea of framing them or sinking them into cement, just to remind myself I was skidding out of control. I went home and played *Lady in Autumn*, a Billie Holiday album I consider to be something of a personal memento, since it was because of this sublime singer, a Billy Wilder film, and Michael Jackson's "Billie Jean" that Lucy-Ann and I decided to name our daughter Billie. It was also because of my nickname, of course, which superseded my full name when I started school, and Jacques Lacroix, my first real friend, started calling me Bill, while I called him Jack. Ever since then, Bill had stuck, so much so that if someone ever calls me William I feel as though he must be addressing a six-year-old ghost or some guy I don't know. William is buried deep under those playgrounds where, if they're lucky, kids are nicknamed Alex, Chris, Bob, or Joe, or, if they're not so lucky, Ratface or Fatty. This name of mine only exists on official papers now, but it doesn't define me in any way. I also write my books under the name Bill, because I can't see how anyone could publish as William after Shakespeare, Faulkner, and Blake.

But Billie was my darling's real name, and she used to wear it like a queen — and don't even think about coming after me because I'm speaking of her in the past tense here. There's no better tense than the imperfect to express the absurdity of a life that has to pivot backwards to avoid face-planting into a brick wall. My own life leans in that direction, to the side of yesterday, to Billie's side, and I never conjugate in any tense beyond the imperfect so as not to get caught up in illusions and become as pathetic as those mothers waiting for their sons to return from the war even though they've already been shipped home in seventy-five pieces in a coffin draped in the country's flag, accompanied by the national anthem. Our Billie wore her name just as magnificently as the eternal Lady Day, and when we saw our newborn's crumpled-up little face, her feminine little Bill features, we immediately knew we hadn't made a mistake in choosing her name. Because Billie looked like me, because she'd inherited my nose, my forehead, my lips, but was a hundred times better looking.

At the time, L.A. and I were disgustingly in love, like blind turtledoves, like a pair of lovebirds pecking each other all day long in a twelve-inch-square cage, proof that our union was founded on a misunderstanding. Lucy-Ann was as proud as a peacock at the idea of her daughter having the same name as the man she often gazed at with astonished eyes, as if wondering how she could ever have stumbled across such a nice guy. And she was actually the one who suggested the name, as a way of clearly establishing Billie's parentage. Had she wanted this parentage to be established in the maternal line, I would have understood; I had no objection to calling our baby Anna, for example, or Marie-Lucie, but for Lucy-Ann this was out of the question. She'd had enough problems with her name, she wasn't about to encumber an innocent child with it.

Lucy-Ann's real name was Lucienne, and she'd never forgiven her parents for saddling her with a name that made her sound like some old aunt from Abitibi. She was right—I don't know what they were thinking, giving such a name to a girl born in the sixties. It made her a target. She was mocked at school, at the swimming pool, at a crappy summer camp not far from Shawinigan, where she'd almost lost her virginity prematurely. By the time she was eighteen she was fed up, and she started the legal proceedings to officially change her name to Lucie-Anne, so that her friends and family wouldn't be too disoriented, and to avoid any further identity problems. Turning yourself into Marie-Christine when you've spent your life in the skin of a Lucienne might be somewhat disturbing, I imagine, and I understand why she opted for Lucie-Anne, even if that was probably the biggest mistake she ever made regarding her identity. Frankly, I don't know what she was thinking either. The people who knew her continued to call her Lucienne, and they passed this on to people who didn't know her or who were hard of hearing, the end result being that she was still a Lucienne.

Eventually, before starting university, she decreed that from now on people had to pronounce her name the American way, *Loosey-Ann*, and spell it in a way even a child could figure out, *Lucy-Ann*. This decision partially solved her problems, especially since her roommate nick-named her L.A., like the city of Los Angeles, conferring on Lucy-Ann, who was tanned year-round, a hint of exoticism that suited her like a lace glove on a courtesan.

She'd been called Lucy-Ann for years when I met her in a bar near the office tower where she worked. After three tequila sunrises, she told me to call her L.A., inclining her cleavage towards me, evoking the roundness of the California mountains, and then she reeled off a load of nonsense, which at the time struck me as brilliant, about the potential resemblance between the city of Los Angeles and her own internal topography. She claimed the names we choose for ourselves reflect our deepest nature, mark-ing our fate as surely as our more-or-less successful pas-sage through the Oedipal phase, and defining us better than any biography. I hadn't known her in her Lucienne period, and the parallels she traced between herself and the City of Angels seemed logical to me, especially since L.A. was smoking hot, capable of giving her body, however delicate, the dimensions of a megalopolis. From that very first evening, I knew the intense seismic activity of the San Andreas fault was not a myth, and I understood why someone might want to become a seismographer merely to get close to L.A.'s sun.

We had some good times together, even some amazing years. If L.A. hadn't entered a period of climate change after Billie's birth, we might have carried on feeling the earth trembling beneath our feet while the buildings collapsed around us in clouds of red dust. But the temperature cooled little by little, and the girl whose mere initials could heat up my atmosphere started travelling north, head lowered, and finally put her luggage down somewhere around Whitehorse.

I do take some responsibility for the appearance of what we might call our preglacial period. I claim the privilege of being as emotionally constipated as the vast majority of men on the subject of relationships, conjugal diplomacy, and post-coital harmony. But God, did I ever miss the old Lucy-Ann, the girl I used to call L.A. when I wanted to press myself up against her laughing body on humid nights.

I don't know exactly when the real rift started, but the name of the woman I thought I'd love until the last glacier in the galaxy melted was suddenly bereft of all meaning. When I called her L.A., I no longer felt the sweetness of angels or the scent of the Pacific slip under my tongue. *L* and *A* were now nothing more than two dead letters allowing me to communicate with the woman living alongside me. With time and the hardening of the cold in our wintry light, these letters became loaded with everything about Lucy-Ann that I disapproved of, wrongly or rightly, and eventually I could only call her L.A. with a hint of scorn, which had no purpose other than to reproach her for having failed to keep her promises, for having been incapable of living up to the fire that made Los Angeles sparkle. I was gradually moving my disappointed heart away from the city of Lucy-Ann while remembering the

94

beauty of the first days of the trip, when the tequila sunrise was the exact colour of the sun setting in the ocean behind the Santa Monica beaches.

The sun was still burning on the horizon like a giant blood orange sliced in half the day Lucy-Ann announced that she was pregnant. We met up for a pre-dinner drink on a patio in a rear courtyard, where there was a display of several post-macramé works of art imitating urban furniture, fire hydrants, streetlights, traffic lights — anything to create the impression of living in a city. L.A. had arrived before me, and she was unwrapping her afternoon's purchases on the table, shaped like an axletree, where a pitcher of sangria stood waiting. She'd bought herself a little white camisole that skimmed her body at the very limits of decency; a hideous pair of yellow sandals, "to go with my sunflower dress, you know, the one with the big yellow flowers"; a DVD of Billy Wilder's masterpiece *Sunset Boulevard*, which was set in one of those villas on the mythical boulevards that cross Los Angeles from Hollywood to Pacific Palisades; then a double Billie Holiday album, *Lady in Autumn*, which I would inherit a few years later.

Apart from Motown and a few old country airs, L.A. knew nothing about music. She hated jazz, thought Miles Davis was Sammy Davis Jr.'s brother, and could never tell the difference between a trumpet and a sax. But we'd come to an agreement. I kept my mouth shut and put up with a little Motown every now and again in exchange for being able to listen to Mingus and Parker without L.A. immediately grumbling. This last purchase didn't really match up with the yellow sandals, so when she slid the album over to me, all in blacks and oranges, the hue of a summer night encircled by flames, I assumed she must have done something wrong and needed to apologize.

"To the two of us, baby," she said, clinking her sangria glass against mine, little sparkles in her eyes, beautiful little sparkles that were slightly golden, indefinable, like her Los Angelean irises.

"To us," I replied, leaving out the *baby*, which I reserved for the intimacy of enclosed spaces, where no vicious ears can mock you for your terms of endearment.

"There's still one thing I haven't shown you!" she exclaimed, rummaging in an enormous leopard-print bag. She pulled out a pack of crumpled tissues, tubes of lipstick, and other grooming items no woman can leave home without, apparently, without the fear of bumping into George Clooney or Clive Owen that percise day. She finally found what she was looking for and brandished it: a little pink soother with a blue ribbon.

"To the three of us, baby," she whispered as she placed the soother on the table. It took me a few moments to work out what she was trying to tell me. When her eyes answered *yes* to the question I couldn't bring myself to ask, I felt as though the patio was tilting, carrying L.A. head-first towards the treetops and the galvanized metal streetlamps.

I downed my glass of sangria and poured myself another one, murmuring "Dad," smiling like an idiot who has discovered his dick for the first time. I wanted to clutch L.A. tightly, but you can't move too fast with the weight of a tiny child on your shoulders. In the end, L.A. was the one who took on the guy's role. She moved close to me, leaned on the nearby fire hydrant, and took my hands in hers to kiss them.

A million questions were racing through my head, a million happy questions surrounded by sparkles that tumbled around and prevented the words from coming out of my mouth. Through L.A.'s barely convex belly, I could already see a little round, creased face floating in the darkness of the amniotic fluid, waiting for the moment to head to the exit. A child was taking shape in this belly, and I wondered whether we'd have to buy it a girls' or a boys' bicycle, dolls or trucks, and if the child would love me as much as I loved the woman who at that moment was getting cherry-flavoured lipstick all over my hands.

"What shall we call it?" I ended up saying, as I gulped my third glass of sangria with a smile so wide I really would have needed to drink from a bucket to make it worthwhile.

I realized L.A. already had ideas on the subject when she pointed to the *Lady in Autumn* CD case, where Billie Holiday's face shone from the darkness of a night that would envelop her until her death.

"Billie's a pretty name, and Billy isn't bad either," she said, examining the case of the Wilder movie. "Billie Richard sounds good, don't you think?"

The message was clear. L.A. had chosen our child's name, and I would have a hell of a time trying to change her mind if I went down that road. But I had no intention of opposing her choice, because it was the choice of a woman who loved me enough to want her child to have both my first and last names.

"You're right, L.A., it's a damn good name, almost as good as Lucienne," I said, and I dodged the maraschino cherry that flew at me from the other side of the table as Lucy-Ann burst out again with her open-hearted laugh, a sound that would harden several years later when the cherries were replaced by sharp knives.

I picked up the cherry with the intention of chucking it back at her when the voice of Michael Jackson singing "Billie Jean" sounded from the speakers installed at each corner of the patio. It was a sign from destiny, there could be no doubt about it; the omens were being sent to us through the voice of a god of pop. We stared into each other's eyes until Jackson finished singing, as happy as Adam and Eve before the whole apple tree incident, and totally indifferent to the kitschiness of the omens that made our chairs wobble in time to "Billie Jean." And all the while, in L.A.'s womb, the little bundle of cells that would become our very own Billie continued to multiply.

It was as simple as that. Whether it was a girl or a boy, it would be Billie or Billy. I raised my glass to Billie-Billy and L.A. did the same, pointing out that it would be her last drink for the next few months, she'd be dry until April, until the first cries of the child whose weight on my shoulders and whose warmth, the sweet dampness of babies swaddled in wool, already seemed tangible.

On April 20th of this year, Billie would have been

twelve, and I often wonder what she would have wanted for her birthday. Probably another cat, since that old flea-bag Pixie had croaked just a few days before I moved to Rivière-aux-Trembles. Maybe he hadn't wanted to get used to another place; maybe he didn't have the strength anymore to face the journey, the storm, the unknown smells, but I think it was more likely that he understood that Billie wouldn't be wherever we were going and so he just stopped breathing at the same moment he stopped hoping. He had clung to life only to be able to say goodbye to Billie and nuzzle her one last time, a nose kiss, "much nicer than a mouth kiss, Papanoute," but the days and the months went by, and boredom transformed his desire to feel his young mistress's hands rub his belly into a kind of bitterness that breaks the ones who lose their faith. I certainly noticed he'd been declining for a while — he no longer pricked up his ears any time footsteps in the hallway might have been those of his princess — but I strictly forbade him to die. "If you die, Pixie Richard, I'll feed you to the pigeons as ground-cat meatballs." But threats are impotent in the face of sadness.

I found him one morning in his Campbell's tomato-soup crate. He was lying on the little blanket Billie had made for him out of my old flannel pyjamas, with his eyes closed and his mouth half-open. When I noticed that his big Garfield-style gluttonous paunch wasn't rising and falling with his breath, I went crazy. I started shouting and yelling that he had no right to do this to me. I ordered him to wake up, "Jesus, Pixie. Breathe!" and then pressed myself down beside his little house and cried and cried, until the need to take a piss forced me to get up. If I didn't have a bladder, I think I might still be there, begging him to come back, to open his damn big green eyes and go see the surprise I had for him in the kitchen, "a lovely tin of Clover Leaf tuna, Pixie, you can't turn your nose up at that, for Christ's sake!"

By dying, this cat had taken away everything of Billie that I had left and annihilated my last hope of seeing her turn up at the corner one sunny morning, a morning so beautiful I couldn't even describe it, even if I tried until my old carcass had been buried at the base of a silver maple. Pixie had given up the ghost because he knew that to keep hoping was useless. His knowledge of life, of death, of pain, of simple well-being had led him to understand that our darling would never come back to scratch his ears. Pixie knew what all animals know when they consent to close their eyes: the end of their world has arrived and there's no point fighting it. If I were as intelligent as Pixie, I would have got myself my own tomato-soup crate, where my heart could quietly stop beating, but part of the stupid human in me still wanted to believe in miracles, in those fairy tales where, against all logic, princesses come back to life and reappear some beautiful morning with arms full of wildflowers.

I remember the day, not long after the Dumas kid's accident, when I rolled Pinocchio under a train and challenged Gepetto to patch him back up. At the end of the story, Billie gazed at me with big round eyes. Then a little smile turned up the corners of her mouth and she punched me on the shoulder, exclaiming, "That's impossible, Papa, you're making things up again. Pinocchio can't die, come on!" Without waiting for my reaction, she went out to play in the yard with Pixie, convinced that the characters in fairy tales could no more die than heroes could, and that her own father was playing a mean trick on her. In telling her this story, I was stupidly attempting to give her a life lesson, to make her understand that nothing and nobody is immortal, and that she should watch her back. But she was the one who was right: heroes can't die any more than little girls can. Now I have the proof of it every time I look at a photo of Billie and see her come back to life, tie her first shoelace, or take her first steps on grass, as immortal as the memory of humankind.

Cats can't die either, especially not Pixies; that's what I told myself that morning when I found him in his crate and wondered what I would do with him. The only other pet I'd ever had was a goldfish that answered to the name of Conrad—which is just a manner of speaking, because if Conrad had ever answered to his name, no one noticed anyway. But this indifference certainly didn't mean Conrad was an idiot. Rather, it was proof that humans don't understand fish, or that fish just can't be named Conrad, end of story. When Conrad defected to the other side, as my father—a man who could never have had a career in diplomacy—put it, my mother was the one who handled it, thus depriving me of the fundamental experience of burying or flushing Conrad myself. Faced with Pixie's inert body,

I felt utterly useless, because nobody had ever allowed me to learn how to deal with the bodies of dead animals.

I ended up phoning a vet, and out of all the choices available to me I opted for freezing, because I couldn't bear the idea of Pixie being thrown into a crematory oven with dozens of creatures he didn't know and would have absolutely despised if he'd met them. So it was out of the question to send him to a hell where he would be jammed in pell-mell with a gang of tomcats to be reduced to dust.

I would have liked to bury him behind our house, underneath Billie's bedroom window, but the snow was too thick, the ground too frozen, the summer too far away for Pixie to last that long without being invaded by maggots and other necrophiliac bugs. So freezing seemed the ideal solution in that it spared me having to decide too quickly what would happen to Pixie's body. The old moggie would probably have been none too pleased that I pressed pause on the process of decomposition and thus delayed his fifth or sixth life, but he was Billie's cat and I felt obliged to see him off with the funeral rites worthy of the love my daughter felt for him.

So Pixie travelled with me to Rivière-aux-Trembles, shut up in a cryogenic crate like Walt Disney, the difference being that Pixie will never wake up in a future full of defrosted Tinkerbells. If one day a cure for death is discovered, neither he nor I will still be around to swallow the Mephistophelian potion that will stir up trouble among the immortals.

When I arrived, I stored the crate in the cellar to wait

for spring, and I started thinking that the real Pixie was no longer there but instead somewhere with Billie, in what people call Eden or paradise. Whenever I'm in a bucolic mood and want to have a good bawl because my kidneys ache from holding all these torrents of salt water inside me, I imagine the two of them in a scene like the one in *What Dreams May Come*, a movie with Robin Williams in which people who love each other are reunited after they die in a paradise more beautiful than nature, with all the trees, flowers, and landscapes you could possibly want, so beautiful that it makes you want to die right then. L.A. must have watched that movie a hundred times during the week before I left the house, tears in her eyes and a tissue pressed to her nose, pausing the film at every opportunity to howl, tears mixing with the laughter the spectacle of joy incites, then diving once more, her heart turned inside out, into gardens that deny death. I reproached her for being addicted to the representation of a beyond she didn't even believe in, for torturing herself with chimera that would explode in her face like over-inflated balloons, but secretly I was doing the same thing, as well as wallowing in naive allegories of eternal happiness even though I'd buried God a long time ago.

People who lose a child have no choice but to believe in paradise, otherwise they are forced to believe in hell and imagine the devouring flames out of which their little one's screams emerge. As for me, I have my paradise days and my limbo days. I immediately exclude purgatory, since children have nothing to expiate but other people's sins.

But I actually prefer the limbo days because I know it's possible to emerge from limbo, especially since the Vatican abolished it, making this zone partway between good and evil even more imprecise, although I don't personally feel quite ready to scratch it out from my map of the heavens. I know you can come back from limbo but not from paradise. And anyway, who would want to leave joy to go back to hell? It's only in Wim Wenders movies that angels are stupid enough to want to experience the good old daily suffering of *Homo sapiens.* So I prefer those days when I manage to imagine Billie in the misty scene of a twilight world from which she will re-emerge one beautiful morning—yes, one beautiful morning—to tell me that neither hell nor heaven ever existed.

MARNIE, SQUEERELLE, OWL, AND SUPERMAN

After my father was buried, I flew back to New York to sort out my affairs, then I left the city in a head-long rush, knowing that if I thought calmly about my decision to move to Rivière-aux-Trembles, I would immediately realize the absurdity of returning to my roots like this. I arranged everything in less than two weeks. I sold my flower shop, A Rose Is a Rose, at a ridiculously low price to my assistant. I met up with my few remaining friends to say my goodbyes. And I phoned Harry Fields, a wild man lost in the heart of New York, in whose arms I sometimes consoled myself about my own exile. I announced my news somewhat brusquely, because Harry wouldn't miss me any more than Gregory Holmes, Dave Cohen, and Jake Danowski, the more-or-less loving lovers I'd kept waiting on my doorstep until they abandoned me in the ray of light filtering in from the outside. These men had only left a few shallow traces on the entrance mat, and Harry

Fields, along with the others, would not hold up against the sweep of the broom I was preparing to whisk across my existence. I kissed him one last time and I closed my door.

That was forty-eight hours ago, and as the heavy late-February snows dump their silence over the countryside, I pace the rooms of the house wondering what I'm doing here, in the middle of the boxes, the memories, and the faded flowers. After I left for the United States, I set foot in Rivière-aux-Trembles only once or twice a year, because this village had become foreign territory to me. Only my father's house maintained some kind of reality in the middle of the bare forests. I generally came back for the Christmas holidays, preferring to avoid the summer months and anything that might remind me of the throbbing storm that had taken Michael away.

My father would bring out the wreaths, the glass baubles, and the angels from the attic for me. While the turkey was roasting in the oven, we decorated the tree while drinking kir and listening to Bing Crosby sing "I'll Be Home for Christmas." Sometimes my father would invite a few friends over, but most of the time at Christmas it was just the two of us, in the glow of the candles that cast our silhouettes on the walls, like a father and daughter whose friendship was cemented long ago by unhappiness. I would tell him about my flower shop, describe my latest visit to the Museum of Natural History, the Guggenheim, or the Central Park Zoo — "They even have lions, Pop, poor old lions who've never breathed the scents of the savannah and probably think New York is in the heart of Africa" — and he would tell me about the book he'd read most recently, an essay by Stephen Jay Gould, or a poetry collection by Renaud Longchamps, reading that reinforced his link with the earth and helped him gain perspective about man's importance. Then he would leave Longchamps' Miguasha cliff and reach the St. Lawrence via Chaleur Bay before slowly drifting towards his rosebushes, his trees, and the plans for his new greenhouse.

During our last Christmas, I'd told him all about my trip to the Hayden Planetarium at the Rose Center for Art and Space. While I was trying to convey the vertigo I felt seeing these cosmic collisions and the supersonic impacts narrated by Robert Redford's spellbinding voice, I suddenly felt that my father was leaving me, that his spirit was slipping out through the window into the distance, where Redford's voice was also disappearing, while his body was collapsing in his old cracked-leather armchair. A few minutes later, his face turned to the dark, he quietly told me about his imminent death.

"Two months," he murmured as Bing Crosby finished singing "Holy Night." "Maybe a little longer, maybe a little less." And then his voice exhorted me not to cry. "It's normal, Marnie, there's nothing more normal than death," and his voice seemed to come from the starry night and lose itself in the numbness that took hold of my limbs during the shock of that death announcement.

If I hadn't told him all these stories about gravitational tides, or collisions between nebulous and cannibal galaxies, he might have kept quiet about the illness that devoured him, but the awareness of his smallness in contrast with the immensity had given him confidence. He must have thought that if I was capable of admitting that galaxies could devour one another, recreating new worlds and making life reappear amid an explosion of atoms, I could certainly acknowledge the movements that, on an infinitesimal scale, had brought about the galaxial collisions occurring in his sickly organism.

He was right. It's easier to accept death when you gaze at the stars. But this wisdom from the infinite always dissipates at daybreak, when you notice your father tottering in the early morning light with a trembling cup of coffee in his hand. That's when you realize he's already started to disappear: his words are becoming rarer, his steps smaller, and he has given up the gestures that propel bodies towards the future. A future without a tomorrow had already established itself in my father's body, and he now only moved within the limited circle of a near future in which he would not allow me to take part. I begged him for hours to let me stay with him, but Alex Duchamp was categorically opposed to my being present at his decline. He wanted to die alone, without anyone seeing him fall apart.

When on the morning of February 6th the phone rang in my apartment right in the heart of Brooklyn, I didn't pick it up because I already knew that my father was no more. I'd heard the cry in the night, the cry from Blueberry River, the scream of death. Wrapped up in my heavy covers, I dreamed I was walking in a vast snow-covered field where long dry stems, like the plants that grow along riverbanks, emerged here and there. It was neither day nor night, neither morning nor evening. I was moving forward in a time frozen between two lights where even the snow wasn't cold, in a large, windless, noiseless, lifeless corridor. Then the shadow of a bird appeared on the snow, just on the spot where a few hare tracks disappeared into the distance, and it stayed there even though there was no bird flying above this dark patch. When the shadow finally fell onto the field of snow, the shout rang out—the cry of a man and the squeak of an animal at the same time—and I woke up.

From four until seven in the morning, I remained sitting up in bed until the ringing phone informed me that the dream had not been just a dream. I let the call go to voicemail; "Hi Marnie, it's Phil, call me," my father's best friend said hoarsely, and I put on my coat to head out to the Rose Center for Art and Space. I shivered in the rain as I waited for the doors to open, and, sitting in the darkness of the Hayden Planetarium, I watched my father fly away among the stars, just as Michael Superman Saint-Pierre had once flown away, seized by the strength of attraction of a fate that dragged him towards Krypton's red sun. A few hours later, I took a flight back to say my goodbyes to a man whose spirit was drifting through the time of the galaxies.

"I'm leaving you everything, Marnie—the house, the greenhouses, the land—do what you want with it," he had said after telling me how little time he had left. In my mind, everything was clear. I refused to live among ghosts. I would put the house up for sale as soon as my father was no longer living there. But all it took was the cry of a ghost, a little while later, for me to travel towards the past. And so here I am again in Rivière-aux-Trembles, wondering what the hell I'm doing in a house that only my father's presence could warm up.

When I arrived, I resolved firmly not to let myself fall into the nostalgia trap, but I didn't find anything better to do than to wallow in memories of my father. The day before yesterday I discovered that the last movie he ever watched was Alfred Hitchcock's *Marnie*. The DVD was still in the player, and the box was lying half-open under the living room coffee table. So I watched it in turn, seeking my origins, since I was named Marnie because of Tippi Hedren, Alfred Hitchcock, and a novel by Winston Graham. Marnie is "a pet name, easy to remember," as the man played by Sean Connery affirms when he brings Marnie back to his house, "a pet name," the name of some small creature, a carefree little animal that is nonetheless pursued by fear.

Apparently I had been conceived after a screening of the movie, with the full blessing of Alfred Hitchcock and Phil Morisset, who introduced my mother to my father and vice versa — Marie, Alex, Alex, Marie — under the awning of a repertory cinema where Cupid's arrows had kindled Eros's thunder, electrocuting Marie Beaupré and Alex Duchamp along the way. Who knows, maybe I'd have been called Scarlett or Willard if some other film had been playing that night, but it just so happened during those years that destiny had a preference for Hitchcock movies.

That was why my parents decided to call me Marnie, but also because my mother looked like Tippi Hedren, and her beauty made my father weak at the knees. Be that as it may, I never really understood why they chose to name me after an insane character. It's possible that my mother, who claimed people should not resemble their names, wanted to trick fate and make sure I would be nothing like Hitchcock's Marnie. I don't know, but I'd have preferred to be called Marion, Mary, Margaret, or Martha — any one of Marnie Edgar's numerous pseudonyms. It wouldn't have changed anything; it would have still been one or another of the names of Marnie's craziness, but the link would have been less direct and I wouldn't be left wondering, every time I sat down to watch that fucking movie, whether my parents had transmitted that girl's obsessions to me as they made me.

I saw the French version of *Marnie* — very economically translated as *Pas de printemps pour Marnie* — for the first time in the '80s, shortly before VCRs became a feature of our lives. I must have been around sixteen, and just a few days earlier my father had told me all about how he met my mother. Ever since, I'd been dying to meet this Marnie who'd given me my identity in a way, and whom I considered a kind of twin sister from whom I'd been separated at birth. I wandered the aisles of three video stores before I found a copy of the movie, and when I returned home I got myself all set up as if I was attending the grand premiere of the greatest masterpiece of all time. I closed the living room curtains, the double doors separating this room from the dining room, and then, when Bernard Herrmann's music erupted over the first image of the opening credits, I ensconced myself in my chair and knocked back a handful of still-warm popcorn.

A few minutes later, the cooling popcorn was still in my mouth. My twin sister was a thief, a liar, a criminal without scruples who changed her identity every time she changed her handbag or hair colour. Marnie's numerous names swirled around me like a mist of lies — Marion, Mary, Margaret, Martha... Was my name, too, based on a fraud, or did it just designate a person with no real face, someone who gravitates mechanically around a pole as smooth as oblivion?

Even with a lump of popcorn stuck in my throat, I carried on watching the movie, only to pause it in the middle of the scene where Marnie totally loses it and becomes hysterical during the storm that turns the curtains in her boss's office red — her boss being Mr. Rutland, her future husband. I had even screamed along with Marnie when a tree struck by lightning crashes through the window right where she stands. And perhaps I too had been invaded by a red tide, Marnie-red, blood-red. But there was nobody to take me in their arms and kiss me passionately, neither Rutland, nor Superman, nor any other rescuer.

I stared for a while at the living room curtains, convinced that a stroke of lightning would set them ablaze any minute, even though we were in the middle of winter, then I burst into tears. Something was eluding me, something that had a link with time, anteriority, posteriority, with the unforeseen conjunction of fates. Had my parents known that when I grew up I would suffer from the same phobias as Marnie, the same terror of thunder? And if so, how could they have guessed that my life would be turned upside down by a storm, and that the slightest rumble of thunder would immediately throw me into a catatonic state just like the one that had immobilized Michael in the rain? It was impossible; they couldn't have anticipated the storm or foreseen it in some premonitory dream that had imprinted the name Marnie on their subconscious. Only one explanation seemed plausible to me. My name had sealed its own destiny. For life, until death, my fate was linked to Marnie Edgar's.

I had waited until the next day to watch the rest of the movie. When I asked my father why he and Maman had chosen the name of a deranged girl for me, he burst out laughing, clearly not understanding my discomfort. In his mind, Marnie was just a way of naming the strength of the feelings he'd immediately felt for my mother, the famous thunderbolt that was striking me today like a ton of TNT. I wanted to retort that they could have called me Alfred while they were at it, but I didn't argue the point. My father had no idea of the heritage he and Maman had burdened me with.

I had got hold of Winston Graham's novel, Hitchcock's inspiration, in case the director's twisted mind had completely reinvented Marnie Edgar from head to toe. I would have been relieved to learn that the original Marnie wasn't as cracked as her Hitchcock clone, but that wasn't the case. The plot of the novel, and the movie, rested on Marnie's fragility and the amnesia that had struck the traumatic events of her childhood from her memory. Hitchcock and his scriptwriter had done a good job. No twisting of the main facts, no Arabian prince in the background, no jack-in-the-box jumping out at you. Classy.

For months afterwards I wondered if Officer Desmarais and the whispering voices might have been right. Was it possible that I'd forgotten everything and I really was behind Michael's disappearance, as Desmarais believed? Was it possible that the horror the storm inspired in Marnie Edgar had been revealed in me that day beside the magic swimming hole, causing me to harm Michael, making me dig my nails into his flesh while in the grip of someone else's madness, and then going to the shore of Catfish Lake to dump his shoe, far from the scene of Marnie Duchamp's crime? But then, where would I have put the body? In which crevasse or cave could an eleven-year-old child have hidden a body, away from the noses of sniffer dogs and the pain of an angry father?

I tortured myself for months, alone under the clouds that obscured the stormy sky. I relived the moment when Michael stood, frozen, thousands of times, seeing him turn slowly towards me, whispering his secret with a disoriented expression, *Foggy day, ma'am, foggy day*, and then running off into the forest at full tilt, where there was no path, no clearing, no side road or cut-through.

I tried to recreate the scene from every angle, but the most accurate one was my own, Marnie Duchamp's, the viewpoint of the little girl who'd seen her best friend succumb to the pressure of a terror that he transmitted to her without explaining its cause. I had forgotten nothing, and thus I managed to convince myself: I had forgotten nothing about what happened before, during, and after this episode, yet almost thirty years later I felt the need to come back to the scene of the drama to reassure myself it wasn't the scene of a crime.

When I found *Marnie* in my father's DVD player, all the memories flooded back from those months when my fear of amnesia had almost pushed me to confess to a murder about which I knew nothing. So I closed the curtains, unearthed a bag of Orville Redenbacher popcorn from the kitchen cupboard, popped a beer, and settled in for a cozy little movie night.

By the end of the movie I no longer knew who I was. The doubts I had entertained in earlier years rushed right back in, accompanied by their armada of trick questions. "What did you miss, Marn? For fuck's sake, what didn't you notice?" The voice of naughty little Marnie Duchamp's guilty conscience was back, thumping the walls, "What are you hiding? What have you forgotten?" trying to create cracks through which I would be sucked towards the past only to finally discover, in the slightly yellowing film unspooling behind the fissured walls, whose hand had dealt the blow to Michael Saint-Pierre.

A mute anguish mixed with the anger I felt towards

Michael, towards the river, towards that cursed place, and towards Alfred Hitchcock. Without thinking, I ejected the DVD and stomped on it until no image of Marnie Edgar could survive. I'd just destroyed one of the things my father had left behind and I didn't give a damn. My mental health was definitely worth a little infidelity to the memory of the dead. I put on my coat and my boots and went out, slamming the door behind me. I intended to go back to the magic swimming hole with the idea of interrogating all the damn trees that had seen Michael go into a trance, but the snow, the cold, and the darkness prevented me. So I walked along the streets of Rivière-aux-Trembles, kicking at all the chunks of ice that had the misfortune to be in my path. I walked around the village three times, kicking the same dumb ice chunks, and finally ended up in front of Michael's house, where Victor Saint-Pierre's enormous shadow was bowed behind the curtains. The house had barely changed. The huge porch under which we sheltered from the sun or the rain was still there, as was Victor Saint-Pierre's workshop behind the house.

The workshop was where Mike had discovered a dozen Superman comics the summer he turned ten. The comics were in English, but his father had agreed—given Michael's excitement—to translate the outline of *A City Goes Dark* for him that very day. Ten minutes after his father had finished telling him the story, Mike called to tell me he'd just discovered a superhero even stronger than Batman and the Incredible Hulk put together. "Come over, Marn, I have to show you this." This was how our devotion to a universe in which the superbeings made up for the shortcomings of mortals had come about. All through the summer his father gave him rough translations of the other comics in the box, and then Michael told me the incredible adventures of the child from Krypton, adding some of his own details, and our lives were transformed. Mike immediately identified with Superman, "the greatest exponent of justice the world has ever known," and I became the impetuous and courageous Lois Lane, the super-reporter who followed Superman closely, and whom he protected from all dangers. In the space of a few days, the squirrel and the owl—our previous alter egos—disappeared.

Phil, his eyes sunken under his Vermont cap, was the first person to say I looked like a squirrel, always darting here and there, skipping and climbing everywhere. July was at its peak, and he was sitting with my father under the pergola, drinking a beer and sheltering from the sun while I danced pirouettes in the yard. After a particularly daring somersault that earned enthusiastic applause from Papa and Phil, I asked the latter to redo my ponytail. "My hair's all messed up, Phil, can you tie it back up?" He smoothed my hair, tied it up with one of those multi-coloured elastics I was always losing, and told me that my red ponytail was like a squirrel's tail. "Don't you think she looks like a squirrel, Alex, with her shiny little eyes, a mischievous little squirrel?"

Papa had gone along with it, giving me a smile so full of love I felt obliged to look away so as not to be swallowed whole. Ever since that smile, I became his little squirrel. A few days later, he borrowed Phil's English word *squirrel*, which he clumsily pronounced *Squeerelle*, and the nickname stuck. He would continue to call me Squeerelle for the rest of his life, a smile playing about his lips, whenever he was choked up by emotion or he saw in me the carefree child I'd been before Mike disappeared.

I actually met Michael shortly after that first patented squirrel pirouette. His father had come by the house to buy a dozen roses for his wife's birthday ("Give me your most beautiful ones, Alex,"), and he brought Michael with him. While Papa wandered around the garden with Victor Saint-Pierre, I dragged Michael into the workshop to show him the birdhouses my father built. Then, point-blank, I told him I was a squirrel. "So what are you?"

He looked straight at me with his big round eyes, not entirely certain what my question meant, and then he said, "An owl. I'm an owl."

"An owl? Why an owl?"

"Because an owl can see in the dark, and because it sees everything, Marnie, absolutely everything."

"Well, Michael, owls see squirrels too, and they eat them."

He remained silent for a few moments, probably trying to come up with some animal that didn't eat squirrels but was a bit more imposing than a sparrow or a mouse, then he replied that the kind of owl he was only ate fries. I was happy with that explanation, and then, sitting cross-legged underneath the workbench, we invented our first squirrel and owl story, a story that took place in the middle of the night amid the thorny bushes surrounding the Mailloux pond at the hour when owls see everything.

Thus our friendship was born out of the meeting of a squirrel and an owl addicted to fries. Amid the nocturnal croaks rising from Gustave Mailloux's pond, I became Squeerelle, his friend for life, and he became my friend Owl, cross my heart and hope to die, until we discovered Superman, Clark Kent, Lois Lane, and Jimmy Olsen and left behind the squirrel and the owl, who had spent more than three years climbing pretty much all the trees and poles in Rivière-aux-Trembles.

I don't remember exactly when Michael started calling me Lois, but whenever he slipped into Superman's skin and we played at saving the world from the endless dangers threatening it, I was no longer Marn, or Marnie, or Squeerelle, but the incomparable Lois Lane. When he was with me, Mike no longer answered to any name other than Superman, which I generally shortened to Supe when certain tense situations required us to be laconic and speedy. Nobody else called me Lois, and nobody else called Mike Superman. They were our secret names, and we promised never to reveal them, even under torture, at the risk of compromising our missions or awakening the suspicions of Superman's enemies, who were scattered all over the planet, including and especially Rivière-aux-Trembles, the new metropolis that was now the centre of the crooked activities of the international underworld.

Whenever I turned into Lois Lane, I was no longer a

little girl but a fearless heroine beyond reproach, walking in the Man of Steel's wake. We mostly just pretended we didn't know that Lois and Superman were in love, an idea that in our childish prudishness we found stupid, except when the Man of Steel took my hand as we crossed the churning rapids of Alex Morin's stream — Morin was an immense man whom we cast as the redoubtable Lex Luthor — or whenever we had to press up against each other in a tight space so our pursuers wouldn't discover us. At those moments I became a little girl with bright red cheeks, wondering if it was her own heart beating so hard or the heart of the boy whose Baby's Own shampoo she could smell so close to her. Sometimes I would regret not having chosen to identify as Supergirl, the girl with the protoplasmic body who could turn herself into a street-lamp or a wild rabbit.

At the age of nine I was already, in my own way, in love with my friend Michael Saint-Pierre. How long would this exclusive love have lasted? I don't know, but it's highly likely one of us would have slowly moved away and become interested in a roller-skating girl, a guy with a baseball-card collection, or a gang of potbellied Jethro Tull fans. We'd have grown wistfully apart, feeling mildly guilty, and would have ended up looking back on this period of our lives as a distant Eden, where our only concern was getting up early enough not to miss anything, neither the dawn chorus of the birds, nor the arrival of the sun behind the hill overlooking the Mailloux pond, nor the last call of the blackbird. We'd have drifted away from each other, and on beautiful summer evenings Michael would tell his wife about his childhood friend Marnie Duchamp, a little redhead with the nervous movements of a squirrel, a girl with whom he used to watch the Perseid showers and play silly dares.

I imagine we would have still crossed paths, bumped into each other in Rivière-aux-Trembles at holidays, family celebrations, funerals. We would've kissed awkwardly on the cheek as we left the church or the grocery store, a little anxious, a little shy in front of a person with whom we once shared everything, right down to our final gumball, to whom we promised we'd never be apart, and about whom we now knew almost nothing. Then one day, Mike would tell me he had a new baby girl. "Her name's Lois," he would confess, blushing at being caught out in his nostalgia. As for me, I'd congratulate him and ask questions about the new baby—age, hair colour, eye colour, ordinary details that he would give me with his young father's smile, a man convinced that his child is the first and only marvel the world has ever seen. And then I'd return to my father's house, trying to staunch the damn tears that sprang up at the mere mention of the name of a cartoon heroine, a fictional character, a little girl who was dead and buried in the light of the past.

Sometimes I imagine scenarios in which Mike and I never grow apart, because it's hard to tear off a limb just like that, because you can't separate earth and water without causing drought. I imagine stories where we grow up together, gradually abandoning the Superman universe for the cinema of Huston or Leone, for hikes in the Adirondacks or wild camping in the Gaspésie.

In these scenarios we're like those happy old couples who've only loved one person in their lives, their child-hood sweetheart, stronger than a barricade of 78-carat diamonds, more real than the naked truth, and we have a whole gaggle of children, none of whom are named Lois, Clark, Marnie, Superman, Squeerelle, or Owl, because we have no regrets, because nostalgia is only useful for people whom life has expelled from paradise.

In these scenarios, Michael is alive and he has a beard, a red pickup, a collection of volcanic rocks, and two or three hundred country music CDs. As for me, I still look like an overgrown squirrel, and even though I might jump at the slightest noise, ready to climb up to the highest branches of my tree at top speed, I'm not afraid of storms or of oblivion. My name is Marnie, but I don't give a shit. I still wonder what my parents were thinking when they named me, but it's no big deal really, because I feel no link to Winston Graham and Alfred Hitchcock's creation, except maybe for the fact that I like horses, but who doesn't like horses?

PART TWO

A funeral procession was travelling down the main street of Rivière-aux-Trembles on February 9th, 2009, when Bill Richard arrived in the village at the wheel of his two-ton U-Haul, his head weighed down by what he would later think of as his Australian fever. He had got on the highway at the edge of the city and driven for almost two hours on the straight road without passing a single vehicle, with the exception of a tanker truck whose driver must have been inflamed, just as Bill was, by the Australian wildfires. Then he'd taken a side road and stopped to consult the map on which he had traced—with an orange highlighter borrowed from Billie—the route that would lead him to the house where he was going to try to remake a semblance of life for himself.

On more than one occasion he thought the pain splitting his skull would force him to stop in some skuzzy motel, where the temptation to slash his veins would end the career of the maid who would later discover Billie's name written in blood on the walls papered with yellow flowers, golden buds or sunflowers that had long since asphyxiated in the absence of what he called healthy light, the light of a happy house with sparkling tiles and sheer curtains. He must have been crazy to hit the road while reality was dissolving at the edge of his feverish field of vision, but he must have been crazier still to imagine that total isolation was in any way going to make up for the emptiness of the absence.

After his first experience of heartbreak, an unexpected split that had given him a little hint of the misery of the Romantics, he had affixed a line from a poem by Alphonse de Lamartine on the back of his door: "Sometimes, when one person is missing, the whole world seems depopulated." He stuck the piece of paper above the dartboard, where he'd pinned the photo of the girl who'd slaughtered his illusions, and sometimes he practised shooting darts before going to bed. While he lay moping in his cold sheets, he often thought hard about whether Lamartine's words were true. Did loss really cause depopulation, or on the contrary, was it the beginning of an unbearable overpopulation?

Ever since Billie's disappearance, this question kept resurfacing, as perplexing as ever, a bitter reminder that the solitude of the bereaved can be defined equally well in the light of the void and the light of the multitude. Some days it seemed to him the world was incredibly full, saturated with insubstantial faces and bodies hiding his daughter's face from him. At other times he could see Billie everywhere, in every picture and every thought, on every street corner, and she was the one overpopulating the planet. But he knew that this overpopulation signalled a kind of depopulation highlighting the futility of excessive numbers. Thus that morning he had no idea whether he was heading towards a house whose halls would be haunted by the same face multiplied many times over, or if he would end up in a place that looked as though it had been hit by a cataclysm, with one sole survivor casting a shadow over the desertification of cities.

When he saw the hearse in all its sinister cleanliness, he immediately thought another world was being depopulated. This welcome was hardly a good omen. If he'd known he would be setting foot in this unknown territory at the same time as death marched through the streets, he might have opted for the motel, where he could have sunk into the drumming of the February rain on the dirty tiles, while listening to country songs in rotation on the radio, songs lamenting wandering and lonely souls. He could have waited there, in that world filled with alcohol and men who ate road dust, for his fever to abate and for the spirit of the dead to leave the force field of the living.

Since he had not yet fallen low enough to behave badly, he parked near the sidewalk while the procession passed by and took the opportunity to get out for a bit of fresh air. Leaning on the back of the U-Haul, he was counting the stones bleached by the coarse salt when the spotless Lexus that followed the cortège drew level with him. Instinctively, he lifted his head and saw the woman in the back seat, red eyes gazing into the distance at nothing, who seemed to be imploring this nothingness to break the spell that had reduced her to immobility. Then their eyes met, and a brief pain in his chest, as rapid as a dagger thrust by an expert hand, mingled with shudders that ran down his whole body.

For a moment he was certain he knew this woman. Then the dagger slipped out of his chest and he understood that what he had recognized was actually the pain, the pain and the reddened eyes that now implored him, at the heart of this devastated landscape, to hasten the desperate time of grief. He recognized the pain, and its expression, which resembled L.A.'s when she demanded the impossible of him—do something, Bill, bring my daughter back, bring my little girl back... Then he would see his own eyes, cold empty circles frozen in the mirror like marbles at the bottom of a pond, incapable of ordering his body to move a little. Sometimes he stayed there for a thousand years, standing in front of the mirror, just standing there, empty.

The woman's red eyelids plunged the world into the same lethargy, and it seemed to him that the hearse was no longer moving forward, that the wind, which had stopped blowing, held a leaf torn from the ground suspended between heaven and earth. The feeling that this woman was burying her son, her laughing child, in the distant eternal laughter of the dead children, paralyzed him, because who else but a child could stop the wind?

Leaving the immobile leaf for a moment, he turned towards the occupants of the other cars, looking for little blond or ginger heads, classmates, boys and girls in Cub Scout or Brownie uniforms, and he felt an intense relief when he realized that there were no children in this procession, and that the deceased, according to all the evidence, had reached an age that hid somewhat the indecency of death. At that moment the spell broke and he got back into his truck, blaming the disturbance that had penetrated his chest with the cold efficiency of a knife on the crazy kangaroo fly or some other virus imported directly from Australia.

In the car behind the hearse, Marnie Duchamp followed this stranger, whom she thought of as the feverish man, with her red eyes. It was a similar fever that had struck her and was embedded under her eyelids. A long fever that would never relinquish him and would leave in him the memory of the body struggling against mirages.

When he moved out of her field of vision, she seemed to see the aura of heat circling his forehead, a yellow aura speckled with red thorns, like a field of grass burned by the August heat in a Vincent Van Gogh painting. Then the image of her father, Alex Duchamp, took its place in the parade of drab trees bordering the cemetery, until the hearse came to a stop and two white-gloved undertakers slid the bronze coffin, which no sun could make shine, out onto a trestle. Then she bent over the coffin, touched it, dampened it with her tears and embraced it, transmitting her warmth to the dead through the cold metal—"Love you forever, Pop"—and then Phil Morisset, her father's lifelong friend, put his arm around her shoulders. Through her tears, the feverish man's dark eyelids appeared to her for an instant, floating in the middle of the gathering of grey men who had come to pay one last homage to the gardener of Rivière-aux-Trembles. Then she forgot the man as the doors of the chapel, where the coffin would be stored until spring, closed with a definitive creak.

A few Mary-Jean petals fluttered as the doors squeaked, heads lowered as people crossed themselves, and the grey bodies dispersed. As for Marnie, she wandered through the village streets, then along the road around Wolf Hill, torn between the forces of attraction and repulsion for a countryside whose contrasting colours, black trees on a white background, somehow reflected the drabness of the universe she felt she lived in, always wondering if she deserved the world's beauty.

A little later, when the only remaining light came from some vague blue patches behind the clouds, a cry from she didn't even know where brought back her childhood and its bright colours, and she'd decided to come back to Rivière-aux-Trembles, where everything had begun and where everything ought to finish. If the beauty of the world was waiting for her somewhere, it could only be in the place where it had been taken away from her. As she passed by the cemetery again, the image of the stranger she'd noticed earlier came to mind, but she quickly shrugged it off, just as she shrugged off the shiver that prompted her to pick up the pace and pull her black coat more tightly around her.

I.

BILL

February to
April 2009

On the roof of the framed-in outbuilding next to my new house, Ronie the Flying Toad was testing out the Supertoad cape I had drawn for him last night around midnight, at that fateful hour during which anything can happen, including sleep. But since sleep still refused to encroach on the crowded terrain where my thoughts jostled one another, I got up, pursued by the ridiculous idea of Supertoad. If I didn't think about this batrachian now, his croaks would cut through the silence and prevent me from sleeping until morning.

Rather than writing down the beginning of his adventures, I decided to draw Ronie with his cape first, telling myself that the story would come to me more easily if I had my hero in front of me. I had wanted him to wear a cape like Batman's, but I had trouble with the folds, so I wrote "cape" on the cape in question, in case my future exegetes wanted to know what was hanging from the toad's back. The result would surely have been just as dreadful if I hadn't messed up the folds, but the goal of the operation was not to win a drawing competition. I simply wanted to occupy my mind and, one way or another, keep at bay the silence that descends over this godforsaken hole as soon as you turn off the radio or the TV, a silence so intense it walls you in and makes you start to wonder if you might actually be the lone survivor of some catastrophe the news anchor failed to announce. It's useless trying to sing to frustrate this oppressive calm, because the silence is still there all around you, giving your voice a metallic note that compresses the miserable song and reduces it to almost nothing, all the while highlighting the void that surrounds you.

Before I moved to this house, I could never have imagined that silence could stop a man from closing his eyes and keep him on the alert for the tiniest creak of the floorboards or the softest sound from downstairs, yet now my ears were attuned to anything that disturbed the silence, listening for the furtive shufflings of matter, of animal life, of the secret life of objects.

Night after night, I discovered that silence was an almost palpable absence that revealed hidden things, and thanks to this absence I was able to perceive objects moving around under the surface of the silence. This silence taught me that places breathed, that after dark the forest was inhabited by presences that were invisible to humans, and that I was never alone in the desert I'd tried to construct deep in the heart of winter. In Rivière-aux-Trembles I understood that all voids were full and that the world moved ceaselessly. The busyness of city life had not prepared me to face life in its calmest, slowest manifestations, and I had to learn that although a man can isolate himself from other men, he can't cut himself off from life.

I'd almost forgotten this silence because I'd only known it in the past, in the summer camps where my parents sent me to ponder my only-child sadness under the starry vault of the northern hemisphere while they enjoyed a holiday in the antipodes.

For my entire childhood, I was convinced that the term "summer camp" was a synonym for adult hypocrisy. They made you think they were giving you a holiday, but this forced retreat to the kingdom of campfire songs and sleeping bags allowed them to swan off and live the good life without having you under their feet. In the splendour of July, this was a "holiday" for parents only, and I later swore I would never send Billie, my daughter, to one of those colonies for children, abandoning her to the bugs, bears, leeches, and other creepy-crawlies that bloomed in the pure and life-giving air of the countryside.

I had kept my promise. Billie had never had to chant "Valderi, valdera!" at five in the morning, and the urbanite in me was not unproud of this when he remembered the distress he experienced in the dawn light, the fog rising above Trout Lake or Perch Lake, with the loons' piercing lament lifting above it. I was six, seven, eight, and I used to wonder if the loons were crying too, if their bird tears increased the lake's salinity. My stays in damp log cabins or wood bunkies had taught me nothing but distress. And here I was again, in the middle of nowhere with a silence more disturbing than that of the chilly Perch Lake dawns, reiterating the promise I had made to Billie back in a time so distant it seemed to belong to another life: "But no, pumpkin, no, you really think I'd send you away to get eaten by mosquitoes?"

That February morning there were no mosquitoes at Rivière-aux-Trembles, but there was a child, a small Billie whose presence took on such invasive proportions that I had to take refuge with a toad dressed in a cape that could only be made to flutter by a hurricane in order not to suffocate in the close quarters of this house, which was too full of Billie calling for help. "Hold tight, Billie, hold tight!" shouts the flying toad, "Bat-toad's coming," but Bat-toad isn't worth shit, he's as crappy as Superdad, who in three whole years of research hasn't been capable of tracking down the butterfly hairclip that could guide him to the lair of the giant who had kidnapped his daughter.

This was why I had headed to Rivière-aux-Trembles, in an attempt to flee the image of this man or nip in the bud the doubt that devoured me when I went crazy, whenever Ménard came over to wipe his huge dirty boots all over my dreams, or whenever L.A. spat her bile all over my white hands. My reaction was absolutely normal. All animals flee in the face of fire or gunshots, all living creatures, and the trees flee too in their own way, moving away from desert zones or swamps that swallow their limbs.

Given that I was alive and not totally crazy, I had fled, unaware that the beast I was trying to shake off had made itself a nest in my very entrails, not knowing that man is a fucking Trojan horse carrying everything he needs to self-destruct and poison his life in his own guts, beginning with the paraphernalia of painful memories that lacerate his body with every false step. We are powerless in the face of the tumour that spreads from the brain to the stomach. The only way to escape your own memory is to have a lobotomy. I wasn't quite at that point yet, but I did sometimes consider this option when time stretched out in every direction and the doldrums, with their load of slimy thoughts, seized this moment of universal stagnation to leap on me. Solitude tried in vain to keep my hands busy, but always gathered itself up in the middle of this void without which it cannot exist, this vast silent plain where it spreads out, naked in its truth, face to face with itself.

I didn't regret having taken refuge in Rivière-aux-Trembles. The complete change of scene the place offered sometimes allowed me to forget I was Bill, a man whose daughter had been a screaming tabloid headline. I wouldn't exactly say I'd unearthed the sacrosanct peace no life form can aspire to, but now and again I was able to dream in toad and become a writer once again for a few hours. And that was already something, a few hours without the pain of Billie, but when my watch stopped I would have preferred to find myself just about anywhere else, somewhere with noise — a symphony of car horns, drilling jackhammers, fireworks, and trumpets — because during quiet moments, instead of calming down, the brain always chooses to plunge into the darkest, slimiest pit it can find. When the second hand freezes on the clock face, I take a quick dip and surface, not far from a sleeping body of water, with a little Billie in my arms, a spineless, soaking-wet little Billie, a child whose cold skin no longer breathed.

And I start howling. "What have you done to my darling, you fucker? Why did you take her, you fucking sicko? Why? Why?"

I had asked myself this question dozens of times, and I would continue to ask it. Why Billie? Why my daughter? Invariably, all the unspeakable secondary questions this presupposed came up en masse, because if evil hadn't attacked Billie, would it have dropped its big black cape on another little girl? On Anna-Sophia Smith, ten years old, last seen at her gymnastics class wearing a white T-shirt with red stars, as she said goodbye to her friends? On Juliette Masson, age nine, who went missing at the bus stop, where her little snow-encrusted rubber boot was found two hours later by her hysterical mother? On Mathilde Dumas-Benoît, nicknamed Mattie, age eight, who went off to go to the bathroom and never came back?

Whenever I got bogged down in this kind of reflection, I looked around me desperately for an object that might be able to offer me some kind of distraction and at the same time erase these little girls' names, silence their cries, and stop me from suffocating, because it was intolerable to imagine another child, another little girl wearing a pink or white parka, the kind you see everywhere, as the prey of Billie's attacker.

But nonetheless these thoughts invaded my mind. What would have happened if Billie had been sick, if she'd stayed nice and warm at home on the day the scumbag decided to put on his assassin's gloves? What would have happened if she'd left school a little earlier or a little later?

Would Anna-Sophia Smith have evaporated in the January cold in Billie's place? Would the man watching from his steamy car have waited for another day, or would he have launched himself on the first girl to pass by, Juliette or Mathilde, lost in thought, humming a nursery rhyme she would later sing to her dog or her cat or her goldfish or her favourite doll? Billie always used to do that. She used to come home from school and recite her lessons to Pixie. She taught him the times tables and showed him where China and Greenland were on the globe. "They have polar bears there, Pixie, they're all white, see? And here's where they have pandas. They eat bamboo." There can't have been a better-educated cat in all of North America, and if fate in all its evil had not taken my darling far away from Pixie, the old fleabag could probably have become a math teacher or an anthropologist.

But fate *had* taken her, and nobody would ever know if Billie was just in the wrong place at the wrong time or if the attacker chose her particularly, if she'd been targeted by some crazed monster with childhood memories of lightweight coats and fine hair blowing in the wind — objects he needed to possess at any price to deaden the anguish he felt when he saw the sweet parade of girls from his past, skirts rustling on their bruised thighs. It's futile putting children on their guard in every possible way; it's not enough, they are too trusting to discern the stench of lying. Purity is the downfall of those we lose. To suspect evil, you have to be capable of conceiving of it, and Billie was absolutely not capable of that, otherwise I wouldn't be here constructing all these hypotheses to sharpen my own instruments of torture.

L.A. too had become a past master on this subject. Not a day went by when she didn't wonder what would have happened if I had, or if she had, or if we had, or if the whole world had done something differently and turned in the opposite direction, driving everyone who hadn't adjusted their watches crazy, thinking that China was snoozing while they were eating their cornflakes. She tore herself apart with great slashes of claws and teeth, putting the past tense into the conditional and cursing herself because she didn't have the power to go back in time and abolish the woulds, coulds, and shoulds.

Two or three months after Billie disappeared, L.A.'s mother had dragged her to a group meeting of families of loved ones who have disappeared, but L.A. was in such a catastrophic state that she couldn't bear the slightest contact with people who claimed to be experiencing suffering like hers.

Then Régine had tried her luck with me, on the off chance that I could pull Lucy-Ann out of this hole by rubbing up against other people's pain, but I gently turned the invitation down. Not that I refused to help Lucy-Ann, not that I doubted the importance of such groups. But I was the solitary-knight type of guy, the kind who prefers to suffer quietly in the corner rather than spill his guts in front of a crowd while drinking godawful coffee from a polystyrene cup. Everyone has their own rituals. Everyone has their own way of licking their wounds. Unlike L.A.,

I had no difficulty believing other people's misery could be as bad as my own. I just preferred to bleed alone, without anyone's help.

In any case, you don't need to seek out other people's misery to have it shoved in your face. It comes to you through the television, the radio, through billions of online images; it slips into your kitchen with the kid who delivers the newspaper, and the acceptable limit is right there between image and reality. As far as I was concerned, I could not align myself more closely to universal suffering. If I did I would die, go mad, or become a missionary, and I wasn't the calibre of guy who decides one random morning to ditch everything and head off to eradicate AIDS in Africa. Billie might have done that, Billie might have had that sort of courage or expansive soul, but not me, I had been cut out to stew in my shitty little pond, into which a few rocks from the outside sometimes plopped, big or small depending on the day.

During my first two weeks in Rivière-aux-Trembles, you'd have thought all the damn pebbles on the planet had plotted together to jump into my muddy pond and splash me as much as possible. All I had to do was open the newspaper to come across a photo of a missing teenager, or some sweet-looking kid last seen getting into a dark vehicle; to see spread out in front of me the details of the funerals of two little ones, two tiny angels, assassinated by their own progenitor; to hear the screams of two other sweethearts, also angels, savagely stabbed by a psychopath; to hear the mothers' and fathers' and brothers' laments of denial. I would sit down in front of the television only to be bombarded with the same absurd violence: "Shooting in Cleveland!"—two women and three children killed. "Carnage at German high school!"—nine students shot, their blood mixed with that of six other innocent victims.

I would swear as I turned off the TV, and a photo of my darling would inevitably superimpose itself on the black screen, the one with the mischievous smile that lifted up her left cheek, the one published in all the provincial newspapers and sent to all the police forces on the continent, posted on all the telephone poles, bulletin boards, and plywood sheets nailed to the badly lit walls I passed on my rounds. Billie Richard. Eight years, nine months. Brown hair. Hazel eyes. At the time of her disappearance she was wearing a pink coat with a hood, a butterfly in her hair, two butterflies on her socks. Also looks like an angel. Generous reward for any pink butterfly captured in an angel's wake.

It was impossible that nobody had noticed her, and yet no lead had led us to her. Every call the police received came from people who were nuts, pathetic losers seduced by the scent of money, pitiful old ladies trying to overcome the emptiness of their existence by inventing chimera, or people so eaten-up with guilt or visceral fear because they had chosen not to act when it was necessary claiming that they saw Billie everywhere. In every case, the child in question turned out not to be Billie, but one of a dozen little girls wearing a coat the colour of cotton candy, flowers, or strawberry milkshakes.

Some girls preferred yellow or blue, but Billie's pink period had been going on ever since she learned how to say the word. We went to the market together that summer to buy big baskets of strawberries from the Île d'Orléans, red and juicy, and Billie couldn't wait to squash them in plain yogurt or vanilla ice cream as soon as we returned to the house. "Look what a pretty colour it makes, Popinouche," she said, and burst out laughing because she'd called me "Popinouche" again, even though I was always telling her my real *dad* name was "Papanoute," emperor of the Noute dynasty, to which only nice people belonged: Mamanoute, Papanoute, Billienoute, Pixienoute.

Billie loved pink the way some people love the scent of lavender or lilacs, the way some people surround themselves with these flowers. She loved the pink that burst forth in June in the city gardens, the pink that spread across the sky in the evenings after dinner, and the pink she knew how to make with fresh fruit, but after January 20th, 2006, none of the little pink coats walking along the streets of this crappy city that had stolen her from me was Billie's. Even *I* thought I'd seen her several times. It took just a hint of pastel pink bobbing about in the crowd to get me pushing past people and shouting her name. Every single time, I ended up, bathed in sweat, in front of a father on the verge of punching my face in, or a mother ready to gouge my eyes out with her nails if I didn't get the hell away. So I would smile at the little girl and go back to my place, nowhere, in this overpopulated city that was incomprehensible without Billie.

I carried on stalking little pink coats for three years, watching for them even in the summer, even on the hottest July day, but there was no Billie hiding behind these flashes of colour breaking up the greyness. Billie had simply disappeared. Billie had vanished, and nobody ever saw her again, nobody knew where she was, except for the man with the rough hands, the driver of the dark car. He alone knew if she continued to grow up and whether her little coat had to be replaced. This man knew, this bastard had touched her plump little hands, maybe her face, her child's hair that smelled like peach-scented shampoo, perhaps, and this idea drove me insane.

I would have preferred it if Billie had been run over by a truck like the Dumas kid, or if some drunk driver had knocked her over after a clandestine poker game in a dive, or even if one of those damn illnesses L.A. and I tried so hard to protect her from had carried her off with the snow. At least I would know. At least I wouldn't be forced to imagine the unimaginable or to wake up with the image of a big dirty fucking hand stroking my Billie's soft hair, dead or alive.

But Billie wasn't there anymore, that was the only truth that counted, and the miserable semblance of survival my memory offered wasn't worth two cents. I could spend a hundred years imagining rocking Billie, but no Billie would feel the warmth of my tired arms. The idea that the dead live on in the hearts of the people who love them is frankly bullshit.

"It's all fucking bullshit!" I yelled, toppling over the

chair I'd been sitting in since the morning, watching Ronie the Toad while I waited for the minute-hand of the clock that regulated my days to start moving forward again. While I was at it, I pushed the table over too, which took a couple of chairs with it, thus breaking the silence with a long-awaited fracas. Time had finally restarted its onward march, and I had survived this breath-holding dive into its narrowest corridors.

I headed over to the sink to dunk my head under cold water and make my hands stop trembling, and then assessed the state of the damage around me. On the floor, the two slices of toast I hadn't touched were soaking up cold coffee next to fragments of broken crockery, shards of glass, and a milk carton whose contents were slowly seeping towards the black coffee stain. It would take me a good hour to put the kitchen in order and wash the floor. So that was something to do, and I wasn't going to complain about having a diversion. I still didn't know how I'd occupy myself for the rest of the day, but I would do it somehow; I had to in order to forget that everywhere on earth, even in Rivière-aux-Trembles, giant men could spy on little girls who hummed tunelessly as they walked home from school.

I woke up this morning right in the middle of a dream in which Australia was burning, forcing all the animals to flee, including some miniscule koalas that were trotting along trying to hook themselves onto my legs, just like the ones I'd seen in sad-eyed processions on the internet the night before, in between a few red-eyed tree frogs and the image of Billie blotting out all other pictures. I'd managed to trick the day's lethargy by cleaning the kitchen and dragging my mop around the rest of the house until it got dark, when I got sucked into a screen showing other people's happiness, hoping that the marvellous universe of Google would distract me from both my own pain and the abyssal world developing in the hollow of my navel.

After doing some research on the behaviour and habitat of tropical frogs, from the túngara frog to the phantasmal poison frog, several species of which I intended to include in Ronie the Toad's adventures to inject a little colour into the relatively green amphibian world, I stumbled across a site with pictures of koalas taken during the atrocious heat wave that had recently blasted Australia. I scrolled through the photos dozens of times, then went to get myself an enormous glass of cold water, thanking the heavens I'd been born in a country that had no drought, not really, not the kind that forces even the wild animals designed to survive water shortages to beg people for something to drink.

The first two photos showed one of these little chaps gripping onto the legs of a cyclist who was giving him a drink right from his own bottle. In the other pictures, one of his brothers or sisters was having a bath under the deck of a house, in a basin where he'd taken shelter to protect himself from the forty-four-degree heat that had been baking the Australian earth for days. He looked at the lens with his little round eyes, too thirsty and too exhausted to be afraid.

Once again I thought of Billie, who sometimes looked at me with eyes like that, distraught eyes that said, "I'm too little to understand, Popinouche, too small to face this all by myself"—life, hunger, thirst, the dark. I thought of the stuffed animals still lined up on a shelf in her bedroom, because nothing looks more like a stuffed animal than a koala. I thought of old Pixie, who had died from being deprived of Billie, and I turned the computer off, cursing Australia. I didn't know what that country wanted from me, but I'd had enough of its fires, its droughts, its desperately thirsty koalas, and yes, its kangaroos, who also had to leap about under a leaden sun in search of a trickle of water.

Australia haunted me even though I'd never set foot there and only knew that part of the world from images gleaned from the internet, television, or *National Geographic*, which I sometimes flicked through at the dentist or at Billie's pediatrician. One day I explained the details of marsupial embryonic development to my daughter, and for a week afterwards she hounded me to draw mommy kangaroos. "Pink ones, Papanoute, with pink pouches, not grey ones, they aren't pretty." So in my mind, Australia is a country populated with pink kangaroos, half chimera, half folklore, an Australia whose unpredictable landscapes borrow a large portion of the relief and the vegetation from Africa and South America. In my nightmare, the fire was devouring with the same fury an improbable forest of eucalyptus and palm trees, from which a horde of terrified animals was escaping.

And I was running with them, suffocated by the spreading smoke, tripping over stumps that teemed with ants abandoning the ship, and still running, mystified by this country that was forcing me to flee my dreams.

The sun was rising when I pulled back the living room curtains, but it was a hazy day darkened by snow-laden clouds. The woman on the weather channel, despite being perched on summer heels, had announced the day before that a large part of the province would see flurries or worse. The more easterly regions were likely to endure a storm that would dump a good twenty centimetres of fresh snow on the crunchy ground. I was overjoyed by this prospect, because we'd had almost no snow since I arrived in Rivière-aux-Trembles, only some wintry rain, and after seeing the dryness in Australia the absence of precipitation gave me visions of apocalyptic landscapes suffocating under grey dust. I kept an eye on the clouds' arrival and wondered what would become of the squirrels, foxes, skunks, and toads if water became scarce. People would manage to find a buried spring, but how would the animals survive?

I was thus hoping for clouds and snow the way you hope for spring after freezing your balls off when the mercury sinks to the bottom of the thermometer in winter. However, it seemed that the Rivière-aux-Trembles landscape on this late February day was going to be hosed down by a storm violent enough to make the animals run away. The day darkened as the hours passed, but I had to wait until early afternoon for the first flakes to start falling. I turned on a lamp near the old leather armchair pushed up against the living room window, from where I could watch the trees bowing in the wind's fury, their branches disappearing in the blizzard, then reappearing thanks to a momentary lull in the fierceness.

To celebrate my first storm in the countryside, I opened a bottle of Chianti and drew a line halfway down the bottle. This was the line I must not cross, the border between pleasure, headache, and the ramblings of a lonely man. I'd imposed this rule on myself long ago and intended to follow it while I was in Rivière-aux-Trembles: half a bottle from time to time but no more, because I had no desire to become the old alcoholic on the 4th Line, the wreck sipping his beer in a dirty undershirt with his paunch hanging out on the scorching porch, spending his days belching out hoppy burps and wiping his big cushiony lips with his tattooed arm.

After my darling disappeared, as I did the rounds of the bars with her photo, I would frequently come within a hair's breadth of throwing myself into alcohol for good. I had a few serious back-to-back benders; when I found my socks in the fridge one morning, I realized I was well on the way to proving right all those people who thought I was crazy. It had to stop. In any case, I couldn't stand alcohol and I hated the furry-tongued blur of the mornings after the nights before as much as I scorned the scum who bawled into their cheap whisky as they poured out their life stories to barmaids who just wanted to give them a kick up the backside. The odour of nausea burned my larynx at the thought of all those men, ranting and spluttering at sticky bar counters, men who pissed themselves, vomited all over themselves, or drank themselves into oblivion. I refused to become one of those red-nosed wrecks who might have been good men once upon a time, before the misery, before the fear, before they started trembling and losing their memory in their drunken ramblings. When my mirror started to look me up and down with its glassy eyes and my fridge started to smell of sweaty feet, I reversed direction at full throttle, because Billie deserved better than a father who could only half-remember the dazzling, harrowing beauty of his child. I started drawing lines on the wine bottles with one of Billie's markers to make the message even clearer, and if I made the mistake of exceeding the prescribed dose, I forced myself to vomit until it seemed as though my very guts were coming up out of my throat.

I drank two mouthfuls of my Chianti, thanking Billie's memory for saving me from degeneracy and its consequences. The snow started to intensify, blown diagonally by the rising wind. After half an hour, the wood of the porch, the roof of the car, and the gravel driveway leading to the house had taken on the colour of the clouds opening up over Rivière-aux-Trembles, the colour of the atmosphere. The nameless space that humans and animals normally move through was filling up with this white stuff, and I could no longer see into the hollows, gaps, and openings visible in clear weather. The world was suddenly full.

I finished my second glass of wine in the state of semi-hypnosis we are often plunged into when we watch clouds drifting overhead, or rain pouring down outside the window. Lost in the heart of the wind and the blowing snow, I was no longer sitting nice and snug in my living room, with all its empty space, but in the heart of this compact mass, where all contact with my surroundings was rendered immediate, with no horizon and no future. The city and its truncated skies had no real horizon either, but here enclosure took on a whole other dimension. I suddenly discovered that it was possible to be confined even in the biggest of wide-open expanses.

I could have died right then, watched myself die in this inertia and imprisonment, and the empty spaces of my very existence would also have been filled with it. Every crack through which unhappiness and pain could seep in would have disappeared, sealed by the blizzard, and no regret would have slipped through. I simply needed to stop breathing, open my mouth to let the snow in, and become a frozen statue, a lifeless being with a smooth body. I was on the point of abandoning myself, just lying down and dying, when the ringing of the phone penetrated the space that I thought had no cracks. I stood up quickly, knocking over my glass of wine, and a stain appeared on my sweater, "blood red, Billie" just like the blood on the finger pricked by the witch's bouquet.

The phone never rang in this house. The last person I'd spoken to apart from Ronie the Toad was my insurance agent, and I was the one who called him. In Rivière-aux-Trembles, this mute machine had a one-way function, from inside my house to outside, never the reverse, and it didn't know how to talk. That it was addressing me seemed as patently absurd as if I had tried to call 911 by tapping on a fence post.

I grabbed the receiver, convinced that the voice on the other end of the line could only bring me bad news, inevitably connected with Billie: she'd been spotted near a pond, a little pink angel rising out of the morning fog, trampling on the bouquet that had made her fall asleep in the magic forest.

"Yes?" I breathed into the phone. Yes, I'm here. Yes, I'm listening, aware that this simple three-letter word, when uttered in certain circumstances, puts you entirely at the other person's mercy, in a position where you're ready to receive anything, including a slap in the face. Sometimes you only have to say "yes" for fate to swerve. Three letters, and suddenly you're curled up at the foot of the altar, in the boss's bed, or behind prison bars. But I still said yes, I'm here, I'm listening.

"Bill?" murmured a feeble voice many kilometres away.

"Yes," I repeated. Yes, let's get it over with.

It was Régine, L.A.'s mother, her nose all stuffed up from too much crying and sniffling. If she were standing next to me, I'd see the cracked skin around her nostrils and the crumpled tissue she was wadding up in her trembling hand. I imagined her manicured hand on her thigh, fiddling with the tissue, fidgeting with her skirt, dropping the tissue, and sometimes flapping up in a gesture of powerlessness. "What can you do?" the hand said, and I had no answer to this question other than the blissful silence brought on by the waves of numbness that were taking over my immobile body.

A few hours earlier, while Australia was going up in flames, L.A. had slit her wrists with a kitchen knife. Régine was asleep in the guest bedroom when the knife pierced L.A.'s too-thin flesh. "She was nothing but skin and bones, Bill." Régine's maternal instinct had woken her up with a start. Hearing the bathwater sloshing around gently, she smashed the bathroom door open with a pickaxe. But in the time it took her to go down to the basement to get the pickaxe, her nightdress tangling in her legs as she ran, her crying colliding with her screams of denial, the bathwater had taken on the tinge of despair that nobody could struggle against any longer.

As Régine described to me the colour of the water with little hysterical hiccups, "Peony red, Billie, poppy red, the colour of crushed-up flowers," I thought of the pulsing arteries pushing the blood intended for the heart out of the slashes, and I wanted to yell at Régine to shut up, to hurl her phone at the wall, and to race into the bathroom to pour hot water over L.A.'s limp body. If the blood stayed warm, maybe it would be possible to resuscitate her, to make warm blood flow through her veins once more. "Run, Régine, run," said the voice strangling me, but Régine, her clothes covered in snow, was now wandering through the silent corridors of the hospital where L.A. had been taken, having traded the horror of the red for the coldness of the white. "It's all white walls, white sheets, white uniforms, Bill." The entire world emptied of blood.

"I'm cold," Régine murmured.

This tiny little phrase encapsulated Régine's misery—she hadn't even thought of pulling a sweater over her trembling shoulders, slumped under the burden of the strange and terrible disorientation of mothers trying to track down the cries of their little ones under the fallen trees. For a moment I could no longer hear anything but her cold, laboured breathing as she whispered, "It hurts, Bill, it hurts." Powerless, I simply received this cold breath as one among the many gusts that whipped Rivière-aux-Trembles. I should have been there, right there, to wrap a sweater around those bent shoulders, to take her in my arms and grip her hand, her little nervous red hand, which was still endlessly fiddling with the damn tissue. But I had chosen exile, I had deserted the battlefield, and four hundred kilometres of blizzard separated me from the place where my impotence could at least have thawed Régine's hand.

I searched for the words most likely to produce the warmth that Régine's devastation required, and finding nothing that could soften the cold at a distance, I promised I'd come to her as soon as the storm was over and the roads were clear. "It's a terrifying storm, Régine," I said, and then I hung up.

Inside the house, there was nothing but silence, but outside, voices yelled, inhuman voices picked up by the wind under the branches trying to rub up against the whitened trunks. I grabbed the bottle of Chianti and refilled my glass, not giving a shit about the orange line. "To you,

L.A.," I mumbled, collapsing into a chair with the slowness of a soldier who doesn't understand that he's just taken a bullet from a Ruger AC-556 right in the chest, and that the sudden weakness in his legs is caused by the reddening hole near his heart. An ugly hole edged with bloody flesh and chunks of soaked tissue.

The news Régine had just announced still wasn't filtering through to reality for me. L.A.'s death was one of those abstractions the mind can't immediately grasp as it tries in vain to associate death and its stillness with the features of a person it has only known while alive. I put my head in my hands. Without realizing it I dropped my half-empty glass on the woven carpet and swung back and forth until the words that expressed the irreversible burst into the semi-darkness of the storm.

"L.A. is dead, dead," I murmured, bearing down on the words one by one to extract their meaning, and then a few tears flowed, tears of anger that I tried to stifle until I felt that the weight of the snotty cries held in my throat would strangle me. "Why, L.A.? Why?" I shouted, hawking up mucus, but this time I knew the answer to the question I repeated as I swayed. "Because it hurt too much, I know, L.A., I know, because it just wasn't possible to go on imagining our baby's body split open by the fucking bastard's hairy dick, which someone should have torn off with their teeth the day he got his first erection, because a mother has the right to rest at some point, of course, L.A., and to go and see if the grass is greener on the other side, or the flowers bigger or the children happier."

Incapable of refilling my now-empty glass, very empty indeed, I glugged the dregs from the bottle as a stream of disparate images from married life flashed across the walls. I put aside the darkest ones, the pictures that hadn't come out well, and extracted from the muddle the most beautiful and the most painful, the ones that reminded me of the good times L.A. and I had shared: our holidays in Cape Cod, our inevitable and amazing trip to Los Angeles, our silly-faces competition, our coast-to-coast swims from the cold waters of the Pacific to the icy waters of the Atlantic, which always warmed up a few degrees whenever L.A.'s laughter plunged into it and reverberated across the waves.

As I clutched the bottle to my chest, I remembered the backlit shining skin, blond and spangled with sea water, the salt-whitened skin I licked from ankle to temple, from ear to navel, over and over, at the risk of needing a kidney transplant before my fortieth birthday. After the skin, I tried to resuscitate the hands, the breasts, the scar on the small of her back, but L.A.'s pallid body, lying on an enamel surface by a pool of stagnating red water, "blood red, Billie," invariably took the place of the warm body, and I wondered miserably, stupidly, whether she had poured a capful of her favourite oil—Désir d'Orient, I think it was called—into the bath, and if the subtle perfume of the orange tree mixed with the scent of blood had infused the room with a scent similar to that of sex, a stench so intimate and primitive that Régine, on discovering the body, would have screamed in horror and vomited.

I finished up the Chianti, thinking about viscous

chunks of vomit on the tiled floor, "Why did you do that to your mother, L.A.?" still incapable of telling her what I really thought of her, fucking egotist, fucking heartless bitch, because she looked too small lying there, too pale and vulnerable in the reflections from the sharp knife, and because I suddenly felt horribly guilty for not having loved her enough to prevent all this, the knife and the blood, but how can you love a mother who is so loving she ends up hating everything that reminds her of her child, which is basically all people and all objects?

As numb as if I'd chain-smoked three joints without taking a breath in between puffs, I stood up shakily, and after a detour past my box of Scotties, I went down to the basement to tell Pixie the news. That's what you do when someone dies, you tell the people who knew them. The old moggie must have already heard the news somehow, but I needed to say something, to actually put L.A.'s death into words, out loud, even though the animal I was speaking to was as deaf as a refrigerated corpse.

He was sleeping in his crate—what else could he do?— stretched out behind the wall where I'd pinned a photo of him with a fake mouse in his chops, a mouse with pink polka dots, chosen by Billie, who loved pink, mice, and polka dots. The mangled mouse lay beside Pixie in the crate now, along with his other treasures: a fluorescent-green tennis ball, a frayed shoelace, and a bundle of catnip. I'd placed these objects in the crate because it's what Billie would have wanted, since she believed that cats, like pharaohs, carry on living in the afterlife.

I sat down in the shabby armchair the former owner had left there and asked Pixie Tutankhamun if it was true, if there really was an afterlife where you wake up with the same head as before, with the same hair, the same shoes, the same pimple on your back. And if it was true, he was perhaps at that very moment snoozing in an enchanted scene out of *What Dreams May Come*, close to Billie and L.A., all three of them divinely happy, their paws and their feet warm in the white sand while I froze my ass off between the 47th and 48th parallels of Planet Earth.

If there was anyone in this house who could answer my question, it was this darn frozen cat. My eyes were riveted to his crate as I waited for him to speak to me. I was hoping for a sign of life, knowing full well that death doesn't speak — it says nothing to you that you haven't already imagined yourself. I wanted death to lie to me, to tell me a good joke about Newfies in hell or transmit a message by tapping on the walls, which I would then decode with my rudimentary Morse code, some extrasensory power inspired by my desire to hear Billie's voice from beyond the tomb. L.A. must have hoped for the same thing, a sign from the beyond, a sentence dropped from the clouds. Exhausted from waiting, she had invented a lie. At the end of her tether, she decided to check for herself whether paradise existed. She seized the knife she'd been eyeing for days and went to look for Billie in the only place the cops hadn't been able to cast their net, leaving me alone on the other side of the divide and obliging me to stay there, because one of us needed to stay and wait for Billie on this side of the world. "L.A. is dead," I murmured, and then I let Pixie digest the news.

It was just starting to get dark when I closed the basement door behind me. The storm was still raging outside, cut through with those inhuman voices. I was about to close the curtains when, through the living room window, I spied a shadow coming out of the forest. My heart leapt just once and I swore, convinced that this apparition was talking to the devil. For a moment, I thought this shadow emerging from the tangle of trees represented the lie I was waiting for from the other side, and then I saw the red scarf encircling the shadow's neck, too concrete, the colour too garish to have travelled from hell or the kingdom of heaven without alteration. This shadow was alive, just like all the shadows that cover the earth.

I watched it for a few moments as it trudged forward in the blizzard and struggled against the wind, wondering what kind of lunatic would abandon the warmth of their living room to throw themselves into the heart of the tempest. "He's going to be buried," I muttered, and then changed the pronoun, "She's going to be buried," because the shadow leaving the forest behind it was too frail to carry the body of a man. This shadow was the shadow of a woman bent under her pain. It was the woman from the funeral procession, I thought, certain from her posture and appearance that it was the same woman, the red-eyed crying woman who only showed up alongside death. I opened the door a little to call out, warning her that I could already see her red scarf disappearing beneath the snow squall that would flatten her to the ground, after which she would be visible against the fields' deserted whiteness as a piece of pigmented fringe reminiscent of the grass in a Boris Vian novel. But my warnings were futile—they were carried away by the wind in the opposite direction to where the shadow was heading. So I closed the curtains, leaving the bowed silhouette to ensure its own survival, and collapsed into my armchair. Then a few tears burned my eyes, and in brimming over they carried away the burning, while L.A.'s smile, the ravishing smile from the time we walked barefoot in the backwash of the Pacific or the Atlantic, began its erosive work.

L.A. had refused to be cremated. In a letter setting out her final wishes, she also expressed the desire to be buried without being embalmed, no coffin, so her body could travel intact in anticipation of meeting Billie, unaware that the physical integrity she aspired to was only possible at the cost of being mummified. She was afraid that if she was subjected to fire and reduced to dust, her hands would no longer be able to stroke the forehead of her daughter, whom she would finally rejoin among the gardens of her hypothetical paradise.

Régine had agreed to bury Lucy-Ann's body, even though she believed in reincarnation even less than she believed in a benevolent God, but there were rules she could not ignore and L.A.'s body was embalmed. Despite all her willingness, Régine wasn't up to fighting the laws that control our lives even when our bodies are rotting away after death. "I tried, Bill, but they kept shoving all this paperwork in my face, hygiene clauses, stories about carrion-eaters raiding the graves. I don't care about all that, but what was I supposed to do?" Nothing. Régine couldn't do anything, or she risked hearing a judge's mallet behind her—a judge who didn't have any choice in the matter either. In any case, L.A. had drained her own blood, thus setting in motion the process she wanted to spare her body. This inconsistency was not like her, but who can be logical with a butcher's knife at their throat?

Whispers resonated at the back of the half-empty room where she was stretched out in a virginal white shroud Régine had chosen for her. Her hands were clasped together in a gesture of piety, even though she had only discovered the relative virtues of prayer after Billie disappeared, clutching at this last resort, imploring and castigating God at the same time. "Do something, God...Please, God...I can't do this anymore, for Christ's sake..." So many empty words addressed to a god she didn't believe in but whose existence could be put in parentheses in case of distress. Every atheist who was raised as a believer has the same reflex: they have recourse to God when their guts are gripped with fear and they're breathless with terror. It's another way of appealing for help to childhood's sweet reassurance.

But no god answered L.A.'s appeals, even though her emaciated face evoked a martyr forcing herself to fast or to undergo self-mortification for the salvation of lost souls. I had never seen her so pale, despite the blush the undertaker's makeup artist had applied to her cheeks. Her waxy skin was a drained white under the powder, and I was certain that L.A. was not benefiting from the rest the dead are promised, the eternal beatitude some living people cling to as a way of consoling themselves for the immobility of corpses. L.A. was not at rest, she was not asleep, and she felt the peace of silence no more than the peace of unconsciousness. L.A. was dead. L.A. no longer existed. In one sense, it was not even her body that was laid out on the satin surface, dressed in a too-severe blouse bought for the occasion, but an anonymous cadaver. The stiff, cold body stretched out in front of us was nothing more than an object that used to be a woman and to which I could find nothing to say.

Since Régine had told me about Lucy-Ann's death, I actually talked to L.A. more often than I did during the last years we lived together. At first I pitied her fragility, then I called her every name under the sun—merciless words like traitor, coward, deserter, reserved for suicides and everyone else who confronts us with the *fait accompli*, leaving us to sort ourselves out with their mute pain. I had confided in the only woman I ever really loved, but I had nothing to say to this pretend L.A. lying in front of me, hands together and shirt buttoned up to her neck. Any contact I had with L.A. from now on would imply that I believed in ghosts or was sinking into my happy memories.

"Goodbye, L.A.," I managed to say to my ex-wife's corpse before they shut the coffin lid over her, then I put my arm around Régine's trembling shoulders, so small in her black dress, and together we walked to the car the funeral directors had reserved for us, a car that smelled like dead flowers and wreaths of withered gladioluses. The procession then moved off to the cemetery, and I felt as though I was reliving the scene I'd experienced when I arrived in Rivière-aux-Trembles, the difference being that I was now the one in the cortège. As a crucial element of this perfect coincidence, where the roles were reversed, a young woman stood on the sidewalk and waited for the freshly washed cars to pass by before going on her way. She looked just like the woman I'd seen in the Lexus going down Rivière-aux-Trembles's main street, the same type of woman anyway, recognizing herself in the distress contained in the mourners' silence, with the same look of a widow or an orphan, the same aloof stiffness. All that was missing was the February rain to give the impossible materialization of the unknown woman in Rivière-aux-Trembles her place in this picture, where coldness had the grace of sadness.

The wind seemed to have doubled in strength when we got out of the car, after driving through the cemetery paths to the chapel where L.A.'s coffin would be stored until the earth ceased to resist the blows of shovel and pickaxe. Régine, more fragile than ever, clung to her hat with one hand, while with the other she gripped a bunch of yellow and white flowers. After the coffin had been slid onto the trestle, Régine placed the bouquet on the coffin, pressed her cheek to the cold metal, then kissed it, leaving the imprint of her lips, "Cherry red, Billie, Maman's red blood under her skin and bones." Behind us, the sobs of L.A.'s faithful, tearful friend Patricia rose up in the wind's whistling, opposing death with one last refusal. Then we left the cemetery and its grey trees behind.

In the lively streets of the city, a single idea filled my head: return at full speed to Rivière-aux-Trembles without attending the reception organized by Patricia. I didn't want to face the pitying looks of the former friends of the couple L.A. and I used to be, or endure their subtext, or yield to their dismayed faces. I didn't want to touch — again — all the hands that had hesitated to reach out for mine at the funeral, people wondering if I was a legitimate part of the bereaved family, and then adding their hypocritical murmurs in order to evaluate the extent of my responsibility for L.A.'s death; perhaps from my distant retreat I had somehow handed her the sharp knife with which she'd drawn two definitive lines over her past life.

These people knew nothing. They had no idea what it took to stifle your tears with a stuffed toy that smells like your little girl's cheeks, or to talk to her dead cat, or to risk fainting every time the phone rang, or to pick up dirty underwear while cursing the entire world. These people understood nothing.

Out of affection for Régine and Pat, I kept my civilized-being mask on and went to the reception. After a glass of Sauternes and a crab puff pastry I could barely choke down, I slipped out, promising Régine I'd stay in touch. "You're all I have left of them, Bill," she said, pronouncing Billie and Lucy-Ann's names in the most heart-rending language in the world, which was probably invented by Eve when Abel died. I tore myself away from her maternal gaze before it could devour me in its confusion and hightailed it out of there without saying goodbye to the dozen or so pale faces of those who still claimed to be L.A.'s friends, even though they only came to the house one Sunday in ten, during visiting hours for the elderly and the sick.

Before I hit the road, I allowed myself a brief detour past Jack and Jack's café to refresh my memory and see whether the guy who wore a red scarf and sipped a cappuccino while his daughter left school for the last time was still sitting on the bench at the back. I imagined a little frost on the windows and the January faces around him, and I saw he was still there, his face serious, unaware that the foam from his cappuccino had given him a clown mouth, made only more ridiculous by the severity of his expression. I raised my hand to him, his image evaporated, and I got back in my car. This man was innocent.

On the way back, I stifled my dark thoughts by pressing on the accelerator, then I calmed down when L.A.'s voice, coming from our thirteen years of life together, ordered me to slow down. "If you won't do it for yourself, do it for Billie. You're all she has left." L.A. was right. Régine was right. I was now nothing but the shell of a man, a shadow, what's left of the memory of the dead when everything has flown off and you need a moron to guard the fort.

As I blinked, the portion of the highway heading north divided into four blurry, wavy lanes. Before I could crash the car or mow down a bunch of innocent revellers on their way back from a family dinner, I veered right, crossing three of the lanes that snaked in the headlights, and parked on the shoulder. With my head resting on the steering wheel, I wept over everything I hadn't dared to cry about in front of Régine because she'd needed the little bit of me that was left not to dissolve right in front of her. When I set off once more, there were only two lanes in front of me again, two lanes edged with shadows and spectres that rose up out of the darkness.

Once I was back in Rivière-aux-Trembles, the perfect silence of the winter night plunged back over me like an anvil hurtling off a roof—and what the hell was it doing up there anyway? I was alone, and this is what my life would look like from now on. It was the life of a father without a child, a husband without a wife, a man without the desires of a man—an automaton at best, an empty vessel carrying the blood that keeps the feeling of loss and vacuity at bay to the brain and the vital organs.

I was tempted to draw the curtains as a way of erecting a barrier between the two silences surrounding me— the one of the black fields and the other creating its own resonance between the walls—but it's always better for silence to circulate freely so it can show you how big it is and demonstrate its ability to give chase if you attempt to escape from it.

Since I was neither hungry nor tired, I shuffled in my slippers over to the armchair, the spot where I was sitting when the phone's shrill ring had dragged me from my lethargy five days earlier. The window beside the chair was white with frost, and on the lower part of the cold pane, the storm had created a wavy ribbon that resembled a chain of lunar mountains, with a few peaks rising up and summits disappearing into a frosty cloud. Through this white screen, the countryside appeared a compact, immutable black, and I had the impression I was navigating inside a vessel moving noiselessly through the galactic night.

Perhaps this was where L.A. had washed ashore with Billie and Pixie, swerving into another silence. I imagined them in a state of weightlessness, released from the heaviness of their bodies, then I transported them onto the lunar mountains standing out against the night. Just as the earth's shadow covered the moon, a howl rose up in the forest behind the house. A new moon or full-moon scream. For a moment, still haunted by the scent of faded gladioluses and the neat line of snow-covered tombstones, I was tempted to take this cry as a sign from L.A., whose soul had perhaps been following me on the road when I saw it double, half angel, half liar, to tell me that the afterlife was nothing but a trick, that the only afterlife possible consisted of this intermediary space where the mind drifts for the time it takes the bed of the deceased to cool down.

But I no longer believed in all this twaddle to which loneliness clings so desperately. The cries could only have come from a few coyotes, wolves, or stray dogs gathered together to hunt. I didn't know if there were stray dogs in

Rivière-aux-Trembles, but I swept that possibility aside. In my mind, these packs of famished animals could only be associated with the savage expanses of Nevada, Texas, or some other state where *Homo americanus* still lived in the age of the cowboy. In fact, I would rather it be wolves or coyotes, less dangerous, less sad than herding dogs, huskies, German shepherds, or Labradors abandoned to their fate overnight, without food, without affection, without voices guiding their steps: sit, lie down, stay. I hadn't grown up in one of those families where bonds are cemented around a dog whose photograph takes pride of place on the mantelpiece beside pictures of children and grandparents, but this didn't stop me from wanting to vomit at the stupidity and cruelty that pushed certain bastards to dump the animals they'd formerly adopted. I didn't understand how you could drive towards the forest, open the car door, whistle for the dog to jump out, "Come on, boy, out you get, Jeff," and then zoom off at full speed while the poor animal wonders what's going on, thinks it's a game, maybe, then panics and tears off into the dust, runs until he's out of breath and then, in the rear-view mirror, becomes nothing more than a minuscule dark spot in the settling dust.

It was Billie, rather than God, Jesus, or Greenpeace and all their saints, who had taught me to respect life. It was her frightened voice that stopped me from squashing the bugs that innocently crossed my path.

"Stop, Papanoute!" she used to shout whenever the shadow of my foot threatened to crush a spider or an ant, and my foot would change direction and the spider would creep off. It was her sleepy little head on the pillow, expressing all the vulnerability of someone who doesn't even know what a wolf is. It isn't possible to live with someone who catches beetles to shelter them from the rain, a little creature whose survival depends on our vigilance, without questioning the concept of survival of the fittest, or realizing that the strongest doesn't always eat the weakest or abandon it in the woods, but sometimes protects and nourishes it, at the risk of its own survival if necessary. So I preferred the cries breaking through the frosty summits where L.A. held Billie's hand to be those of a pack of coyotes that could make out the reflection of the moon behind the clouds.

I moved closer to the window, in case I could see a shadow with the bent back of two or three species of canid at the edge of the woods, but I saw neither wolf nor coyote nor stray dog. In the thick darkness, I could only make out the silhouettes of the trees lined up behind the house like a range of sentinels protecting me from the forest spirits, or, who knows, guarding the forest from the intrusion of men. For a moment I thought of the cypresses guarding Arnold Böcklin's painting *Isle of the Dead*, a reproduction of which I'd hung in my office a few years earlier to counterbalance the covers of my books, which also hung on my walls. Each time I lingered in front of the picture, I felt the weight of an anguish as white as a death sheet, and I felt the same in front of these trees that forbade me access to the forest. I turned on a light, the way one does to destroy the monsters hiding under children's beds, and went upstairs to sleep. In the forest, the crying quietened down, making way for the hidden noises that shape the silence.

It took me a long time to fall asleep. I was disturbed by the hiss of my own breathing, which lengthened into a slow whistle whenever I was about to drop off. Rather than count sheep — or thirsty koalas — I concentrated on the small cracking sounds coming from the wall just behind my bed, trying to discern some kind of pattern, a mathematical or algebraic formula that connected the three points from which the noises seemed to originate, and that would allow me to determine their rhythm. I had decided on a musical model in two-time for triangle and orchestra when my muscles finally relaxed.

When I woke up, the previous day's howling still in my head, I swallowed down a hasty breakfast before going out, muffled up to my ears, planning to look for tracks at the edge of the forest, the tracks of animals or aliens that had picked up the wolves' howls from the very depths of space and thought it was the language of two-legged creatures who seemed compelled to annihilate others.

The snow at the edge of the woods was pristine, and I walked a few hundred metres under the tree cover, reassured that my tracks in the snow would lead me back, but found nothing except a can of 5W30 motor oil sitting under a pine branch near an old brown sock, so I picked both items up with the intention of putting them in the garbage. The products of human activity know no borders, so I wasn't surprised to find these unusual objects in a place where nobody needed oil or a holey sock. I'm sure if people ever set foot on another planet they'll discover empty bags of Humpty Dumpty chips, shirt buttons, and orphan socks of all colours, just like the thousands of lonely, forsaken socks you find abandoned on wet sidewalks, parks, or roadsides, as if humans are actually one-legged animals that enjoy taking one shoe off in the middle of the road and leaving a single sock behind.

With the can in my hand and the sock in one of my coat pockets, I made my way among the tangled trees and eventually reached the river that gave the town its name. Someone had passed by the same way not long ago, a man or a woman whose tracks had not been entirely covered by the most recent blizzard. The tracks went along the river, penetrated a few metres into the forest, and then descended to the crevice where the river would form a pool when it wasn't frozen. The marks in the snow grew wider here, indicating that the person had lain down or slipped into the river, sweeping a good chunk of the accumulated snow along with him or her.

Clouds began to amass in the sky, which until that moment had been an intense blue. Through the branches of the bare trees, I could see them pushing gently forward. One blue patch, one grey patch, one white patch made up of tiny particles swirling around. Hypnotized by this movement, I too lay down on the ground and started flapping my arms and sliding my legs back and forth, like we did when we were children, like I used to do with Billie in the backyard at home. We used to call the shapes we made snow angels or snow owls, depending on whether we felt closer to the earth or the heavens. "Do you think we could fly in the snow?" Billie had asked me one day, and I imagined the two of us gliding close to the ground, crossing the snowbanks and pulverizing them with big flaps of our wings.

This same thing was happening to me now. I was flying through snow, half angel, half owl, raising clouds of powder that fell back on my face. I was flying on my back, seeing things from the perspective of an owl or an angel skimming the whiteness of the snow, when a cry rang out in the forest, the scream of a torn beast, as definitive as death in person. I stopped short. A squirrel had just departed this life, or a hare, caught by the angel or the owl. Nothing was moving. The scream had absorbed all other calls and movements. Its echo slowly imprinted itself into the hares' memory, a new cry in the repertoire of fear assuring the survival of the weakest. As I sat on the frozen river, I observed that my hands were trembling as I waited for the next cry. I stood up carefully, afraid to disturb the silence, and looked around me. No angel, no owl flew or fled by the river, yet dozens of eyes watched me, creatures turned to stone by the cry, waiting for the forest to start breathing once more.

I picked up the oil can and set off into the forest, following my own tracks to find my way through the trees, disturbed by the vague but powerful impression that I was not alone, that I was being tracked by an animal disturbed by my presence. Quiet cracking followed me, becoming silent whenever I stopped and turned around. Given my pursuer's precision — it never took a single step more than I did — I concluded that these cracking sounds were made by my own footsteps, by the noises travelling between the trees. But still the feeling persisted. This place was unhealthy. There was something off about the river. When I came out of the woods, a heap of dark clouds was piling up behind the house. A grey mass, then a black mass. Another storm was going to break over Rivière-aux-Trembles. I might have taken this as a bad omen if the worst hadn't already happened to me, but I let it go. I made sure the door to the shed wouldn't bang in the wind and went back inside.

With the oil can still in my hand, I went into the kitchen, threw the can into the garbage, and searched in vain for the sock, which must have fallen out of my pocket when I was being pursued through the silent forest by the unknown animal that wanted to make sure I really left the woods. While the clouds gathered to the north, I made myself a three-cheese, lettuce, and mustard sandwich to eat in the basement, where a pile of planks waited for me to turn them into a workbench. It wasn't an urgent job, but I needed to keep my hands busy to ease the discomfort the scream in the forest had provoked.

Once I had eaten my sandwich, I set to work, telling Pixie — still waiting in his crate for the arrival of spring — a story starring the Cheshire Cat and Puss in Boots. I put the pair of them in an enchanted forest, which is pretty much obligatory in a fairy tale, with ridiculous fairies, one-legged people, or belly dancers to pass the time. I described Puss in Boots' boots — princely boots, not to be confused with seven-league boots — then lingered over the Cheshire Cat's floating smile, not a very reassuring kind of smile, and interrupted my story just at the point when the latter meows a rather indignant "oof." It was either that or kill it off. This cat had always got on my nerves, and I didn't plan to wait for the next storm to cross it off my mental landscape. With no transition, I started talking about Ronie the Supertoad to test out Ronie's metamorphosis on an audience, and thus went from cat to ogre and from ogre to super-batrachian until my piles of planks looked something like a workbench.

By the time I went back upstairs it was dark. A timid circle of clarity, crushed by cumulonimbus clouds, was vanishing in the dark sky. I barely had time to walk over to the window before it disappeared in the darkness of the treetops. By this point, no light remained over the countryside except for the feeble halo glowing on the porch that came from the bulb by the door. I reached out my arm to turn it off and observed the night, which seemed to be devoid of life. But I knew that there were wolves on the hill, coyotes or wolves, and that birds of prey perched on branches, keeping an eye out for little animals scampering over the snow. I would hear their cries and then everything would become quiet again. This was life at its most authentic and cruel, and there was neither a booted cat nor a fairy world in which deer and wolves slept alongside one another. The truth resided out there in that silent darkness, exempt from the lies with which people surround their existence.

The storm I had predicted was even more violent than its predecessor, a spring storm combining snow and rain that transformed the yard into an enormous pond, the wind furiously whipping up chaotic little waves over the drifts of granular slush that formed a kind of bank for this new pond. Days after the storm, as I gazed at this wind-dried pond, I thought about the river, whose waters must also be agitating under the increasingly thin ice cover; I thought about the cry I heard, about the furtive footsteps that stopped behind me, and I shivered a little just like the slushy pond, nothing serious, a little frisson that wrinkled my forehead and pushed my eyebrows down over my eyelids, giving me the appearance of a guy thinking about serious things. But most of the time I treated myself like a cowardly urbanite who didn't know the difference between a beaver grunting and a woodchuck chucking.

I still waited a while before going back to the river, pretending I had no desire to wade knee-deep in icy water or to sit down beside a stand of stoic spruces that were waiting for me to speak first. Then, one morning in early April, I had just come to the end of a new Ronie the Supertoad adventure when I realized that my fears were as insignificant as a heat rash compared to the climatic tidal waves shaking the planet. CNN had just informed me that torrential rains in Namibia and Zambia had caused several rivers to flood, exposing the victims to crocodile and hippo attacks, snake bites, bilious malarial fevers, and painful diarrhea. In comparison to this, the threat of hares and squirrels here in Rivière-aux-Trembles didn't seem so bad.

The weather had warmed up and a light rain was falling over the countryside. Since the last storm, the snowbanks had been shrinking daily, revealing yellowed grass. In a few weeks I would be able to sit on my porch watching the wildflowers grow and getting eaten alive by mosquitoes. As I looked at the rivulets of rainwater and melting snow carving up the gravel in the yard, I wondered if the river had thawed and if it too was going to burst its banks. The ridiculous fear that the water would overflow as far as the village, causing a family of beavers to settle on Main Street, did cross my mind, and it set off one of those crazy laughs I hadn't thought I was even capable of anymore, a crazy head-to-toe experience like Billie used to have, a deranged laugh with all the frankness of open-eyed innocence, the kind that washes your brain clean of the nonsense weighing it down and gives you major stomach cramps.

Three quarters of an hour later, I was crouched near the river by the edge of the basin. In the tumult of the current that swept the winter detritus along, I could hear neither my heartbeat nor the distant cries that rose up from the forest. There was nothing but the sound of water. As I looked around for a log or a tree trunk to sit on and listen to the torrent, I noticed a little wooden cross at the entrance to the trail, the kind that are placed on the road by a deadly bend, to mark the spot where death carried out its work, discreet little crosses with wreaths of faded artificial flowers and laminated photos of the person who lost their life at the scene.

On the cross, which stood in the shade of the trees, someone had carved the name *Michael* with a pocket knife or a chisel. There were no decorative flowers, but a little owl made of straw and bark swung in the wind on a string that was attached to its head but had become wrapped around its neck. It looked like someone who had tried to hang themselves but had miscalculated how much rope they would need and had been forced to glue their head to the ceiling so as not to fail. This owl was frankly sinister, with little yellow eyes that seemed to catch the tiniest movement around them, the slightest change in the landscape. When it stopped moving, I felt as though it was watching me, trying to evaluate whether an anomaly like a man in the middle of the forest was something to worry about. Then the wind made it swing around just as a ripple shivered over the river.

I went closer to the cross to see if it had anything else inscribed on it, but Michael was the only name on the worn wood, gnawed away by time and insect larvae. No date, no epitaph, no mention of the age of this man or child named Michael. But I had a feeling it was a child, a boy who had fallen into the river and died. It was harder to imagine an adult coming to drown himself in a pool that could hardly be a metre deep in summer. But I could see a child running into the basin, yelling, climbing out with his hair plastered to his skull, then starting the whole routine over, again and again, until cramps twist his stomach, and later a man armed with a mallet, face ravaged by alcohol, anger, tears—everything that devastates a man who pisses his son's blood out of every pore—comes to hammer in a cross by the fucking river that snuffed out his little boy, thus putting God and his creation in opposition and insulting him with his swearing.

This father who resembled me, who clung to a cross because he was unable to cling to a god, filled me with both shame and pity. I thought of Billie, who would never have her own cross or her own coffin, because Billie was everywhere, because she was nowhere, and because I would have needed to hammer little pink crosses over the entire world to be sure that somewhere, under this macabre crop, lay a Billie like the one I had known, the great architect of the alternating overpopulation and depopulation of my universe.

Missing children don't have a right to their own grave. They only have the right to a hole, or the corner of a dump, or the edge of a slimy swamp where cattails grow. The man with the rough hands, the January man, knew where this hole had been dug, knew where the water of this swamp stagnated, but there was no way he had placed a cross among the cattails because such a bastard cannot believe in God. I didn't believe in him myself anymore, but obviously for different reasons, and I didn't see how an object that a martyr's blood had flowed over could provide comfort to anyone, no more to a criminal than to a poor innocent crying over a missing body. Christ's cross was nothing more than a morbid symbol, and the same was true of little Michael's cross, as gruesome as the owl somebody had hung there. The owl was still staring at me with its bulging eyes, identical to the eyes of every hanged person, popping out of its skull and accusing we'll never know who of tying the rope around its neck.

I was wondering who could be twisted enough to come up with the inspired idea of hanging a bird on the cross. Maybe the kid's mother, who had gone postal, or his father, as drunk as he was crazy, or maybe his psychopath sister. Who knows? I didn't give a shit. I unwound the string strangling the bird and muttered a cursory prayer to the child Michael, "Say hi to Billie, Mike, hug her for me, take care." My first impression had been correct after all: there was something about this place that was not right. This sinister river was haunted by the ghost of a child.

The rain was still falling, fine and icy, my clothes were soaked through, and I was shivering as much as if I'd actually fallen into the river. I made a gesture of goodbye to Michael X, Y, or Z, wherever he was, and got out of there before the next ice age could begin. Followed by soft cracking sounds, I ran through the trees, unsure which path to follow, tripping over my bootlaces, faithful to the stereotype of an urban scaredy-cat who only feels at ease in a concrete landscape.

I had found it easy to follow my tracks in the fresh snow the first day I ventured down to the river, but today the ground was only covered in mud, dead leaves, and sparse patches of snow. Now and then I could make out a partial footprint, but I no longer recognized the trees or any of the landmarks I'd passed earlier. I eventually managed to make my way out of the woods by following the footsteps I thought were mine but which turned out to be those of children, the footprints of two or three children wearing shoes with different soles, one with diagonal stripes, another with horizontal lines.

What were these children doing in the heart of a forest haunted by the memory of a little boy? Maybe they had known little Michael. Perhaps they'd come here to gather at the foot of his cross and throw stones into the water, unafraid in the slightest of the creaks of their own footsteps, considering the forest a place of safety that kept them at a distance from the adults they would become. Children who grow up under the trees know that the woods are only hostile to those who never learned to make out their shadow in the pitch black. I didn't need to worry on their behalf. If ghosts were a part of their games, it was only in accordance with a lie that they bitterly protected. When I eventually came out into a field, I discovered I had walked in the wrong direction. I had exited at the other end of the road, about two kilometres from my own house.

I trudged those two kilometres in the rain, convinced I was going to catch my death. I heard a stifled ululation, like a child's cry, at the edge of the woods as I set foot on my porch, but it was only the wind, just the wind, and the fever already heating up my forehead.

For the next three days I was once again subjected to the agony of the Australian flu. I would wake up with my sheets soaked in sweat and tears for Billie, for L.A., for all the suffering people in the world, and only got out of bed to drag myself to the toilet, where the mirror reflected the image of a man as pale as a corpse, whom I had trouble recognizing. "Bill? Is that you, you old fart?" Every time, my reflection tried in vain to reassure me by forcing a smile — not my smile, but that of a man disappearing behind a wintry fog that had entered his house along with the fever. I would swallow two Tylenol and go back to bed, wondering if I might actually be the dream creation of a cruelly unimaginative forest spirit.

Maybe I had somehow swallowed my birth certificate at the wheel of my rental truck on my rambling journey to Rivière-aux-Trembles two months earlier, missing the last turn, the one you never see coming, and thrusting myself into the section of road that forks at the last moment, turns into an inescapable dead end, and sends you shooting out into infinity. If that were the case, perhaps the funeral convoy I had seen driving down Rivière-aux-Trembles's main street was my own, led by the tearful woman I could have loved if my immune system had not declared war on Australia. But perhaps I was just the woman's dream, a tragic dream, at the end of which she reached out her hand to me as my U-Haul took off with a crunch of metal. From the depths of the nebulous space where I drifted, I could hear her sobs and cries of denial as she kissed my blood-covered forehead amid the cooling engine's clicking sounds.

I didn't know what might be happening in the head of a guy who had suddenly been catapulted into the middle of a dream. If I could go by the people I met in my own dreams, they never really seemed to be thinking about much. But what did I know? Until that point, I'd always thought the postman who rang the doorbell when I was deep in a nightmare wasn't even aware of his own existence, but what if that wasn't the case? Maybe the postman had feelings, fears, worries. Maybe the poor idiot was ruminating on prime numbers before tumbling down to the bottom of the steps, mailbag slung over his shoulder, and being propelled into the kingdom of dreams without being asked.

It was only when the mercury dropped below forty, where it had been for seventy-two hours straight, that I gradually gathered my wits and decided I wasn't anybody's dream, and that the postman doing his nighttime rounds in my subconscious had been a product of my mind alone. This fever had certainly left a mark, and I couldn't stop thinking about the boy named Michael, who had been the start of it all. A boy whose death had demolished an entire family and perhaps pushed his mother under the wheels of the train that stopped every Monday and Thursday at Saint-Alban, the nearest town to Rivière-aux-Trembles, twenty kilometres to the northwest. We had seen that before, fathers and mothers who blew their brains out or bled themselves dry—right, L.A.?—because dying is less painful than breathing, especially since it doesn't last as long.

The entire village except for me must have known what happened to that boy and his family. The whole region must have heard about the train-mangled mother, or the boy's unrecognizable body, spotted by a fisherman downstream of the swimming hole. After three days of insomnia interspersed with nightmares, I needed to know too, if only to get this little boy out of my dreams and stop the dying owl who watched over him from slipping in after him. My cupboard was already full of skeletons and ghosts, and there was no room left for a drowned boy or a hanged owl. But I couldn't exactly picture myself showing up at the grocery store to ask Max the butcher about the kid who must have died years ago. The Rivière-aux-Trembles welcoming committee hadn't arranged a reception for me with fanfare and a mayoral address when I showed up unannounced.

I was the outsider, the bizarre guy who had recently moved into the former house of a man named Lucien Ménard, who did "every kind of lawn maintenance," who spent his life trying to kill the dandelions whose roots he was now fighting with, which goes to show that obsessions really do endure. Even though people were polite to my face, I could hear them whispering behind my back every time I left the hardware store or the grocery store. The rumours that rose up from those little huddles of two or three customers at Max the butcher's meat counter had nothing to do with my sex appeal or the desire of one of the local women to lasso me into her bed. These overheated rumours were all about suspicion that would cling to me until I married a local girl on either a reconnaissance or a kamikaze mission who would testify to my innocence while she was out buying sausages.

They must have come up with a thousand miserable reasons to explain why I showed up in this godforsaken hole, or assigned me questionable origins, or invented shady dealings to explain my seclusion. Above all, they would have told their children and teenagers to be wary of me. Single men aren't popular, and it's easy for people to paint them as satyrs or pedophiles. My status as a single man made me a creature on the margins—safer to be distrustful. If I had rolled into town with a wife and kids they might have opened their arms a little wider, but my solitude made me seem suspicious, and I would be given no credit until I proved I wasn't Ted Bundy's grandson or some other sleazy serial-killing bastard, which would probably take me around twenty years if I skipped the marriage option.

Since I had no hope of getting the information I wanted in the village, I fell back on the internet, but without a date or a surname I might as well have been looking for a needle in a haystack. In any case, the event had happened too long ago. Nobody archives the death of ordinary people, people who didn't make a fuss and hadn't had their splattered brains splashed all over the front pages of the tabloids. I would do better gleaning scraps of information here and there in order to expel this child from my thoughts. While I waited, I would focus on the April rain and Myrtle the Turtle, the new character the rain had inspired. Her name made no sense, but I liked how it sounded. Myrtle the Turtle, the genius of the magic bottle. I was writing any old rubbish to kill time and forget that the daisies weren't anywhere near blooming.

On the morning of April 12th, the day of Christ's resurrection, I phoned Régine. She hadn't been doing much; like me, she was waiting for the arrival of the heat instead of the Messiah, hoping that the sun would finally warm up her perpetually icy hands. We talked about everything and nothing, avoiding the topics of L.A. and Billie, even though that was all either of us could think about, even though we were both thinking about the eggs L.A. used to hide in the garden for Billie, rain or shine, every Easter Sunday. She would paint chickens on the eggs, or flowers, or simple blocks of colour in the style of Mark Rothko or Kenneth Noland. Billie must have owned close to a hundred of L.A.'s painted eggs, the best of which she kept in a wicker basket tinted yellow to match the fluffy chicks L.A. would sometimes arrange beside the artistically crackled eggs.

I didn't know what had happened to that basket. Régine had dealt with L.A.'s things. She'd done orderly sorting-through of paperwork, drawers, and wardrobes, her nose covered in dust, being crucified by memories. When all the drawers were empty, she put the house up for sale. I had left everything with L.A.: the property, the furniture, Billie's toys. This freed me from the responsibility for the objects as well as the objects themselves, whose sight had become unbearable to me.

I had abandoned L.A. in a cowardly fashion amid all the soft toys and pink skirts, and the only thing of Billie's I kept was Pixie's corpse, which I would soon return to the earth. I didn't want her dolls around me, or her damp-eyed teddy bears following me from room to room, clinging to my legs and trying to talk about her. So I burdened other people with the job of dealing with this poisoned legacy. But today, as Régine's voice disappeared behind the sound of the bells returning from their pilgrimage to Rome, I would have liked to have Billie's egg collection with me, which would also have talked to me about L.A. I finally broke the silence in which we had shrouded L.A. to ask Régine if she knew what had happened to those eggs. "They're right here on the table in front of me," she said, and after she described to me one of the last ones L.A. had painted — a dark dot circled in yellow like an owl's eye — I hung up.

I had never seen this egg, but I immediately imagined it with the face of the owl that hung down by the river, flanked by two bulging yellow eyes that could read thoughts. I pushed away the image of this owl's-head egg before I'd started making absurd connections between L.A. and the Rivière-aux-Trembles mysteries. Rather than drive myself insane by fretting about Régine's very palpable pain for the rest of the day, I forced myself to go out for an hour's brisk walk, three kilometres north, three kilometres south, there and back in the gloom. When I returned, there was a cat sleeping on my porch, a yellow and white male that started meowing as soon as I put my foot on the porch step, a scruffy old tom that looked like Pixie. I walked around him and ordered him to go home. I had absolutely no desire to adopt a cat, even less a cat that could have passed for Pixie's reincarnation if you took away the cirrostratus-shaped mark over his forehead. I closed the door on his meowing, but it still came through the door, albeit more muffled.

This cat had sensed what I was: the kind of person who gets attached, the kind you can wear down, and he would persist until he got what he wanted. Images from the time when Pixie used to order me around with a swish of his tail spooled across the misty horizon of this dreary Easter day, pictures of Billie rocking Pixie and petting his big Whiskas seafood-stuffed paunch, and I realized I was fucked.

From the pantry I unearthed a can of Clover Leaf tuna that in earlier times I would have saved for Pixie, and I served it to my visitor on the porch in a Tupperware container from my former life. While he was stuffing his face, I noticed that the old fleabag resembled Pixie even in his way of eating, casting sideways glances to make sure I wasn't planning to take away the fruits of his exhausting fishing trip.

If I had been just a little drunk or just a little more unhinged, I would have raced down to the basement to make sure Pixie hadn't had the brilliant idea of leaving his crate to come and haunt me. I could have assumed that the cirrostratus was just one of the multiple effects of the freezing or the reincarnation, and I would have shut the cat in so I could watch it out of the corner of my eye 24/7, just in case he decided to transform himself into a magician or a shaman when I was sweeping the floor. But I was neither drunk nor crazy. This cat was simply Pixie's double, a kind of brother, a quasi-twin who had inherited the same stupid appearance, and who inspired in me the same burst of sympathy. Pixie and Dixie. As I petted the head of Pixie's twin, I announced that if we saw each other again I would call him Dixie, in memory of Pixie, and I didn't want to hear any grumbling about it being a damn mouse name. If it wasn't Dixie, it would have to be Pixie Two, and nobody wants to be called Two.

He didn't listen to a word I said, but he finished up his tuna and rolled onto his back so I could stroke his belly while his contented purring thrummed through the air. "Listen, Popinouche," Billie used to say when Pixie, on the brink of ecstasy, used to coo like a pigeon on its wedding night, "listen, he's making his contented cat sounds." Billie didn't say happy but contented, because the idea of happiness is an adult notion, a concept for people who have left behind the simple pleasures of childhood and are hoping for an inaccessible nirvana instead of being content to be content. Happiness is too complicated a concept for children to bother much with it. They laugh, they play, they simply are, and they don't spend their time wondering whether they could be laughing more or guffawing in a way that conforms to their idea of laughing. "Listen, Popinouche, he's making his contented cat sounds." For Pixie, this was the peak of existence. He could never feel any better than he did right then.

I sometimes thought we should have a nomenclature for the sounds that express contentment, the noises happy animals produce, from the chirruping of the sparrow to the grunts of pleasure of the pig at his trough. I thought we should have recorded the sounds with the idea of giving remedial lessons to the millions of depressed people on the planet, starting with myself. But I had no intention of saddling myself with evening classes with a cat on my lap. This old tom with the stinky breath had nothing to do with me. I wouldn't be his next victim, the next imbecile to stand and peer through the curtains to watch out for his return while he got fed Pacific salmon or Nicaraguan tuna at a random stranger's house.

"There's no way I'm adopting you," I announced to the furball, who still wasn't listening to me. I left him on the wooden porch to freeze his nuts off. Billie would not have approved of my behaviour; she would have wanted me to open the door wide to this mangy old cat and never close it again. But I refused to give sanctuary to a creature that would then become the centre of my bachelor existence and would play the dirty trick of disappearing just when I least expected it. The cat, understanding my dilemma, watched my lips move from behind the window and responded with a sincere yawn. Three minutes later, Dixie hopped off the porch and stretched before returning to wherever he'd come from. I watched him cross the road with his rolling gait and disappear behind a thicket of alder trees.

As for me, I left my observation post and plunged back into the adventures of Myrtle the Turtle, to forget, to kill the unkillable, and to trick myself about the dispersal of boredom across time. At nightfall, a few cat yowls were added to the sounds of wolves, children, and owls who inhabited the forests of Rivière-aux-Trembles.

Ronie the Toad and Myrtle the Turtle are wearing their party hats today. I can hear them singing "Happy Birthday" to Billie between the covers of the notebook, which I quickly shut when Ronie attempted a Tyrolean yodel.

I forced myself to silence these voices, but even if I strangled Ronie and shipped Myrtle off to a South Pacific island crawling with predators, they would still keep on singing in the sweetness of this April 20th, because Billie would have turned twelve today and would come running down the stairs as she always did to see what was waiting for her on the kitchen table. No doubt it would be a Dixie, a Pixie Two with a blue bow, the illustrious descendant of a dynasty of Pharaoh cats that had become alley cats. Aside from that, we'd probably give her an iPod or some punk CDs. The tastes and interests of girls that age were utterly alien to me. Billie was the one guiding me through, year by year, and she would continue to lead me through the fog by telling me she didn't want any more dolls, pink sweaters, or movies starring talking animals.

It would hurt like hell to see my little girl growing up and refusing to sit on my lap any more while I told her about Captain Ahab defying the lightning, but I would keep it to myself and try to follow her in this astonishing tango, which, at this age, forces you to take two steps back for every step you manage to go forward. I would even try to keep my big trap shut when she spouted the idiotic claptrap all teens and pre-teens use to claim a justice that applies only to them. I would dodge the daggers in my daughter's eyes and we'd escape unscathed. We'd abandon the battlefield brandishing our white flags and we'd go to the latest Woody Allen movie together, remembering the days when I put up with both *Antz* and *Monsters, Inc.* in the same afternoon.

This is what those loud voices singing their poignant "Happy Birthday" had driven me to: imagining a future whose arrival relied on a miracle. Ronie and Myrtle's tune forced me to remember the good moments from the past, such as my little girl's first birthday when she ate half the candle on the cake; the time she had a tantrum because she wanted Geoffrey the Giraffe to have a slice of cake, after which Geoffrey spent two hours in the bath holding his breath, and when he got out he had holes along with spots, which triggered a whole new crisis, forcing me to trudge all over town in the pouring rain to track down another giraffe that answered to the ridiculous name of Geoffrey.

Even the orange-vested zealot who slapped on me — because I was encroaching ever so slightly on the space set aside for disabled drivers (which was empty) — is part of my happy remembrances of the day. I thought the officer would stop writing up the ticket when she saw me galloping along the sidewalk with a happy giraffe in my arms and a smile even the most hardened pessimist couldn't resist. But somehow, she did resist, proving that civil servants truly are recruited for their atrophied zygomatic muscles. With her cap pulled right down over her eyes, she brandished her pen, remaining unmoved by my arguments whether I invoked Billie's tears or the fact that there were no disabled drivers anywhere in sight.

Faced with her professional stoicism, I slammed my door and made a giraffe face at her, regretting the fact that Geoffrey wasn't a llama, and then I had to stop in the very next disabled parking space I saw, because my llama idea turned out to be one of those utterly ridiculous jokes that nonetheless sent you into uncontrollable hysterics. When all of a sudden you think you're funny and you want to enjoy it for a while.

My good mood lasted until I got home, where I waved the parking ticket in front of L.A.'s face, laughing like a weirdo. L.A. wasn't amused by the fine or by my llama joke, but this didn't stop my meeting with the para-constabulary forces from being one of my happy memories.

I had dozens of these good memories, hundreds of them, most of them associated with Billie. I had a lifetime's worth of them because a child fills up your existence in the blink of an eye, but I would rather become amnesiac on the spot than be reduced to remembering that I was once happy. There's nothing sadder than a happy memory when the little girl you should be sharing it with is no longer there to prompt it or to ask you what happened to Geoffrey the First after his catastrophic dive into the bubbly water.

Ronie and Myrtle still refused to shut up, so I went down to the basement to look for a bottle of red wine, avoiding looking at Pixie's crate, where he was probably drowning in happy memories. I had warned Billie that today warranted a drastic approach, so I would not be drawing a line halfway down the bottle in orange pen. In some circumstances all the rules fall by the wayside, such as when your only daughter doesn't show up on her own birthday, or the life of the woman you used to love drains out with the bathwater and you're tempted to do the same thing—in other words, drown the toad whose singing has gotten inside your skull.

Halfway up the stairs, I unscrewed the cap of my fifty-dollar bottle of Cigare Volant and had a birthday slug, after which I sang, "Whiskey is the devil in his fucking liquid form." I couldn't remember any more if it was the Bailes Brothers, the Bailey Brothers, or the Blues Brothers who sang "Whiskey Is the Devil (in Liquid Form)," and it didn't make the slightest bit of difference. Baileses or Baileys, those brothers were talking about the same mornings after the nights before. The warning made sense—alcohol is just one representation of the demons that eat away at you—but I would return to this wise aphorism later, when copious amounts of alcohol would no longer seem to be the only way of getting through this grim anniversary. For the time being, I just wanted to get smashed and forget my happy memories while I listened to my demons singing the blues. My aim was simple: to feel a little more lizard-like with each sip, because I had a certain amount of admiration for the way lizards behave. They don't bother splitting hairs, but are content to dart their tongues out when they're hungry and sleep squarely on the ceiling if the walls are full.

I hadn't eaten anything since that morning, so

I swallowed down my first glass of red with a Jos Louis cake, dedicating the first bite to Billie. One mouthful for Billie, one mouthful for Papa, one mouthful for Maman. The first mouthful went down fine, but the next two got stuck in my esophagus. Then a few tears sprang to my eyes, and the bites dedicated to a child named Billie continued on their way with a loud swallowing sound that nobody heard, so who gives a shit.

In other circumstances, sadness would have put a dent in my appetite, but because I was eating for Billie, I swallowed down the rest of the Jos Louis in a few seconds. I even licked the wrapper, where a little chocolate still lingered, telling myself that Billie would definitely have liked these half moons and Jos Louis cakes if L.A. had agreed to buy them, and then I emptied my glass and hummed a tune with no beginning and no end, with no other goal beyond silencing those voices we refuse to hear, in this particular case the voice of Lucy-Ann Morency.

I had no desire to endure Lucy-Ann's remonstrances from beyond the grave, or to think that my ex was some bourgeois asshole whose fancy tastes had deprived our daughter of the pleasures of Quebec's industrial patisserie. If she had been allowed to eat them, Billie would no doubt have loved half moons and Jos Louis cakes — all kids do. You should always behave as though kids are about to disappear any second, as if a tsunami is about to sweep them away, as if monsters stalking them from cars are always seconds away from opening the door to reach a hand out to the first little girl who happens to be passing by. Had I known Billie was going to vanish without warning, I would have abolished all those stupid bans that go against children's simple desires and let her eat lemon tarts for breakfast and ice-skate around the living room if it made her happy.

"You're losing your marbles, Richard," Lucy-Ann's voice breathed into my neck, "you've gone off the rails completely." And then she started crying, her breath on my burning neck, and I started singing again, blocking my ears, "Je l'ai connue la la, en dansant le yaya, ah ah (ah ah)," but L.A.'s voice refused to leave me in peace, "You're losing it, my love," which in turn brought up a whole bunch of memories that tasted like the seaside and salty skin. Realizing that I had no chance of pushing away the ghosts that haunted me, I allowed myself to cry for a few moments, my tears mixing with L.A.'s tears, which eventually ended up diluting my second glass of red wine, and this time I didn't dedicate any swallows to anybody other than me.

I was in the process of becoming a lizard, moments away from the reptilian indifference I aspired to, when a car braked outside the house. Then two car doors slammed and I saw two guys appear at the front door, two men who looked like Ménard and Dubois, the inspectors who worked on Billie's case. They weren't actually Ménard and Dubois, but the two guys screwing up their eyes and peering into my house were cut from the same mould and had the same air of sinister sullen cops, which did not bode well.

I immediately thought they were coming to officially inform me of Billie's death, that Ménard and Dubois had off-loaded this dirty task onto them, to tell me that a young couple or a woman in her fifties walking her Doberman in the woods full of orphan socks had discovered a skeleton that had been identified because of a few pearl buttons lodged in its sternum. I suppose it could have been the opposite—that they were the bearers of good news, but such cold faces, without the slightest light of joy in their eyes, could not be bringing good news.

I had waited desperately for this kind of visit for three years, but right now I didn't want to know, not on her birthday, not when Billie was barely twelve and Ronie the Supertoad was celebrating the event in the company of a tortoise that had dragged itself out of lethargy for the occasion. I ignored the fists hammering on the door and burrowed into my armchair as if it had the power to make me invisible. The banging intensified, and one of the men yelled that they had a warrant and would break the door down if I didn't open it.

This threat confused me. Why did these two police-men need a court order to tell me that a day or so earlier a woman had run out of the woods screaming hysterically, or hiccuping breathlessly, after vomiting near what had once resembled a child? Why did they need an official docu-ment to tell me I was now a father without a daughter, a kind of reverse orphan, since there's no word to describe a mother or father who has lost a child? These parents aren't orphans or widows or exiles. They are nothing. They are fathers and mothers for life, with no word to describe their new status on their tax return. These creatures are anonymous forever, walking around with gaping holes in their stomachs, without the benefit of a single word to attest to their shredded identity.

I staggered over to the door, following the undulation of a ray of sunlight that stretched out diagonally across the floorboards whose very solidity suddenly seemed in doubt. I leaned on the frame as I opened the door and the two cops showed me their ID, Marchessault and Doyon, from the Sûreté du Québec. I was waiting for them to tell me the reason for their visit, but they headed towards the kitchen and invited me to sit down with them. Cops have a soft spot for kitchens, unless this is some kind of atavism peculiar to the Québécois, some kind of nostalgia for kitchen parties that particularly affects the police. Who knows? When Marchessault scraped his chair over the floor, I felt as though I was reliving one of the innumerable scenes Ménard had forced upon me by showing up unannounced, and I waited for one of the two men sitting at the table to start speaking.

"Does the name Michael Faber mean anything to you?" Marchessault, the taller of the two, asked me. He was going to lead the interrogation, playing the tough one and making out that the other guy was the wimp, while the wimp in question would file everything in his big bald head and jump me the first chance he got. I knew this script. I hesitated for a second before answering, since the child's name engraved on the wooden cross near the river was stuck in my mind. Could this be the same Michael, the boy I had thought was long dead and buried? And if so, what had happened to him? I tried to worm something out of the men, but they remained frigid. Silent and stoic, they watched to see if my eyelids fluttered or my voice trembled when I answered their question, when I confirmed without stammering that no, I didn't know anyone called Michael Faber. Because I wasn't lying. I didn't know any Michaels, including the one who had drowned — or not — in the river. But I was certain they had come to tell me this boy's story and explain how it was connected to mine. So I let them start, even as I dreaded what they might reveal about this child.

First they asked me some questions about how I spent my time, glancing meaningfully over at the counter, where the level of wine in the bottle was definitely lower than the invisible orange line, and thumbing their noses whenever I asked why I was being subjected to this interrogation.

"All in good time," grumbled Doyon, the bald one, stroking the moustache he grew to demonstrate that neither his body hair nor his virility had given up the ghost. "You'll answer our questions first, am I making myself clear?"

I couldn't tell them much about how I spent my time because I was just killing time, day after day with no respite, like an assassin who sees his victim come back to life every time the sun rises and then becomes obsessed with light. But I told them about Ronie and Myrtle, about how I earned a living, because life does have a price, everyone learns this sooner or later. I told them about the flying toad who had allowed me to buy a house for a woman who painted the bathroom red, a house that would now fetch a reduced price because nobody really cared for the red L.A. had chosen, "Blood red, Billie, red running through your veins."

They weren't interested in my bread and butter any more than they were interested in how L.A. and I had spent my money. They glossed over the subject and their questions became more specific.

"Mr. Richard, what were you doing on the day of April 18th?" April 18th was the day before yesterday. In principle I should have had a clear memory of how I spent that Saturday, but since all my days looked pretty much the same, that memory was lost in the unchanging gloom of repetition.

"Come on, try harder, it wasn't exactly a long time ago," muttered Marchessault, leaning his elbows on the table and bringing his face so close to mine that I could guess what he had for breakfast. The stench of half-digested fried eggs made me recoil, and as I swung back in my chair, I returned to Saturday, April 18th, hour by hour in reverse, and finally remembered that on that morning I learned, when I opened a two- or three-day-old newspaper, that little Ashley Tara Bravo Gonis was finally going to be able to leap into her father's arms after being declared missing for two years. I remembered that this news had made my chin tremble, because it proved you could still be alive even while living in darkness. I had followed the case closely, like every other father in my situation, I suppose, in solidarity with their wounded brothers. After I learned that Tara had been kidnapped by her mother, I began to hope that Billie had been kidnapped by some unhinged person who put her own infertility above all moral considerations. Frustrated in her desire to become a mother, and after ejecting one after another the eggs that her impotent husband kept failing to fertilize, the crazy woman had stolen Billie from us to take her to Mexico or Argentina and make her call her Mama. In my most despairing dreams, Billie used to thwart Mama's vigilance and escape by jumping out of a window. The rest of the story featured multiple variations, but it invariably had a happy ending worthy of Hollywood's cheesiest era.

I had wasted my saliva, because Marchessault and Doyon did not find Ashley Tara's liberation fascinating either. But they had pricked up their ears at my interest in missing children. In the face of their accusations, I brought my fist down on the table and demanded them to tell me if their presence here had something to do with my daughter and if Michael Faber was connected to her disappearance.

"All in good time," Doyon repeated, visibly unimpressed with my anger. "Tell us about your day first of all. You'll have plenty of time to destroy your furniture once you've clarified a few things for us."

"I'll reply to your questions on April 18th next year, asshole," I thought, sealing my lips together with an imaginary zipper, but Marchessault took over with his fried-egg breath and I understood I was exhausting myself needlessly by saying nothing. So I racked my brains and remembered that after I read the paper I had taken a shower and then gone to the grocery store in Saint-Alban. When I unzipped my lips to say the name "Saint-Alban," they suddenly became agitated. They immediately wanted to know what time I went there, what time I came back, how many people had seen me there, and if anyone could confirm the time of my return. So I got annoyed for the second and last time. I demanded an explanation immediately, warning that I wouldn't open my mouth again except to call a fucking lawyer who cost three hundred bucks an hour.

Marchessault and Doyon stared at each other like guys who can read what the other is thinking from the tiniest flicker of an eyelid. Doyon pointed his chin at Marchessault and the latter launched into a bewildering story about a twelve-year-old kid, Michael Faber, seen for the last time on Saturday, April 18th, near Cave Way, halfway between Saint-Alban and Rivière-aux-Trembles, around one in the afternoon, while riding the brand-new bicycle he'd been given for his birthday. A bicycle he'd been asking for since Christmas, in anticipation of warm weather, and which he only stopped riding when he was asleep or in class. It was a blue bike with a pear-shaped horn. As I understood it, the child had been heading towards Rivière-aux-Trembles. The bike had been discovered four kilometres from the village in the ditch that ran alongside the road. These two cops were combing the area and interrogating anyone with the slightest connection to any disappearance, which included me since Billie's case had never been solved. So far, I and one other suspect were the only ones in the entire region who met the criteria, so it was in my own interests to cooperate and tell them whether one or more people could testify to my comings and goings on April 18th.

I was so stunned I couldn't get a single word out. These men were crazy, even crazier than Ménard and Dubois, who at least never treated me like a psychopath. I asked for a time out so I could go to the living room and get my glass of wine, then I downed it in one gulp. I could have told the men to get lost and meet me at the station, where I would pull up in my shady lawyer's BMW, but I had done nothing wrong. Unfortunately, I didn't have any witnesses to provide, except for Myrtle the Turtle, one of whose adventures I'd finished writing during the afternoon of the 18th. The date and time recorded on my computer would prove that. As for anyone who had seen me in the vegetable aisle or browsing the cleaning products in the supermarket, there were dozens of people, mainly women, I must confess, since I don't want to lie about the persistence of certain social phenomena and the partial failure of the feminist revolution. They could also talk to the cashier with orange hair, who would no doubt remember seeing a man who matched my description wearing a red scarf at around ten thirty that morning. All they had to do was ask.

"We'll do that as soon as we've finished here," snarled Marchessault, and then, armed with his warrant, he and Doyon searched the whole house with a fine-toothed comb for Michael Faber's cap, or the neon handlebars he'd put on his brand-new bike, or worse still, his corpse wrapped in wax paper or cling film. The jerks even forced open

Pixie's crate, declaring that I was stark raving mad. Little Faber's cat had disappeared at the same time he did, apparently, and Pixie matched the description. I tried in vain to explain that this was my daughter's cat, and I owed him a decent funeral, but they immediately classified me as one of those sickos who tortures animals and then freezes them for breakfast. But the sicko wasn't me, it was them, for profaning Pixie's temporary coffin and tromping through the house with their big dirty shoes.

When Marchessault told me he was taking Pixie away as a piece of evidence, I clenched my fists, ready to take a swing at him, but Doyon, foreseeing my action, intercepted me and pinned me against the wall before I had time to crush the other guy. Thirty seconds later, I was handcuffed.

"Assault on an officer of the peace!" Doyon shrieked. He then read me my rights, advising me to use the phone call I was allowed to contact the best criminal lawyer in the province. According to him, I was going to need it, but his assault story wouldn't stand up since I hadn't touched a hair on Marchessault's head, and he was the one holding the big end of the stick. Since I was well aware that when a child goes missing the cops don't have the heart to laugh or let themselves get upset by morons, I shut my trap and the five of us set off: Marchessault, Doyon, Pixie, my computer, and me. Marchessault and Doyon had that worried look I had often observed on Ménard's face, while Pixie and I looked like we were being buried. When Doyon closed the door to the house, Ronie and Myrtle fell silent.

"Happy birthday, Billie," I murmured as I sat down in the back of the police car, from where I spotted Dixie the cat, who had come for his helping of tuna. I tapped on the bullet-proof glass that separated me from the guys in the front, trying to get them to look at Dixie, who also matched the description of the missing cat, but I might as well have been begging a regiment of deaf soldiers for help. Marchessault and Doyon had heard so many men knock on this window over the course of their careers that they just ignored it.

The bells of an invisible church chimed midday as the car pulled up in the parking lot of the Saint-Alban Sûreté du Québec station. Through the car's closed windows, this sound evoked the happiness of family Sundays, dresses billowing in the spring wind. I was drunk and Billie was twelve.

II.

MARNIE

February to
April 2009

The Saint-Alban owl was swinging in the dark window, which shook with the last gusts of the storm, mixed with snowflakes that fell silently on the dust the February rains hadn't washed away. And it was talking to me again, telling me that little animals disappear in the middle of the snowy forest, little Mikes and little Marnies, some leaving a little trail of blood behind them, others leaving nothing at all, not even disoriented tracks or a flapping of wings.

My father had given me this owl, and I secretly named him Mister Holy Owl, alias Mr. Holy Crappy Owl, because it was born on Christmas Day, kind of, and because I hate the bitches of owls who stare at you in the darkness and speak to you at daybreak. I had seen this owl in a souvenir shop in Saint-Alban two days before Christmas, while my father and I were shopping with the feverish joy of the season. I immediately sensed that this inert little animal was watching me, me and nobody else, and felt he was calling to me. Every time the store door opened, he swung on the end of his cord and turned his little yellow eyes towards me. Every time.

I moved casually closer to him, and suddenly Michael's bulging eyes were superimposed on the owl's, confirming that *owls see everything, absolutely everything, Marnie*. In an instant I was swallowed up by his gaze and whisked off somewhere else, into another time and another place, alone with the owl in some area of my memory where clouds were gathering. The walls of the store disappeared along with the harried customers, the Christmas music, and the snow whirling outside the window, leaving only the owl, who opened his eyes wide in the face of the stormy sky. "Michael, is that you? Michael?"

The days when Michael and I used to pretend to be a snowy owl and a red squirrel were so far in the past that I had forgotten the way Mike used to let out clumsy hooting when he came to get me after dinner. The sound of three or four "tu-whit, tu-whoos" would come in through the open window, and I would respond to the owl's call by racing outside as fast as a squirrel running down a tin roof. This game lasted a little over three years, but long ago I stored this owl, simply named "Owl," in a closet of my memory and never took him out, because I preferred to imagine Michael as a superhero who had flown off to a secret destination.

The sight of this little bird made out of bark led me to reopen the closet and recall that in a time before robots, interdimensionality, and futuristic genetics, there had been a forest, trees, and animals. Before Michael became invested with Superman's powers, it was the powers of a nocturnal bird that had kindled his childish imagination.

A shiver zigzagged up my back when my father rested his hand on my shoulder. I blamed the flush suffusing my face on the stifling heat in the shop. "I need some fresh air, Pop, I'm going to the cake shop to buy our Yule log," and then I abandoned my father in front of a display of gnomes and goblins.

Before I even reached the cake shop, I was tempted to go back and buy the damn owl, but I stopped myself. *Marnie, if you do that, you're fucked. You're going to start talking to doorknobs and believe they're answering you.*

Despite the cold, I was bathed in sweat when I walked into the cake shop, and I had to sit down to catch my breath. Luckily there were no owls or squirrels in the store, only chubby-cheeked Santa Claus heads, sprigs of mistletoe, and garlands. I focused my attention on Santa Number Two, the one that faced me, defying his big, decapitated head to start talking to me. Since the fellow remained mute, I finally relaxed, but was then suddenly seized with a fit of hysterical laughter so intense I had to race to the washroom of the café next door. "A total nutjob," people must have been saying, and I kept repeating to myself in the mirror over the sink: "For god's sake, get a grip on yourself!"

For the rest of the day, and even the following day, I barely gave the owl a thought. The memory of his little head bristling with fake feathers occasionally crossed my mind, but I immediately chased it away. I figured that by then someone had bought the owl to hang on their Christmas tree, unaware of the revelations the bird was going to whisper in their ear between the turkey and the sugar pie.

On Christmas Eve I devoted myself to my father and our reunion, decorating the living room and embellishing a strawberry meringue in the shape of pine trees. This is what creates the Christmas magic — surrounding yourself with pink pine trees, reindeer with bling-studded harnesses, and tiny fairies dressed in muslin. Papa and I drank a kir, we listened to Bing Crosby, and then at the twelfth stroke of midnight I handed him his first present. A pile of multicoloured wrapping paper accumulated around us in the joyful chaos of nostalgia. As I was dabbing the perfume my father had given me behind my ears, he slid a little box towards me. When I unwrapped it and saw the little black and yellow beads sunk into the bird's head staring at me, my heart lurched. I looked up at my father with a stupefied expression.

"Where did you get this?"

"In Saint-Alban, the day before yesterday. I saw you looking at it, I thought you liked it. Don't you like it?"

"Yes, yes, of course. It's just that I wasn't expecting this at all."

I had never been so right about anything, but it was unthinkable to spoil my father's joy with my ghosts. All night long, that damn owl watched me, noticing my slightest movement, absorbing every word I spoke, and it was an enormous relief to shut him back in his box two days later when I packed my bags.

He stayed in that box for nearly two years, and every time I opened the closet where I had stored him, I was sure I could hear Holy whispering and scratching the sides of the box, giving a weak hoot just like the ones I used to hear coming through my curtains as they fluttered in the breeze. The easiest thing would have been to just get rid of him, but I could never quite manage to do so, in case a fragment of Michael's spirit, soul, or body was somehow contained inside him — perhaps, thirty years ago, little Michael Saint-Pierre had rubbed against the bark the owl was made of, maybe he had leaned against the tree the owl came from, leaving the imprint of his breath or his blood, and it was this imprint that now seemed to shine through in the gaze of the owl from Saint-Alban.

I was still irrationally convinced that this object was the bearer of a message and that even if I shipped it to Afghanistan, the owl would find his way back sooner or later to tap his little beak on my window while flapping his wings. Any shrink would have interpreted this as yet another manifestation of my repressed guilt, but I persisted in my belief that the discomfort I felt around this animal was not merely a figment of my haunted imagination. This alone stopped me from hurling the fowl into the trash or losing it somewhere in Central Park.

The same reason prompted me to take him out of his box and hang him in the kitchen window. And this very day, as the flurries became a blizzard, Holy Crappy Owl started speaking to me, swinging on the end of his string and using his luminous little eyes to point out the direction I should follow, over there, near the river's frozen waters.

I was finishing my noon coffee and the first flakes had started whirling down when I heard the owl's call, the distant call that used to make me run out into the yard full of Mary-Jeans and Golden Girls. I was slumped in my armchair quietly leafing through the newspaper when the call rang out from the kitchen, from Holy Crappy Owl's window. It must have been the wind, it could only have been the wind making the barn door or the pulley attached to the house squeak, or setting the roof shingles clattering. But I knew that none of those sounds resembled an owl's call.

This time, I didn't hurry. I walked slowly towards the kitchen window murmuring, "What the fuck, Holy? What the holy fuck?" and grabbed the bad-luck bird by the tail, positioning him to face me. But the stubborn creature resisted, and, with a jerky movement like a bird hopping along a branch, he once again pivoted to face outside, his eyes focused towards the invisible waters of the Trembles River, one of whose branches passed behind the forest close by.

I don't know how long I remained standing by the window. All I remember is the snow intensifying along with the wind, and when I looked down I saw the porcelain cup inherited from my mother lying in three or four pieces in a pool of cold coffee at my feet. I could feel one of the pieces piercing my slipper and going right through into my flesh, but I went upstairs to get dressed without even bothering to bandage the wound, which left a reddish trail on the stairs. Ten minutes later I was outside, wearing my father's snowshoes. Mister Owl watched me from the window, his eyes boring into my back and the Rivière-aux-Trembles woods.

I hadn't been on snowshoes for over a decade, and I cursed the inventor of the stupid things for a good half kilometre before I got back into the rhythm of it, stretching out my legs, holding my back straight, and keeping my balance. Even then, it was hard not to curve my spine against the violent wind, but I faced it and pushed on, pushed on, because I had no other choice. If Phil Morisset knew where I was headed, he would almost certainly come after me, take me back to the house, and call me harebrained, because ever since my father's death Phil had watched over me as if I were a fragile little thing, a Marnie to the power of ten who needed to be protected from the ambient idiocy. That's what men of Phil's calibre do, they take care of dead people's treasures without pillaging them, and I was damn lucky to be able to count on him, because this man I used to call Uncle Phil was the only living person who could stop me from going off the rails. Without this bridge between my past and my present, Rivière-aux-Trembles would lose its consistency. I needed Phil Morisset's rugged intelligence to keep me moored to reality, which had been disrupted by my escape.

During my years in New York, I had managed just fine by myself and made peace with my past. I hadn't forgotten Mike, but his face became as hazy as some of my mental images of Rivière-aux-Trembles, lost between snow and fog. Little by little, he stopped haunting my nights and I was able to sleep without being oppressed by the feeling that I had no right to rest. The guilt I used to feel was no longer mine. It belonged to the little girl some people called sorceress, Marnie the Witch, and I knew that witches didn't exist. If I had stayed in New York, witches would have carried on not existing, owls would have remained in the forest, and I would have led the life of any average woman, with its own dramas and fear of storms.

My return to Rivière-aux-Trembles put an end to this utterly artificial insouciance. In the space of just a few days, more than twenty years of my life disappeared, doubt floated to the surface along with little Marnie, and guilt took on the appearance of a straw and bark owl whispering in my ear that my life was nothing but a trap. I had to avoid the trap, and Phil could be of no help to me in this game. It was up to me, and me alone, to evade the owl's craftiness, to follow the tracks of small paws sprinkled in the snow in order to tell the real tracks from the fake. So I went ahead, my blood-red scarf weighed down by tiny lumps of ice created as my breath hit the frosty air.

I had just one aim: to make it to the magic swimming hole and get there fast, because that's where everything had started and everything had ended, and everything would begin again. I didn't try to understand the nature of my urgency, or explain the how or the why of it. I simply obeyed the instinct, nothing more, convinced that this compulsion could only lead me towards revelation.

When I arrived at Lucien Ménard's house, I hesitated a little due to the intensity of the blowing snow sweeping across the field. This was where we always used to cut through, Michael and I, keeping an eye on Ménard as he worked outside around his house. On good days he would wave and tell us to be careful of the river's water level, mama bears carting their cubs around, or wasps' nests, but if he'd overdone the gin the night before, a constant stream of swear words accompanied us until Luc choked on the spit from his pipe.

Despite the biting gusts of wind blasting the void, I ploughed on through the field, facing the wind and my childhood memories, and headed towards the forest. I should have been able to spot the trail easily, but everything had changed over the past thirty years. Some trees were no longer there, others had grown. The unredeemable apple tree that had produced hard, inedible fruit we stuffed ourselves with until our stomachs hurt had disappeared, and there were no longer any landmarks other than a row of trees that resembled the one from my childhood, except that it was different in every way. Somehow, I managed to spot an opening between two pines that looked like the entrance to a path, so I set off towards it.

I had taken barely ten steps under the tree cover when the storm began to ease off. The wind groaned in the treetops; I could see them blowing in all directions above me; a scattering of snow from the top of the world came tumbling down from the hemlocks and spruce, but despite the tempest raging outside, the forest was unnaturally calm. I was in a sanctuary being shaken by the fury of the northeast wind flaying the canopy, but the storm stayed on the outside, beyond the dark walls enclosing the light of the snow. In the heart of the sanctuary the impregnable silence of the woods reigned.

I closed my eyes for a few moments to better feel the peace enveloping me, welcoming me into its asylum, and I was propelled back in time, to the days when Michael and I would stop in the middle of the path to hear what couldn't be heard: the breathing of trees, the brushing of branches against the light, the descent of snowflakes. "Listen, Marnie, you can hear the snow falling." And we heard it as it landed softly on the white ground. How could I have moved away from all this? How had I believed it was possible to find my way in places named Forty-Second Street or Fifth Avenue when everything I was made of resided in the sound of the snow burying Rivière-aux-Trembles? Everything was here, in this moment under the trees, all the seasons and all the places. I could have died right then and my life would have been complete. And who knows if I might not have understood, as I trained my ear towards the falling snow, what had happened to Michael. But I continued on my way. I opened up my eyes and I walked on.

What I had thought was a path suddenly came to an end, and I had to make multiple detours, crouching to squeeze under branches, manoeuvring around stands of trees that grew so close together it was impossible to fit between them, until I finally reached the river, which looked like a snowy road dug out in the middle of nowhere, without streetlamps or road signs, and without any travellers who might lend a hand in the midst of the storm. Here too, all my landmarks had disappeared and I was alone. The magic swimming hole was somewhere close by—it had to be—but it was hiding from me, along with everything else I needed to see, and I would probably have to wait until spring to be able to find it properly.

I watched the long drifts of blowing snow rolling over themselves in the open road of the river, sheltered as I waited for the frozen waters to tell me the beginning of my story. Crouched next to a tree, I contemplated the clouds catapulted by the wind towards the horizon, lost in the memory of a distant evening when Mike and I stretched out underneath the trees counting the stars through the branches. It must have been August, because the sky was so full it seemed to want to suck us in. We stayed silent for a long time, fascinated by the lights that swarmed above our heads, and then Michael pointed out the Great Bear, saying, "Marnie, this is what squirrels and owls must see when they're in their nests."

After that night, every time we lay on the ground to watch the clouds, the stars, or the snow shooting down on us, we'd think of the squirrels, snuggled in their nests at the tops of the trees, who must be able to see things that we couldn't. "If we could climb up into one of their nests, Marn, I know we'd see new stars, and species of owls we don't know about, and flying saucers," Michael whispered as he brushed away mosquitoes or snowflakes whirling around his face.

The time had finally come for me to climb a tree, to get a squirrel's- or an owl's-eye view if I wanted to see the stars Mike had gone towards and guess what he had seen behind the storm at the magic swimming hole. My mind bursting with memories from other winters, I left my shelter, took off my snowshoes, and lay down along the edge of the river, where I extended my arms and legs the way children who grow up in the snow have always done, to imprint the shape of an angel or a bird on the ground. Michael and I used to call it "making an owl" because that's what it was called in Rivière-aux-Trembles.

Eyes firmly fixed on the storm, I spread out my wings in the powder, offering up my face to the thousands of flakes leaving the pull of the sky to land on me, like the thousands of stars watching over sleeping squirrels. As I imagined them spinning in the chill of the atmosphere, I made a wish that one day Michael and I would lie down in the snow together and cover the frozen river in a parade of twin owls, reuniting at long last the past and the present.

I stretched out one arm, and at the end of my mitten I felt Michael's mitten, his old red nylon mitt closing around my woollen one. "Don't cry, Marnie, don't cry," Michael's voice exhorted me. "If you cry, you'll turn into an ice statue." The voice was right. If I opened the floodgates, my gaze would freeze in the river water and the owl who was supposed to decipher all the signs gathered in the forest would be nothing more than a blind owl. But Mike's mitten, his damn moth-eaten mitten, closed around my throat and I felt the warmth of tears dampen my cheeks before sliding down towards my ears and soaking the edges of my hat.

I could have stayed there and nobody would really have been affected, except for good old Phil. He would curse all the saints in heaven — whom he addressed only to yell at them — he would curse himself and pillory me, and then he would go to my father's grave and cry, apologizing for being an old fucking imbecile. Every year during the harshest February storm he would have brought roses to the river, Beauty Marnie roses that the gusts would bury beneath the hooting of owls, until the day he finally decided to lie down with me among the snowy roses. Phil would seriously resent me for wrecking his last few years, but in the end he'd understand; Phil understood everything, starting with the inconsolable sadness of children. As for the people in the village, they would decide that those old rumours about me must have had some truth to them, that little Marnie Duchamp was absolutely stark raving mad and she'd finally gone to join Michael Saint-Pierre, her first victim, God rest his soul, because her guilt was strangling her or because there was such a thing as divine justice — this is what those bigots would claim, crossing themselves with trembling hands before going off to sting another innocent child with their forked tongues. The gossip would start up even worse than before, and I would become a legend, a tale of witches and evil spirits to be told to naughty children and bad seeds so they wouldn't be tempted to sneak into the ogre's lair.

Lying down beside the screaming river, I frantically mocked the gossip and the chatter of the goody two-shoes. I was in the eye of the cyclone, at the very centre of the tempest, in a place of complete peace and perfect silence. All my strength was leaving me. My wings had stopped beating, broken by the excessive burden I had laid on them, and suddenly I had just one wish: to cry myself to sleep and finally forget that Michael Superman Saint-Pierre might have saved the city of Kandor if that nasty little Marnie Duchamp hadn't existed.

I closed my eyes to better feel the snowflakes land on my eyelids and my forehead, and I imagined spiders, white ants whose feet turned to liquid on contact with my skin. Smooth landscapes, moons shining under tangled creepers, and mountains rolling towards stormy rivers scrolled past in the iridescence of my weakly backlit blood. I would find peace there, on the sides of mountains covered with white spiders. Sleep was the answer, eternal sleep. Beneath my eyelids, which were now too cold to drink insects' feet, the light dimmed, the iridescence took on rusty hues, and night slowly fell.

I was just about to give myself up to the sweet numbness climbing up my legs and slowly enveloping my torso when a rumbling of thunder surged from the clouds, somewhere beyond the thousands of snowflakes falling on my motionless body. A shiver from the depths of the river slithered along my neck, where a few tears had flowed before freezing, and I instinctively curled up into a ball.

It wasn't the first time I had heard winter thunder. It happened sometimes when the sky was so full it behaved like a summer sky swept by the north wind, but this clap of thunder didn't come from the turmoil of the skies. It came from the fury of Kandor, from the month of August 1979, or from what people call fate. But I wasn't disposed towards reflecting on the non-existence of chance. I had been tempted to let go there, by the river, without even trying to push away the hands that kept me pinned to the ground, hands sunk deep into Michael Saint-Pierre's red nylon mittens. A couple of more minutes and I would have let the hands' gentleness drag me into a whiteness more infinite than the one that fell from the sky. I would have fallen asleep as frost moons unfurled and dreamed of white galaxies until my body lost the ability to dream.

I had never wished to die, even when everything seemed to be going wrong, even in the small hours of insomniac nights when the accusing voices of Rivière-aux-Trembles continued to harass me long after Michael had disappeared. I'd never felt the call of the chasm between the rails of two subway trains speeding off into the inviting darkness of the void. However, it had taken just a few snowflakes to tempt me to give up the fight and race head-first into the depths of the abyss.

My thoughts were jostling for position, each one more ridiculous than the last, but for the moment I had other worries. I had to move faster, get the blood circulating in my veins and warm up my frozen extremities. After struggling to my feet, I started hopping around like a disabled toad, doing leg bends, punching my body all over; then I sat down, took off my boots, and massaged my feet until I could feel dozens of stings burning my blanched skin. I stood back up and jumped around a bit more, swiping at the air with my stiffened limbs like a boxer whose survival depends on the number of left hooks he can land in the heaving stomach of his adversary, until I slipped and fell ass-over-teakettle on the ground.

Nearby, the owl wings I'd drawn earlier had uncovered

large patches of ice. I scanned the river around me quickly, realizing at last that I was actually right in the middle of the magic swimming hole—and that the bloody basin had tried to get rid of me just as it had gotten rid of Michael. I withdrew to the bank, scraping my knees on the sharp edges of the ice striating the swimming hole, where I waited for the ground to tremble and the ice to crack open under pressure from the water. But the earth remained stable, the swimming hole smooth and white. After one last glance back at the owl as it rested, wings spread on the river, I quickly strapped on my snowshoes again and plunged back into the woods, right where Michael had disappeared thirty years ago. I then followed my own tracks—which had not been entirely covered over by the snow—thinking that perhaps they were Mike's footsteps welling up slowly from the earth and my memory.

At the edge of the forest, I thought I heard an owl's hoots mixed with the lament of the wind. A thin voice exhorted me to be careful, but I didn't ask Michael if it was him calling me. Instead I murmured, "It's okay, Mike, it's okay, I'm starting to understand you," and continued on my way. It was dark by the time I got home. Mr. Holy Owl was calmly waiting for me in the dark, hypnotized by the ongoing storm.

I didn't sleep that night. I curled up in my father's old chesterfield and listened to the storm lash the Rivière-aux-Trembles fields, fascinated by the patterns created by the fine layer of snow as the wind plastered it to the windows. When the big clock in the living room chimed three in the morning, I got up and walked to the kitchen to ask Holy Owl what he thought about the morbid power of attraction held by certain locales, and whether during his innumerable watchful nights he had ever felt as though he were being sucked up into a time vortex.

I grabbed his small coarse body and waited for him to blink, for his pupils to shrink at the memory of a too-bright light, or for his beak to open and allow all the winds he had ever known to speak. Then I realized I was actually waiting for an answer from Holy Owl. I let go of him and took a step back, the way you might recoil if you saw a face in the mirror that wasn't yours. The bird pivoted to the left, to the right, to the left, his neck buried in his shoulders, and finally came to a stop facing the gust-swept night.

"You're losing your grip, Marnie," I said to myself as I backed out of the room, "you're seriously losing it." After checking that the front door was properly locked, just in case any other Holies wanted to come in and warm up next to Crappy, I went upstairs and took shelter in my bed, avoiding my reflection in the mirror standing at its foot as a weak light travelled across the other end of the room.

I lay until the small hours, pondering the possibility that thirty years ago Michael had been snared, like I was, by the light of a chasm he had simply been unable to resist. I wondered if I had merely imagined Mike's mittens, or if my hand had really and truly brushed against that ragged fabric. Then I remembered all the stories about revenants

I'd read or heard over the course of my life, trying to find one that explained how phantoms sometimes come to seek the living. I ended up concluding that I was delirious and neither Michael nor any other spirit had tried to command my will down by the magic swimming hole. "You're just going mad, Marnie Duchamp."

When, despite its wintry chill, the sun finally rose from behind the trees, I thanked heaven I didn't live at a latitude where people were plunged into polar night every winter. After a scalding shower, I decided it was time to pay a visit to Victor Saint-Pierre. Since leaving Rivière-aux-Trembles, I had seen him only at my father's funeral, gathered with the men in dark suits standing together in the fug of tobacco that dominated the funeral home's porch. A dozen grey-haired men who had lived through the beatnik era talked about yesterday in clouds of white smoke rather than the pot smoke of yore.

Victor Saint-Pierre had aged terribly since the days when he used to belt out "Back in the USSR" on Saturday mornings, unaware that the winds of catastrophe were gusting forward in the blue sky. However, in spite of his bowed shoulders, he was still the man who had seen the arrival of the scourge, the horse that reared up at the red glow of the inferno, in the throes of a pain that made him seem like a giant. When he reached his hand out to me, I instinctively recoiled, like a child afraid that all the fury of this colossus, who struggled with a procession of bloody images, would erupt over her head. Then our eyes met and I understood that Victor Saint-Pierre was just a wounded horse, a hurt father still waiting for his son to come back. This old man could only harm me by showing me his injury, a wide gash from his neck to the base of his stomach. After hesitating for a few seconds, I took the hand he held out and tried to find the words to sum up the past. But it was futile, neither he nor I needed words. He showed me his wound and then he went home.

Today, though, I felt that Victor Saint-Pierre could help me by talking about the Mike only he had known, about the duplicity of the storms that lashed the rivers, the shadows, and the spirits that haunt the living. But above all I needed his absolution. I spent the day wondering how to approach this overly silent man. Then a little before dusk, I pulled on my boots and put on my coat.

A lamp was lighted on the ground floor, showing the hunched silhouette of Victor Saint-Pierre behind the curtains, like a cardboard puppet being moved by invisible hands moving around behind rice-paper veils. I took a deep breath and stepped onto the porch, where little Emmy-Lili's dolls sat slumped, soaking up the light of that final August.

He answered on my first ring, as if he had been simply waiting for my visit. He immediately recognized me under my hood and gestured that I should come in. He led me to the living room and went to make coffee while I sat down. Barely a thing had changed in thirty years, not the furniture, or the lampshades, or the floral-patterned cushions, except for the photos of Michael that appeared on every wall and every piece of furniture. This profusion of photos gave the room the feel of a sanctuary and only accentuated Mike's absence. In a place where a single photo would have revived Michael's living memory, the accumulation of images merely signified his irrevocable disappearance. Wherever you looked, there was a child—pale, insubstantial, talking to you about death, and again about death, reminding you that his smile no longer existed and that he had never grown up. You could feel his cold skin, his cold breath on your neck, his bland, acrid, condemned-child scent, and wished desperately to turn all these photos to face the wall so nobody could see them anymore. This frozen-in-time living room reeked of withered flowers; no presence haunted it except that of a boy who had become anonymous among all these gilded frames.

"It was Jeanne, my wife, who put all these photos up," Victor Saint-Pierre mumbled behind me. "After she died I didn't have the heart to take them down. I felt like I'd be betraying both Mike and Jeanne."

I had learned from my father that Jeanne Dubé had succumbed to a long illness a few years earlier, an illness that the doctors were incapable of identifying but was simply called Mike, Mike sickness, the sickness of a mother who can't hold on anymore and ends up just letting go. All her life, Jeanne Dubé had waited, baking cakes for Mike just in case, just in case, dusting the photo frames and adding new ones whenever she stumbled across old pictures at the bottom of a drawer or between the pages of a prayer book. And then she died of it, of waiting, of the incurable Mike sickness, right in front of the powerless eyes of Victor Saint-Pierre, who didn't know how to cure her or how to stop loving her so it would hurt less, to not clutch onto every one of her smiles like a life vest that would puncture in his arms.

"It's terrible to say, but some days I don't even really see them anymore," Victor Saint-Pierre said, putting a photo back on the dresser and inviting me to sit down. "At the beginning, all these pictures of Mike drove me absolutely crazy, and then they just ended up blending into the wallpaper. That's what happened to Michael, Marnie, he became a painful pattern in the wallpaper."

He swallowed a mouthful of coffee and ask me if I had settled back in to Rivière-aux-Trembles. I lied — what good would it do to tell him that the forest wanted me dead, too? — and then we talked about Émilie, who had graduated from the national police school with honours, and for a few years now had been in a job that allowed her to track down killers, lunatics, and child abductors.

She had never got over Mike's disappearance either, or the smell of cake embedded deep in the paintwork, but instead of getting bogged down in sorrow she had gone on to something new. Now she spent her days handcuffing shitty little rapists who had the misfortune to cross her path, forcing them to spill the beans in an interrogation room where she would shut herself in along with them and her hatred. She made those bastards pay and felt not one iota of compassion for the ones the system tried to make out to be victims. She was a classic case. She substituted herself for the ones who couldn't be bothered to find her brother, collaring all the fruitcakes who poisoned the world for little Emmy-Lilis. She was getting revenge for Mike, day after day, barely aware that her entire life was being guided by her brother's hand, Michael, her god.

"She's going to come at Easter," added Victor, after describing the house Émilie had just bought to live alone with her killers and their corpses. "You should come by and have a drink." The invitation was sincere, but I wasn't sure I wanted to see Emmy Saint-Pierre again after all these years. In my memory she was a child broken by loss and anger, a child who didn't understand that sometimes fairy tales end in the ogre's belly. I would prefer not to get mixed up with that anger. Emmy had grown up in my dreams and nightmares and that was enough for me. We had nothing to say to each other. Shipwreck survivors can never tell each other something the other one doesn't already know. Our only connection was Mike, and that link had been broken by my actions, or at least that's what little Emmy-Lou must have thought when she tore her dolls apart and threw them against the fly-spattered wall. And despite what Victor Saint-Pierre seemed to think, she wouldn't be too pleased about the idea of seeing the person who had dragged her brother away on his flying bicycle — "Look, Lili, we're flying" — and never brought him back. I thanked Victor Saint-Pierre and told him I'd think about it, Easter was still a long way off.

"You can call me Victor," he said, "you and I are old trench mates."

He was right; we'd been in the wars together, we were

connected by spilt blood. Ignoring the fact that I used to be his enemy, Victor had just given me, in some fashion, the absolution I had hoped for. Our antagonistic positions had, however, dug a pit between us, a trench where at the bottom we had not always shared our provisions, and this forbade me from getting too close.

He didn't wait for me to answer, knowing full well you can't change the habits of a lifetime so quickly. Instead, he asked how my life in New York had been and told me he'd visited the city a few years earlier in memory of Mike and his fascination with Superman. "Remember, Marnie, all your crazy games with those capes?" He smiled at the memory of the day Mike had ripped his cape on a thorny bush, and then, without transition, asked me why I had come back to live in Rivière-aux-Trembles.

"Because it's my home, because I want to understand."

"If there were anything to understand, Marnie, we'd have understood it a long time ago. The forest took Michael and that's all there is to it."

"What do you mean by that?"

"Exactly what I said. Mike ran off into the woods and was never seen again. There were no signs of abduction or violence, no tracks, no suspects, no clues except for that damn shoe all by itself in the mud at Catfish Lake."

He stayed silent for so long that I started to wonder if I should leave. Then he cleared his throat and looked at me the way you look at a small animal that has forgotten it punctured the ball it wants to play with. I immediately sensed what Victor Saint-Pierre was going to say to me,

229

but instead of running away as fast as my legs would carry me, I sank down into my armchair and waited. I was there so that Victor Saint-Pierre could reveal what was eluding me. Fleeing would get me nowhere.

"Don't take this the wrong way, Marnie," he said finally. "I know you didn't do anything to Mike, but if there's anyone who can explain why his shoe sank in Catfish Lake, it's you. You've forgotten things, my girl. It's not your fault. You were scared to death and you forgot. That's the only possible explanation. Somewhere in your memory is the lost key to the mystery."

While Victor Saint-Pierre evoked the madness of another Marnie, an entirely invented Marnie from movies and novels, little dead Mike's smile multiplied around me, opening mechanically to tell me his secret: "Foggy day, ma'am, foggy day." All the intervening years hadn't changed a thing. Time was still stuck at the storm, and I was still the keeper of the secret that could have explained the abduction of Mike Saint-Pierre. "Rainy day, monsieur, foggy day," I thought, as a curtain of rain began to fall between Victor Saint-Pierre and me, an unbreachable wall behind which he couldn't hear me.

"I don't know," I answered simply, hoping some of my words would be heard over the noise of the rain. "Maybe I have forgotten, Mr. Saint-Pierre, but I don't know how to recall what I've forgotten." I ended on that note, resolving never to call Victor Saint-Pierre by his first name. You can't be on a first-name basis with a man who is waiting for you to bring back his son. Victor was a name for a friend, and the only real friend I'd ever had was named Mike. I didn't know any Vics.

Victor Saint-Pierre led me to the front door insisting I should come back and chat with him another time. I stood on the porch a few moments with Emmy-Lou's dolls and their accusatory plastic and porcelain eyes. I apologized, "Sorry, Emmy, shame on me," and then dragged my feet to the sidewalk, while behind me the bright light on the ground floor of Victor Saint-Pierre's house went out, and Victor's silhouette disappeared behind the opaque curtains.

Then I walked to the cemetery, to the chapel where my father was waiting to be buried, mangling some stupid song about love at the end of the line and kicking all the chunks of ice still blocking my way.

Swearing calmed me down, lashing out relieved me, so I swore and lashed out in rage. "Don't cry, Marnie, or you'll turn into an ice statue," whispered Mike's voice in my ear, but the tears flowed along with laments, curses, nonsensical words from the song that made rhyming an absolute joke. How could I not remember this anymore? How? I'm not crazy, dammit! After I spent a few moments kneeling in front of Jeanne Dubé's tomb, apologizing piteously for all the evils in the world, I hammered on the chapel door with both fists, "Answer me, Pop, answer me, I'm begging you," crying even harder and gradually transforming into a statue made of frost and ice.

Around me, other statues stared at the horizon, some facing east and daily renewal, others facing the cold of the north and of hell, Virgins, doves, angels with broken wings, Christs who couldn't be bothered to answer me anymore, their stone eyes closed over the secrets of death and the resurrection. I left my father in peace and railed against the statues, against dirty Christs with their moss-covered feet. Once the crisis had passed, I automatically started walking towards Phil's house, where I knew it would be warm.

I must have been a terrifying sight when I knocked on his door, because Phil pulled me into the living room with my boots full of slush, where he forced me to sit down before giving me his best cognac in a water glass. The warmth of the alcohol had an immediate effect. My limbs relaxed, my trembling lessened, but the alarming sensation of being inhabited by someone else's lunacy did not leave me. That someone was behind me, speaking alternately though the voices of Mike and Victor Saint-Pierre, whispering words in my ear whose meaning I did not comprehend, "How can you manage, ma'am?"

Phil pulled up an armchair to face me, perched on its edge, and waited for me to start talking. But how could I talk with all these voices in my head? I knocked back the cognac and focused on the photographs of beavers, marmots, and deer on the walls. These animals must all have died since they'd been photographed, but their presence on the walls didn't convey an atmosphere of death. They were living animals in a living house. This place had also lost a few of its occupants, but it had retained happy memories of them. Unlike Victor Saint-Pierre's house, whose walls, impregnated with a foggy damp, could give rise at any moment to pictures suffocated by remorse, Phil's house did not hold on to its dead with an atmosphere of guilt and regret.

"You've added some new photos to your collection, but these three were here even when I was little," I said to Phil, my voice nearly inaudible, as I pointed at the three black-and-white photos featuring two birds of prey and a young bear. "You even gave them names, remember? Harvey, Hervé, and Irving."

Phil remembered. He also remembered me constantly bugging him to tell the story of Irving, the baby bear, and then the story of Jésuite and Récollet, the two racoons who had been destroying his garden for generations, as tenacious as Jesuits and whose names never changed.

"Once upon a time lived Jésuite and Récollet," I murmured. I smiled at Phil, took his warm hand in my cold one, and then, head down, launched my question, "Have you ever forgotten things, important things, Phil, as if you'd fallen into a black hole, things that might have changed your life if the hole hadn't absorbed them?" I waited a few moments for an answer that didn't come, then went on, "Crucial things, that could have changed the whole trajectory of your existence? Answer me, Phil. It's not that difficult." But Phil's face was not that of a guy who wanted to talk about forgetting. It was the face of a man who couldn't stand seeing his best friend's daughter suffer anymore. "You're still going on about the Saint-Pierre kid's disappearance, huh? Jesus, Marnie, it was nearly thirty years ago."

Phil had been a witness to the events of the summer of '79, Mike's disappearance, and my becoming an outcast.

Despite the shock that had shaken the village, he never understood how supposedly sensible adults had turned against me instead of trying to help me, how they had poisoned my life to the point where my father was forced to take me far away from Rivière-aux-Trembles. Faced with the imbecility written all over the villagers' faces like an eruption of purulent zits, he almost left too, but was incapable of taking the final decision. He had spent his life in Rivière-aux-Trembles, and its forest, its lakes, its rivers were in his blood. Leaving his patch of countryside would have been like suicide for him. Nonetheless, the drama had affected him deeply, and his anger rekindled whenever the subject came up as time compressed around him, forcing him to screw up his eyes against the poisoned sun of the summer of 1979. Recently, time had compressed around me too, crushing New York, whose horizon was now nothing more than grey dust, reducing the years I spent there to a heap of debris that had only taken a few seconds or a few days to destroy. Between yesterday and my childhood, there was nothing but this dusty sky.

"What happened, Marnie? Which fucking piece of shit is still hounding you about that?"

"Nobody, Phil, nobody. Just me. I'm trying to understand, and I think maybe people were right about me hiding things, except I must have hidden them so well I can't find them."

I didn't want to tell him about Victor Saint-Pierre, the man who had spent his life digging up the ground in Rivière-aux-Trembles in the hopes of exhuming one of his son's bones. Victor Saint-Pierre wasn't to blame. He was only staying alive in order to learn the truth. I couldn't really hold it against him if he considered me the only person likely to allow him a peaceful death.

"Stop torturing yourself, Marn," Phil implored. "We remember more of our miserable times than we forget. If you had lost your marbles, your memory would have spat them out long ago. They would have come back to the surface, otherwise you would have cracked, you'd be fit to be tied."

"That's precisely what I'm wondering, Phil, if I could be going crazy."

But Phil didn't want to hear any talk of insanity, neurosis, psychosis, or anything like it. For him, madness existed only in books, wars, and massacres, or in families where children break their legs before they even learn to walk, but not in our people, not in our houses. Little Marnie all grown up could not be afflicted with any kind of madness. He took my hand in turn and led me to the kitchen, where he made us pasta while I set the table. "We'll eat, that'll get us seeing things clearly again. You open us a bottle, Marnie, a Chianti, from the cupboard back there. Go and get the candle holder from the living room too. We have three or four things to forget, so we'll do it in style."

I avoided the subject of Michael for a considerable stretch of the meal, even though his voice was there just behind me, along with his father's voice, talking to me about foggy days and how you can manage, when the storm was raging and there was no fog at all. As we sipped our coffee, I let the voices talk, with the help of the wine and the fatigue, because I couldn't hold them back anymore. Since neither the dead nor the Christs and their doves wanted to answer me, I really had to fall back on the living. I merely wanted to know if Phil had ever felt sucked in by the woods in Rivière-aux-Trembles, had ever felt his will bend and abandon him by the river or at the edge of a path. He'd lived in Rivière-aux-Trembles too long not to have felt the call of the forest.

I wanted him to describe this call to me, I wanted him to talk about the times when you wanted to sink into a snowbank or start running and never stop — to hell with the past, with death and the afterlife, to hell with this farce, with the damn shit that sticks to your shoes — but I was getting tangled up in my thoughts, stumbling over the broken branches on Mike's path, while on the other side of the table Phil's large beagle eyes grew misty behind the spent candles that were now no more than heaps of misshapen wax trying to plant their roots in the candle holder's metal.

"I'm not following you, Marnie, I'm not following you at all," he murmured, fiddling with his sauce-stained napkin, but he was following me at a hundred miles an hour according to my stubborn brain, he was following me as well as Holy Owl, otherwise his face wouldn't have crumpled as though I'd announced that Barack Obama had declared war on Saskatchewan. Since the branches on Mike's path were blocking my way, I stood there right by the path and said to Phil, "In my opinion, Mike could have vanished all by himself. That's what I've been trying to explain to you, that maybe the forest took Mike and he let it happen."

Phil put down his sauce-splattered napkin, which looked like a crushed duck, a poor half-red duck that would never be able to quack again after being crumpled like that, stood up, and came over to stroke my hair.

"Don't put ideas like that into your head, Squeerelle," Phil's voice murmured into my hair, like a warm wind that smells of vines and grapes. "Please don't blame the trees for the crimes of men. A man took Mike. Only a man could do such an awful thing, a monster with a tumour where his brain should be, and monsters don't live in the bark of trees."

But I had believed otherwise for a long time. Wherever I was, whenever a storm forced me to take shelter in music that rivalled the storm's power, I would see once more the hairy arms wanting to rip away from the trees near the magic swimming hole, and I could believe that one of them had managed to do so, that it had left the tree and coiled itself around Mike's neck. After the storm, however, after the blaring music ended, the tree limbs took on the form of human arms, and I would decree, in line with Phil, that only a man could have made Mike's face turn so pale. But no eye, no panting mouth, came forth out of my distraught memories. It was perhaps this eye, too much like a man's, that my memory had blocked out.

"It's possible, Phil, anything's possible," I said quietly, and Phil held me in his arms, strong like the old vine stock impregnated with the scents of wood and earth, until the tears that had come to my eyes when I heard the word Squeerelle, spoken with such tenderness, at long last stopped burning. Then Phil washed the dishes in silence while, hypnotized by the crumbs scattered over the plastic tablecloth, I tried to breathe calmly. One by one, I picked up the crumbs with the tip of my index finger and swallowed them, one mouthful for Papa, one mouthful for Squeerelle, and then, seeing that Phil's shoulders were a little too hunched, I decided it was time to play the clown.

I had refined this technique as a child and resorted to it whenever my father's face grew dark at the memory of Marie Beaupré. I would start hopping around him and turning a series of squeerelle pirouettes. It usually worked. Marie Beaupré vanished behind my pirouettes after blowing me a kiss, happy to see the expression of joy slowly spreading over my father's face, just enough joy to spread over his heart at the same time.

I had always hated clowns and their stupid red-ball noses, their Albert Einstein mouths painted all the way back to their bald heads, as if Einstein deserved that. But as soon as I became too distraught to act intelligently, as soon as my fear of facing reality triggered a commotion in my terrified neurons, I called in the clowns as backup and played dumb. So I wheeled out my old jokes about self-hating clowns, but neither Phil nor I had the heart to laugh. We had both known for too long that sad clowns weren't real clowns, they were poor girls and boys that had fallen from heaven into a circus ring and weren't cut out for the stupid job.

Phil turned off the ceiling light in the kitchen. A drop of water hit the sink every three seconds, as annoying as a broken clock or a bread crumb left on a tablecloth. Then he went to make up a bed for me. I was sleeping at his house tonight, and that was an order. He gave me the green bedroom, the colour of freshly cut hay or the barely budding leaves of May. Before I fell asleep I counted ducks, red ducks and white sheep, and recalled the story of Irving the bear cub, who got lost in the forest while out looking for honey. Depending on the day, Phil would change the ending of the story. Sometimes Irving would be saved by his mother, other times by a gamekeeper, or by little Marnie when she was out for a walk in the woods. Tonight it would be Marnie who saved Irving, but in order for this to happen she needed to remember the storm that had carried him off, to find the piercingly blue eye or the magic formula that would open the door to the antechamber where the bear was shut up. It was simple. Marnie had to remember. Irving had to be saved.

Marnie had to remember... These words obsessed me for several days. I would be turning on the shower, brushing my teeth, cleaning the coffee maker, and they would cross my mind at the speed of lightning, as if the obligation to remember belonged to someone other than me, to a little girl born in some strange fairy tale whose plot escaped me.

It wasn't me but this little Marnie wearing boys' overalls who had the task of finding Michael Saint-Pierre. Not me, but the child from the fairy tale enveloped in mist. If I managed to shake this little girl and place her on the path where Irving the bear cub had run off, the past would become clear. When that phrase struck me, I froze mid-gesture, plunged into an almost trance-like reverie. Time stopped, the outlines of objects blurred in the flow of time, and I was propelled into that little girl's forest, in a futile attempt to follow her, because she invariably vanished behind a tree or into a patch of fog, where her body disintegrated, leaving behind nothing but her childish laughter. I almost got to the point of telling myself that this child had no connection to me when finally, as I stood before the swaying of a captive sea, I managed to locate her bursts of laughter.

I had to go to my father's lawyer in the city we lived in for six years in order to finalize some details of his estate. I was very early for my meeting, and I looked around me as I sat in the waiting room, a bright room with modern, almost spartan, furnishings. Apart from the certificates hanging on the wall and a few photos scattered across the receptionist's desk, the only object decorating the room was a little wooden hoop animated by continuous motion. Inside the hoop was a rectangular block of glass half-filled with coloured water. As the hoop moved back and forth in perpetual balance, the water hit the sides of the glass, folded back in on itself, and then rose up again.

At the age of forty-two, I knew nothing about the sea. I'd seen the Atlantic where it met New York, but the grey stretch of ocean hurling itself up on the beaches polluted by the smell of hotdogs didn't match my idea of the sea, not the real sea. I had fantasized about my own sea, dreamed about it, and in my imagination it looked like the glass block inside the hoop—a mass of perpetually blue water that moved with calculated randomness. I rejected the wild seas and steep rocks, preferring the image of a sea breaking on itself. I had tried to imagine the blue scent of this dream sea for a long time, but some elements, such as the wind and the putrefying seaweed, were missing. I had had numerous chances to stay near the sea and discover its scent, but I always refused to see it as it was. I preferred a sea that looked like my lakes and my rivers, and didn't risk supplanting the fascination that fresh water exerted over me. I didn't miss the sea.

I was thinking of words to express the iodine aroma of the open sea when the receptionist leaned towards me to say softly, in keeping with the muffled atmosphere, that Maître Legendre would be with me in about ten minutes. I smiled at her and then focused my attention back on the hoop, where the sea projected its foams and its blues against the glass walls enclosing the universe. Bewitched by the object's movement, I closed my eyes as I dreamed that Marnie needed to remember, and the sea withdrew to the mouth of the Trembles River, calm and peaceful under the August clouds. Michael and I were swimming in the unreal atmosphere of dreams. Michael was laughing at who knows what joke, then he dived to the bottom of the water to collect rocks, which we would sort into two groups. The first would be reserved as part of the treasure he hid in the hollow of a tree, in a pouch that also contained marbles, old jewels, and foreign coins, while the second was for the games we played where we invoked the river's secret powers.

The rocks shone, and the frilly skirt of my striped bathing suit floated around my waist like the corolla of a strange flower. "It looks like a yellow-and-red water lily, Mike, look, a water lily made of Jell-O." And Mike laughed, dived, and then resurfaced with some stones, mauve and white, which he set down on the riverbank.

And then suddenly, with no transition, we're in our hut. Twenty-five rocks are arranged by size and colour in circles in front of the door. There are five circles altogether, five perfect circles that form another circle, increasing their powers. They are magic circles, bewitched by the river spirits, allowing children to fly or jump from the tops of mountains. Around us, the air is weighed down by the scent of pines whose softened needles imprint designs on our knees that resemble fossils, centipedes, and tiny skeletons of dead insects. No noise reaches us from the outside, the birds have fallen silent. Mike and I know this silence; bad weather is on the way. I hear Mike whisper, "Bad weather, it's gonna thunder, Marn," and he shows me the clouds rushing along the river. "Don't move, I'll go grab our bathing suits." As he runs out, he stumbles, breaking the circle of ochre stones. Lightning flashing through the tree canopy bleaches the sky as our swimsuits dangle from the ends of Mike's arms, but I only see the broken circle. It's a bad omen. It's bad to disturb the order of the ochre stones. I'm trying desperately to remake the circle when another streak of lightning lands at the entrance to the shelter. Outside, Michael leans and sways, staring at his running shoes. Our bathing suits have fallen to the ground. Beneath the dense, heavy rain, he reels off absurd words in a monotonous voice, then he tells me not to move — "Don't come near me!" — with bulging eyes. "Go away, Marn, go!" After this a cry rips through the heart of the storm, the cry of death and the drowned, darkening the sky, and suddenly everything turns black. Amid the entanglement of the forest, clouds fall on Mike. I crawl and shout beneath the rain, I scream, I pick up a rock and stand up, ready to attack the enemy, the man with the crystal eyes, then a voice seeps into the din surrounding me. I breathe and the sea reappears, projecting its waters in the light. Maître Legendre's face is there, lit up by the sea, and she's asking me if everything is okay.

It took me a few seconds to pull myself together, to recognize this woman who owns objects that reflect a section of the ocean, and I asked for water, fresh water, remembering the words Mike had spoken, his terrified words hammered down by the rain. "Go away, Marn! Foggy day, go!" I chased the images knocking on Mike's words and followed Suzanne Irène Legendre into her office without taking in half of what she was saying. Then I signed the papers she held out to me, mechanically answered a few questions, and escaped, slamming the door to reception, where a sea withdrew into the darkness of its depths.

Outside it was just starting to get dark and the March

dampness pierced through to my bones. I ran to my car and locked the doors. The truth was there on the threshold of my awareness, the man or beast that had attacked Mike at the same moment the clouds came down around him, while the mute words exhorting me not to go near him were getting muddled up in my mind. Mike's lips were no longer saying "Foggy day, ma'am," but "Go away, Marn, run to the village," as though he wanted to protect me, keep me away from the faceless enemy who had transformed him into a mechanical doll.

I wiped the sweat off my forehead and turned the radio up to maximum volume, then I left the illuminated city. By contrast, the road going to Rivière-aux-Trembles was extremely dark. On the screen of this darkness the river landscape spooled by in fast-forward, its trees blending in with the ones the car's headlights swept over. On the radio an analyst was discussing the Iraq War, while I, channelling the great Marlene Dietrich, hummed *Lili Marnie, Lili Marleen, Lili Marnie fell asleep, Lili Marleen will fall asleep, goodbye hello Lili Marnie*, endlessly in a monotonous voice, my eyes fixed on the white ribbon that ran alongside the dark highway.

After I'd been driving for about an hour and a half, I had to stop for a coffee. I took an exit that led me to a restaurant-bar called Le Madrid. Here, the universe seemed to have completely changed. The yard was filled with plastic and fibreglass dinosaurs that stared with bloodshot eyes as though demanding what the hell they were doing in the back of beyond when they could have been starring in a

Steven Spielberg movie. The banality of this Jurassic scene, combined with the ambient artificiality, was exactly what I needed right then. I needed kitsch and fiction.

I ordered some fries, which I barely touched, and a black coffee, which the waitress topped up between my every sip, while a guy in his fifties sitting at the end of the horseshoe-shaped bar leaned morosely over a glass of beer, which he, too, barely touched. It was immediately obvious that this guy was missing people — his wife, his children, his dog, and women in general. All it would have taken was a kind word, a hand on his shoulder, to make him start bawling about everything that was stopping his beer from going down. I looked away; my coffee wasn't going down either, "Go away, Marn," and picked up the newspaper lying beside my plate.

"Macabre discovery," blared the front page of the tabloid under a photo of a pretty young woman who smiled at the camera in the same way as Mike smiled in Victor Saint-Pierre's living room, in the same way as every missing person on the planet, and all the dead people we force to smile so we can forget their tears. Mélinda X, the woman on this garish front page, had disappeared three months ago after leaving work and had not been seen since. Yesterday, Mélinda's car, with Mélinda inside it, had been found beside a lake, half-buried in snow. At first it looked as though she was sleeping with her arms folded over her head. But Mélinda wasn't asleep, Mélinda wasn't smiling. Someone had taken her smile and her sleep, a man, presumably, a crazy man who wanted Mélinda's beauty.

As I closed the newspaper, my eyes met the waitress's—Teresa, according to the label sewn onto her uniform. She was also looking at the photo of Mélinda and wiping her hands with a cloth. "Poor girl," she murmured, trying to find something to say without betraying with clichés the suffering and the fear hidden behind the paper's black ink. I gave her a feeble smile and lowered my head. There was no need to add anything else. We were women, just like Mélinda, and a single look was enough to express the compassion we felt by contagion, in a way, just from the fact of being women, as a result of the chromosomal relationship that had taught us to be distrustful of the night, deserted parking lots, dark passages, and stairwells. Teresa didn't understand the violence incited by the scent of women and children, and I didn't understand it either. "Go away, Marn!" I laid the paper face-down to give Mélinda a brief break from the indecency of hands rubbing her smile, and I left the restaurant.

In the empty parking lot, under the watchful eyes of a few descendants of prehistory as reinterpreted by Hollywood, a fine snow fell from the opaque sky, an owl snow that hit the ground with a sound so close to a sigh that you had to hold your own breath in order to hear the augmented fall of the snowflakes as they expired on contact with the ground. "Listen, Mike, you can hear them sighing."

Along with the snow, I was plunging into a familiar melancholy when the creak of a door made me start. The lonely man from the bar, his shoulders hunched, was leaving the restaurant. I reached my car, crushing the dead snow, and started the engine.

In my rear-view mirror, the dinosaurs shrank along with the hunched man, the restaurant — which was right out of a bad photo of Las Vegas — disappeared, and I rejoined the darkness of the highway, deep in the heart of which roamed the degenerates who strangled the Mélindas and the Michaels of the world. I turned off the radio, which was playing an old Enrico Macias song, and for maybe the thousandth time repeated Mike's words in a low voice: "Go away, Marn, get out of here, run to the village," trying to figure out what had scared Mike so badly that he'd become unrecognizable to me, because it wasn't Mike swaying in the rain but Mike's body emptied of Mike, the white-faced child who was dematerializing in the jumble of the branches.

In the overheated car, Lili Marnie fell asleep along with Lili Marleen, but the Marnie who held the steering wheel with two hands stared with eyes wide open at a past that poisoned her existence. Among the owls, the smiles, and the rocks strewn across the road, she was looking for the man Phil had told her about, she was looking for the monster and for redemption, the trembling hand that had gone astray.

During the last section of the highway, along the pine-bordered bends lit up by the headlights, I could see virtually nothing. The effects of the caffeine had worn off, and I followed the Rivière-aux-Trembles streetlights in a state of quasi-hypnosis. When I arrived at the house, I felt as exhausted as if I had cried for a thousand dead people, and all I wanted was to fall asleep watching an old comedy starring a nice old clown like Charlie Chaplin, who would make me forget everything to do with Michael Saint-Pierre. But I still greeted Holy Owl, who watched the three silver maples to the left side of the house, which he desperately wanted to perch in. Captivity wasn't for Holy, or indeed for any bird, but Holy had had the bad luck to be born with tiny little wings that couldn't fly. I opened the window to let him know his freedom belonged to him and no one else, but his little wings stayed affixed to his bark and wood body. The wind plunged into his coarse feathers and he simply followed the northeast wind's lead, spinning and hitting the dust-covered windowpanes with his beak or his tail.

In the kitchen, which was lit up by a single streetlamp on the other side of the road, this tapping accentuated the intensity of the silence. I tried to get Holy to straighten up, but he carried on beating in time with the wind, which was fickle and disturbingly perfect. The wind is like the sea, it's the epitome of chaos, like the sea and the storm, I thought, as the curtains brushed my face. I listened to its whistling in the tops of the trees, so beautiful it can drive people insane, and I closed the window before this beauty could incite me to rush down to the magic swimming hole.

I hadn't been back there since the storm I named Owl Storm. Every day I would put on my boots with the intention of heading there, and every day the fear of being seduced by the forest's strange peace convinced me to put off the expedition until the next day. I would go when the winds were less violent, when the snow had thinned out across thousands of tiny ponds and formed channels that sank in the mud. Then the ice covering the magic swimming hole would have come away from the banks and I would no longer take the risk of lying down on it.

I heated up the frozen pizza I'd bought a few minutes earlier at the village depanneur and spent the evening killing off brain cells in front of the television. From time to time, I thought I could hear Holy Owl's beak tapping on the windowpanes, but it was the shutters clattering, the naked branches of the Mary Matthews bushes rubbing on the siding. Around eleven, I dropped off while watching the image of the sun peeking out from behind clouds, numbed by the soporific voice of a weatherman warning of violent winds across the province.

All the conditions were in place for me to dream I was being carried off by the wind. But there was never any wind in my dreams, never any wave-like rustling or shushing. They took place in a climate-free universe where it's impossible to feel the heat of the sand or the water covering my feet. Instead of dreaming about the wind shaking the house, I dreamed about the sea imprisoned in Maître Legendre's office, being tossed around between its glass walls without a breath of wind ever touching it, without the noise of the backwash ever reaching me. Propelled by an absurdly regular ticking, it poured soundlessly into the river. The world was surrounded by hermetic partitions, smothering even the noise of my footsteps and my breathing. I dreamed of the sea and of silence.

The wind had dropped by the time I woke up, but the sea was still undulating in all corners of the globe, just as the water would be flowing beneath the river's icy crust. It was cold in the house and daylight languished behind the clouds. In order to trick the boredom trying to work its way into me along with the cold, I filled the tub with piping hot water and, after tipping in two capfuls of Mr. Bubble, sank into it.

When I was a kid, I used to love baths brimming with bubbles, and my father always kept a bottle of Mr. Bubble for my rare visits because he knew I had enjoyed my childhood. Along with Caramilk bars, Cheez Whiz, and Rice Krispies, Mr. Bubble bubblebath was one of the few products that had survived unchanged since then. The others had all disappeared in the great tide of interchangeable consumer items that western society apparently cannot live without.

Mr. Bubble's bottle was in the shape of a bear or a panda, it wasn't clear which, and Papa and I gave it a new name every day. Some nights he was called John, John Bubble. Other evenings he was Martin, Clement, or Dominique, and he always had a story to tell me about the shapes I sculpted with the foam. Today, the plastic bear was called Michael, but he refused to tell me the story of the river whose bed I had carved out on the water's foamy surface.

In order to wake the bear up, I shook his translucent little body, which made a wet noise as the bath oil stuck to his sides. Then I forced him under the water and held him there, thinking he might be more inclined to talk if he was afraid of ending his days in this lifeless pool of water. A few eddies rose up through the foam, Michael Bubble kicked his feet, and I released him, asking if he was now ready to reveal his secret, the one carefully guarded by the broken circle of ochre stones for three decades, maybe for several centuries. He was still silent, so I plunged him underwater again, a little deeper this time and a little longer. Mr. Bubble's plastic face continued to smile as his eyes widened and his features dissolved in the languorous waves that slosh the foam around. "Foggy day, ma'am, foggy day," Mr. Bubble hiccupped. Far below the bluish surface, Mike's equally blue eyes said, "Go away, Marn, get out of here," synchronizing perfectly with Mr. Bubble's plastic lips. I let go of the bottle with a start. Mr. Bubble popped up to the surface, his eyes filled with foam, and drifted on the lapping water to the far end of the bathtub.

I looked at my trembling hands, then grabbed Mr. Bubble and hurled him at the wall. For a brief moment, these hands gripped Mike's neck, submerging him in the river as the August sun heated it up. Through Mr. Bubble's smile, I had seen Mike's frozen smile as he repeated, "Go away, Marn, foggy day," his lips surrounded by three perfectly round little bubbles that had escaped from the bottle.

"It's not me, for Christ's sake!" I yelled, beating my arms and banging my elbows on the sides of the tub and the wall of yellow-and-white tiles, splashing the floor with soapy water and then slipping on the enamel, nearly knocking myself out or breaking a limb. "It's not me! It's not me! It's not me!"

My stubborn need to shine a light on the hypothetical

shadows covering my memory of August 7th, 1979, was becoming an obsession. If I didn't pull myself together, Phil would soon be compelled to admit that even little Marnies could go crazy. I forced myself to breathe calmly, then gazed up at the immaculately white ceiling. White, white, nothing but white.

"What if there are no missing images?" I muttered to Mr. Bubble. "What if the arm of the monster that attacked Mike was invisible, or his claws were disguised among the profusion of greenery?" Perhaps nobody except Mike had ever seen this man's arm. Nobody except Mélinda.

I climbed out of the bath shivering, pulled on a dressing gown and some wool socks, and then I rang Phil to hear him call me Squeerelle and remind me that some mysteries can't be solved.

The rain had almost stopped the evening before when I got back from a drive that had no other purpose than to distract me from the banality of my nights at home, which typically unfolded with a bowl of popcorn and boring television. Thick fog was rising over the snowy fields, the houses of Rivière-aux-Trembles disappeared in the heavy vapour, flickering lightly, and the smallest objects — garbage cans, woodpiles — lost their stability behind the mist. The glow from the streetlamps formed yellow halos, similar to the soft beams of flashlights that sweep the summit of the trees on the outskirts of villages when a child doesn't come home for dinner.

I had seen these lights coming out of the woods during the night of August 7th, 1979, drawing an irregular perimeter around Rivière-aux-Trembles crisscrossed by the voices of men calling out for Michael. The echo of the westbound shouts was dying on Wolf Hill, which had fallen silent along with the coyotes in the face of the commotion in the woods; the eastward shouts were disappearing into the humid air, meeting nothing but obstacles that absorbed the sound of their distress.

Mike's name was being shouted everywhere, in the fields, in houses, in the darkened sky. Then the name was carried off into the distance, where it was soon nothing more than a breath hitting against hazy boundaries where the wind goes to die. Mike was there, right where his name went silent, in the wind's dead zone. When I heard the echoes tumbling from the summits of the hills, I burrowed under my covers, attempting a short prayer, and I waited, waited for the trees to bend and sway again in the wind, hoping Mike's name would hook onto a gust that would lash his face.

I had seen these jerky lights in movies before, tracking men who were fleeing, or racing over to a muddy shoe belonging to the little girl who was sent to buy milk at the corner store. Sometimes the camera showed a close-up of the shoe, and you saw that it was pink or white, and these colours added a sense of gravity to the drama. These images disturbed me a little more each time, not only because they were always superimposed over Michael's running shoe, but because the shoes were always muddy, and this was always the object discovered first, a dirty shoe that indicated the child had stopped running right next to their final footprint. My father could never understand why I stayed riveted to the television whenever it showed a movie about a child's disappearance. "Go to bed, Marnie," he would say. "How is watching this going to help you?" But it was stronger than I was, I had to see, I had to know, I had to understand. Yet all these movies taught me only one bitter truth: missing children never come home for dinner. A shoe is discovered, sometimes a body, sometimes bloody clothes, but rarely a hungry tearful little girl or boy.

The fog that enveloped Rivière-aux-Trembles reminded me of those evenings spent searching during the summer of '79, when confusion reigned over the village, when its contours were blurred, and I could see nothing any longer except through a kind of nebulousness that affected the flow of time, making it slower than usual, moving through the thickness of the ethereal stuff that surrounded faces and objects. For five nights, the lights projected in the undergrowth had searched for Michael, and then there was just one lamp, that of Victor Saint-Pierre, who shouted louder than all the other men.

I crossed the misty village in the fuzzy numbness surrounding these memories and parked outside the house, where I listened to the irregular patter of raindrops falling from the trees onto the car roof. The sound was like a lullaby; I recalled how much I used to love the rain, all kinds of rain, before my life was ripped apart in the fury of a storm. "Why can't you leave me in peace, Michael

Saint-Pierre? Why won't you leave me alone? Why?" Then tears joined in, trickling slowly down to the bottom of my chin, slowed down by the viscous snot and saliva blocking their way.

Idiotic with tiredness, I cried until my numbness doubled up as vertigo and forced me to open the window to catch my breath and get some oxygen to my brain. Outside, the eavestroughs filled with autumn leaves overflowed, a few happy rivulets multiplied their branches in the gravel, and the air smelled ripe with the end of winter, polluted snow, the mud of trampled leaves. I took advantage of this lull to wipe my face, then I walked calmly up to the house while I asked Mike why I was no longer capable of loving or smelling the rain.

Holy Owl was waiting for me in the kitchen, just like he would until the end of time if I left him hanging in front of his window. Suddenly I didn't want Holy to wait for me anymore, reminding me of Mike until the Final Judgement. I went down to the basement to find my father's portable floodlight, his big spotlight, the very one he'd used to search for Mike while Julie Lacroix looked after me and bombarded me with questions, her eyes wide and shining, so she could tell her friends how she had grilled Marnie Duchamp, the crazy kid, who gave her plenty of grisly details about the disappearance of the Saint-Pierre boy. Julie Lacroix was a damn liar who poisoned my existence more than any of the others. I told her to go fuck herself, wished her tongue would get ripped out by a train, and went back up to the main floor, where I put on a raincoat and a pair of waterproof boots before going to get Holy Owl from the kitchen.

"This is the night you get to fly away, Crappy, I'm giving you your freedom," I whispered, pressing my mouth to his little fake-feather-covered head, and I stuffed him into my raincoat pocket. I had been wrong to accuse Mike. He wasn't the one who prevented the rain from falling on me. It was the phantom that I nourished day after day with enough bad faith to feed a whole army of zombies. My problem wasn't called Mike, it was called Marnie Duchamp, alias Marnie Hitchcock, alias Squeerelle. If I wanted Mike to leave me in peace, first of all I'd have to expel him from this phantom zone, where I'd imprisoned him without even realizing it. I'd always been fascinated, with a fascination close to terror, by carceral enclosures, the kind of phantom zones straight out of Superman's futuristic universe. The eternal sequestration that lawbreakers were subjected to, shut up in these spaces, drifting for eternity, seemed to me the most atrocious kind of punishment imaginable, worse than all the hells people have imagined up until this point, yet this was exactly where I had kept Mike prisoner. In my desire to keep his memory alive, I had created a new hell for him, no longer reserved only for criminals but also for beloved people who have become ghosts, captives of this love that dooms them to an absurd immortality. I had to get him out of there and free myself at the same time.

Before I left for the river, I called Phil so he wouldn't have a sleepless night if he paid me one of his surprise visits and found the house empty. I gripped Holy Owl's beak shut as he wiggled in my pocket and told Phil I was going to bed early to listen to the rain. We would have dinner together the next day, my treat. "Five o'clock, Phil, good night."

The rain had surged back eastwards while I was gathering my stuff together, but the fog was still thick enough to cut with a knife. I went through the village, trudging through the puddles of melted snow, then headed up the 4th Line. When I reached Lucien Ménard's fields, I ducked into the forest.

The trees took on another dimension in the brightness of my father's floodlight. There was something human about them. I discovered trees I'd never seen before, trees whose twisted branches blocked access to other paths — secret, sinuous paths, forbidden to walkers, or belonging to children who no longer existed. A light mist sometimes still lingered at ground level, where the earth was warmer, but the forest repelled the fog that encircled it. Shapes that were invisible in the clarity of daylight stood out on the damp tree trunks, totemic figures of spirits seeking to extricate themselves from the substance that had swallowed their souls. The artificial light I held out in front of me or angled onto some dark hollow surprised the night in its intimacy with the trees. At this late hour, a person intruding on the chatting and whisperings rising up out of the mist was not welcome. This hour was the kingdom of fairy tales and demons, stories of werewolves and fear-inducing beliefs. This was where the ogre and the wolf were born.

Perhaps Michael was there, in one of the excrescences that took on the appearance of tortured bodies desperate to escape from these rugged trunks. Perhaps he'd disappeared just like children in fairy tales disappear, captured by the trees, shut away by some witch who fed on virgin blood. Frightened by the storm, perhaps he'd tripped over the scrawny legs of the sorcerer of Rivière-aux-Trembles, stretched out across the ground like roots, oozing a bitter sap, and had landed deep in the heart of an utterly changed forest that had no exit other than eternal loneliness.

Some people had thought I was the witch, which made me wonder if I wasn't the product of incubuses who mated when they visited my parents' bed to create Marnie the Witch, the sorceress of Rivière-aux-Trembles. The ridiculousness of this hypothesis might have earned me a straitjacket if I hadn't finally managed to knock it into my skull that witches were purely chimerical creatures who only showed up in fairy tales. And my life was not a fairy tale. However, as I moved forward among the unreal trees, nothing seemed impossible. Perhaps there were dimensions whose depths we were unaware of, supernatural or maleficent forces that struck adults and children indiscriminately. The fog rolling around at my feet might also enchant me, but I pressed onwards. If the forest had wanted me, it could have taken me long before this, and if it wanted me today, any efforts I made to counter its plans would only exhaust me, and I would sink, head down, into isolated areas that only opened inwards, towards the bottom of the world.

After I veered around a group of cedars that grew so close together they stifled one another, I finally heard the river flowing under the ice, whose edges had been eroded by the rain. The hidden path snaking through the twisted trunks had led me to where I wanted to go. Instead of losing me the way it had lost Mike, the forest opened out in front of me. No evil spirit would be stealing my soul today. I followed the sound of water, and two minutes later I was at the magic swimming hole.

I directed the floodlight's beam onto the trees along the river, among which I could detect no quivering or trembling. Pine, birch, spruce, but not a single specimen of the tree that had given its name to this body of water. The quaking aspens had apparently disappeared from its banks after the river had been named, unless the men who did the naming had been mistaken, mixing up birches and poplars. I would have to ask Phil if he knew what fate had befallen the river's trembling trees.

I carried on sweeping my light across the moonless night. The glow from my lamp brushed the squared-off end of a piece of wood, blackened by water, that I didn't recall seeing there before. Slowly, I swung the beam back towards the spot where I thought I saw the wood, and I froze. A few feet away from the magic swimming hole stood a cross, whose funereal appearance perfectly suited the atmosphere of this lugubrious night. It was just a simple little cross emerging from the snow, the kind you might see on a dangerous curve or in a movie where the horror is tangled up with holy symbols. I got closer, taking care to not make a sound, afraid of waking up the person sleeping under the cross. Then I saw that there was a name carved on it — Michael — with no date or any other inscription.

A single word, Michael, the weight of which made the cross lean over into the shadows. I took a few steps back, staring at the cross, which forced me to imagine Mike's body six feet under the blanket of earth, his mouth and eyes crawling with all the tiny little beasties that live in the soft soil. But I knew that even if I scraped away at the soil until I tore my nails off, my hands would never reach Mike's face, because nobody — neither Victor Saint-Pierre, nor God, nor the police — had ever found the slightest evidence of his death.

For a moment I wanted to tear down the cross, which made official a death that had never been confirmed and gave the Rivière-aux-Trembles witches licence to carry out their pagan rituals around this symbol of the resurrection. It must have been Victor Saint-Pierre who put it up one spring or summer day, maybe accompanied by his wife or Emmy-Lou. He must have carved Mike's name on the wood in his workshop, being careful to make the letters straight and of equal size, without embellishment, as dry as death, and then armed himself with a mallet to stake Mike's name in the cursed forest. Victor Saint-Pierre had lowered his arms and entrusted Michael's memory to an object whose appearance, unusual in this particular place, could only provoke deep unease. If it were up to me, I would have made it disappear, but I had no right to destroy this cross, which Victor no doubt came to visit every year on August 7th.

As I looked more closely, I noticed the wood of the cross was rotting. It had probably been put there a long time ago, when Emmy was still playing with her shabby dolls. For all these years, I had been unaware of the existence of this gallows, whose shadow, on sunny days, must have reached the entrance to the path by which Michael had fled. Given the configuration of the place, the shadow of the rotten cross would lengthen towards the path. Its only function was to indicate absence, flight in the direction of the trees.

I had left the house with the intention of hooking Holy onto a branch overhanging the river, abandoning him to the mercy of bad weather. But as I examined the cross, I had the idea of burying him together with Mike's absent body. His place was there, underneath this rickety cross. I pushed up my sleeves, swearing that Holy Crappy Owl would join Mike, plunged my bare hands into the snow, and dug and dug until I reached frozen earth. Unable to cut through its icy surface, I ran to the river to find a sharp stone and tried to dig some more, my forehead dripping with sweat and my hands stiff from the cold, but the edge of the rock snapped and I tossed it behind me, cursing all the saints in heaven. The sound of the stone dropping into the water, so much like the noise of all the rocks Mike and I had hurled into Catfish Lake and the Mailloux pond, pierced the night with a clear sound. Crouched down in the melting snow, I looked at my raw hands and black nails. I heard myself panting, and I was afraid. "Don't go crazy, Marnie!"

My hands still trembling, I replaced the soil, the snow, and the wet leaves I had scattered at the foot of the cross, then I took Holy Owl out of my pocket. No bird is meant to be in captivity. No bird is meant for the earth. I pressed my lips to Holy's little beak. "Good luck, Crappy," I whispered, and I tied his string to one of the arms of the cross so that his shadow could follow the same trajectory as Mike's, and maybe one day he would perch in a treetop. That's where birds should live, and that's where they should die, in the trees or in the clouds. After assuring myself that Holy wouldn't fall off with the first gust of wind, I took a few steps back. In the light from the lamp I held in my outstretched arm, the cross cast its shadow on the snow, along with the shadow of a small hanged creature swaying gently. "Arrivederci, Crappy, maybe we'll meet again. Say hi to Mike for me if you bump into him," I said, and then left without looking back.

As the rush of the river faded behind me, rain began to fall again, amplifying the whispers that echoed between the branches. From time to time, a cracking sound made me jump, but I carried on my way, inhaling the scent of melting snow and soaked wood that rose up from the earth. I was alone, Holy was watching over the magic swimming hole, and around me birds of prey and wolves sighed in harmony with witches. I wanted to walk more quickly, but I stumbled over one of those roots that only emerges above ground in the dark. With my face in the grainy snow, I searched frenetically for the lamp, which had slipped from my hand when I fell. I patted the ground all around me, finding only things that were viscous or putrefied. Just as a hand with nails like claws—I was sure of it—crept towards my leg to pull me backwards, "It's coming, Marn, it's here," I caught sight of the glow from the light behind a stump. I crawled over on my elbows, convinced that the hand was going to dig its nails into my flesh at any second. I grabbed the floodlight, turned around, and shone it in front of me. Everything was motionless. The hand that was pursuing me had slithered back into its lair.

I was out of breath by the time I reached Lucien Ménard's clearing, but I didn't stop. I ran until I got to the road, oblivious to the water dripping down my neck or the pain from my fall and my attempt to bury Holy Owl alive. Perhaps an owl was hooting in the distance, but I didn't hear it, any more than I heard the cry that once rang out on Blueberry River.

"Nanamiu-shipu, Trembling River, is probably the Innu word the name Trembles River comes from," Phil explained to me as we sipped our coffee after dinner, not long before the candles went out. "People must have called it the 'rivière Qui-Tremble,' and then the name gradually got distorted into Trembles River, even though not a single trembling poplar lies anywhere near that river."

We were sitting at the dining table, chatting by the light from a wall lamp and three candles that burned down slowly on small glass plates, since I couldn't find any candle holders. Phil had knocked on my door around five o'clock and we made dinner together as we each drank a bottle of Belle Gueule blonde. Phil grated the cheese, I grated the zucchini, while Miles Davis took care of the music, approaching the sublime with his soundtrack to *Ascenseur pour l'échafaud*.

Faced with Holy Owl's empty spot in the window, I tried to forget the wooden cross from which I had hung this glassy-eyed bird. I danced to "L'assassinat de Carala," a piece of music composed for the scaffold, not for dancing or for carefree behaviour, but I seriously didn't give a shit because I felt an urgent need to play the clown, to protect my innocent Bozo smile while Jeanne Moreau desperately looked for her lover, Julien Tavernier, who had just pulled off the almost-perfect crime. So I danced, I staggered around the scaffold, and I stumbled about to the sound of the languorous trumpet. To forget. To play the clown.

When I got back from the river the night before, I lay down on my bed hoping to fall asleep to the rain's percussive beat, but I stayed awake until the small hours, watching the shadow of the cross appear on a wall of my bedroom and then seeing its reflection in the full-length mirror, where the silhouette of my stretched-out body lay. Just like the wicked stepmother in a fairy tale, I had taken Holy into the woods to abandon him there, and now I was afraid he would retrace our path by following pebbles scattered along our route. My desire to get rid of Holy constituted my first attempt to free myself from Mike, to find my own life and to feel the rain once again, but its chances of success seemed very slight. This is why I was dancing, as lazy as a carp after the spring thaw, as ridiculous as a teenager pretending to be Madonna or Elvira Madigan, trying to convince myself that Mike's cross was a sign from heaven rather than hell, that I simply needed to entrust Mike to God to finally be free from my torments. Essentially, I needed to take refuge in a very simple truth. Mike was dead. Carala was dead. Marnie was alive.

"What's up with you, Marn? It's ages since I've seen you in such a good mood," said Phil, and I told him it was the spring, the spring and the rain, the snowdrops coming in three weeks, Phil, do you realize that? The warmth will make buds bloom and hatch out swallow eggs. Phil was happy to see me dance, and despite his powers of perspicacity, he couldn't make out the hideous clown nose I'd put on under my cracked plastic mask.

During dinner, riding high on my exhausted-clown good mood and the effects of the Château Timberlay Phil had brought over, we talked about everything and nothing, the rain—again—the impossible temperature in Quebec, all while commenting on the record number of consecutive apostasies due to Pope Benedict's words on the use of condoms, the earthquake that had caused three hundred deaths and destroyed the homes of seventy thousand people in the Abruzzo region of Italy, while I was walking through a forest where the only things that trembled were my hands.

I waited until the end of the meal to tell Phil that Mike was dead, and that it was, in a manner of speaking, his tomb I had been dancing on earlier. I was lying, a fine puff of air was still able to escape from Mike's throat, but I wanted to call Phil as a witness to his imminent death. "It's about time you let him die at last," he sighed. "Old ghosts, in the long run, become exhausted and can get nasty."

Phil's smile was almost happy, and I was suddenly ashamed of announcing the death of a dying person. I felt like one of those writers who has to prepare the obituaries of people who are still alive, but whose death has been predicted for several weeks. The piece has to be ready in advance so it can go to press the minute the old guy or old gal kicks the bucket. "It'll settle down, Marn, you know as well as I do that you end up getting used to death," Phil added, before getting up to make coffee.

The candles flickered on the little glass plates, where melted wax formed piles of red lava. I passed my hands over the flames and thought of summer, hoping for summer the way you hope to finally be reborn, throw your old running shoes out and buy a pair of two-hundred-dollar sandals, only to realize at the end of the day that it's better to run around barefoot, with nothing between you and the grass or the soil. I was putting stakes in the ground by the Mary-Jean bushes, barefoot and bareheaded, when Phil came back with the coffee.

"What are you thinking about, Marn?"

"Pop's rosebushes, I need to take care of them."

And then, from Mary Hope to Mary Kay, I ended up near the river, totally incapable of spending one hour without having that damn water course surge into my field of vision. I rushed past Mike's cross and leapt over the magic swimming hole to ask Phil what he knew about the river's trembling aspens. It was a simple question, and I expected a simple answer. "Nanamiu-shipu, trembling river," Phil murmured, as the candles flickered, almost ready to go out. According to him, the Indigenous people had probably given this name to the river after the earthquake that violently shook the region in October 1860, a quake felt as far away as Nova Scotia and New Jersey. "I read somewhere that the river might have deviated from its course when a rift formed," Phil continued, "so the Innu gave it the name 'Nana-shipu,' meaning vanished river. Some experts claim that the river's real name was actually Nanamassiu-shipu, river of thunder. The first white settlers in the area mixed up the words nana, nanamiu, and nanamassiu, so they gave different names to the river, and this confusion led, after fifty years, to Trembles River."

Phil was speaking, piling up words that seemed alien to me. The candles were flickering, Miles was playing "L'assassinat de Carala" again, and all I could hear was nana, nanamiu, nanamassiu: disappearance, trembling, thunder, Michael and Marnie in the storm. The words of the ancient Innu who had named this river for its moods, for its revolt against the heavens, or its tumble into the earth's fault lines, could not be a lie. It was the aspens that were lying, the white words born of a misunderstanding, but not nana, not nanamiu, not nanamassiu. Tremble, storm, dazzle, and ravish.

My forehead was once again dripping with sweat, its rancid smell was impregnated in the armpits of my sweater, nanamiu, nanamiu-shipu...I was repeating these words nobody had taught me, even though they encircled my destiny the way fire surrounds besieged villages. They revealed the true nature of the river, Nanamassiu-shipu, which wanted to carry me off during the last tempest. Phil had been wrong when he claimed we couldn't accuse the trees and the rivers of crimes. Mike's disappearance was beyond comprehension because it had been caused by the resurgence of the river's distant trembling during the lightning, because Michael, with his unlaced shoe, had fallen into one of the rifts that were immediately covered over with water.

"What's up, Marnie?" asked Phil, sounding worried.

"Nothing," I replied. "I was walking in the rain yesterday, I must have caught a fever."

He touched my forehead; it was burning hot. The fever was well and truly established. "You go to bed," Phil ordered, "I'll sort out the dishes."

But I stayed at the table, watching the candles flicker as they went out in the shapes of red lava frozen on the glass plates, asking myself about the rivers in Abruzzo, wondering whether some of them had flooded and carried away missing children. I gathered up the crumbs scattered across the tablecloth and sorted them according to shape and size before arranging them in circles, five little circles that evoked witch's rings, at the centre of which the mad and the doomed lured demons with frenetic dancing. Five little circles reminiscent of the stones Mike had fished out of the Trembles River, "Let's group the white ones together,

Marn," before the splattering of the rain, before the thunder, before the children all started shouting, *sorcerer, bitch, witch, Marnie the Witch!*

At eleven o'clock on the dot, the house was all in order and Miles Davis had gone back to the uncomfortable backstage area between death and immortality. As for Phil, he had figured out that I had just dug Mike up out of his tomb.

The fever lasted for several days, during which, in my near-delirious state, I resuscitated Mike in order to return his body to the river, where his blond hair stroked his cheeks in time with the current. I followed the slowness of his movements in the gentle water and wondered why no painter had tried to depict the tranquil face of a drowned person under the features of a man or a boy. Surely some gallery or museum must show the faces of tortured men rising from black seaweed, but to my knowledge no peaceful Ophelia drifting among the nenuphars bore the name of a man.

When I wasn't imagining him at the bottom of a river or a ravine, I saw Mike arriving by Hook Hill, which was named thus because its outline used to go around the western flank of the hill it crosses today. He had dirty hair, a long beard, and was carrying over his shoulder a shapeless bag containing all his possessions, which consisted of a few clothes and books. This was the resuscitated Mike, the prodigal child who had taken thirty years to return to his village. If Victor Saint-Pierre hadn't died it was because he was waiting for this Mike, the one who belonged in the category of children who prolong the existence of the undead in spite of themselves. People wait for them, people hold off dying or get a reprieve from death, and they end up believing that immortality is simply a disguised version of waiting.

As I was resuscitating Mike, I had wanted at times to run over to Victor Saint-Pierre's to tell him not to die before he had seen a blurry silhouette standing in relief against the summit of the Hook Hill in the summer light, but the fever stopped me, making me shiver from head to toe even though my body was drenched in sweat. This was the trembling fever, nanamitshiu-akushu, caused by the rain that had risen from vanished rivers.

Phil showed up every day at the end of the afternoon, bringing me oranges, Campbell's chicken soup, or black molasses, but only the finger of gin with honey he poured for me after dinner brought me any relief. Nothing other than childhood memories force nostalgia to bring out its arsenal of placebo effects. That's what I told Phil as I held out my glass for a second dose of gin. In the middle of the evening, after a hot bath to which I no longer invited Mr. Bubble, I fell asleep to the scent of juniper while Bones identified femurs on television.

Then the fever left as suddenly as it had come, like a traitor sneaking out the back door after he's stabbed you in the kidneys. I dragged my feet for a good week longer, not knowing if I was suffering from the symptoms of convalescence or grief, and then life returned again. I tried not to think of Mike, focusing on the notebooks my father had kept about the care of different kinds of rosebushes, filling orders for young plants, and tidying up the workshop and the greenhouses.

While the trembling fever did its worst, I seriously considered leaving Rivière-aux-Trembles, but then, gazing out at the melting snow in the yard, I understood I had missed my childhood too much to renounce it now that Mike's memory was fading, and I could hope, little by little, to become the Marnie who would sometimes whistle "As Time Goes By" under the New York skies.

Since I had inherited it, I would take care of my father's little business and pick up my childhood right where I'd left off, under the blooming pergola. I would live here from now on, amid the aroma of roses and dry hay, the scent of pines exuding their bitter sap in the Rivière-aux-Trembles summers. I would evoke these summers, the crunch of the hay, the sand sticking to damp hands, and I would stretch out beside the occasional enormous waves that rolled up the beach as far as the sandcastles. I would take off all the screens and allow the hues of childhood to enter my father's house. Only the colour of rain would challenge me, because nobody has ever been able to pin down the hue of summer rain. People who think rain is grey have never really seen rain. They've seen only wet ground and clouds.

So I waited for the fever to abate and then plunged into my work with a single aim in mind: to recreate certain happy childhood states. I was in the greenhouse, where I'd been working since early morning, when two car doors slammed outside the yard. Phil was pretty much the only person who ever came to see me, but it couldn't be him. Phil wouldn't slam his door twice, Phil didn't throw salt over his shoulder or jump over cracks in the sidewalk. Phil was as rational as a right angle, and his only reason for not walking under a ladder was to avoid making the guy who was painting his eaves fall down, a guy who hoped nobody would be stupid enough to risk walking under his ladder. The normal flow of events was about to come face to face with the instability that was a daily threat to the millions who believed themselves to be protected from chaos.

I put down my secateurs and walked towards the greenhouse door. The slamming doors were attached to a Sûreté du Québec car, and the men who had slammed them were striding up the steps to the house two at a time. I instinctively hid at the back of the greenhouse. These uniformed men had come to arrest me. They'd discovered the missing link, the detail that incriminated me, the one I'd searched for in vain by reading Winston Graham and letting myself be lulled by the waves of a non-existent sea. As I leaned against the workbench, I heard them knock on the door, shouting my name, "Madame Duchamp, Marnie Duchamp, open up!"

I closed my eyes and counted to one hundred. If they were still there when I opened my eyes, it would prove they were real. I was at sixty-five when I heard a voice in the greenhouse doorway. "Don't open your eyes, Marn," Mike's voice implored me, "you need to make it to a hundred if you want them to disappear." But the voice got closer, accompanied by the sound of footsteps. "Madame Duchamp? Officer Marchessault, Officer Doyon. We'd like to talk to you." I opened my eyes when I reached ninety, thus depriving myself of all possibility of knowing whether these inspectors were real. Standing in front of me, the two police officers waited for me to confirm my identity. The taller one had hair while the shorter one was bald with a compensatory moustache. Apart from this difference, they looked the same. If you transplanted the short guy's moustache under the tall guy's nose, and implanted the latter's hair onto the bald one's head, it would have changed nothing. Their chilly attitude would not have warmed up by a single degree.

After they showed me their badges, they asked if we could talk somewhere more suitable. The greenhouse seemed to me no less appropriate than the Sistine Chapel for what they had to tell me, but I didn't object. I led them over to the house and invited them to sit down in the living room, but they preferred the kitchen, just as Desmarais and McCullough had the first time they'd interrogated me about Mike's disappearance. The only one missing was my father, whose place was occupied by the bald guy, and Victor Saint-Pierre's silhouette in the doorway. To gain time, I brushed together the crumbs on the plastic tablecloth, noticing how much my hands were trembling, which Doyon also took note of, gesturing with his chin to Marchessault. I tried in vain to picture them as two bumbling doofuses to quell the panic that was tying my guts into knots, but these cops were anything but idiots.

They knew what they were doing. They could sniff out the scent of fear from inside a diving suit.

I was waiting for them to reveal irrefutable proof they had unearthed allowing them to pin Mike's disappearance on me, but Marchessault launched into a description of his grandmother's kitchen, which had cupboards entirely made of laths just like mine, and the pantry where his grandmother kept huge orange cookies in a stoneware jar. He wondered if they really were enormous or if he just saw them that way because he was small. He finally concluded it wasn't because he was child-sized — they truly were big, crumbly biscuits that melted in your mouth and left a little orange powder on your fingertips.

I didn't know if he was talking to Doyon or to me, if he just wanted to irritate me or if he was soliloquizing, lost in the splendour of a childhood where he never had to put up with a bald colleague or to make arrests on Monday afternoons. Cops often used the most implausible methods to make you confess, which included old ladies in flowery aprons who force-fed them cookies until they were twelve. You couldn't believe them or their touching memories. When he finished raving about the flavour of those orange cookies sprinkled with grains of sugar, the kind of biscuits people didn't make any more, he turned to me and asked how I had spent my day on Saturday, April 18th.

I sat there with my jaw hanging open. What possible connection was there between April 18th and Mike's disappearance? Why April 18th and not December 25th, 1940? I hadn't done anything on April 18th that could have any link to Mike. I hadn't spent a quiet moment at his cross or gone to Catfish Lake, I had only left the house to go to the hardware store in Saint-Alban, which sold a special kind of fertilizer I needed for my roses.

So that's what I told them, that I'd spent the day in the greenhouses before going into Saint-Alban to run errands. They seemed interested in the fact that I'd been to Saint-Alban. Once again, Doyon jerked his chin at Marchessault, who leaned towards me and asked if I liked children — little boys. His big hairy hands were almost touching mine, and his face was so close to mine I could see the sweat pearling on his forehead, just like the beads that had trickled down Inspector Desmarais's forehead in the August sun. Marchessault was sucking all the air out of my personal space, and his proximity was making me nauseous.

"Little boys?" he repeated, bringing his face even closer to mine, and I leapt to my feet.

"What the hell are you talking about? I have no idea what you're talking about. What do you want from me?" I shouted, backing up slowly towards the door, waiting for my father to appear and bang his fist down on the table to make this interrogation stop. I knew full well my attitude made me look guilty, like a crazy woman who wasn't in control of herself, but I continued retreating. My fear didn't go unnoticed by the two men sitting at my kitchen table; my panic made their faces glow, as if they had thwarted JFK's assassin.

"Sit down," ordered Doyon.

"Not until you explain what you're doing here," I answered, pulling a tissue from the box to blow my nose.

Marchessault waited for me to finish sniffling. Then, assigning the mute role to the other guy, he explained the reason for their presence. His voice was calm. The uninterrupted flow of his words filled my kitchen with a kind of drone, constantly peppered with the name of a boy, Michael, a boy whose brand-new Superman-blue bicycle had fallen into a ditch. But Marchessault was spouting nonsense. He was mixing up facts, dates, seasons. Mike's bike hadn't fallen into a ditch, he'd hidden it there along with mine, and he wasn't wearing a red jacket; it was too hot, nobody wears a red jacket in the middle of August.

"That's not what happened, you've got it all wrong," I told the two men, who watched me with bated breath, like two cats crouching by a rain puddle where a few innocent sparrows are drinking. I smoothed the tablecloth with my moist hands and explained how Michael had run off while I was in the fort, kneeling in a broken circle of rocks. I described to them the sudden force of the wind, the words Mike had spoken — he didn't say anything about a foggy day, no sirree, he told me to flee: "Go away, Marn, run." They were wrong about every single detail. I was in the fort, Michael was by the river, and there was a storm between us.

The tablecloth was now smooth and the two inspectors were staring at me with their feline eyes wide open. With his fists clenched, Doyon demanded to know where the boy was, where I had hidden Michael Faber. This name had cut through the buzzing a few moments ago, but I hadn't lingered on it, it had slipped over Michael's name and tumbled into a vast space where neglected words gather up in a higgledy-piggledy pile, useless and powerless. While Marchessault insisted in turn that I tell them where I'd hidden Michael Faber's body, I understood they were talking about a different boy, a different Michael.

The buzzing suddenly stopped. What the fuck, Holy?

I saw little pearls of sweat shining on Doyon's moustache and covering Marchessault's forehead. "I don't know," I stammered, wiping my mouth, annoyed by the damp moustache with its coarse hairs forking at the corners of his lips. "I don't know anyone called Michael Faber, I haven't hidden anyone, and I'm not insane. I'm not insane, do you hear me? The forest took Mike." But Doyon and Marchessault refused to listen to my explanations and justifications. From their point of view, I had more or less confessed to kidnapping a boy named Michael Faber. Despite my shouts and protestations, one of them, I don't even know which one, slipped handcuffs on me, read me my rights, and walked me to their car parked outside the door. I tried to struggle, to explain that their story didn't stand up, but the one who led me pushed me gently into the car while I wriggled and squirmed like a worm on the end of a fishing rod. Then he shut the door, sure I wouldn't be able to escape, since there's never a damn handle on the inside of the doors that close as abruptly as a rat trap on little Marnie, and he went back to join the other guy inside the house.

I don't know how long they stayed there, but it seemed as though they would never come out again. As soon as

I had resigned myself to being left alone to suffocate in this car, which was drenched with the scent of artificial pine to mask the reek of vomit from the drunks they picked up at the side of the road every Saturday night, the front door opened and Marchessault appeared on the lawn followed by Doyon, who held a plastic bag inside which I could make out the Yankees cap I'd bought in New York, long after my Expos hat had given up the ghost. And here too the police were wrong, mixing everything up — past and present, royal blue and navy blue, the Expos and the Yankees, who played no part in this story. Doyon put the bag down on the steps, then he and Marchessault started inspecting the garden. They scrutinized every square centimetre of the land, lifted up everything they could lift up, moved everything they could move, and then disappeared into the greenhouses, Marchessault into the one for hybrids and Doyon into the other. Once more I thought they were going to spend their entire lives in there, but then Marchessault came back out, calling to Doyon. They talked for a few moments, gesticulating with their arms, and then headed to the workshop.

Huddled on the back seat of the car, I tried to understand what was happening to me. A child had been kidnapped and I was the one they had come for. They'd come back to Mike and concluded I was guilty twice over because of their names and their blue bikes, the colour of Mike's rain-soaked T-shirt. Evil Marnie had come back to the scene, and it was a race to stop her before she could abandon other victims along the trampled path. But all this made no sense. I hadn't touched Mike, I hadn't kidnapped some kid called Michael wearing a red jacket, but a little voice inside me was whispering that I had no idea, memory is forgetful sometimes, and people don't always remember where the bloodstain that has soaked into the stitches of their sweater came from.

When Doyon and Marchessault got back in the car, I was no longer sure of anything and still didn't know if the two cops were even real. I could see two blue bikes, Superman blue, riding side by side on county road 4. I could hear laughter. I saw a mud-encrusted running shoe and a New York Yankees baseball cap together in a plastic bag. I saw two Michaels, one smiling, the other with no face, entering the glass bottle that imprisoned the city of Kandor.

From the front seat, Marchessault was still soliloquizing. Because of the glass partition separating us, I couldn't hear what he was chattering about, or if he was still blathering about his grandmother, but I knew he was buzzing, that Doyon was cocooned in the vibrations of this buzzing and the murmur that would soon escape the car announcing to the whole of Rivière-aux-Trembles that nasty little Marnie Duchamp was back.

PART THREE

I.

THE INQUIRY

As soon as I arrived at the police station, I started biting my nails, like Billie, like Lucy-Ann after Billie, because the situation was out of control and my nerves were shot, an unexplainable phrase you can only truly understand when it happens to you. Instead of wallowing in self-pity over my own fate, I thought about Pixie's fate, imagining him being sent off to a laboratory to undergo DNA tests, have dental imprints taken or whatever, but the speed with which they decided Pixie wasn't Nuage, the missing kid's cat, eliminated this possibility. Those cretins must have been okay with just opening Pixie's crate and asking the terrified father to bend over it and identify this cat carcass some sicko had put in a box. If the guy wasn't already destroyed, the sight of the stone-dead cat would have done him in. I'm talking about the father because it's generally the father who is there when they lift up the white sheet covering a dead child's face. Nobody dares inflict this sight on the mother, so we go by the principle that the man is stronger and will get over it, he won't have a meltdown that will force you to restrain him and call a doctor to plunge a syringe into his deltoid while two burly guards struggle to pin his arms down by his sides.

Once I felt reassured about Pixie's fate, the image galloping around my head was that of a man with shadows under his eyes and a red-veined face, puffy from insomnia, even though there was nothing to prove that the mother hadn't insisted on seeing Pixie and threatened to rearrange Doyon's moustache on his forehead if he blocked her way. With Lucy-Ann, I had clearly seen the ferocity of mothers calling for their children, and I learned that nothing would stop them from lifting up a ton of bricks if they thought their child lay underneath the rubble. The supposed strength of men, compared to the violence born from women's stomachs, wasn't all that impressive. That made two faces standing over the crate, two destroyed faces that would continue to search for Nuage, calling out his name and hoping their son would reappear running behind the cat.

Marchessault and Doyon also found nothing compromising on my computer, which they decided to keep for a few days anyway to submit to a specialist examination, just in case I'd tampered with it so as to be able to send images of mutilated children hidden behind photos of Billie. I tried to plead my case, telling them the computer was a work tool, but Marchessault was deaf to my arguments. He left me in the room with the two-way mirror, and I killed some time by conjuring up the expression of the guy—maybe a cop, maybe a psychologist—behind the mirror, stroking his chin, trying to determine if my attitude and nervousness were those of a guilty man.

Marchessault left me hanging for two hours, probably while he hassled the other suspect in the case, before coming back to tell me I was free to go, although he was visibly annoyed that he had to let me leave. He could have invoked the supposed assault that had caused him and Doyon to jump on top of me a little earlier, and thus keep me in for another night or two, but he must have realized the paperwork wasn't worth the hassle. There was no evidence to allow him to detain me, so he had no choice but to send home the monster who froze his own cats. "We'll be keeping an eye on you, Richard. Don't leave the area, we'll be seeing you again soon."

After a short chat with the girl who lurked in the corridor, Marchessault disappeared and the girl led me to the front desk, where someone returned Pixie's crate to me, staring as if I was the craziest person ever born. Then I found myself outside on the wet sidewalk, counting the dirty cars carrying their drivers home after the week's first workday. My mind completely empty, I walked through the gentle rain to a shopping street, where I hailed a taxi whose driver agreed to take me to Rivière-aux-Trembles as long as I paid his usurious fare up front.

The driver was one of those people who has an opinion about anything and everything, along with a solution to all the scourges that plague the planet, so I let him reel off his nonsense, every now and then producing a grunt that could have been taken as agreement. Challenging the truths that his great good sense doled out to me would have required me to demolish — with a swift swipe of my hand — the North American right wing in its entirety, and I had other fish to fry.

On my right, a landscape unfurled where trees and sopping fields gathered in the silence. I thought about the fact that I hadn't mentioned Dixie's visits to the inspectors. To assuage my guilt, I moved on to examine the beauty of the female inspector who came to relieve Doyon during my interrogation. There was nothing wrong with her face, but her gaze attacked you straight-on. She had enormous eyes that enfolded you like the huge wings of a bird from some paradise lost and gave the impression that nothing that you might confess while in the bluish shade of those wings could possibly land you behind bars.

This woman's presence beneath the blinding fluorescent lights relieved my fatigue, and I was almost happy to confide in her warm voice. With confidence, I entered the zone of azure shadow that surrounded her expression, then an alarm bell sounded inside my skull: I had to stay on guard and, above all, remember that this woman was a cop, even if nothing in her appearance suggested that under her mask her mug was as ugly as Marchessault's or Doyon's.

To start off with, she asked me the same questions those guys had asked, in case I happened to add to my statement any detail that would allow her to trap me, which wasn't going to happen since I hadn't done anything wrong. After she jotted down my movements on April 18th and asked me to explain who Ronie the Toad was, she opened a large envelope and pulled out a close-up photo of Michael Faber that showed the kid laughing with his head thrown back, as if someone was kneeling just outside the frame tickling his belly button.

Seeing this photo was like a slap, because deep down I knew Michael Faber wouldn't be laughing anymore. Then she slid another photo across to me, this one of the boy standing next to the bike he was given on his twelfth birthday, a ten-speed CCM in sparkling blue on which Michael had fitted a basket for his cat, Nuage. "Take a good look at this child, Mr. Richard," the woman said. "Take all the time you need and tell me how the idea that someone kidnapped him makes you feel."

The cruelty of this remark took my breath away and I felt my cheeks start to burn. This woman knew as well as Marchessault and Doyon did that my daughter had gone missing. Therefore she should know full well that anything that might remind me of her disappearance would rip out my heart. But she dug the knife in deeper and pushed it around in my still-living flesh, using Billie to destabilize me. I told her it made me feel bad, worse than she could possibly imagine, and then I shut my mouth, end of answer — because her gentle voice, I noted bitterly, was a trap that had been set in front of me with the sole purpose of outwitting the moron who would let himself get distracted by her bait and switch.

She saw that, given the state of my soul, I couldn't formulate any more commentary about Michael Faber's disappearance, so she started attacking from a different angle. She pulled another photo out of the envelope, this one of the boy and his cat, to show me just how much the cat looked like Pixie, whom she too had examined in his crate. But the resemblance proved absolutely nothing, and if she was under the impression that I went around freezing every cat that reminded me of Pixie, she was totally off her rocker. I pitied the poor wretch who would have to deal with her obsessions the day she lost her mind.

But I picked up the photo she held out to me and glanced at the boy. He wore ripped jeans, a Canadiens jersey, and running shoes that had a flickering light in the back of the heel. In this photo, the lights weren't flickering, but I could make out the brief flashes with which it must have streaked the twilight when Michael straddled his bike after dinner, just before the Canadiens game. An ordinary boy, to all appearances, just like any other, but one whose smile crushed your heart the moment you knew his fate was not the same as any other boy's.

I left little Michael in peace to concentrate on the cat, whose forehead had a mark in the shape of a cirrostratus cloud, and whose goddamn big green eyes glared at the lens, goddamn big eyes just like those of the cat who waited for his serving of tuna outside my front door. Up until then I hadn't been certain that the cat that came to my porch for dinner was Michael Faber's, but any final doubts were now dispelled. Dixie was Nuage, Nuage was Dixie; it was pointless to expand on the subject any further.

I still didn't see what the cop was driving at with this cat, but I had no reason to lie to her. I was just about to reveal the truth when I noticed her eyes fixed on me, no longer a blue that evoked the clear skies of summer but the metallic grey that announced the inevitable advent of cold weather. "This girl has set a trap for me," I thought next, "a damn bloody trap, and I'm rushing into it like a starving rat." Nor did I have any idea what this trap was precisely, but a surge of suspicion mixed with paranoia inspired me to backtrack. I pushed the photo away, claiming that at the most the cat could pass for one of Pixie's cousins by marriage. If I talked about Dixie and his lost-cat face, I was convinced two big pairs of arms would immediately show up in the interrogation room and drag me into a cell looking out onto the stunning view of the natural resources of Quebec subsoil, or a concrete yard filled with short shadows, where other big arms would stub out their cigs in the crooks of their elbows while admiring the effect of burned flesh amid their tattoos.

Now that the first houses of Rivière-aux-Trembles appeared in the distance, I was no longer convinced I should have kept Dixie's recent arrival in my entourage hidden. I had set the bloody trap for myself. If the cops ever figured out this cat had been visiting me, my silence on the matter would make me doubly suspect. I had wanted to avoid further twisted interrogations that would lead nowhere and pushed away my mental image of Billie, whose childish features were now blurring together with Michael Faber's, but at the same time I had hidden a potential clue to finding a missing child. I had behaved not only in a cowardly fashion but also in a criminal manner, because I knew better than anyone the importance of the smallest detail when a child's life is at stake. If some cretin had behaved so stupidly while there was still a flicker of hope for Billie, I would have been the first to grab his throat and dig my thumbs into his trachea until he spat out the information.

Today I was the utter cretin, the unscrupulous man who had run for his life instead of trying to catch hold of a child lost in the same nebula that had swallowed Billie up. Through the driver's endless babbling—he had just decreed that Parliament needed to be thoroughly reformed from top to bottom, and the salaries of our elected representatives lowered—I could hear Billie's voice in the distance, her soft voice refusing to admit her father was a fucking bastard. "It's not true, is it, Papanoute? It's not true?" And I stayed silent, silent as the motionless trees, silent as the gravestones lined up in the Rivière-aux-Trembles cemetery, which had just disappeared behind me with its frozen dead and its thousands of blackened bones.

Just as the loquacious driver turned into my driveway, I started to tell him to turn around, to drive back to Saint-Alban at a hundred and forty, but then I noticed Dixie on the porch. He must have been hungry and thirsty, so I opened the car door—yes, Billie, like a coward, like a wimp justifying his actions by hiding behind a pack of lies that would have made him vomit just a few hours beforehand—and, along with the crate containing Pixie, melted into the fog that surrounded the house.

෴

A row of grey footprints spotted the floor and led up to the sofa where Dixie was snoring. My uneasy conscience had tugged at me to let him in, just long enough to determine whether I should call the cops, thus offering up my head to an indifferent executioner who wouldn't think twice about slicing open my jugular. I sat in the rocking chair opposite the sofa and watched Dixie sleeping, wondering if little Michael Faber had named him Nuage because of the lightness evoked by his long white hair, which was starting to get matted near the skin, or because of the caramel mark on his forehead in the shape of a cirrostratus cloud whose edges blurred a little towards the ears. I said his name, Nuage, to see if he would react, but Nuage was travelling through the land of dreams, his nose tucked between his front paws, his body jerking as he met another cat in a halo of lamplight down a dark alley.

At eleven on the dot, I stood up, picked up the phone, and left a message at the Saint-Alban police station for Marchessault and Doyon, informing them that Nuage was at my house. This revelation was more or less equivalent to suicide, but at least I could walk towards the gallows with my head held high, no longer worrying that Billie would be ashamed of her father. I put a bowl of fresh water down near the sofa and went upstairs to lie down. I knew I wouldn't sleep, but it was worth a try, just in case the feeling of doing something for the good of a child—who had loved the same cat as Billie, plus or minus a cirrostratus—would envelop my body with the happy numbness that allows tormented souls to forget their lives for a few hours. In any case, I had nothing better to do while I waited for Marchessault and Doyon to show up and take me to the station.

After I switched off the lamp, I let my eyes get used to the darkness and stared at the ceiling, where the knots scattered across the planks of raw wood formed a network of dark constellations spiralling around a nucleus that kept them from dispersing. The universe's balance relies on these poles of attraction; billions of worlds gravitate around them and might one day collide to recreate original chaos. In the midst of these worlds—assuming it's even possible to talk about the middle of infinity—the earth and its sun progress, humans live and die as they spin around other poles of attraction that prevent them from dispersing and convince them that, for the duration of their lifetime, they are at the centre of an infinity they have reduced to their own size.

Billie was my centre, the midpoint of the billions of worlds whose vertigo she spared me, and now through this child I don't even know, people are accusing me yet again of being the cause of my universe's collapse. But how could a planet destroy its own sun? Those who accused me of burying the heat and the light my very survival depended on were unaware that this accusation went entirely against all the laws of physics.

Harassed by questions all day long, I hadn't had the time to reflect calmly on the new explosion the fragility of children had provoked in my narrow life. Now, darkness brought the calm I needed to observe that history was repeating itself, and unless Billie's real attacker was caught, I would be considered a dangerous man until I died. I hadn't touched a hair on Michael Faber's head, but by withholding Dixie-Nuage's presence, I had backed myself into a sticky situation. From the police point of view, this lie by omission would be more evidence of my guilt. Only by admitting my cowardice could I hope to be exonerated.

Covered in rancid sweat, smelling of sickness and fear, I pushed the sheets off and went to brood on my remorse under a scalding shower, where I tried in vain by massacring "Guantanamera" to silence the voices of those who wanted to put me on trial. It had been centuries since I'd sung that song my father loved so much, and months since I'd even thought of my father, who we used to hear whistling through the sound of water as he shaved or had a bath. The interval between the moments I devoted to thinking about my father grew longer the more distant his death became, and perhaps one day it would come to pass that this man who I had idolized would no longer be a constant part of my thoughts. And yet after months of absence, he still had the ability to suddenly appear in my shower in the middle of the night. It must have been his way of giving me an encouraging slap on the back, "Don't get down, kiddo," or letting me know I had no chance of forgetting him, "because the dead won't be forgotten, son, any more than the missing will." I could ignore my fears, my father sang to me, Billie's image would never leave my mind, she would appear less frequently but also more joyfully, just as it was with the cheerful man slathering foam over his face in the steamed-up mirror.

I thanked my father for the unexpected visit, and the notes of "Guantanamera" stayed in my head as I waited until morning, when I would see, coming down the road along the 4th Line path, from the curve partially hidden by a stand of trees, the car driven by a man named Marchessault, whose fetid breath would poison my day.

Even if Doyon hadn't introduced her, I would have recognized her right away — Emmy, Emmy-Lili, Émilie Saint-Pierre, who had grown up to look even more like her brother. Only the colour of her eyes was different, but not their shape, or their gaze, like a night bird that missed nothing. Emmy Saint-Pierre had stared at the river for so long its colour had imprinted itself on her eyes. The river would flow in her forever.

"Lieutenant Saint-Pierre," Doyon muttered after the introductions, "will be leading this inquiry." Then he picked up his pen and left me alone with this woman who stood silent with her hands stuffed into her pants pockets. Leaning against the wall, Emmy-Lou Saint-Pierre measured me up, Emmy-Lou Saint-Pierre evaluated me, probably wondering what I was doing still in her hair and whether she would be able to break me.

"It's been ages," she said eventually, coming to sit down opposite me. She worked for the regional investigation office at the Sûreté du Québec, and she had specifically requested to be put on this case. She considered Michael Faber's disappearance to be her own personal business and had no intention of letting anyone mess with her.

She would take this inquiry all the way. "I don't know what you've been doing for the last thirty years," she said, "but I've been doing just one thing: looking for Mike. So I want to get one thing straight between you and me: we don't know each other, and I'm not going to be giving you favourable treatment just because you thought you were Supergirl."

The situation couldn't have been clearer. Emmy Saint-Pierre hated me—contrary to what her father claimed—and she would continue to hate me no matter what I said or did. In the head of the little girl who saw Mike head off with me on our chrome bikes, nothing had changed. The image fixed in her mind was me taking her brother away forever, and at the same time kidnapping her mother, Jeanne Dubé, who ever since then had only loved her through Mike's memory. Her hatred came from this image, and nothing could alter it. I had thought I was armoured against scorn and anger, but I felt myself shrivel up before Emmy's coldness. Her expression reawakened my guilt, and I hated myself in turn for ceding to the accusations of a girl who allowed herself to judge me when she didn't know a single thing about my fucking life and had no idea what it cost to grow up with a big black hole in your brain.

"I have no idea why I'm here, Emmy, but go ahead, ask your questions and let's get it over with," I retorted, grabbing the glass of water someone had placed in front of me, which suddenly trembled as if an earthquake shook the room I was confined in.

"Where were you exactly on April 18th?" she asked. "Parts of your statement are still unclear. Describe your day to me in detail."

I had already answered this question in minute detail, but I was ready for this. They'd asked me the same thing over and over, with so many different inflections, that I started contradicting myself, mixing up the times, no longer able to remember if it was the day I ate a sub at Mike's on the way out of Saint-Alban or a four-cheese pizza from the pizzeria downtown. In the silence, which was barely disturbed by footsteps in the corridor coming and going at irregular intervals, I talked about the rose-bushes of my father, Alex Duchamp, who had died from a cancer that had stolen his voice. I mentioned the fertil-izer I had needed to buy, the sun that warmed up the car, making it feel like the middle of summer. I also spoke of the happiness I felt at the prospect of scraping my fingers raw in the rosebushes and seeing the drops of blood on my soil-stained skin. Then I described the hairstyle of the waitress at the pizza place—two red braids like Sassette Smurfling—which stood out because braids and the Smurfs were both a little dated.

Staring at the glass of water covered with sticky finger-prints that betrayed my nerves, I didn't forget a single detail—the rubbery mozzarella on the pizza, the hurt finger of the assistant in the hardware store, the too-heavy bag of fertilizer. At the end of my account, my throat was as scratchy as sandpaper and my thick saliva made embarrassing suction sounds that I tried to disguise by articulating certain syllables with exaggeration. I needed a drink of water but didn't dare touch the glass for fear that my hands would shatter it to hide their trembling. Around the glass, the table was immaculate, not a crumb, not a speck of dust on the grey steel, which had been brushed with a product that made its surface and edges shine. Counting crumbs, stains, or dust motes would calm me down, so I looked for scratches on the cold metal, lines I could link up to draw shapes, and then I burst out, "Can someone tell me what the fuck I'm doing here?"

My voice, pitched too high, echoed off the white halls, the footsteps in the corridor paused, and I grabbed hold of the glass of water, which quivered even more. Two or three sips dribbled down my chin and on the old overalls I'd thrown on to work in the greenhouses, and I realized I was dirty, my squirrel tail was wonky, and my nails were encrusted with dirt.

"I have to go to the washroom," I murmured.

"End of the hall, turn right," Emmy replied. "I'll give you five minutes. I'm sure you're smart enough to come back."

I left the room with my head down, ashamed that my filthy nails had been seen not only by the perfect Emmy—who had not a single hair on her head out of place—but also by the unknown people who observed us from the other side of the two-way mirror in the interrogation room. The blackened nails placed me in a position of weakness and were one more item on the list of things against me. Murderers have dirty hands, I thought as I slowed my pace, not remembering from where I'd dragged up this phrase, and then the little voice that served as my conscience seized it and began repeating it. Murderers have dirty hands, murderers have dirty hands, soiled hands, the voice insisted, while I tried frantically to scrub my nails under the boiling water gushing out of the tap, and plunged my face into the sink after lathering it with a layer of hand soap that would have made an effective paint stripper.

The reflection the mirror showed me when I lifted my head back up was that of a woman on the edge of hysteria. I almost smashed the mirror but then got hold of myself. "You can't crack, Marnie," the voice commanded, "you just can't." I took a deep breath and tried to fix my hair, smoothing it down with my fingers, red from the hot water, and twisting the elastic around it, and then I bit my lip. "You can't crack," I said, walking back to the interrogation room, leaving the scent of cheap soap behind me.

"Six minutes, thirty seconds, Marnie," Emmy announced, tapping her watch, as I sat back down across from her. I didn't say anything. I had no way of recovering those few rebellious seconds that offended Emmy Saint-Pierre's almost military strictness. I waited for her to carry on and stared at the glass of water, which some charitable — or sadistic — soul had refilled. My sticky fingerprints were still visible, making the fresh water appear cloudy. As for Emmy Saint-Pierre, she was staring at my face, which was covered in red patches from the hot water and soap. Without taking her eyes off me, she moved forward, rested her arms on the table, and tossed out yet another of those comments intended to destabilize the poor idiots already teetering on the edge of a pit, at the bottom of which a bunch of starving lions prowl nervously.

"Marnie, you claim you've never seen this kid, so I don't understand how you know what colour his bike and his sweater were. Can you explain that to me?"

I had never mentioned the boy's bike, or his sweater, or his damn shoes. Marchessault and Doyon had slipped those elements into our conversation themselves so they could later claim I'd confirmed what they said, but those jerks were wrong, they got everything mixed up, confusing Mike's bike with Michael's, the T-shirt of one with the sweater of the other. But how could I explain to Emmy Saint-Pierre that I too had muddled up Mike and this other Michael? If I admitted to this woman that I sometimes felt guilty about Mike's disappearance, I'd be practically begging for a hanging or a lethal injection. On the other hand, Mike Superman Saint-Pierre was my only way out of this situation.

"I was in shock," I replied. "I didn't know what I was being accused of, and my first thought was of Mike, his blue bike and his red T-shirt. You're not the only one who hasn't forgotten Mike, Emmy, and it's not my fault if kids all like the same colours."

When I stopped speaking, Emmy's imperturbable face was flushed red like mine. Little circles of heat blotched her cheeks, and for a moment I thought she was going to lose her poise and jump at me.

"Don't bring Mike into this," she warned me. But Mike was the only reason I was there, nobody else, and I pointed this out to her as I looked at my hands, my nails. I hadn't managed to clean them properly; instead I had forced the dirt right down into the tender flesh below them. An urgent need to wash, to scrub myself until I flayed off my own skin, gripped me again. I needed to leave that room immediately and plunge into a bath scented with sugary fruit and overflowing with Mr. Bubble foam.

Without waiting for Emmy's next attack, I stood up and announced I was leaving. She had nothing serious enough to detain me, no concrete proof, no fingerprints. I was free to hit the road if I felt like it.

"I wouldn't advise that," she retorted, but I ignored her and headed towards the door. If I hadn't been wearing the shapeless overalls, she would have noticed my knees were twitching, and if she had just raised her voice a notch or two she would have crushed me and sent me docilely back to my chair. But I walked straight ahead, opened the door, and went down the hall to the exit without turning around, convinced that one of her henchmen would come and grab me by the neck to bring me back to Emmy's lair.

When I finally set foot in the building's forecourt, I felt as though I was walking in a dream. Day had given way to night without my seeing the sky darken behind Wolf Hill. In my absence, time had withdrawn into the light just as it had done near Trembles River. The glow from the streetlamps reflecting on the shining road seemed unreal, as if painted with a lacquer that slowed down the rain's spasms when it came into contact with the ground. I was disoriented in the sudden darkness, watching the rain soak my skin without feeling its coolness. Its scent of rotten leaves gave way to the oily odour given off by a snack bar's deep fryers, and I felt deprived of the simple pleasure that water from the heavens can bring to those who delight in the approach of clouds.

For the last thirty years, rain hadn't affected me unless it was propelled by a stormy wind, and Emmy Saint-Pierre had just given it another reason to fall beside me, so beautiful, though, so melodious. Moving like a sleepwalker, I reached the road and sat down on a soaked bench. The nightmare was starting again. Once more the witches were going to chase off the phantoms.

Mr. Bubble has rejoined the ranks of family friends. Standing on the edge of the bath, he offers me his smile of days gone by, when we used to tell each other stories that always had a happy ending. I invent another one for him in which there are no missing children, no drowned pandas or bears, but a little girl called Squeerelle, who has just been saved from the perils of the river by Superman and taken to a castle built on the summit of an ice mountain. I sculpt the castle for Mr. Bubble, this fortress where nothing can reach me, and shape Krypto the dog, Superman's faithful ally. Then I sink under the water, letting the castle drift towards my face, and rise to the surface holding in my hands the ruins of an indestructible fortress, far from which, on a delicate skiff of matter unknown on earth, bobs Krypto the dog.

On the wicker stool, my watch indicates that I've been soaking for one hour and four minutes—no more and no less, Emmy-Lili—in Mr. Bubble's foamy strawberry-scented soap, my favourite forever, ever since Michael Superman Saint-Pierre, crouching down in a patch of wild strawberries as big as Liechtenstein, told me about Lois Lane's predilection for these little berries. In that hour I'd had all the leisure in the world to tell Mr. Bubble a whole pack of stories. He was astonished to see me in such a good mood, and even more to hear me sing in the middle of the stories ancient airs his predecessors had taught him: *Here comes the candle to light you to bed and here comes the chopper to chop off your HEAD.* On the last word I pressed my hands together; too bad for the one who got caught, the last ones are always the last. I crushed the little foam body, which would soon be reincarnated as a beaver or a rabbit, with ears made of sparkling iridescent bubbles whose curves reflected the violets and the periwinkle blues of a fairy-tale sunset.

Every ten minutes I pull out the plug to let some of the water trickle out, replacing it with water so hot that scrolls of steam rise up from the eddy of bubbles escaping from the pressure of the water. I add a little more Mr. Bubble, just a tiny bit, just a quarter capful, to build other stories and melt off the muck from the Saint-Alban police station still clinging to my skin. My nails are clean now, so is my hair, the red skin on my hands and feet is as wrinkled as an elephant's, but there's still dirt, I can feel it, that will never go away until the end of my final story, the story of Mike and Marn at the river, whose ending I will write one day. I'll sing that story at the top of my voice and Mr. Bubble will flap his hands as I fling foam up to the ceiling. For now, though, Mr. Bubble is cold, Marn is tired, Marn wants to go to bed, but she knows this is impossible because nobody can sleep when the past meets up with the present and the two work in league to assail you with questions, like in school on days when you've forgotten all the facts you used to know. "Who discovered America, Marnie? Who invented the wheel? Who said this, or that, and why? Who, who, who? Where were you on April 18th, Marn? What did you do to Mike? What colour was his blue Superman bike? What are you hiding, Marn? What? What? What?"

Before the final question, Mr. Bubble flies against the wall again; too bad for him, the last ones will be the last ones. I pull out the plug and the water gurgles away. As the water level drops, my body is left covered in iridescent foam. It looks like one of those old trees colonized by lichens, those trunks that gobble up lost souls, confined in one of the circles of hell. This is where Emmy Saint-Pierre had sent me back to: the heart of a silent forest containing the cries of the damned, where the only sound is that of my voice calling Mike.

I had hardly expected Emmy to clamour to be president of my fan club, but I had at least hoped to find an ally in her, someone who would hold out a hand to me in the forest. But instead, Emmy hated me, Emmy accused me, barely disguising the word "witch," even though her narrative was supposedly founded on the rational analysis of facts and clues.

"I've never seen Michael Faber, Mr. Bubble, do you hear me? I never touched his bike and I never pushed it into the ditch. Do you hear me?" But Mr. Bubble isn't listening any more than Emmy Saint-Pierre was. Caught between the water heater and the laundry basket, he's humming the song I was just singing, tapping the rhythm with his stiff little plastic feet. He isn't happy, I get it, and he's going to sulk until I apologize. We'll see about that later. In the meantime, I have to rinse the scum from the tub, remove all the grime, rip off the lichen, and get out of the forest. "Here comes the chopper..." Mr. Bubble continues, "to chop off your..." and then he claps his hands just as my foamy body is about to reach the edge of the forest, and I fall, I fall on the icy tiled floor, while Mike's muffled voice travels through a clump of red stars, a swarm of flashing red dwarfs, to whisper in my ear, "Run to the village!" The words that have been torturing me for thirty years disappear in the fog that enters me. "How can you manage?" becomes shrouded in mist, while Mike keeps repeating "Run to the village, run to the village..." And I understand that Mike was simply exhorting me to run silently far away from the devilish circle opening up near the magic swimming hole. "Run to the village!" I understand that the hand Mike was so afraid of was not nasty little Marnie's hand.

Marchessault wasn't involved in Operation Nuage. When the car pulled up by my porch, I saw Doyon get out first, a Sherlock Holmes–style cap plonked on his bald dome to protect it from the rain. Then he clumsily tried to pull on a raincoat that was partly inside out. For a moment I thought I was in an Inspector Clouseau movie. I expected to see Marchessault struggling to haul his carcass out of the car, cursing the bad weather, but it was the girl who got out, impeccably dressed in her oilskin jacket and brown leather boots. Immediately, the atmosphere altered, and the scenario switched registers. Clouseau folded his raincoat over his left arm and took a cat crate out of the trunk, then followed the girl, both studiously avoiding the puddles of water in the yard. The punchline misfired. Standing by my bedroom window, I waited for them to knock before I went downstairs. I took my time, aware that these moments of liberty were perhaps my last for an unspecified period.

"Where's the cat?" Doyon demanded without even bothering to say hello.

The last time I'd seen the old fleabag he was lying on the sofa licking his tail thoroughly, but he must have run off to hide when he heard the car engine or the banging on the door. Cats don't like cops.

I set off to look for Nuage with Doyon—who hadn't even bothered to take his boots off—on my heels, adding his enormous footprints to Dixie's delicate tracks, which meant I'd have to wash the entire floor if Dixie didn't show up pretty quickly. "Here, Dixie," I called. As for the female officer, she stayed by the door, sizing up my living room inch by inch, probably looking for other footprints, other clues, the kind of evidence an imbecile of my ilk would never have suspected might hasten his path to jail before he even had time to call his mother.

I finally spotted the tip of Dixie's tail in the kitchen as he tried to contort himself around one of the legs of the buffet under which he had taken refuge. It was a job and a half getting him out of there, but with Doyon's help I eventually succeeded; he lifted up the buffet while I grabbed hold of Dixie. Once again, we were in *Pink Panther* territory, minus the music, although I was seized with the desire to hum a little bit of the tune just to mock Doyon. He told me to shut Dixie in the cage as soon as I could get hold of any part of his anatomy other than his tail. We would laugh some other time. Dixie was dead set against me picking him up, so he treated me to a brutal swipe of his claws, gouging two long grooves along my left arm and drawing fresh blood—"red, Billie, the colour of late-August apples"—and then gave me the dirtiest look, containing a curse borrowed from the alley-cat lexicon and printed in capital letters. I was ashamed to trap Dixie like this, but I didn't even try to make excuses, knowing full well he would just spit them back in my face. Cats don't like traitors.

I told Doyon and the girl to wait while I went to attend to my wounds. When I came back, I found them scrutinizing photos of Nuage and comparing them to Dixie, who stubbornly kept his head tucked between his paws. I could have helped them in their task by certifying that Dixie was Nuage, but I felt as though I'd cooperated plenty for the time being.

"You'll be coming to the station with us," the girl said, taking my coat down from its peg. I suggested that we all sit in the kitchen instead—cops like kitchens—but I guess the girl didn't care for the furniture or the décor, because she tossed my coat at me and gestured for Doyon to bring the cage.

Three quarters of an hour later I was once again sitting on the uncomfortable metal chair that had been gathering dust since the previous day in the Saint-Alban police station's interrogation room, waiting for the arrival of the lawyer I'd hired a few hours earlier while I paced up and down my living room to the tune of "Guantanamera." I wanted to play it safe, so I dragged Béchard, my literary agent, out of bed before dawn and tasked him with immediately tracking down a criminal lawyer who liked the great outdoors. After just forty-five minutes, Béchard called me back with the news that one Jean-Pierre Maheux had agreed to take on my case in return for a fee nobody dared say out loud. I quickly realized that a bandit would be more qualified to defend me than an honest man, and I asked Béchard for Maheux's contact details. I would call him myself, with no middlemen to inflate the fee by ten percent. After I explained the situation to him, Maheux told me he'd be in Saint-Alban by noon, and I started breathing again.

I was waiting alone in the interrogation room while Doyon and the female inspector attended to their business. I couldn't bring myself to call Émilie Saint-Pierre just by her surname, even though I called Doyon Doyon without any problem. It must have been a gallantry thing, or maybe machismo, depending on what you call the social skills certain backward people try to demonstrate, but be that as it may, Émilie Saint-Pierre's name didn't fit at all well with her job, and would have been more appropriate for an actress on a children's television series. This impression probably came from my unconscious creating its own stereotypes, but a name like Jane Adamsberg or Harriet Bosch would have suited her better, just as Doyon would have been more credible as a Marlowe. Émilie was far too gentle a name, too innocent to be getting involved in the criminal world. Judging from her appearance, little Émilie must have needed sharp elbows, and had maybe had to nip a couple of swaggerers before her colleagues would take her seriously. If she'd climbed the hierarchy this quickly, it was because she knew how to fight, and land a few blows below the belt if necessary, just as a way of crushing the balls in her way. Despite this, I found it easier to cast her as Snow White.

Since they had refused to allow me any reading material to pass the time, concerned that I might try to choke myself by eating newspaper or maybe slice my veins open with the staples from a brochure about eradicating street gangs, I was making up stories about Émilie Saint-Pierre's life. Marchessault and Doyon were also part of these stories, playing the role of good guy and bad guy in turn, preferably the bad guy. My animosity towards Marchessault and Doyon wasn't personal in the slightest. It was simply a product of our positions, our respective roles. We weren't standing on the same side of the fence, so when I saw one of them approaching the border that separated us I would shoot immediately.

I could have used the wait time to prepare my defence instead of letting my imagination get carried away about honest workers, but since my lawyer's clock had already started ticking, it seemed like a pointless waste of energy. I could have also tried to figure out how Michael Faber might have disappeared, just in case a genius brainwave allowed me to make a connection between the kid's disappearance and Dixie's appearance, because I truly hoped with all my soul that they would find this boy. But visualizing him at the back of a barn or the bottom of a grain silo was beyond my capability. I'd already been through this gallery of horrors with Billie, and I knew each painting was more hideous than the last. I had no desire to take another guided tour of the place. This burden belonged to Michael Faber's parents now, and even though it was something I wouldn't wish on my worst enemy, nothing could stop them from pushing open the door to this grotesque museum. The only way they could come out of it without going completely crazy would be by instinctively relegating the worst images to some part of their brains that could be hermetically sealed at the first sign of craziness.

When the door to the interrogation room opened at last, Émilie Saint-Pierre, wearing a princess veil, was pursuing a drug dealer at a hundred and fifty an hour on a snowy highway, accompanied by a Marchessault who was sweating even more than he did in real life. Émilie Saint-Pierre came into the room, not visibly affected by the ordeal I'd just been putting her through, followed by Doyon and a short guy in a suit who could be none other than Jean-Pierre Maheux, my lawyer.

Considering the rate the lawyer charged, it would have been nice if Béchard had found someone a little taller; at least I would have felt I was getting my money's worth. Maheux didn't suffer from dwarfism, but from my perspective sitting there on the chair he looked short enough to walk across the room and under the table without hitting his head. This element of his physique annoyed me, because how can you take seriously someone who trips over his own tie, or who has to ask clients to stay seated if he wants to speak to them face to face? However, it quickly became clear that Maître Maheux knew his stuff and, like Asterix and Napoleon, compensated for his small stature by a ferocity equalled only by his perspicacity.

After the customary formalities, Émilie Saint-Pierre informed us that Michael Faber's parents had identified the cat I had supposedly taken prisoner, and it was indeed Nuage. "So, Mr. Richard, please explain to us how the cat ended up at your house."

I replied that I had no idea whatsoever. The cat had shown up on my porch one fine April afternoon, I fed him, and he came back. That was the absolute truth, but neither Doyon nor Saint-Pierre seemed inclined to believe me.

"Which fine April afternoon was this?" Doyon enquired, gnawing at a wooden pencil that had already been assaulted by teeth—hopefully his own, for hygiene's sake.

"The twelfth," I replied without needing to think about it. I remembered because it was Easter Sunday, I had just talked to Régine earlier in the day, and I was devastated. I went out for a walk after the phone conversation, and when I got back the cat was waiting for me.

Doyon couldn't have gone any redder if I'd slapped him. As for Émilie Saint-Pierre, she took out her pen and battered me with the waves of her oceanic eyes, clearly hoping to catch me in the undertow. "Mr. Richard, this cat disappeared at the same time as the boy, which was the eighteenth of April," she clarified, emphasizing the date, "so either you're mistaken, or you take us for idiots."

I wasn't mistaken, and I didn't think they were idiots, although I would have definitely chosen a word in the same syntagmatic field to describe them. I could see only one solution to the problem: contrary to all appearances, Dixie was not Nuage.

But when I uttered this blindingly obvious truth, Doyon repeated what Saint-Pierre had just said, and wanted to know if I really thought they were stupid. A heavy silence fell over the room, then Émilie Saint-Pierre took control of the interrogation. Her questions came one after another like gunfire: clear, precise, direct. But every time I was about to open my mouth, Maheux ordered me to stay quiet, or stated bluntly that the inspector was going too far. "Don't say a single word more, Richard. My client doesn't have to answer such questions. You're out of line, inspector," and other such formulaic responses that made me look seriously guilty, just like everyone who is ever represented by a lawyer. But Maheux was right; if I had tried to answer these ridiculous questions, I would have necessarily contradicted myself because Émilie Saint-Pierre's allegations made absolutely no sense.

When the two hands on the wall clock reached 12 with an audible click that made me jump, Maheux gathered up his papers and decreed that the interrogation was over.

I had told them about Dixie's existence thinking it would help Michael Faber, but the end result was that I'd merely managed to mix up the cards and cast myself as the two of spades, or the halfwit who skids on a banana skin he didn't spot on the smooth slope he thought he was walking on. I had hoped to leave the police station with a happy heart, a lighter conscience, my soul at peace with the world, but Doyon and Émilie Saint-Pierre had loaded a half-ton bag on my shoulders. Before I crossed the threshold of the interrogation room, I turned back to remind them that I was on their side in this, that I wanted to see Michael Faber come out of the woods safe and sound just as much as they did, that the damn cat had an amazing talent for being everywhere at once, and that I was anything but guilty. When Maheux heard me pronounce the word "guilty" he tried to stop me, but I ploughed on. I was prepared to subject myself to the most absurd lines of questioning to help save this child, and I wanted them to know it.

"So tell us the truth then, Mr. Richard," retorted Émilie Saint-Pierre. A riptide hit me and I had to hold on to the door frame.

I had been told the same thing once before, long ago. Another cop, sitting at my table with his hands folded, had accused me of lying. History was repeating itself, and it was just as incomprehensible as it had been the first time around. I had lost my daughter, my precious little girl with hazel eyes, and in the same instant I had become a monster.

"I'm going to drive you home," Maheux murmured, taking hold of my arm.

I told him I needed some air and left him standing there with his clock ticking.

When I opened my eyes again, my surroundings were nothing but a jumble of colours, shapes, and corners I couldn't understand. If I'd had the brainpower right then, I might have thought I was dead, but the concepts of life, death, and survival were beyond my understanding. I felt absolutely nothing, and my mind was entirely empty of thoughts. I was nothing but two eyes without awareness skimming over nameless objects, because there was nothing behind the eyes, no soul, no past, no memory that could label reality. The person doing the looking knew neither the word "I" nor its meaning. The person doing the looking didn't even know himself.

Then, gradually, words that expressed how I belonged in the world started to surface, and I remembered who I was. I was a woman, my name was Marnie, I had fallen. The images scrolled through my mind again: Mr. Bubble, the foam, Michael, the scalding water, and Krypto the dog. "Run to the village!" And then I felt the cold. My frozen feet twitched, a searing pain split my skull, and I slid over to the wall to grab the towel hanging on a hook there. Fighting the pain, I struggled into a sitting position and wrapped the towel around me, one buttock still on the sopping wet floor.

I was shivering like a child who has been pulled out of an icy river. A few tears ran down my cheek, but I didn't know if I was crying because I had so narrowly avoided a stupid death or because I was still alive. I imagine people who wake up after jumping off a bridge or out of a fourth-floor window must feel the same way: a sudden and profound understanding of the void in parallel with the feeling that everything's all fucked up and now they have to start living again, start washing their clothes, putting their shoes on, walking the dog, answering the phone.

If my head had struck the tub I would probably still be there, stone-cold dead on the chilly tiles, covered with dried foam, my skin red from the blood seeping from every part in contact with the floor. That's how I would have been discovered—my eyes bulging, my hand reaching out towards Mr. Bubble—or else in the calm pose of dead people who didn't see it coming, suddenly struck by darkness right in the middle of a sentence.

I shivered a little at the idea that death could be so sudden and unexpected. All it takes is a wet surface, a dangerously placed carpet at the top of a staircase, a moment of inattention while you're distracted by the memory of a happy day, and suddenly you're no longer there. Your life is snuffed out in an instant, and the only witness left is a mute corpse. Seen from this perspective, survival verged on the miraculous. Assassins understand this fragility. Maybe they murder people just to experience it. A quick blow of the hammer and pouf, the victim no longer exists, except as a victim whose skull has been turned into mush. In my own way I had also experienced life's precariousness when Michael and I stomped on the sand where grasshoppers hid. Each insect made a dry crunch underfoot, like a bone being crushed, and suddenly the creature no longer existed except as a purée.

But for all that, I wasn't a criminal. Mike had told me so before I went to sleep on the icy tiles, Mike had whispered it to me, "Run to the village," while he waved his arms around to create a diversion, leading the enemy far away from me, like a bird pretending to be injured to protect its chicks. Mike hadn't been struck with some kind of craziness during the storm; no stupor had overcome his lucidity. He had seen what the trees stopped me from seeing, and then he laid his broken wing on the ground, offering himself up to the creature being lit up by the flashes of the storm. In the space of a moment, he became a bird and transformed his wounded animal dance into a sacrificial ritual with no other purpose than to keep me away from the evil advancing through the forest. All the elements of this puzzle I had been trying to put together for years fell into place during the brief moment before I fainted, all except one: the piece that showed the face of the creature, man or beast, that had compelled Mike to act out his crazy alarm under the pouring rain to save little Marnie.

Should I rejoice about this revelation or, on the contrary, should I accuse the child in the story of stupidity, this little girl dressed in boys' overalls who was unable to recognize the reality under her friend's pallor? But the question no longer needed to be asked because it was too late to go trawling back to examine my conscience. The child in the story could not rewrite the plot. All that mattered now was the fact that the other child had distracted the wolf and led it off into the forest to spare the little girl from its fury.

I tried to stand up, but a burning, stabbing pain radiated out from my right hip, forcing me to change position and press my knees up against my chest, flopping over to the side. I waited for the burning to ease off while I thought about how Mike had saved my life with a few words that would have actually signed my death warrant if I had heard them. If fear had not effectively paralyzed me, and if I'd understood he was telling me to run, I would've tried to pull Mike along with me — that's what children do, that's what best friends do, friends who hold hands as night falls — and then the thing would have caught both of us near Catfish Lake or somewhere else, this monster that would disorient the Rivière-aux-Trembles sun. Thanks to Mike, I was alive, well and truly alive, and yet pain was forcing me to move. I gripped hold of the edge of the bathtub and, supporting myself against the wall whose ceramic tiles quivered in the intensity of the light, I managed to stand up.

I swallowed two Atasol without daring to look at my reflection in the mirror and hauled my sorry ass to bed. Despite the weight of my winter blankets, it took a long time for me to warm up, and I fell asleep out of sheer exhaustion just at the moment when Michael, near Catfish Lake, lost his running shoe under the storm-washed sky.

Behind Wolf Hill the final sun was setting. "I can hear you, Mike, I can finally hear you."

My pounding head awoke me a few hours later. Behind the church a sombre dawn was breaking, shot through with a light that extended the night's darkness into the deep blue of the clouds. As I felt my neck, I figured out the cause of the heavy throbbing between my ears. An enormous goose egg, covered with a scab of dried blood, had grown out of the back of my skull during the night. I needed a shower, which I took sitting down in the tub. I had just finished drying my hair when the phone rang. I immediately thought it must be Émilie Saint-Pierre, thinking she must have heard me screaming the words her brother had spoken. As my father's old answering machine clicked on, I strained my ears to hear. The voice coming from the living room was a stern voice, difficult to make out because it was whispering and holding its breath. The sound, absorbed by the walls, carpet, and furniture, was nothing but a distant rustling, like the murmur of an insect colony chomping through a wooden door from the inside.

At the beep that indicated the end of the message I went downstairs to the living room with a towel wrapped around my body. I rewound the tape and pressed play. "I guess Michael Saint-Pierre wasn't enough for you, hey?" the voice whispered hoarsely. "You needed another one. Another defenceless child. But it's gonna stop right here. If the police don't lock you up we'll take care of you ourselves. We want no more of you in Rivière-aux-Trembles, Marnie Duchamp!"

Leaning on the back of an armchair, I felt faint as the words, spat rather than whispered, spooled out. This man understood nothing, nothing about anything. He had no idea that my only crime was that I hadn't heard Mike properly. Secure in his crass ignorance, he couldn't judge my innocence. "You don't understand," I muttered, "you just don't get it, you jerk," and then the beep that indicated the message was over rang out, waking up the crushed grasshoppers — Nasty, evil little Marnie, they chanted — and their song mingled with the scratching of wood-eating insects, longhorn beetles or termites whose jaws worked away gnawing at the wood of the door that was closing on me.

"Call Marchessault, Marn, call him right now, don't let the gossips break your cursed little life a second time," ordered the voice inside me, which had slipped in through the muffled snacking of the longhorn beetles and replaced the other man's hoarse voice. "Call before it drives you crazy!" I had just picked up the phone when, through the big living room window, I saw an ambulance zoom past the house, followed by the barking of the dogs that belonged to my neighbour two doors down. I was suddenly hurled backwards into the sun-warmed forest, where the yapping of Rex, Chet, and Lucy grew louder, a series of excited calls indicating that they were tracking down a child and hunting his attacker, whether assassin, kidnapper, or witch. With numb limbs I walked to the kitchen window, convinced that a group of men armed with batons and guns were preparing a pyre for me in the garden. But the yard was empty. My executioners were hiding, just waiting for me to make one false move before streaming out from inside the greenhouses or behind the trees.

In the distance, towards the river, the dogs were still howling. Rex, Chet, and Lucy. I splashed my face with cold water and went back to sit in the living room. The clock indicated it was eighteen minutes past nine when a dead silence struck the house. Then the ambulance drove back in the other direction. Michael Faber's body had just been discovered.

After I abandoned Maheux at the police station, I wandered aimlessly, wondering what the hell I was doing in this dreary little town, where the passersby stared at me as though I had rabies. I stopped to examine my face in a store window, to see if my hair was all messed up or if there was a thread of drool trickling down my chin. I looked normal, I thought, assuming that a man walking at the slow pace of someone who no longer knows where he is going can fade into the noon bustle without raising the slightest concern.

This is what people must have noticed, the aimlessness and lack of faith that made my face look blank. I did have one goal though: to forget this entire story. But how can you forget something when it impregnates every particle of the air you breathe? If at that very moment I had been crossing a high enough bridge, I think I would have thrown myself off, since I could see no way to forget other than by interrupting the freefall of my thoughts with an impressive dispersal of grey matter. I would have jumped into the wind with my arms outstretched. The choppy surface of the water snaking under the bridge would have become my destination, and the serenity of a brief faith would have flashed across my face. Besides the peaceful shimmering that surrounds death, this was probably what had driven L.A. to get out her kitchen knife—this faith, this certainty of meeting Billie in the long hallway leading up to heaven.

Frozen at the junction of Saint-Alban's two main arteries, I was thinking about death—how it is the only truth worth anything, the only unerring certainty—when a police car stopped at the red light. In the back seat, a woman, who also seemed to be devastated by an absence of hope, stared at the indistinguishable pedestrians who dissolved into the anonymity of a scene whose "why" escaped her. Then a car horn made her jump and she turned her head towards me. I knew that face, the oval with the reddened eyes frozen in the pallor of a statue. It belonged to the woman from the funeral procession that had welcomed me on my arrival in Rivière-aux-Trembles, the widow or the orphan being dragged along by life against her will, and it also belonged to all the women dressed in black who stand at dawn in front of the horizon devoured by the sea or the mountains. Not a single thing in this woman's face had changed since the convoy passed, not the fear, not the sadness, not the incomprehension, all of which were crushing her.

I lifted my hand mechanically, as if greeting a friend, and her clouded expression cleared for a moment. The lights turned green and she pressed her palm to the car window as she recognized me. Then she spoke a word, the same one several times. "Run," her lips said, "run," then her face was carried along by the flow of traffic. So I ran,

I raced stupidly after the car, with no idea why I was running or if I was heading in the right direction, and then I stopped, out of breath, as the car turned into a street that aspired to be a boulevard.

My heart was still pounding in my chest when I staggered into the McDonald's whose enormous sign dominated the buildings on one side of the street. I wasn't hungry, but I ordered an apple pie along with my coffee to reassure the cashier, who must have thought I was either suffering from chronic asthma or had just escaped from a gang of armed pursuers. As she poured my coffee I glanced around the half-empty restaurant. Curiously, there were very few children colouring in pictures of Ronald or stuffing fries into their mouths. The customers were mostly workers who distractedly swallowed their Big Macs or Quarter Pounders, or retired people reading the newspaper and discussing prostate issues over trays filled with crumpled wrappers and disposable cups.

I chose an isolated table near a window on which someone had drawn a smiley face with ketchup. You don't need any special artistic talent to draw a smiley face, but this one was actually pretty stylish, almost as though it had been painted with acrylic and a spatula. The limbless head was probably intended to make people at this table smile, but it was futile on my part to hope for a semblance of joy when fate had reset the counters to zero and would restart yet again every time a bad thing happened within a thirty-kilometre radius of me. This is how it would always be. I had been branded by the disappearance of the love of my life, and I would never be forgiven for it anywhere.

As I poured packages of sugar into my coffee I gazed out at the drizzle, which had been constant since the day before, trying to chase away the image of the infinite spiral gaping open in front of me, and I wondered what had got into me to make me run after a total stranger. Madness, maybe, the violence that was barrelling into my life again and making me cling to the slightest hint of sympathy or recognition.

I knew nothing about this woman except that she was pale, but I felt as though she and I were in the same boat, tossed around by the current, with no oars to steady the vessel, which was spinning as we headed into the rapids. And anyway, what was she doing in that police car? Had she been intercepted as she tried to ram her own car into a concrete block with a family photo taped to the dashboard? Had she disturbed the peace, broken a window, stolen a ton of romance novels to prove she was still alive? She didn't look like a thief or a drama queen. I would have put her more in the category of girls who would knock back a pint of cheap gin to ensure she wouldn't have the strength to hurl herself out the window. A girl who had many, many reasons to jump overboard, but clung to the idea that the sea was beautiful.

I was turning all these hypotheses over in my head — pointlessly, because my instincts were quietly telling me this woman had been arrested for the same reason as me. I hadn't noticed the cops who were with her, but

I would bet anything one of them was called Doyon or Marchessault. She was the other suspect. Her son or daughter must have vanished in the forest years ago, leaving no trace, and the crime had never been pinned on the piece of shit who did it, and so people had decided to give this piece of shit a name—her name—so they wouldn't have to live with the uncertainty. They had stuck a label to her forehead: "Keep away from children." People pointed at her, stealing her chance to quietly mourn her child, and she was a suspect every time some kid lost all concept of time and came home later than expected, their head full of exploits that they decided not to relate when faced with the heavy, reproachful atmosphere in the kitchen, where the cold dinner had turned hard on the plates. With the exception of minor details, her story had to be something like that—in other words, the same as mine.

I chucked the coffee and apple pie into the garbage—to hell with scruples—and made my way out of the restaurant. At a table near the door, a young father stuffed his face in the company of his little girl, age around six or seven, one of only two kids brightening up this old fogeys' haunt. While the father ogled a girl passing by on the sidewalk, the child finished a jigsaw puzzle that contained most of the farmyard animals, from the hen to the pig via the cow, whose relative the dad was currently chewing. Next to the puzzle, a local tabloid showed a full-page shot of Michael Faber, smiling his big, happy-kid smile. I wanted to grab hold of the father's shirt and shout in his face that he must never let his daughter out of his sight, never, but instead I merely asked him if I could borrow the newspaper. With his mouth full of half-chewed hamburger, he nodded yes, and I folded up the paper and slipped it into my coat pocket. They could add this minor theft to the other crimes being pinned on me.

Unsure how to fill the next few hours, I paced up and down outside the McDonald's for a while. Eventually I pointed my feet in the direction of the police station. If I wanted to help the child smiling deep in my pocket, I could only do so with Doyon, Marchessault, and Émilie Saint-Pierre, too bad if they handcuffed me and shut me up at the same time. With a bit of luck, my voice would carry through the prison bars, despite being notoriously airtight to the shouts of shackled men. With a bit of luck... In any case, if they had arrested the woman from the funeral procession, it must mean there was something new in the Michel Faber case. There was no point in paying for a taxi to Rivière-aux-Trembles only to find a car outside my house, waiting to take me immediately on the same journey in reverse, minus the blue flashing lights. Might as well get it over with right away and save the taxpayers the cost of a few extra litres of gas.

I asked to speak to Marchessault or Doyon. I didn't trust Émilie Saint-Pierre's contained aggression, which might explode in your face if you had the misfortune to press the detonator hidden somewhere inside her shirt, buttoned up three-quarters of the way. Marchessault and Doyon had the advantage of being clear and direct, with no grey areas. If you got on their nerves, the reaction would be immediate. They might hurl their bad temper at your face, and you'd understand you only had a fifty-percent chance of keeping your balls intact if you persisted in playing the clown.

"They're busy," Officer Tremblay replied as he filled in forms behind the reception desk. Then he pointed at the row of chairs against the wall: I could wait for them there or come back later. I chose the row of chairs and unfolded the newspaper I'd stolen from McDonald's. One of the two articles devoted to Michael Faber's disappearance described the young boy's habits and reported comments from his tearful parents, their neighbours, the child's classmates, his teacher, the guy from the corner store, the guy who delivered the flyers, and his cousin by marriage. If there had been any way of interviewing the little boy's cat, the pseudo-journalist who wrote the article would no doubt have found a way of attributing two or three bits of nonsense to him.

As a bonus, the reader was rewarded with a photo of the abandoned bike, its caption dripping with false compassion. It all brought back memories of the gang of vultures who had gotten hold of pictures of Billie in order to increase the print run of their rag, and had hassled L.A. and me, trying to get us to cry into their microphones and blow our noses on their shitty newspaper. I wanted to damn well set fire to this heap of crap, or tear it into a million pieces and flush them down the shittiest toilet in the men's washroom, whose door, adorned with the asexual representation of a fellow who'd never pissed in his life, was at the end of the hallway where the row of chairs stood. But I wanted to read the other article first, the one devoted to the police investigation.

First, Sergeant Gilles Marchessault, well known in Saint-Alban, was quoted, claiming to be following several promising leads, then it was the turn of Lieutenant Émilie Saint-Pierre, originally from the area and specially assigned to this case from the SQ's regional offices. According to Lieutenant Saint-Pierre, the police already had two suspects in their sights and were expecting to wrap up the case very soon. She added that they were still hoping to find Michael Faber safe and sound. To this effect, she appealed to the public to help the police by reporting the tiniest detail that could be connected to the boy's disappearance.

In a macabre twist, the journalist then proceeded to give an exposé of Émilie Saint-Pierre's private life, telling the reader her big brother had gone missing thirty years earlier and that she was considered the police force's fiercest investigator when it came to catching child attackers. And there we had it: everything became clear. Émilie Saint-Pierre's attitude was rooted in a broken childhood. Your childhood is taken away from you and everything gets fucked up. You spend the rest of your life searching for the child who's been stabbed to death. This was the quest Émilie Saint-Pierre had dedicated her life to. She was hunting for the person who had murdered *her*.

Now I could rip the newspaper to shreds. It could no

longer teach me anything. I took it to the washroom but contented myself with throwing it in the garbage can. A noise like hollow metal rang out in the narrow room, reminding me of the definitive, morbid sound of the first bell announcing the death knell, and I pulled the paper back out, taking care to avoid touching the garbage can's sticky sides. I couldn't throw out this photo of a child who might at that very moment be crying for his father to come and rescue him. I carefully tore off the first page of the *Écho de Saint-Alban*, folded it in four and tucked it in my pocket. It would go with the photos of Billie, with all the other photos that left ink on my fingers and that I couldn't bear to get rid of, because you can't simply bury a child's face among objects that evoke no memories, splattered with mud, sweat, or cold coffee.

My face, on the other hand, would have felt right at home among all the dirty tissues. My skin was grey, my eyes were ringed with black, the two cuts I'd given myself during my morning shave had bled, and I needed another shave with a blade that wasn't dull. It was only around thirty hours since this whole circus had started, but I felt as though it had lasted a week already, a long week during which I'd neither slept nor eaten. I stuck my face under the tap's cold water, smoothed back my hair, and returned to my row of chairs.

At the reception desk, a guy I would've guessed was around seventy, but who looked likely to reach a hundred while still splitting his own firewood, was yelling at Officer Tremblay and threatening to bring a suit against the police for abuse of power and doubtful process. Tremblay remained calm; he'd seen it all before, and he repeated the same thing he'd said to me earlier, namely that the guy could read his newspaper and wait quietly until one of the inspectors handling the case in question was free, or he could come back later. Realizing that he was going to get nothing out of Tremblay, the man made the same decision as me and reluctantly chose the row of chairs. He tapped his foot for a few moments, then stood back up to pace from the entrance door to the washrooms.

This man's anger was so palpable it created a kind of magnetic field around him, and anyone who came near, uninvited, bounced off of it. He moved around inside a mineral aura that gave him a certain resemblance to Clint Eastwood on a bad day, and I wouldn't have been at all surprised to see him draw a gun if someone tapped him on the shoulder. I pitied the guy or girl who had to negotiate with him. After three trips from one end of the hall to the other, he sat back down and asked me if I had any cigarettes. I did not. He didn't smell of smoke and probably hadn't smoked in years, but the situation that made him want to snap Tremblay in half must have reawakened his taste for nicotine, and he would have chain-smoked two or three in a row if I'd been able to cater to his temptation. As he stuck a matchstick in his mouth, I moved away slightly so as not to be caught by the attraction of his magnetic field, and a silence settled over us, disturbed every now and again by the metallic sound of filing cabinets that Tremblay was opening and closing behind his counter.

A quarter of an hour later, a door opened, another door—or maybe the same one—slammed, and Émilie Saint-Pierre came down the hall with the woman from the funeral procession, who looked like someone who's just seen a graveyard full of ghosts. The guy beside me leapt to his feet and rushed towards her shouting, "Good God, Marnie, do you want to explain what the hell is going on?"

I immediately thought the name Marnie suited this woman very well, even though it had lost its mischief when the world crashed down on her.

"Phil," she murmured, but Émilie Saint-Pierre pushed herself between her and the man named Phil.

"You have no right to talk to her, Mr. Morisset. Marnie's just been put into police custody," she said, then she opened the door to a windowless room into which she ordered the woman to enter.

"What is all this nonsense, Emmy?" thundered Phil Morisset.

"It's confidential, Mr. Morisset. I can't tell you anything."

For a moment I thought Morisset was going to launch himself at her. He clenched his fists so hard his knuckles turned white, as stiff as a crowbar, then he dropped one arm and punched the wall so hard it left a mark next to a light switch. "If you weren't a woman, Emmy Saint-Pierre, I'd smash your face in." Then he told the woman named Marnie not to worry, he would take care of finding her a lawyer right away and get her out of there. At the same moment, Marchessault appeared out of yet another room, came over to the row of chairs, and stopped in front of me. "What on earth are you still doing here, Richard?"

When she heard my name, the girl called Marnie lifted her head in my direction. I thought she was going to tell me to run, to go as fast as my legs could carry me, to leave this town full of unhinged people and never look back, but she stayed quiet, staring at me with eyes like those of a statue. I didn't know what treatment she had received from Emmy Saint-Pierre in the interrogation room, but if there was anything left in this girl that could still be broken, Saint-Pierre had no doubt taken a sledgehammer to it.

Before the door closed on her, Marnie shot me a look that could have been interpreted as a cry for help or an admission of powerlessness, and her face was replaced by that of Marchessault, who wanted me to explain what exactly was going on, for fuck's sake.

The man from the funeral was there, the one with the fever, the bird of misery that seems to pop up every time I'm being towed along in a dead person's wake. He was waiting for me on a street corner at noon today, and again at the police station, to remind me that we are alike, he and I, that the sky fell in on us on a day just like every other day, and nothing is more terrifying for the people who have not yet been struck than a man or a woman who continues to walk through a destroyed heaven. Nobody told me what he was doing in Saint-Alban, but it was easy to guess. He was there for the same reason that I was, because he was still paying for the crime committed by the shit who had destroyed his existence. This was the cause of his fever and the reason he looked like Crappy Owl. Richard, Marchessault had called him. Richard Richard, Crappy Richard, Holy Richard. With a bit of luck, I might find out his real first name with Emmy-Lili's help. She was bombarding me with questions I had already answered. Cradling my head in my hands, I repeated that I didn't know, I didn't remember, I didn't even know what I should or shouldn't know, for Christ's sake, but she remained convinced that I was both a shit and a liar.

When I went into the interrogation room a little earlier, Emmy had placed several objects on the table, all enclosed in plastic bags. She wanted to assess my reaction to these objects, to get an idea of how guilty I was from the nervousness or panic that sent the blood rushing to my cheeks.

Between a mud-stained New York Yankees cap and a small bag that held marbles and stones of various colours, all labelled as pieces of evidence, Holy Owl lay on his back, asphyxiated by the bag he'd been sealed in.

"Holy Crappy Owl," I muttered, reaching out to him, but Emmy forbade me to touch, just as she stopped me from picking up the little bag Mike used to carry his treasures around — his marbles, his rocks, his gemstones. It was impossible for these objects to have ended up as part of this case. Someone had made a mistake, mixing up the dates and the children. These items belonged to Michael and me, and they could only have ended up in Michael Faber's hands by accident. Except for Mike and me, the only person who could have got hold of them was the Faber kid's attacker, assuming he had known Mike's secrets.

"Do you recognize these items?" Emmy asked me.

I nodded yes, since no sound came out of my mouth. Whatever her purpose was, Emmy's aim had been accurate. My cheeks were flaming, and I counted the seconds that ticked by nonchalantly on the clock, sure that I was going to faint, convinced I would wake up in a deep dungeon with the rats, deprived of any chance to explain to Emmy how Mike had saved my life. I was watching Emmy-Lili's trap close around me when I realized that the cap wrapped up in the third plastic bag was not the one Doyon found when he searched my house. This hat did not belong to me. On my hat, one of the legs of the *N* had come undone and the embroidery threads had unravelled. "That's not my cap," I murmured, pointing at it. But Emmy knew that already. She just wanted to verify that I'd seen it before. "Look, the button on the top has come off."

The button had indeed come off. It wasn't my cap. That was all I knew. Emmy put it to one side for a moment, seeing that I wasn't about to upstage everyone by revealing that this hat belonged to Tiger Woods or the Yankees coach, and pushed Holy Owl over to me, just under my eyes, next to my hand.

"What can you tell me about this owl, Marnie?" she continued, tapping Holy Owl's head with her finger through the plastic. Her polished nails were short, nicely shaped, clean, the nails of a girl who gives herself a manicure every week while watching *Grey's Anatomy* or *Desperate Housewives*, just as I'd done during my New York period, when I lost touch with the smell of earth as well as the smell of death. How did Emmy Saint-Pierre manage to play in ditches and garbage dumps and still keep her nails clean?

I looked at my own nails, still dirt-stained, and a wave of hatred of the kind I hadn't felt for a very long time added a second layer of red to the flame that already burned my cheeks. The sensation of numbness that had deprived me of speech a little earlier had disappeared, borne off by anger, and my blood was circulating again. This girl should have been out there digging up the forest with me, on all fours in the mud, our hands occasionally unearthing a blackened femur and coming together in a feverish prayer that this bone might not be human. But instead she was accusing me of having the dirty hands of murderers and lunatics, because lunatics don't wash either. They daub their shit on their bedroom walls in nightmarish frescoes and gnaw their toenails as they rock to the rhythm of ancient nursery rhymes.

Looking at Emmy straight in the eye, I answered that the owl belonged to me, then I asked if she remembered the story of Hop O' My Thumb.

"I did the same thing as Hop O' My Thumb's parents, Emmy. I told Crappy Owl a bedtime story and took him off to the middle of the woods. But it wasn't enough just to lose him, I hung him off your brother's cross deep in the woods. The rocks are the ones he scattered behind me to follow his path, but they were no use to him, poor Crappy. Is that clear enough for you? And if you want to know if I did the same thing with Mike, all you have to do is find other rocks!"

I wasn't shouting any more, I was screaming, and the door opened abruptly to reveal Doyon, who stopped me from lunging at Emmy's throat and ripping out her damn pink nails. But I wasn't the only one who longed for disembowelment. I had mentioned Mike's cross, the sad wooden cross beside the river put up by Victor Saint-Pierre's flayed hands, and had thus strayed over a line beyond which Mike's little sister was ready to kill.

"You're gonna go back over that story calmly, Marnie Duchamp, you're gonna explain where you took Hop O' My Thumb. Start talking!" she yelled, whacking the table with both hands without flinching. She waited, her breath short, her face sweaty, and I felt as though I was falling into a nightmare whose exits were blocked by a motley collection of objects that my dirty hands couldn't clear away.

So I surrendered. I told Emmy I didn't understand anything anymore; everything was all mixed up, Holy Crappy Owl wasn't bad, and I wanted to go back home, back to the past, deep into that August forest.

"I'm going to help you understand, Marnie," she said in a low voice. Then she told me a story in turn, a story a little like Hop O' My Thumb, Hansel and Gretel, Little Red Riding Hood, as bloody and animalistic, mixed in with the howling of wolves, children carrying rocks in their bellies, cookies and little jars of butter in their baskets, orange cookies just like Marchessault's grandmother used to make. But I didn't begin to grasp her story until she mentioned what had made the dogs — Rex, Chet, and Lucy — fall silent.

At 9:18 that morning, Michael Faber, the child with the blue Superman bike, had been found drowned in the Trembles River, his skin icy and his little face all puffed up. An owl made of straw and bark was hooked around his neck, and from the pocket of his sweater dangled a little red canvas bag containing Michael Superman Saint-Pierre's magic stones, a bag Emmy had been searching for for years. "I even looked in your father's garden, Marn…"

Doyon was still in the room, and I could hear his breathing, as well as a heart beating fit to burst, and I think I said, "No, someone's lying, the dead little boy is lying." And then the exits to the nightmare turned white. I think Emmy asked Doyon to take care of the formalities of placing me into custody and then left me alone in the interrogation room. I don't know how long I was there because time no longer moved forward. When I walked down the hall, Phil was waiting for me along with the man from the funeral, Richard Richard, who was, like me, suffering from fever.

Marchessault, who had been silent for a few moments, was drawing arrows on a sheet of lined paper. I'd sworn to him on Billie's head that I didn't know this Marnie woman, Marnie Duchamp is what he'd said, but this wasn't enough for him. In his mind, the oath of a father who still aroused suspicion was not worth a whole lot. Screw him! Billie was the only person in the world on whose head I could swear and genuinely not lie or falsify the truth, and if Marchessault was too stupid to realize that I was offering him my best guarantee of good faith by invoking my daughter's memory, then I wasn't going to crawl on my knees just so a flash of intelligence could light up the darkness where his stupidity comfortably snuggled up.

I closed up like a strongbox with seven combination locks and considered calling Maheux, the gnome who was staying in the only decent hotel in Saint-Alban at my expense, although I couldn't see how he might be useful to me at the moment. I counted the seconds, Marchessault ripped up his arrow-covered paper, and then, like a magician, he swiftly pulled a photo out of his shirt sleeve and pushed it under my nose. I've never liked magicians, or tightrope walkers or jugglers, especially when they take off their baggy pants to dress up as cops, and my heart immediately started pumping my blood around at top speed, although it had been relatively calm until then.

The photo Marchessault had made appear just by clicking his fingers could have appeared in a horror anthology. A boy lay near a riverbank, his white eyes gazing up at the pallid sky, in the middle of which lingered perhaps the wake of pale air disturbed by the flight of what we call the soul or the spirit, a kind of energy or naked shadow that creates laughter and sorrow. His face, in contrast, had taken on the colour of angry skies with gathering storm clouds, his hair extended into frozen spikes that were melting in the sun, and a wide gash sliced the thin flesh on his forehead down to the bone, a gash that looked like a burgundy bolt of lightning in the cloudy sky. But I couldn't have said which was more painful to look at, his eyes or his little swollen hands, one of which bobbed under the water and seemed to want to gather the river up in its open palm.

I dearly hoped they weren't planning to show the parents this photo, which would eclipse all other photos and would condemn them to no longer see their son except with his hand outstretched and the gash over his protuberant eyes, like those of fish stranded on the beach. Horror is a hundred times stronger than innocence, and it's always horror that imprints itself onto injured memory. One remembers the smile, but the bitter rictus dominates, and that's what lingers, abolishing all other smiles.

For months after Billie went missing, I was afraid that Inspector Ménard would show up in my kitchen one day and slide a photo like this one through the clutter, past a fork turned into an impromptu see-saw or a little paper house made by his fat, hairy-knuckled fingers, and now here was this photo on display for me, reproducing the perfect, terrifying image of death.

"Is this the Faber boy?" I asked Marchessault stupidly, pushing the photo of the child back towards him — gently, so as not to damage his battered body even more.

"Who else would it be?" he grunted, before informing me that the child had been found a few hours earlier lying in the Trembles River, just half a kilometre as the crow flies from my house. "Taken together with the cat, this puts you in a very bad position, Richard."

Such precision was pointless. Since I had heard him say the river's name out loud, I felt my legs weaken, I thought of the children's tracks that had led me out of the forest the day I discovered Michael Whoever's cross, and then I wondered if the soles with horizontal stripes were Michael Faber's.

I brought the photo close to me again to figure out if I recognized the stretch of river where he'd washed aground, and I noticed the owl, the same one some nutcase had hung on the other Michael's cross. It now hung around the child's neck, twisted on the end of its string. I hadn't noticed it earlier because the river current had pushed it between Michael's body and his right arm, where it had got caught. But there was no doubt about it, this little heap of coarse feathers nosediving into the river was truly the same owl that had been hanging from the wooden cross under the trees. Had Michael been the one who had hung it there and then taken it back later?

I pointed at the photo, intending to tell Marchessault I'd seen this owl before, but the words tumbled back down my dry throat, creating a logjam that blocked my air circulation, and I threw an imploring look at the cop. I was going to die of asphyxiation, the same way Michael Faber had died, strangled by the owl or smothered by the river. By the time a guy behind the mirror brought me a glass of water, I thought I was going to see my life scroll past in slow motion, but I only noticed the present moment, made up of colours and shapes of startling clarity, in the centre of which Marchessault's enormous mouth yelled that I was going to die on him.

When I eventually got my breath back, all my limbs were shaking. This reaction of a body struggling for survival was normal; shock was shooting through my previously tense muscles and nerves, but mostly I was trembling because I had escaped the asphyxiation that had turned Michael Faber's boyish face purple.

On the other side of the table, Marchessault mopped his brow, waiting for me to be able to speak again. I downed the glass of water, spilling half of it on myself, then I told him what I knew about the owl and the children's tracks. "Holy shit!" Marchessault swore, smoothing down the hair on the back of his head, and demanded more details about the cross, the condition it was in, what was engraved on it.

"Wait here a moment," he muttered as he left the room. He came back with three evidence bags. He asked me if I could identify the owl and to tell him if the other objects were familiar. The baseball cap meant nothing to me, but the red bag certainly did. Billie used to have one like it for keeping her marbles. "Look, Papanoute, this one looks like a sparrow's egg." She used to set them up on the living room carpet while I watched *MythBusters* or some documentary about the difficulties an endangered species was having trying to reproduce. She would then sort the marbles by style and colour, separating them according to whether they were cats' eyes or beach balls, before finally putting them all back in the little bag. Every time she was amazed at rediscovering them, never tiring of observing the way the light travelled through the translucent marbles to give her a distorted vision of the world. "Your face is all crooked, Popinouche."

"Billie had one like that," I said softly, pointing at the bag and at the same time shooting myself in the foot. Marchessault immediately started bombarding me with questions about the bag. I tried in vain to explain that it couldn't actually be Billie's bag, but it was too late, he wasn't listening to me anymore. Among the stones in this bag, which had been stuffed in Michael Faber's pants pocket, there were also several marbles, blues and emeralds, translucent, cats' eyes, and speckled ones like swallows' eggs.

I turned to look at the clock. Four forty-five. It was time to drag Jean-Pierre Maheux out of his hotel room before he went down to the bar for a few Scotches and then set off to discover the charms of Saint-Alban by night on the arm of a girl who would later have to crouch on the floor to give him a blowjob.

Maheux got me out of there before somebody could come up with the bright idea of putting me into custody along with Marnie Duchamp, who was guilty of breaking who knows what immutable rules governing small communities. You only had to look at the woman to realize she wasn't remotely criminal but yet another victim of the prevailing hypocrisy.

Since she and I were alone in the same boat, I wanted to believe I wasn't lumping myself in with a psychopath, but I could well have been way off the mark, duped by her pallor, which might be nothing but a mask, a feature under which Marnie Duchamp hid her icy coldness and her cruelty. Murderers don't always look like murderers, just like pedophiles don't have the word *pedo* tattooed on their forehead, which allows them to roam in peace and collect corpses in the basement of their suburban bungalow or the walk-in closet of their penthouse. This Marnie was still a mystery to me, somehow connected to the occasionally disconcerting depths of the Rivière-aux-Trembles forests, full of unspeakable secrets.

Unlike Marnie Duchamp, however, I was free for the moment. Still in the boat, but free from the shackles that had hobbled my steps. As soon as Jean-Pierre Maheux showed up at the police station with his wonky polka-dot cravat—thus confirming I'd been on the right track regarding the lawyer's pre-dinner activities—he put on his courtroom voice, swept away Marchessault's arguments with the back of his hand, and then drove me home, telling me I was forbidden to talk to anybody unless he was there, probably because he wasn't convinced I was innocent either.

Since I got back home, I'd been ruminating as I examined my cup of cold coffee as if the patterns forming on the sides of the mug could reveal the truth to me. I tried to imagine little Michael's final hours—he was so young he wouldn't even know he would die one day—and I thought of Marnie Duchamp's fragility, which perhaps hid a Mrs. Hyde, and then of the cat named Nuage, who ended up at my place one sad Easter day when he should have been purring in his little master's house.

This cat had only spent a few hours with me, but his departure left a gaping hole on the armchair he'd adopted. The room suddenly seemed devoid of life, as did the whole house, numbed by a kind of ennui that oozed out of the very walls. But I wasn't stupid; this musty smell filling the air around me didn't come from the absence of a cat who'd barely had time to shed a few hairs on a tatty cushion. I was the one who was sweaty, stinking like a shut-in, and no longer had enough energy to believe it was worth getting my butt kicked, or to make soup while singing Charles Trenet's "Y a d'la joie!" or to knit slippers in the corner by the fire while children were dying in the river that flowed behind my house.

Life ran out of me through all the holes it had persisted in digging in my stomach and sometimes in my back, like a real traitor, and I didn't see how I could deal a mortal blow to the moribund colours that tinted the atmosphere. Even if I painted the walls fuchsia, the gloom would remain there, hanging in the air that stagnated around my punctured carcass.

I summoned the strength to go upstairs to my bedroom, just in case I was still alive enough to fall asleep, but I barely had time to fold the covers down when the sound of smashing glass reached me from the ground floor, followed by tires squealing on gravel. I froze for a few seconds, then raced over to the window, partially resuscitated by the surprise and the noise, but all I saw was two tail lights at the end of the driveway, which rapidly vanished behind the bend that led to the village. More or less reassured, I went downstairs, my ears straining.

No sound came from the ground floor except that of the wind, whose coolness reached my bare feet. When I turned on the living room light, I noticed that the curtains in the front window were blowing gently, the way they do on beautiful summer nights when the air is too sweet to imagine a ghost's immaterial body gliding among the folds of fabric, between dark and light. But the cold made me think of this kind of spectre, whose invisible footsteps had sunk into the carpet, which was strewn with shards of glass, in the middle of which sat a rock wrapped up in a scrap of paper and tied with jute—as if I really needed this, as if my living room wasn't ugly enough already.

I picked up the rock, and as I did so I felt the spectre brush past me on its way out, leaving the scene by billowing through one of the curtains. The message I had just been sent could not have been clearer: "Go back home, sicko! We don't want your kind around here." The message was written in red, probably to heighten the dramatic effect, and the paper had been soiled with various substances commonly associated with people like me.

I thought about calling the cops, but nobody would bother coming out in the middle of the night for a bastard like me, who was simply getting pretty much what he deserved. I'd get Maheux on it the next morning; he might as well earn some of his fee. I placed the message in an empty bread bag with the rock and the string, and then spent the next hour clearing up the mess and covering the broken window with pieces of cardboard. Once I finished this job, I sat in front of the television until morning, thinking of Marnie Duchamp and Michael Faber, and wondering if I shouldn't hightail it out of there, as I had been so politely invited to do, or just set fire to this shack and immolate myself for the greater good of humanity.

The next three days were relatively calm. Two uniformed officers came to write up a break-and-enter report before leaving again with my rock and my message. I sent Maheux back to the city until further notice, I contacted my insurance company, and I called a glazier. These various activities shook me out of my apathy, and I came close to having an almost-normal reaction, something resembling emotion, when the sun finally broke through the cloud cover during the day of April 22nd. If the sun kept up its efforts, I might even crack a genuine smile between now and the lilacs blooming.

I also took the opportunity to get back my computer, which had not revealed any shameful secrets or provided any incriminating evidence to the investigators. And after that, not knowing what to do with myself, I focused on Ronie. I took him out of the silty hole where he'd been hibernating while I left him alone and sent him off to the mangrove trees in the Everglades, just to warm up his old hide a bit and at the same time get me far away from the Rivière-aux-Trembles scenery.

Once Ronie had acclimatized to his new environment, I left him to stew, because I had absolutely no idea what to do with him. I could have set him up with a doe from the swamp, with whom he could have blithely hopped around in the tall grass as the sun set, giving my illustrator the chance to explore animal romance. I could have had the rabbit ask him to marry her and given them a large brood of floppy-eared toads, but my heart wasn't in it. Every time I tried to get Ronie to explore the swamp, I couldn't help but imagine him being eaten by a crocodile or an alligator, and that was the end of that.

Michael Faber's purplish, scarred little face wouldn't stop coming between Ronie and me. The boy then sailed down the river to the freshwater swamps of Florida, where he drifted unhurriedly among the egrets and the ibis. Sometimes Billie swam with him, her little girl's hair crowned with orchids, and their hands touched over the slow-moving seaweed. The bigger boy reassured the little girl in the pale, gentle sunlight, and night never fell, because night could not reach these bodies released from pain. This was my new version of heaven and hell joined together, a kind of idyllic vision invented by the devil. I loaded photos of the mangroves on my computer and then superimposed pictures of Michael on his bike and Billie in her polka-dot dress, their smiles bursting through the shadows of the cypress. If it had been remotely possible, I would've bought myself a one-way ticket to the Everglades, with the idea of searching for the doors of heaven and hell, but I was more or less under house arrest. Émilie Saint-Pierre had advised me that I was not allowed to leave the region until the case was finalized; too bad if I got stoned to death while I ironed my shirts.

Since the early hours of Wednesday, nobody had come to smash my windows or hang an effigy on my porch; I had received no threatening letters, no hate-filled phone calls; but at night I was still afraid of waking up to a thunderous explosion of glass or seeing the silhouettes of two or three men armed with baseball bats in my bedroom. I didn't dare to go into the village anymore for fear of confronting the grocery store cashier's naked hostility, or giving Max the butcher the idea of lacing my ground beef with strychnine. I was living like a criminal, even though the only thing anyone could reproach me with was not having kept my daughter in my sight twenty-four hours a day, which would likely have driven her insane or caused her to become delinquent.

The ringing of the telephone yanked me out of my lethargy just as I was splashing around in an imaginary pond with Ronie, as weary as a duck-billed platypus who'd got caught up in the Tour de France. It was Marchessault, his drawling voice showing that he too was short of sleep. I was anticipating a summons, but he merely wanted to check a few details in my statement regarding Dixie-Nuage's visits. The fact that he hadn't come to haul me off by the scruff of my neck meant there was something new and I was no longer on the list of suspects. I asked him if they'd arrested the guilty person, but he brushed aside my question. "You'll find out when you read tomorrow's papers, Richard," he said, and then he hung up before telling me whether I was free to travel outside the region, whether I could pack my swimsuit in a suitcase and fly off to the swamps of Florida. I was tempted to ring him back, but I realized that Maheux would be able to obtain that information more quickly than I could. I dialed his number, and his secretary told me he was in court for the day, but she would deliver my message as soon as she could reach him. Since I had no choice but to wait, I elbowed Ronie aside and sat down next to him, my feet in the slimy water, thinking about Michael Faber, who would never get his life back even when the guilty person was arrested, and whose parents' nightmare would never come to an end. The only advantage they had over me was that they knew where this nightmare had taken place, and in the head of which furious psychopath. I almost envied them for being able to put a name and a face to their misery, for being able to elaborate scenarios in which they exacted bloody revenge for their son. This is the kind of unconfessable emotion people feel when they've been forced to face the void and must now cope with the infinite possibilities that might give some kind of coherence to their ignorance.

Maheux called me back around three in the afternoon, just as I'd finally decided to spring into action and had two free-range eggs sizzling in my non-stick frying pan. I explained the situation; the noise of people coming and going around him muffled his words, and I heard him mutter that he'd call me back in a few moments. My eggs were now smothered in blackened butter, and I was just throwing them in the garbage when the phone rang again. It was Maheux, proud as a peacock to announce that I was now free, and that his bill would be on the way shortly. As for the rest, he hadn't managed to find out any details. I thanked him and hung up, unable to share his enthusiasm. I was free, sure, but the earth would continue producing hundreds and thousands of bastards who would massacre the world's beauty.

Emmy told me the boy who'd gone down to the river with Michael Faber was called Martin, a bland name that could nonetheless turn bad: nasty, vicious little Martie. After several days of silence, Martie had cracked. His parents thought his fever was a result of his best friend's disappearance, but the real origin of his illness was more complicated. Martie's was a post-disaster fever brought on by the gleam of thin layers of ice covering the trees that had fallen into rivers in spate. The virus that caused this fever could strike suddenly; the victim wouldn't see it coming, but he would be plunged into a hallucinatory delirium full of impossible dead people and grotesque corpses.

Martie Jacob had caught this virus around three in the afternoon on Saturday, April 18th, just as the sun grazed the tops of the tallest trees. A piercing cry had rung out, he saw a body floating in the river in a strange position—unnatural, not the posture of someone who was swimming—and then he started running around in circles like an animal trying to find a way out of a stifling pen. He had lost his mind, screaming the name of his friend, Michael, Mike, and adding incomprehensible words that no ear except his own could hear. Then he jumped in the river, where he banged up against rocks and stumbled to his knees. When he saw the bloody tree trunk he vomited into the clear water, spewing up a brownish lump-filled liquid that dispersed as it sank to the sandy depths where a few white stones lay sparkling.

"Wake up, Mike!" he shouted at his friend, loudly enough to burst his lungs as he pulled his limp arm, and then he tumbled down the bank. For a moment the river flowed over his eyes, coming between him and the sky. It tried to penetrate his mouth and he sat up gasping, his raspy breath tasting of vomit and raw fish. After that, he couldn't remember anything more. He called for Nuage in vain, clinging to the image of the cat as proof that nothing he had seen was true, and ran some more. At the edge of the forest, he grabbed his bike, hands and feet frozen, already feverish and cut off from the sounds of the world by the river's cavernous noise in his ears.

The chill of the wind eventually forced him back home. Once inside his bedroom, he hid his soaked clothes in the dresser and took refuge under his wool blankets. He was dreaming when his mother put her hand on his forehead, panicked at the heat radiating from her son's body. She told him Mike's mother had phoned, she was looking for her son. Anna Dickson and Charles Faber, Mike's parents, were out of their minds with terror. An alarm bell rang immediately in Martie's consciousness. Mike's mother must not know. Her eyes must be protected from tears and from the bloody tree trunk. Mike wasn't dead. Mike was going to come back with Nuage, propelled by the warm wind, by summer, which cannot wound. He was the one who had slipped on the tree trunk—him, Martie—and cut his skull on the rough scales of a broken branch. It could only have been him, because he had seen the sky, the blue backdrop against the clouds, through the river that was trying to force his mouth open.

I made the journey to Saint Alban to buy the newspapers. I could have bought them in the village, but I preferred driving the extra kilometres to having doors slammed in my face in a shower of insults. I had a pain in my skull as a result of waiting for the explosion that would pulverize my house, and I felt unable to face the subtexts and the threats of a few bloodthirsty yokels who would like to skin my hide in the village square. I would throw myself into the wolf's mouth when I felt able, and once I'd done some in-depth study of *The Three Little Pigs*. The roads were still misty from the cool morning, and I stopped at the first depanneur I came to, Granny Berthe's place. Granny's inviting smile brightened up the sign that squeaked gently at the start of the road leading to the centre of Saint-Alban, which was as ghostly as a movie set at this early hour.

The door of the store creaked in harmony with the sign as I pushed it open, and I came face to face with a close-up of Michael Faber's face on the front page of three of the newspapers lined up on the counter. I froze for a few seconds in front of *L'Écho de Saint-Alban*, where the little boy was sitting with Nuage in front of a Christmas tree that was so like every other Christmas tree it was as though I was looking at Billie and Pixie on the day L.A. gave her a doll's house.

I came out of my torpor when the door squeaked again, and I took a copy of each paper, forbidding myself to read the headlines right away. I didn't want to discover, between the chips and the household cleaning products, in the musty atmosphere of the store, that Michael Faber had been knocked out and then strangled by his hockey coach or his mother's first cousin. I poured myself a tea-coloured coffee from the coffee maker by the beer fridge and added a few generous spoons of sugar. It would taste like sugary dishwater and I didn't care, I just needed a hot liquid to give me courage and get the blood flowing back to my fingers, which were stiff after gripping the steering wheel so nervously from my house to Saint-Alban.

"The poor child, it's so senseless," murmured a woman who must have been Granny Berthe minus the smile, pointing to the newspaper with a withered old hand, her ring finger so swollen her ring seemed to be embedded in it. The years had caught up with Granny Berthe since she modelled for her business sign. The attractive young woman for whom a future full of promise was opening up had quickly understood that the future is a sky whose horizon constantly contracts, and she probably started to swell in order to push it away. She had a puffy face like those dogs that always have tears in their eyes, and she was moving with difficulty in the narrow space that has shut itself around her obese body.

"It's so senseless," she said again, holding out my

359

change, her little Pekinese dog eyes watching for my reaction. I muttered some imbecility about how existence itself made no sense and got out of there, afraid of having to spend ten minutes listening to her sigh about the fate of generations left to themselves, about the absence of mothers and fathers, about the innocence of children who wait anxiously in the schoolyard and give their hand to the first person to ask for it, start getting high at the age of twelve, and lose their virginity two months later. Over the last three years, I'd heard over and over again all the common themes associated with the sadness of childhood, and I felt indigestion on enough consecutive days to have become allergic to the words dripping with compassion or laden with barely veiled reproaches that people feel obliged to formulate even when the best thing would be to keep their mouths shut.

Once back in my car, I put the papers on the passenger seat, which would henceforth belong to the boy with the printing-ink smile. Chilled by the patches of damp that hovered just above the ground, I turned the heat up to full and looked for a quiet place to park. At the edge of town, I pulled into the muddy driveway of a rest area with no picnic tables, as desolate as a circus big top without ballerinas or horses, and began reading.

Michael Faber had not been knocked out or strangled. Contrary to the first theories, the latest information led to the conclusion that the Faber child had met an accidental end. The results of the autopsy would be available at some point during the day, but the testimony of a friend of Michael's, whose name couldn't be revealed because of his young age, left almost no room for doubt about the circumstances of the drama. The friend in question had apparently witnessed the drowning, but the child had repressed the horror of the scene until the body was discovered. At present, the police refused to release any further details, but the witch hunt was over. No unknown hand—except the hand of a destiny some people call God—had struck Michael Faber's skull when he fell out of the tree blocking the river.

The three newspapers all gave more or less the same version of events. Michael Faber was dead because he loved life. If he had preferred vegging out in front of the television to going out and hurling himself across rivers, he could have continued living in a universe made up of thousands of pixels, while the rivers flowed by themselves and his bike grew rusty as it leaned on the garage door. Chance had struck, the bogeyman didn't exist, and I was now free to come and go as I pleased. The suspicions that had weighed on me had been swept away by a spring wind, but it was impossible for me to find joy in this. A child was dead, and my liberty lost its meaning in the lugubrious echo of the death knell sounding in the distance.

I let the picture of Michael posing with Nuage in front of a Christmas tree drop into my lap, and I wondered if Billie was dead because she too had loved life too much, because she had grabbed the gloved hand that promised her rivers and streams, because she'd docilely followed it in the hope of coming across a vast delta opening out into a sea woven from pink and blue ribbon. Outside, the fog was dissipating, a few chickadees were cheeping, and a blackbird, a harbinger of gentler times, was hopping on the gravel in the shade of the ballerinas and the lost horses. "Billie, tell me that's you, Billie?" The blackbird hopped and the chickadees flew away, but the sky stayed silent.

When I arrived back home I phoned Marchessault, who owed me a few explanations after accusing me of all the crimes committed in the area over the past century, transforming my lack of reputation into the reputation of a scumbag. He gave me the necessary explanations in a weary voice, broken by powerlessness, and I realized how much the life of a cop could destroy a man. But the weary voice did its job; it existed for this reason alone, to try to stop violence and then work its ass off explaining why death had won again. This is how I found out why Dixie ended up in my neighbourhood that Easter Sunday. The explanation was so simple it really shouldn't have taken fifty detours to get there. Everything Marchessault had told me I already mostly knew. I had guessed the answers by observing the photos of Michael Faber published in the newspapers and by learning that he'd floated down with the river with a smile on his lips.

The whole thing could be summed up in a few words. Michael Faber loved his cat, he loved riding like the wind on his bike, and above all he loved throwing rocks into rivers, building dams with broken branches, and catching blacknose shiners after the spawning season. Once his parents gave him his bike, he started exploring the area with

Nuage, venturing a little farther each day, and always bringing his best friend, the only one he would share his Smarties or his PlayStation with, the same friend who had seen him drown and who would never again set foot in a river.

On April 12th, Easter Sunday, Michael Faber, Nuage, and the friend in question ventured as far as the bend in the Trembles River half a kilometre away from my house, squelching their feet in the muddy paths, their footprints allowing the halfwit people from the town, like me, to not gather in the Far North while they thought they were heading quietly towards their houses. It was the friend who had given the police these details and explained that Nuage started chasing a field mouse and only went back to Michael's house the next day. This was how the old fleabag had come to knock on my door and developed a taste for Atlantic tuna. It was as simple as that. The children were playing, the cats were hunting, all was almost right with the world.

Despite the fact that children scarcely obey commands, and cats even less so, I was still troubled by the fact that Michael Faber had drowned behind my house. If I had hiked down to the river on Easter Sunday instead of getting bogged down on the 4th Line path trying to avoid Régine's voice, I might have crossed paths with him, and, who knows, maybe it would have changed the course of his existence, like Edward Lorenz's butterfly. A beating of wings, a branch cracking beneath my feet, and his entire life could have shifted the few millimetres necessary for his foot not to slip six days later.

This boy had played behind my house on more than one occasion, running in those woods where I almost got lost, or wading in the river with his rubber boots with diagonal stripes on the sole, which had helped me avoid a trip to James Bay and had perhaps saved my skin. We had inhaled the same air, the same rotten scent of the damn spring rain, and I had found myself there again the same day he died, very near him, trying to set Ronie up with a tree frog while he needed me to save him in turn. A flapping of wings, and the friend who was beating his head with both fists would have continued drawing a map of a treasure island in the river's mud, Nuage would have gone home in his basket, and Billie, Billie-Billienoute, would have been doing pointe work in front of the wide mirror that ran the length of Mademoiselle Lenoir's dance studio.

In vain I told myself that my wings had been broken for a long time now, and I wasn't remotely responsible for Michael Faber's accident, but not a single hour had passed since Marchessault showed me the photo of his body without me reproaching myself for not having followed his tracks for longer, for not having been there, down by the river, watching death. I am the unmoving man who, almost to the second, could have allowed Michael Faber to get up from his fall with just a broken arm or a hefty dent on his forehead. I am the man who couldn't stop the madness of the January stranger, whose face is only known to a little girl named Billie.

This is all Rivière-aux-Trembles has brought me, a doubly guilty conscience accentuated by silence. Since nothing good seems to be waiting for me here, and the landscape surrounding the river look too much like purgatory, I'm going to pack my suitcases, leave the key in the door, and set off for Florida, Australia, or the Amazon rainforest, hoping not to arrive at a river next to which I will kneel, wondering if a child might at that moment be drowning in the twisting and turning branches of the Trembles. And nobody, absolutely nobody, would lament the departure of the man who just wants to rush to the nearest confessional booth so he can hammer his chest with *mea culpa* blows and accuse himself of not beating his wings in the right direction, just like Lorenz's butterfly caused a hurricane in the middle of the ocean, and then catching a kid losing his footing mid-flight.

B eside a Christmas tree decorated with angels and multicoloured baubles, some frosted with tiny sequins evoking snow or the gold of the Magi, Michael Faber holds a cat named Nuage in his arms. That's what the caption under the photo tells us: Michael and Nuage, Christmas 2008, in the centre of an article informing me that I did not kill this boy.

Emmy Saint-Pierre, having come to the same conclusion, told me I was free to leave a few hours ago. "You're free, Marn, you can go now," she said, which didn't stop Phil from fulminating against her. He's been busy in the kitchen for twenty minutes, slamming the cupboard doors and beating the hot milk as though he wants to kill it. I can hear him grousing through the noise of the beater hitting the sides of the metal bowl, "Silly woman, dumbass, a Saint-Pierre through and through, as if Marnie could ever, not even capable of killing a fly, damn police," but Phil's anger burns out on contact with the images jostling in my head. A few words reach me, devoid of true meaning, while I think of Michael Faber slipping on the ice, or of Martie Jacob tumbling down the slippery rocks, each one condemned by the river. I think of Mike's buried treasure, which Michael had dug up out of a hollow tree trunk, a few marbles, a few stones that had been turned into kryptonite by the magic of faith, with the help of formulas borrowed from Superman's mysterious alchemy. I think of the little white hand weighing the treasure. "Come and see this, Mart, I've found diamonds!" The rest is easy to imagine, because Michael and Martie are just like me, just like Mike and all other children, unaware of death, free to imagine the world.

I'm free too, it seems, free from climbing trees and walking with my head held high, but ever since Emmy-Lili, betrayed yet again by the Trembles River, agreed to tell me what she knew about the story of the two children from Saint-Alban, my freedom has existed alongside another life, that of Michael and Martie, which melts into my own, that of Mike and Marn. I contemplate these two lives and their threads slowly dovetail, like icebergs whose drift has no other purpose than to create new islands. I am this new continent, in the middle of which, precariously balanced, I walk towards a tree trunk fallen over Nanamiu-shipu, the trembling river. A little bark owl swings from my neck — Holy Owl, Crappy Owl, very Crappy Holy Owl — the reflection of Nanamiu-shipu in his all-seeing yellow eyes.

I don't know how Michael and Martie discovered the owl, or how it came to be around Michael's neck, but I can imagine the boy's heebie-jeebies when he stumbled upon a funereal cross with a name, his name, seven letters whacking him over the head like a disturbing message from fate. "Geez, Martie, come and look at this!" And Martie comes running over, swears, then kneels down next to Michael and points at the owl with the yellow eyes. "It's a sign, Michael. You have to put this owl around your neck, he'll protect you." Along with Martie, I thus invent the other Michael's story, the one to whom the cross is dedicated, a story of vampires and deep caves, bony demons coming out of their coffins at night to devour wolves. Since yesterday, I am no longer one person but four, and I don't even try to understand. The forest has its laws, the river its rules: one wanted Mike and the other took Michael.

"Drink this," Phil says, and I reach my hand out for the coffee covered with a mousse that reminds me of a Mr. Bubble landscape. Phil is afraid: afraid I'm losing my mind, afraid I'm getting the two Michaels mixed up, afraid I'm going to lie down at the bottom of the river in the same spot where Martie saw the blue of the sky through the raging current. But Phil's wrong, I can't get the two Michaels mixed up because they are one and the same, one single child just like every other child, burying treasures and discovering them months or years later, as sparkling as jewels stolen by crows, shining in their nests, as fascinating as the diamonds that sparkle on women's fingers.

I savour the white foam Phil has sprinkled generously with cinnamon and reveal to him that the little bag of treasures found by Michael Faber belonged to Mike. "You'd swear Mike gave this boy his heritage, Phil, signed a blood pact with him."

Nevertheless, Mike couldn't have caused Michael's death, any more than Holy Owl could have knocked him over with those surprisingly heavy bark feathers. Death is the result of chance, of a fate that insists on leaving circles of black ice hidden on the trunks of dead trees, circles whose reflections disappear under the clouds. It's always this way: death is chance combined with white water.

"The river killed Mike," I tell Phil between two sips of coffee and, while I'm speaking, a shadow gradually covers the sun at the exact same spot where the film of ice formed that would prove fatal to Michael Faber.

"What's going on, Marn?" I hear Phil's voice from the other end of an interminable tunnel.

I answer that nobody can do anything anymore. Rex, Lucy, and the gamekeeper will never find Irving the bear, it's too late for Irving to be saved. I talk to Phil until it gets dark about the misshapen trees, the almost-human limbs coming out of the wet trunks; I will never know if they were real or simply a product of my terror. I describe my ignorance to him, tiptoeing around the edge of the hole some people think my memories have sunk into, even though there might be nothing but a great void at the bottom of this hole, nothing but non-existent images. And Phil listens until it gets dark, swearing through his pursed lips and trying to hide his fear at seeing me tremble like this. But Phil has nothing to be afraid of. Craziness is far behind me, eclipsed by fate. All it needed was a little ice. All it needed was a few words: "Go away, Marn! Run!" All it needed was the knowledge that my hands hadn't killed Michael Faber.

II.

THE END

Given that I'd soon be leaving Rivière-aux-Trembles and that nobody could accuse me any longer of being responsible for Michael Faber's death, I was past caring what kind of welcome I received in the village. The grocery store cashier, Max the butcher, the assistants in the depanneur and the hardware store would soon be nothing but fuzzy images in my memory of Rivière-aux-Trembles, where I'd only recall a few trees and a poorly named river that would perhaps be rebaptized one day as Two Michaels River, Cross River, Death River. Whether Max, his daughter, his aunt, or his mistress despised me barely bothered me. Their version of the truth was that of people who are bored with their lives and enjoy bad-mouthing others. The banality of their concerns almost absolved them of their idiocy.

It was now April 30th, the weather was glorious, and I'd had enough of racking my brain. I needed a few bits and bobs to close up the house, and I would buy them in Rivière-aux-Trembles. I shouted to Ronie, who alternated as a listening ear and a punching bag, a kind of imaginary friend or whipping boy, telling him I was going down to the village for an hour or so. I put on my smoky crooner's shades and drove the two kilometres separating me from the main street with the windows down, occasionally catching a whiff of the greenery that heralded summer's bright colours. When I went into the hardware store, I greeted the assistant cheerfully as he priced screwdrivers straight out of the box, and I started down an aisle without waiting for him to reply in an equally cheery manner.

I was comparing two brands of masking tape when I noticed her, Marnie Duchamp, struggling with a bag of fertilizer that was slipping out of her arms. I had thought several times about the possibility that this meeting might happen one day, with no hearses or police officers to get between us, but finding myself face to face with this woman who had been handcuffed for no good reason made me deeply uncomfortable. In reality I was afraid to approach her. In my mind, she was nothing more than a face marked by a kind of fatality that scared me because it was too close to the destiny that had struck me. I didn't want her to tell me the name of the deceased she'd been following to the cemetery, or to talk to me about empty graves or the missing child that had given Marchessault and Doyon an excuse to show up unannounced at her house and subject her to their absurd interrogations.

I could pretend I hadn't seen her and run off, but to make that work I would need to feign sudden blindness and immediately find a white cane or a guide dog behind the pyramid of masking tape that threatened to tumble down on top of me.

I risked a timid smile, hoping that would be the end of

it, but I had clearly invented a fantasy about the nature of the relationship between us. This woman had recognized in me some type of kinship visible enough for her to beg me two or three times with her eyes to hurry up and hold out my hand to her, and I wasn't going to get away with just an idiotic smile. But what can you say to a woman who thinks you can help her clamber out of her hole even though you yourself are squatting at the bottom of a ditch into which sharp rocks fall every day? The law of gravity gave me a helping hand at this point, manifesting itself as it always does when we are in freefall, and I caught the bag of fertilizer as it hung between two opposing forces of unequal power: the attraction of the earth and Marnie Duchamp's exhausted arms. She murmured a quick thanks as she pushed a lock of stray hair back behind her ear, leaving a track of brown dust on her cheek in the shape of a comet tail projecting its haze into infinity, then she smiled at me.

This was the first time I had seen her smile, and I immediately thought how it suited her. Something had changed inside her since I'd seen her down at the police station. You could say her body had grown lighter, not so much that she might fly away, but enough for her to admire the Milky Way without crushing her cervical vertebrae because she had her chin pointing to the ground for so long.

I must have looked utterly stupid, standing there staring at her like that, because she burst out laughing, another sign of her transformation, and introduced herself: "Marnie."

"I know," I tried to tell her, but all I could say was, "Bill, Bill Richard."

Without coyness, she immediately accepted my help carrying her purchases out to an old red pickup truck parked outside the store's big window. I was placing a fourth bag of fertilizer in the already-laden truck bed when she asked if I wanted to have coffee with her. "I think we might have a few things to say to each other, and we could do that better over coffee."

This prospect gave me the shivers, but I agreed; we almost certainly had things to say to each other. So we left the hardware store together, under the suspicious eye of screwdriver guy, who probably thought he was letting the successors to Paul Bernardo and Karla Homolka — the new Ken and Barbie of the pedophile diaspora — escape.

He stared at the table as he told me about his daughter, Billie, who went to school one day and never came home. That explained the fever. It explained why he was sitting there opposite me, fiddling with his coffee cup, trying to find an explanation for his nightmare. He and I were in the same untenable situation, not knowing what had happened to our missing people. It had killed us, but we tried to carry on living regardless. The only advantage I had over him was the length of time since Mike went missing, but was that really an advantage? Maybe in thirty years Bill Richard could answer this question and tell me if hope was better than the erosion of faith. I no longer knew. When he put the dog-eared photo of his daughter back in his wallet, I took out the bottle of cognac. The coffee tasted of ashes and we both needed a pick-me-up. We clinked our glasses together and downed our drinks without saying a word, in memory of Mike and Billie and to the health of survivors, the survivors of Nanamiu-shipu and other trembling rivers that stretch their arms into the hearts of cities.

In the heavy silence that followed, he pushed his cup away and started playing with his glass again, turning it one way and then the other under the sun that slanted in through the window. Then he swirled the remaining drop of alcohol in his glass, the drop that had avoided being swallowed, making it move in the same direction as the earth's rotation and then opposite, putting time in reverse, and then started all over again. Maybe he thought if the liquid spun backwards long enough he'd be able to go back to the past and force the earth to bend his nights one after the other. But he must have known that the night cannot be bent any more than the day; on the contrary, we must run and hold back our cries, it's the only way to save ourselves.

I was just about to pour him a second cognac when he repeated his daughter's name, Billie, in a barely audible murmur. It was the first time in months he'd been able to say her name without it hitting the walls' silence. It must have been a relief to no longer be alone hearing it and to know what it meant. So he repeated the name, Billie, and gave a sad smile, a smile that said "What's the point?" while still thanking me for being there and for not being deaf. Then he talked about Billie's cat, Pixie, Ronie the Toad, and the entire menagerie that mated and reproduced endlessly in the memory bank of his old Mac. He focused on cross-species mating so that talking animals would never disappear from the universe of children. According to him, there was nothing sadder than a child who didn't know that trees sing and birds tell fairy tales while snacking on cheese. He earned a living from these picturesque animals, mainly Ronie the Toad, his oldest and best friend, whom he'd invented one rainy day long before Billie was born. If he'd known, he would have invented Billie the same rainy day, and would have conferred superpowers on her so she could swipe away the claws of evil people and slash open their stomachs with them.

A whole heap of chaotic memories came hurtling towards me when he mentioned Supertoad, one of his latest creations, and I left the space-time where his voice was trying to create an indestructible Billie only to find myself in Superman's shadow. When I returned to the kitchen, he was talking about immortality, the worst possible thing, immortality on earth. He would have wanted Billie to be alive, for her to be able to rip child predators into pieces and swing them into garbage trucks, but not at the price of being condemned to the eternal life we try to impose on heroes, who end up dying of loneliness and boredom. He was right: eternity was a punishment innocent people didn't deserve. Nevertheless, I wished so many times that Mike had left this world for glory and eternity, when really I ought to have wished for him a simple life that would last the length of a normal life and would end with the fracturing of fragile bones and the bursting of an exhausted heart.

From talking about eternity we got onto the subject of the little girl's mother, Lucy-Ann, who had drowned in her own blood and departed for the eternal gardens where she believed Billie grew translucent flowers. As he stared through his glass at the patterns on the tablecloth, Bill asked me if translucent flowers really existed. I'd never asked myself this question before, but as far as I knew there was no flower that could blend into its surroundings like that, no flower whose petals were nothing but pure transparency, the quasi-absent colour of glass and water. If Lucy-Ann was right, he concluded, it meant that Billie, in humans' phantasmal worlds, was the only one who grew flowers that were almost invisible. He then apologized for dominating the conversation to describe the paradises dead mothers make for themselves. "Tell me about Mike instead."

I didn't know what to tell him. When I described the storm earlier, it seemed as though I'd told him everything. So I went back to the magic swimming hole to tell him the stories we used to make up, from owls who loved fries to invincible heroes, never short of ideas, dreams, or plans. "We thought we were Lois Lane and Superman," I said, letting out a short laugh that sounded false, and then I crushed the damn pile of crumbs I'd brushed together on the tablecloth while I was trying to describe the magic swimming hole's clear water, the ice fortresses, the owl's eye a yellow eye that let night flow over the forest ground.

As I crushed a crumb into one of the green cherries lost among the tablecloth's pattern, I noticed that Bill Richard was lost in a cloud maybe five or six years old, maybe as much as seven or eight, one of those old unkillable clouds that still lurked over the same heads and filled the atmosphere with a musty smell that only people who aren't absorbed in the cloud can smell. Realizing I was watching him, he brought his cloud close to me to tell me how Billie had loved stories too, like all Billies, like all children. He told her so many stories he sometimes wondered if she might have mistaken her attacker for a character he'd made up for her. "If that's possible, then she went into a fairy tale," he said softly, "a story where maybe she met Mike, because children are always meeting each other in stories where they turn into squirrels or fairies, where they wear capes and magic shoes, disguised in harmless lies. This is how they tame the world and touch it, by going through the surface of mirrors."

He put his fingertip on the drop of cognac, then slowly drew a circle on the tablecloth with it, so slowly that the circle dried, and he said, "That's what happens, missing children become Hansel or Gretel, characters from fairy tales and legends." With his finger still touching the sticky ring, he started reimagining the story of Billie and Mike, inserting his Supertoad into their adventures, and then I made him down another shot, hoping drunkenness might divert him a little from the weight of these fictions we invent in order not to die, but which end up guzzling us up, like vanished children and dreams.

Billie's and Mike's disappearances belonged to the incomprehensible world of chance and the unexpected. Attempting to explain them would have been as futile as trying to understand why God played dice with his utterly worthless adversaries. Nevertheless, caught between Ronie and the seven dwarfs, Bill Richard still looked for a way out of his ignorance, then he started muttering incomprehensible words about birdsong, about Billie's voice trying to cut a path through the twittering chickadees who came to peck from her hand, so tiny and trusting, when it would take just a squeeze of the hand to close those hazel eyes forever.

Bill Richard was sinking, regressing to those first painful days, marching his drunkenness right over to where it hurt the most. It was time to create a diversion before he lay down on the old, ragged tablecloth along with the dead we had laid down in the falling light. I rolled the cognac lid over to him and said that if he associated everything that got away from him with an esoteric belief, he would end up surrounded by crystal balls and Ouija boards that would order him to paint his walls purple and black.

I don't know what happened then, what button I must have pressed, but he burst into uncontrollable laughter and launched into a soliloquy about quarters in the Plexiglas. While he went to mop himself up in the bathroom muttering "fucking quarters," I made a bowl of popcorn, not finding anything else in the kitchen that could be easily cooked in three minutes, and went back to sit down opposite him, at the table over which he'd slid Billie's photo, which he'd taken out of his wallet again to prove he wasn't crazy.

In the silence that had fallen once again, we stuffed our faces with popcorn, crunching the unpopped kernels with our molar fillings, and then we discussed leaving, departure, escape. We were searching for what we might still have to say to one another when, slowly, I slid my hand across the tablecloth, my left hand, the one that wasn't covered in butter and salt. I could pretend to be acting unconsciously, without thinking about it, but that would be completely false. I wanted to touch this man who was getting ready to go even though he'd only just arrived, I wanted to leave an indelible mark on him, something he would carry off with the time bomb ticking in his chest that would rip him to shreds just as easily in Honolulu as in Rivière-aux-Trembles. I wanted, in fact, to give him some regret. But Bill Richard had enough regrets. He didn't need to be burdened with memories of a woman who hung up owls and got tangled up in everything that reminded her of her childhood. He stood up from the table, a little unsteady on his feet, and I watched him cross the road, head down, while Lili Marnie, seated at the edge of the darkness, built a castle out of a few kernels of popcorn.

There's thunder in the air. The unchanging weather is filled with the scent of rain, and heavy clouds are gathering slowly from the west. It will be my first and last thunderstorm in Rivière-aux-Trembles, since I'll be leaving tomorrow, May 10th, to visit Régine and then fly to Australia. My suitcases are packed, the fridge is empty, and I managed to hire a man from the village who doesn't have too many scruples, at least not when there's moolah involved, to look after the house while I'm away. This house will become my place of contemplation, just in case one day I'm seized with nostalgia for the country or want to come and relax near a river that has disappeared.

It was Marnie Duchamp who explained the river's name to me. We were sitting at her table with Billie and Mike when she murmured, "Nana-shipu, Nanamiu-shipu, Nanamassiu-shipu," describing how the quaking of the earth had taken on the shapes of non-existent trees.

This was early on in our conversation, before Superman landed among the dried breadcrumbs, before she slipped her hand over towards mine and I suddenly felt an urgent need for fresh air. She was talking to me then about those images of infinity she said could only belong to the inhabitants of the treetops—birds or squirrels that had the privilege of living closer to the wind. "Closer to the blue," she said as well, referring to the colour that was as ungraspable as the tranquility it was supposed to inspire. Along with Mike, she had tried to touch the blue of Catfish Lake and Trembles River, which dissolved into the water's clearness as soon as you leaned over it. The blue was an illusion she wanted to get closer to, and I was betting she would succeed—she would touch the illusion with her fingertips and in this way would be liberated from the weight of her dreams. She had a house, trees, flowers, and a friend named Phil on whom she could rely if ever the distant horizon overwhelmed her. Marnie Duchamp had taken root in Rivière-aux-Trembles, which meant she could observe the sky without falling over. I didn't have such foundations, which was the reason I needed to leave and try to find my balance again in movement.

The light was starting to dim when I told her I was leaving soon. We were a little tipsy, completely exhausted, and we didn't really understand what had compelled us to spread out our baggage on a sticky tablecloth when we knew perfectly well that as soon as there was nothing left to say, each of us would gather up our old guilty memories and leave again with our bags under our arms.

Perhaps it was this awareness of the pathetic usefulness of confidence that inspired Marnie Duchamp to reach her hand out to mine, messing up the little heap of crumbs she had been endlessly scattering and regathering. Just at the place where a comet had previously left its mark, a little bit of pink warmed up her cheeks, "rose pink, Billie, Purple

Cloud and Rainbow's End roses, the colour of rainbows, of clouds at the end of the day, and of painted flowers lined up on the walls of Marnie Duchamp's house in wooden frames." At the time, I didn't know whether this gesture was a way of wishing me bon voyage or if, on the contrary, it was a shy attempt to keep me from leaving so we could combine our spoiled pasts and together build some kind of future on their rickety ruins.

I put my own hand out as well, just far enough for our fingertips to touch and break the spell. But the gesture didn't ruin the enchantment, and for a moment I wanted to leap on this woman, push her down onto the table and stretch out on top of her, panting, my pants half-undone and my head full of desperate words. We had so much in common, so many sleepless nights spent frantically tearing out our hair and gnawing our nails, that it would be the most natural thing in the world for me to throw myself at the body of this sad woman and wrap my hand in her hair so she could hurl a torrent of curses at me, bite me, hit me, and accuse me of being no better than anyone else who had tried to make her feel better by mounting her like rodeo cowboys.

I hadn't fucked anyone for three years because I was convinced that if I touched a woman my pain and my anger would crush her before she'd had time to spread her legs, but with Marnie Duchamp the situation was totally different. We were on an equal footing, and we'd taken enough blows to be able to block others, even rip out chunks of flesh if it would get rid of the pressure that bore down on us day and night.

I was trying to persuade myself that a bit of nooky was probably the only intelligent activity that could be undertaken by a man and a woman who were holding hands in front of a precipice covered by a plastic tablecloth where the woman's nervous fingers were building tiny crumb mountains only to immediately destroy them, but a force related to a kind of survival instinct kept me riveted to my chair. If I jumped this woman's bones, either I would never leave Rivière-aux-Trembles, or I would leave with my tail between my legs, tormented by the feeling that I'd sullied the only person who understood Billie's name.

I pulled back my hand to touch the photo of my darling girl that I'd taken out of my wallet in order to forget the birds, all the birds that had taken on Billie's voice back when I was still hoping for a sign from heaven or hell, and I told Marnie Duchamp I had to leave. She didn't protest. She pulled her hand back, a little hesitant, a little shaky, and then she built a tiny new mountain, this time out of popcorn. When I left, she was still sitting at the table, looking down and singing a song to the tune of "Lili Marleen." A few stars shone in the dark Rivière-aux-Trembles sky, but not a single patch of blue softened the horizon.

I haven't seen her since that meeting that nearly ended up with us panting and clutching at each other, and I haven't made any attempt to do so. Everything we had to say to each other has been said. If we meet again, we'll be forced to invent a present for ourselves to make the other person believe we have a life worth living.

Regardless, I'm leaving tomorrow, and I haven't the

slightest interest in any present whatsoever. In the weeks, months, and years to come, my life will only be a kind of passage between two places. That's why I chose Australia, which will allow me a change of scenery at will, to visit a country and a continent at the same time, to travel from the Great Barrier Reef to the Pinnacles Desert, on horseback across borders drawn in the very stuff of time. If Australia has a message for me, perhaps I'll discover it in the eucalyptus forests, where a few surviving koalas have escaped the expansion of urban sprawl, forest fires, and the fashion for fur hats and collars.

I'm taking nothing with me except a few photos of Billie and this old computer on which Ronie the Toad breeds. If I have the chance, I'll initiate him into marsupial customs, "with pink pockets, Papanoute, not grey, that wouldn't be pretty," and I will invent stories for Billie where happiness looks like a sleeping teddy bear clinging to a tree trunk. And of course it's possible that the great Australian fever will seize me as soon as I set foot on the continent, but I have to take the risk, just in case a researcher affiliated with the University of Sydney has discovered an antidote to this deep sickness that only attacks people who tumble from ravines into abysses.

There was just one thing left for me to do before I departed: give Pixie the burial he deserved and thus allow him to move up to his seventh or eighth life. The day before yesterday I took him out of the crate he's been freezing in for way too long and brought him out near the maple tree that shades what appears to be an old garden behind the house.

The soil there is workable, softened by the recent rains. He can enjoy the morning sun in this spot, or the shade of the maple when the light is too strong, and he can come out to catch field mice whenever he pleases.

I worked half on my knees and half bent over, reciting impious prayers that would have got me admitted to an asylum or excommunicated if a psychiatrist or a pope had been within earshot. When I had finished praying and digging, I placed the flannel blanket Billie made at the bottom of the tiny grave and gently laid the old tom on top, along with a few toys to allow him to live his best eternal Pharoah life. Then I sobbed, "Sleep well, Pixie, adieu old chap," but I could have sobbed, "Sleep well, Billie, adieu my girl, my beautiful girl, my wonderful girl," and it would have meant the same thing. I was burying Billie, Billie's life, Billie's toys, along with Pixie. I was putting my beautiful, wonderful girl under the ground, and I placed a photo of her on Pixie's still-cold belly, the photo with the mischievous smile. Afterwards, I rushed to cover him up with earth before I could be tempted to lie down beside him myself, pressing Billie's photo to my cheek. Then I wrote the damn cat's name across the width of the garden using a stake that I dug into the ground as deeply as I could so it would be visible from the stars, where perhaps Billie was watching my pitiful efforts at learning to walk without her. I didn't put up a cross, since Pixie didn't believe in God any more than I did, and I had been forcibly excommunicated.

The best thing I could have done after this burial was to go and wash, but I decided to embark on what you might call a pilgrimage. I took the vague outline of a path that leads to the river and sat down near Marnie Duchamp and Michael Superman Saint-Pierre's magic swimming hole, which had perhaps been carved out by a distant earthquake or a minuscule meteorite that had travelled from one of the celestial bodies that orbit in the Kryptonian galaxy.

I almost expected to find a second wooden cross not far from the river, with a bouquet of wilting white flowers at its base, along with a photo of Michael Faber holding one of Nuage's paws in a goodbye wave. Perhaps the father of the second Mike would put up this cross one day, when the desire to throw himself under the train that travels to Saint-Alban every Monday and Thursday evening had left him, unless he turns out like me and no longer believes that invoking this hypothetical celestial being that moves around in the body of the universe could bring any practical help to his child.

For the moment, only the cross of the first Michael watched over the dramas occurring near Nanamiu-shipu, a simple cross that doesn't give the missing child's age or the date when he went missing, and thus becomes the cross for both Michaels, who will henceforth be only one Michael among all the children who have gone missing at the edges of quaking forests. In the place where a withered bouquet might one day bloom, I traced Billie's name, imagining her walking in the river, hand in hand with the two boys.

When I returned from my pilgrimage, I threw my clothes into a corner of the bedroom and had the kind of long shower that would make an eco-warrior scream about the planet's water reserves, starting with the guy who not long ago was worried about the drought drying up Australia. This guy was dead and no longer wanted anything except to lose awareness of time, space, flooding, and the war that would soon pit arid countries against countries that wallowed in fresh water.

I feel I'm achieving this desire, more or less, but today, as the hour of departure grows nearer, memories flood back as if it were the day of reckoning. The only reckoning I can make is that I am henceforth alone with Ronie, without ties, without hope. If it weren't for the storm moving in I'd leave right away, but the wind has already picked up and lightning is streaking across the sky, over the forest, which will soon make the ground and the river tremble as jets of furious rain strike the windowpanes.

This will be my last storm before the storms that make the Tasmanian devils roar and the eucalyptus bend. It will be my last memory of Rivière-aux-Trembles, the memory of a corner of the countryside irrigated by fury and light. If I come back one day, some trees will have grown, others will have died, petrified by thunder or eaten away by worms; Marnie Duchamp will have aged; and a cat with white and ginger fur will perhaps be waiting for me on the porch, the spitting image of an old moggie to whom a child named Billie used to tell, once upon a time, the history of the world.

I was standing at my window when the first flashes of lightning lit up the sky behind Wolf Hill. Not too long ago I'd have quickly drawn the curtains and turned up the volume, playing a Jethro Tull or Led Zeppelin CD in anticipation of the din to come. With my knees folded up to my chest, I'd have rocked in my armchair, massacring "Stairway to Heaven" until the storm was over, then I'd have thrown myself into housework or any other activity that would keep my hands busy and stop me from thinking too much.

This time I remained standing at the window, letting the lightning violently strike my retinas and the rumblings of thunder roll over my moist skin as my heartbeat sped up. In my head, the words of "Stairway to Heaven" spooled by and "rings of smoke" wreathed the trees, but they indicated to me that it was never too late to change direction. Robert Plant and Jimmy Page were right: "There's still time to change the road you're on," and this is precisely what I was attempting to do, sitting in front of this storm and trying, finally, to see the beauty in it.

"I'm starting to feel the rain, Mike," I murmured, as several branches of Mary Delahunty whirled around in the white sky like tumbleweed caught in the desert wind. They spun for a few moments and then smashed into the hybrids greenhouse, whose glass walls lit up every ten or fifteen seconds. I was riveted to the window with fear, but it was tempered by the fragile joy of someone who is learning to walk again. If the sky wanted me, it could have taken me a long time ago... When the rumblings ebbed as the storm rolled east, I pulled on my raincoat and went outside to sit in the garden, under the pergola. The wind had dropped, a fine rain softly hammered the roof of the house, and nature was slowly unfurling after the assault of the tempest. I wanted to live in this calm from now on, in this barely audible sigh that follows the storm.

Of course, there will always been some idiot coming to throw stones in my garden or call me up in the middle of the night, some child raised in stupidity who will shout "Bloody witch!" at me and run away. Ignorance is long-lived. But if the river was able to resist the earth's quaking, I could probably stand up to the increasingly rare after-shocks of the cataclysm that had ruined a good chunk of my life, and whose origin nobody — neither I nor anyone else — could figure out. All I know about the story is when and where it started.

Once upon a time there were two children and a river, is how the story begins. Once upon a time there was a storm, and there was a child alone in the middle of the lost forest, a Marnie who was disoriented among the pebbles. Once upon a time there were two children, and then there was just one. There isn't really any other true story. It's possible,

I know, that a third person slipped between the children and that in my panic I blocked out the hairy hand that strangled Mike and covered it with a thick layer of magic paint to make it invisible. On the other hand, I know the next part of my story begins here, a few weeks before summer, whose suffocating heat and achingly beautiful nights I look forward to. It will be my first summer since the summer of '79, too beautiful to be true, so good that the month of August lost its mind and knocked the sky into Trembles River. My story begins here and now, and I also know that nothing, neither gossip nor meanness, will make me leave this house, where summer after summer I will grow Alex Duchamp and Marie Beaupré roses.

My name is Marnie, and I don't care. I still wonder what my parents were thinking when they chose the name, but it's really not that important, because I'm also called Squeerelle and I'm no longer afraid of storms.

There was no funeral procession driving down the Rivière-aux-Trembles main street when Bill Richard left the village on May 10th, 2009, at the wheel of his 2005 Volvo S40, his only baggage a computer, a Samsonite suitcase, and a photo album. The morning shower had ended, but the rain would start up again soon, making his journey gloomy and discouraging him from leaning his elbow on the open window and belting out hits from the olden days, days which at the time he didn't recognize as blissfully carefree.

In the meantime, he was singing, "Hit the road, Bill, and don't you come back no more." But he didn't know if he would be coming back. He was leaving, that was all. He was moving. He was going somewhere where every day he would wake up to anonymous scenes of grandiose landscapes in the middle of which he would have trouble recognizing his own shadow and where he hoped to be able to forget his own name. He was neither bitter nor sad, but simply relieved to have finally understood that he couldn't live under the same roof for months on end without the roof threatening to imminently collapse from a phenomenon connected to the negative pressure of loss and boredom.

When Marnie Duchamp's house appeared in the distance, his first memory of the woman materialized in front of the windshield wipers, a frail dark ghost that wanted to bewitch him. "Don't look," he muttered to himself, stepping on the gas, "whatever you do, don't look back," but despite himself he turned his head, just like the woman who was turned into a pillar of salt on a sandy road. When he saw Marnie digging at the end of the garden, he braked hard and came to a stop on the shoulder. Fear yanked at his guts, sweat drenched his shirt, but all he wanted was to fling the Volvo's door open and race over to her, jump on her and pull her down into the soaking wet grass. If he didn't know the power of sad women and fear that the Australian landscapes might disappear behind Marnie Duchamp's inscrutable expression that hinted at landscapes filled with roses, rivers, and squirrels climbing verdant trees, he would have ripped off the damn door and run over to wrap himself in that long, red, wind-scented hair. But he knew the power of sad women.

He was just on the point of driving off, his damp hands slipping on the steering wheel, when Marnie turned around. After a moment's hesitation, she dropped her spade and came closer. Once she was near the road, she stopped, leaned on the tailgate of her pickup, and pushed the lock of hair tickling her cheek back behind her ear. She wouldn't come any closer. She raised her hand, the one that had left the imprint of a dark cloud on her cheek, waved it in a gesture of until-we-meet-again, or a final farewell, and then dropped it to her side just as the rain started pouring again.

He raised his hand too, to say until-we-meet-again, and started driving away in the torrential rain, but the image of Marnie Duchamp in her yellow raincoat—lemon yellow, Billie, buttercup yellow and the yellow of wilted dandelion bouquets—her buttocks resting on her old red pickup, her hair wet, followed him the entire journey that took him away from Rivière-aux-Trembles. It pursued him for a long while afterwards too. He would find himself standing in front of the spumy waves of the Indian Ocean, wondering if he'd missed an opportunity that day, an opportunity to rebuild a genuine life in the arms of a woman who drew clouds on her cheeks, clouds or comets flying towards her red-squirrel expression.

As for Marnie Duchamp, she watched the Volvo get smaller in the distance until it disappeared behind Hook Hill, then turned back to her garden. She spent the whole day exhausting herself—digging despite the rain, weeding, trimming the bushes, asking the rain to touch her and smiling when the smell of the fresh water brushed against her dirty hands now and then.

At the end of the afternoon, she headed down to Trembles River at a leisurely pace, not having been back there since the day she had taken Holy Owl. As she passed Lucien Ménard's former fields, in the middle of which stood Bill Richard's closed-up house, she regretted not having gone closer to the Volvo a few hours earlier to kiss Bill Richard right on the mouth, whether he wanted it or not, and give him a very good reason to turn around. Then she told herself that if he wanted to kiss her, he'd come back one day or another, a little older, naturally, but cured of the fever that had darkened his face with sickly shadows.

Then she set off along the path that led to the river and remained seated by the water until dusk, next to a wooden cross on which Michael's name slowly disappeared into the darkness.

ACKNOWLEDGEMENTS

Since he's sitting right here next to me, the first person I'm going to thank is Pierre, my in-house editor, for his multiple readings, his sound advice, and his solid bear's shoulder.

Next, of course, I'd like to thank everyone at Québec Amérique, starting with Jacques Fortin and Caroline Fortin, for their confidence and support, and because they have spared no effort in increasing my readership. I'd be mad at myself if I forgot Isabelle Longpré, my kind and devoted literary director (KDLD) when the book was first published, Marie-Noëlle Gagnon, Alexandra Valiquette, Nathalie Ranger, Mylaine Lemire, and everyone else with whom I've had the pleasure of working at Québec Amérique.

Thanks are due also to Josephine Bacon and Rita Mestokosho, who generously agreed to translate a few terms into Innu-aimun for me, allowing me to better understand the Trembles River's real name. Tshinashkumitin, ladies.

I also thank my friend Yvette, who relieved several of

my linguistic anxieties, and Gilles Mitchell of the Sûreté du Québec, who kindly agreed to answer my questions. I hope he won't be too upset that I've put his fictitious colleagues in situations where they aren't always the good guys. I'll make up for it in another novel.

A huge thank you to my sister Viviane, again, for her photos of thirsty koalas. In some ways, Bill Richard owes his Australian fever to her. And, as they do on television, I'd like to thank the other members of the family: Maman (mamanoute), Odette, Louise, and Tommy, as well as my nephews, nieces, brothers-in-law, and my cats, my gang of Noutes,* for their constant encouragement.

Final thanks goes to the Gabrielle Roy fund, whose confidence allowed me to finish this novel in a place that was, to me, total paradise, and to the Canada Arts Council and the members of the jury who awarded me a grant, without which I would still be floundering in Trembles River.

For the English translation, I sincerely thank J. C. Sutcliffe for having accepted once more to dive into the deep waters of my universe, which she has done with sensitivity, intelligence, and perspicacity. I would also like to thank Noah Richler for his confidence in my work, as well as Leigh Nash, Allegra Robinson, Joshua Greenspon, Jenny McWha, Leslie Ahenda, Tilman Lewis, and all the members of the House of Anansi team who had a part in producing the English version.

You'll need to read the novel to understand what this word means.

NOTE

Although the names of the characters who appear in this novel are common in Quebec, they designate purely fictional characters, invented entirely for the purposes of this story, except in the case of public figures or people who have been in the news. As for the main locations where the story takes place, the author has cobbled various places together to create them.

Anyone who thinks they recognize Rivière-aux-Trembles or any of the characters in this novel should chalk this perceived resemblance up to the randomness of invention or put it down to the fact that one man resembles nothing so much as another man, and the fact that the landscapes, villages, and forests of a country share a colour palette, which only adds to the confusion.

© P.

ANDRÉE A. MICHAUD is one of the most beloved and celebrated writers in the French language. She is, among numerous accolades, a two-time winner of the Governor General's Literary Award and has won the Arthur Ellis Award for Excellence in Canadian Crime Writing, the Prix Ringuet, and France's Prix SNCF du Polar. Her novel *Boundary* was longlisted for the Scotiabank Giller Prize and has been published in seven territories, and the English translation of *Back Roads* was a finalist for the Governor General's Literary Award. She was born in Saint-Sébastien-de-Frontenac and continues to live in the province of Quebec.

J. C. SUTCLIFFE is a translator, writer, and editor. Her translation of *Back Roads* by Andrée A. Michaud was a finalist for the Governor General's Literary Award. Her other translations include *Mama's Boy* and *Mama's Boy Behind Bars* by David Goudreault, *Document 1* by François Blais, and *Worst Case, We Get Married* by Sophie Bienvenu. She has written for the *Globe and Mail*, the *Times Literary Supplement*, and the *National Post*, among others.